MURDER WILL OUT

MURDER WILL OUT

Alyce Chaucer 3

CHRISTINA HARDYMENT

HAUGETUN

*For Dick the dauntless, who has stood by me
through ups and downs alike.*

First published in Great Britain in 2024
by Haugetun Press, Oxford

ISBN 978-1-7391980-6-0 hb
ISBN 978-1-7391980-7-7 pb
ISBN 978-1-7391980-8-4 eb

COVER Crown imperial and broom © Bodleian Library,
University of Oxford, L 1.5 Med.; chough from Eleazar Albin, *The Natural
History of Birds*, London, 1731–38. ENDPAPERS Tintagel Castle from Sir
John MacLean, *The Parochial and Family History of the Deanery of Trigg
Minor, in the County of Cornwall*, vol. III, Nichols & Son, London, 1879.

Designed and typeset in 11 on 14 Dante by illuminati, Grosmont
Printed in Great Britain by Henry Ling Ltd, Dorchester

Contents

FOREWORD

This book's cover refers to the fight for the English throne – with crown imperials for the rightful king, Henry VI, imprisoned at the time of this story but restored in October 1470; broom (*planta genista*) for the Plantagenet pretender Edward IV of York; and the Cornish chough, a pointer to the significance in this story of the piratical rogue Sir John Trevelyan.

The underlying theme of the novels is the power of women in a world torn by war and faction. 'To thrive, you must wive', ran a contemporary proverb. 'The man is the head of the family, but the woman is the neck; she turns the head', was another. The central figure is Alyce Chaucer (1404–1475), only known grandchild of the poet Geoffrey Chaucer (*c.* 1343–1400). She was one of the wealthiest individuals in England: herself an heiress and married three times, she had estates in every county of England south of the Trent. After the death of her third husband in 1450 she chose not to remarry. As a widow, her power didn't have to be veiled in apparent obedience to a spouse. She was notoriously proud and strong-minded. There's evidence that she loved books and had a well-chosen library, which included at least one book by the foremost medieval champion of women, Christine de Pisan.

For much of her widowhood Alyce lived in great state in Ewelme Palace, fourteen miles from the city of Oxford. Little of the palace now remains, but the church that she and her last husband William de la Pole, Duke of Suffolk, rebuilt and the cloistered almshouse known as the God's House and the school they established beside it remain uncannily unaltered. They and the magnificent tomb which describes Alyce as 'Most Serene Princess' (her son's wife was the sister of King Edward IV) are the inspiration for the Alyce Chaucer series. So too is the never solved mystery of who was responsible for the death of Duke William, intercepted on his way into exile in 1450 and brutally executed.

The first book, *The Serpent of Division*, set in September 1466, sees Alyce fighting not to lose her Ewelme heartland and learning that she needed friends to survive the machinations of avaricious enemies: her neighbour Sir Robert Harcourt and Queen Elizabeth, wife of Edward IV of York. In its sequel, *The Book of the Duchess*, Alyce is summoned to London in May 1467 by King Edward's mother, Cecily Neville, Duchess of York, to investigate the murder of a scrivener, only to find herself caught up in a plot intended to prove her a Lancastrian traitor.

In *Murder Will Out* Alyce travels to Tintagel Castle in Cornwall, hoping to discover at last who contrived Duke William's murder. With her ride the faithful Tamsin Ormesby, her bumptious London bookseller friend Joan Moulton and Sir Thomas Malory, now outlawed and seeking to flee England to further the cause of the once and future king, Henry VI. It proves a perilous journey, especially once they reach Tintagel.

In all three books much is imagined – these are novels after all – and many of the characters are invented. Those who were real are capitalized in the 'who's who' below. I have taken liberties with their doings, but none that contradict known historical facts.

Cast of Characters

No need to read now, but useful to remind yourself if muddled.
Historical characters are in CAPITALS.

OXFORDSHIRE FOLK

ALYCE DE LA POLE, Dowager Duchess of Suffolk, described on her tomb as 'Most Serene Princess'. A lover of literature and gardens and granddaughter of the poet Geoffrey Chaucer, she lives in Ewelme Palace, near Wallingford, Oxfordshire.

Tamsin Ormesby, a Ewelme village orphan with a stubborn streak, now Alyce's secretary.

Matilda Lovejoy, Alyce's new maid, acrobatic and flighty.

WILL STONOR of Stonor Park, Alyce's godson, now a lawyer.

Martha Purbeck, Ewelme's chamberlain, fierce but fair.

JOHN GETOUR, Alyce's chaplain.

Farhang Amiri, Alyce's Persian physician, much given to quoting Rumi.

Nan Ormesby, Tamsin's grandmother, Matron of the God's House, warm and wise.

BEN BILTON, Steward of Ewelme, cocky but a true heart.

Wat, now less of a wild boy, still devoted to Tamsin.

Joseph Pek, a sturdy one-armed veteran of the wars in France.

JOHN (JACK) DE LA POLE, Duke of Suffolk, Alyce's heir, growing up at last.

ELIZABETH (BESS), his wife and King Edward's sister, cleverer than both.

Dick Quartermain of Rycot, Jack's squire, shrewd and capable.

Mistress Joan Moulton, eminent London bookseller, four times widowed and as irrepressible as Chaucer's Wife of Bath.

Godith and Gwennol Hawksmoor, witchy sisters.

SIR ROBERT HARCOURT of Stanton Harcourt, a bullying braggart who covets Ewelme.

LONDON

LORD JOHN WENLOCK, of The Royal, Chequer Lane, diplomat to Edward IV and man of mystery.

SIR JOHN LANGSTROTHER, Prior-elect of the English Knights Hospitaller.

SIR THOMAS MALORY, chronicler of the life and acts of King Arthur.

Owen Pailton, his squire.

CORNWALL AND IRELAND

SIMON BRAILLES, formerly of Ewelme, now living in Tintagel.

FATHER JOHN GREGORY, vicar of Tintagel.

Oswald Marrack, reeve of Tintagel.

Jim Perrin, ostler of the Malthouse Inn.

Morwenna, a Tintagel village girl.

Philip James of Trehane, Morwenna's uncle.

Denzil Caerleon, now a captain in the Earl of Warwick's fleet.

SIR JOHN TREVELYAN, Lancastrian courtier and former pirate, now Constable of Tintagel.

LADY ELIZABETH WHALESBOROUGH, his wife and cousin to Alyce.

Sir Reginald Mohun, deputy sheriff of Cornwall.

Guy Despenser, his squire.

John Mawgan, Harbour master of Wadebridge.

JOHN TIPTOFT, Earl of Worcester and Lord Deputy of Ireland. A lover of books and learning; just but merciless in his pursuit of traitors.

LISBET HOPTON, his third wife.

John Hurleigh, his secretary.

RICHARD NEVILLE, Earl of Warwick, Admiral of the royal fleet, later acclaimed as the Kingmaker.

'Murder will out, we say day after day.
Murder is so foul and abominable
To God, who is so just and reasonable,
That he will not allow it long concealed,
Though hidden for a year, or two, or three.
Murder will out: that is my conclusion.'

GEOFFREY CHAUCER,
'The Nun's Priest's Tale'

Tintagel, Cornwall

A procession of flickering candle lanterns wound up the lane to St Materiana's, perched high above the village of Tintagel and prominent for miles around. The sun had set an hour ago and the church was silhouetted against an eerily green horizon. The high trebles of children rang out in the first verse of the hymn to Mary that Simon Brailles had taught them:

> Mary, maid mild and free,
> Chamber of the Trinity,
> Listen, listen, please to me
> As I thee greet with song.

Then came the deep voices of the men:

> Thou art queen of paradise,
> Of heaven and earth and all that is,
> Thou hast born the king of bliss,
> Thou hast righted all amiss.

Exhilarated by the frosty air and the biting wind, Simon joined in, his rich tenor linking young and old in the last verse:

> In thee is God become a child,
> In thee is rage becomen mild;
> The unicorn that was so wild
> Tamèd is by your chastity.

Candlemas was Simon's favourite festival. Last of the feast days of Christmas, it celebrated both the purification of the Virgin Mary after Christ's birth and old Simeon's presentation of the Holy Child in the temple as a light to lighten the Gentiles. Tintagel had its own traditions. On Candlemas Eve the villagers came to vespers carrying as many candles as they could afford, to provide light in the church in the coming year. Vespers was followed by the customary dismantling of the church's entwined wreaths of evergreens – rosemary and bay, juniper and myrtle, holly, ivy and mistletoe – and their burning on a ceremonial bonfire around the ancient Celtic cross on the seaward side of the graveyard. Every twig, leaf and berry had to be removed from the church before Candlemas the next day, for local superstition had it that anything overlooked would turn into pixies and plague the village goodwives until Advent.

As Simon led his flock into the church, he reflected on how much had happened since he came to this remote Cornish parish eighteen months ago. He'd hated leaving Ewelme Palace and his position as secretary to Princess Alyce, but his exile was of his own choosing. Two years ago in London he'd betrayed her. He'd drunkenly boasted to one of the king's intelligencers that he had access to her private papers. Next day he'd been arrested by Sir John Tiptoft, then Lord High Constable and dedicated to rooting out treasons. It hadn't even taken real torture, just a twist or two of the body-stretching rack to make him blurt out that a Dorset manor of hers might hold a dangerous secret. He'd promised to find out more about Newton Montagu and had pored for hours over its estate rolls, but he had only discovered that it was farmed by a family called Downton. 'Keep searching' had been Tiptoft's terse response to this information. 'And report your findings to Sir Robert Harcourt.' Simon shivered. Harcourt held lands neighbouring on Ewelme and coveted more. And he loathed Princess Alyce. Nothing would be a greater betrayal of her trust than to reveal her secrets to him.

Then came a chance of escape. Alyce's first marriage had endowed her with mines in the west country and the patronage of Tintagel's church. A year and a half ago its vicar Father Gregory had written to Ewelme asking for someone he could train up to be ordained and help him with his unruly parish. Simon suddenly realised that in Cornwall he would be beyond the reach of both Tiptoft and Harcourt. And once confirmed as a cleric he would be safe from lay authority. Although only half sure that he was suited to holy orders, he had begged to go. Alyce had been puzzled.

'Why not prepare in Oxford?' she'd said. 'Then I can keep you as my secretary. And when dear old John Getour retires, you could become my chaplain.'

He'd fudged up a tale of finding Oxford clerics daunting and spoken, truly enough, of his interest in all things Arthurian. Eventually, she'd given way graciously.

'Well, Father Gregory couldn't have a more able ordinand. And Tintagel Castle is spellbinding. All but an island. I'd love to return there myself one day.' She'd made him a present of the best horse in her stable and a purse full of silver. Thanking her, he'd felt like Judas.

Father Gregory, who had the bluff air of a countryman rather than a cleric, welcomed him with open arms, proudly introducing him around the parish and offering him a newly built stone house next to the island chapel. 'If you live there, you'll be entitled to the allowance payable to whoever says regular prayers in Tintagel chapel,' he explained with a wink. 'Though there's only God and the goats to hear them.'

Simon was nervous at first, but Gregory was an encouraging and reassuring teacher, advising him wisely as to what bad behaviour to curb, and what to let pass. Now he was established, liked even, and both the services he held in the formerly neglected island chapel and the small school he established in a former hermitage on its western edge were well attended. Gregory warned him of the importance of tolerating local superstitions, especially the one which combined vespers on Candlemas Eve with the villagers' celebration of Imbolc, the pagan marker of the coming of spring on the first day of February.

'Just avert your eyes from their junketings after vespers. As the great cross in our churchyard shows, Celts have been in Cornwall time out of mind, and, since the Imbolc bonfire burns our shrivelled Christmas evergreens so merrily, it seems to me reasonable to let it and Candlemas Eve merge.'

'But shouldn't we stamp out such ungodly practices?' Simon protested.

Gregory wagged a finger. 'You're not in Oxfordshire now. The Bishop of Cornwall rarely travels west of Exeter, and the sheriff, Sir Avery Cornbury, prefers to idle at court. His deputy Sir Reginald Mohun lives in Restormel Castle and maintains the king's writ when he chooses. But lining his pockets and obliging his friends is more important to him than decrees from London. And celebrating the end of winter and the start of spring cheers heart and soul.'

Father Gregory was struck down with an ague soon after Christmas, and much to his own regret could do no celebrating. He lay coddled under blankets in the parsonage, sipping infusions of dried blackcurrant leaves, while Simon led the singing villagers into the ancient church, lit by the wavering wicks of shallow clay oil lamps on the ledges under the windows of the nave. He walked up to the altar, bowed his head, then turned to watch through the rood screen as the parishioners trooped in, handing their candles to the sidesmen, Oswald Marrack the reeve and Jim Perrin, ostler at the local inn. Six were placed in tall candlestands to provide more light, and a warm glow lit a sea of smiling faces as, after a prayer for Father Gregory's recovery, Simon began to intone the canticle of Mary from the Gospel of Luke. An hour later, after the haunting *Nunc dimittis*, everyone set to, reaching up for the evergreens, and bundling them together to be taken outside to add to the huge pile of brushwood and flammable rubbish they had brought up yesterday for the bonfire.

Simon snuffed out the candles and followed his parishioners out of the church, enjoying their high spirits as the fire was lit, and pretending not to notice that some of the village girls were tossing woven figurines into the flames and murmuring incantations. Leather flasks of ale appeared from under cloaks and the clamour grew. On the other side of the blaze, a dark-haired young woman with bright eyes was throwing garlands of ivy that crackled and curled in the leaping flames. She smiled, giving him a quick nod. Morwenna was the daughter of the local washerwoman, and her weekly visits to the vicarage to collect and deliver laundry had become very precious to him. As had their clifftop walks and the rare times when she was able to get away at night and meet him.

Soon after they'd met a year ago, he'd asked Marrack, a thin, bony man with a perpetual frown of suspicion, about her background. 'She's a widow,' the reeve had said, giving him

5

a sharp look. 'Her husband Mark was a fisherman. His boat was lost several months ago in a storm. So she went back to her mother and took up laundry work. Mark left her nothing.'

'She seems...' Simon had hesitated.

Marrack had given a snigger. 'She seems a cut above Tintagel folk, you mean. Could be on account of nothing being known of her father. Rumour has it he was well born, but the only thing that's certain is that her mother married with a child on the way. She hasn't a penny to her name, or I'd consider her as a wife myself. Though she'd need her haughty ways beaten out of her.'

Simon's feelings for Morwenna had grown. She seemed to enjoy his company too, listening wide-eyed as he talked of Ewelme and London and Windsor; telling him in turn how much she loved her own wild and windswept homeland. He longed to marry her, dowerless though she was, but if he were ordained as a priest that would be impossible. And, unless he was ordained, he would be penniless himself.

Then everything changed. Two weeks ago he came across information that he knew would earn him Princess Alyce's undying gratitude and a generous reward: a clue to the identity of those behind the murder of her ill-starred third husband, William, Duke of Suffolk. Knowing who had been responsible for his gruesome execution would finally mend the rift between her and her son. How long would it be before he got an answer to the letter that he had sent to Ewelme Palace? It would take at least a week to reach Oxfordshire. If Alyce was away from Ewelme, or weather delayed the king's messenger to whom he had entrusted it, it could be even longer. And it would take just as long to get her reply. But perhaps by St Valentine's Day...

Standing at the lych gate, he watched the villagers troop down the hill singing raucous and entirely unchristian songs. Candlemas Eve had morphed into Imbolc with a vengeance. He went back inside the church, walked up the aisle, and knelt on the altar step head in hands, praying for their sins to be forgiven – and his own. Then he snuffed out the oil lamps and left, turning the massive key in the iron-bound north door, and tucking it behind a loose stone low in the porch. The moon was rising in the east. It was entering into Aquarius, a sign he hoped that Dame Fortune was favouring him at last.

He started along the track that led to his island lodging. The sea glimmered in the moonlight, and once his eyes adapted themselves to the darkness it was easy enough to see his way. He hoped Morwenna had managed to slip away to meet him at their usual place, a sheltered niche in the rock close to the crossing to Tintagel Castle. Far below, surf crashed around the steep-sided promontory, now almost an island, on which most of the ancient fortress had been built. He started along the narrow path on the seaward side of the high stone walls that guarded the approach to the island. He stopped for a moment and gazed across at the castle, dreaming of using Alyce's reward to establish a new life in Cornwall with Morwenna.

Behind him, metal scraped against stone. Simon turned to see three dark figures approaching, one of them sword in hand. Recognising the hatchet face, scarred and brutal, of Cornwall's deputy sheriff, he backed against the wall, profoundly uneasy.

'B... by the Rood, Sir Reginald,' he stuttered. 'I had n... not expected to see you here.'

As courtesy demanded, he bowed – and one of Mohun's companions dealt his bent head a hammer blow with the hilt of a sword.

Ewelme

Tamsin added more logs to the fire Princess Alyce had asked for in her turret reading room, then went to the window and looked down into the central courtyard of Ewelme Palace. She could see right into Martha Purbeck's room, and watched her berate a kitchen boy for some misdemeanour, then slip him a sweetmeat from a jar on her table. Tamsin smiled, remembering how awed she had been by the chamberlain when she first came to the palace two and a half years ago. Now she was almost nineteen years old and a striking young woman. Her unruly hair was tamed, and gleamed chestnut under an elegant caul of blue silk thread, and she had had more than one offer of marriage. But she wasn't ready to settle down. Will Stonor, the one person she longed to spend the rest of her life with, was utterly unattainable. And service with her courageous, demanding mistress had much to offer. Though since Christmas Princess Alyce seemed to have retreated into herself like a snail in its shell, spending long hours in the palace chapel with her chaplain John Getour.

There was a tap at the door. She went to open it and smiled at the sight of the halo of wiry white hair around the head of Farhang Amiri. A Persian who had been doctor to the Lancastrian queen Margaret of Anjou, Farhang was dismissed by the xenophobic court physicians as soon as he arrived in England with her in 1445. Alyce, who had learnt his value as they journeyed from France, had promptly asked him to be infirmarer of Ewelme's God's House, and he had lived there for over twenty years.

'Lady Alyce said that I might steal you away to teach you about using plants as cures for common ailments. You need to know what's what, or we'll have you poisoning folk. Then I'll reward you with a look at two treasures I bought from John Doll's bookshop last week. One is a marvellously wrought *mappa mundi* which has Noah's Ark perched on Mount Ararat at its centre. Not much good for showing travellers the way, though, except as a guide towards Christian life.'

Tamsin smiled wistfully. 'Which may suit my lady better these days than real maps. She seems weary of journeying. And she's begun formal rehearsal with her chaplain for becoming a vowess. It's as if she's given up on the world.'

'Well, there's no need for you to,' Farhang replied. 'You've got all your life in front of you. With the right man by your side, you...' He stopped, seeing tears beginning to glisten in Tamsin's eyes and remembering what Alyce had told him about the girl's yearning after Will Stonor – far above her in rank, and duty-bound to marry a well-born heiress.

Pretending not to have noticed her turning away to hide her distress, he continued talking. 'And the young duke and his family are coming for the Candlemas Hunt. She won't have time to ponder on her immortal soul once her grandchildren are rampaging around the palace.'

Pressing her sleeve to her eyes, Tamsin gave him a watery smile. 'What's the other book?'

'It's an account of the travels of Marco Polo the Venetian,' Farhang continued smoothly. 'Doll told me it was copied from a version given to the University Library by Duke Humfrey of Gloucester, which was later purloined by the queen's father,

Earl Rivers. As were so many of the Good Duke's books.' He shook his head sadly at the avarice of the Wydevilles.

It was Tamsin's turn to change the subject. 'Let's go to the infirmary. I've got so much to learn. Will you show me how to make up my lady's favourite lemon-scented salve?'

On their way down the stairs they met Alyce coming up. She was wearing a mud-stained gardening apron and a faint scent of manure hung around her. She smiled vaguely at them. Her thoughts were on the signs of spring she'd found in her wintry garden while overseeing Wat and Adam spreading rotted stable dung over her brick-edged raised beds. Poking careful fingers into the earth of the most sheltered one, she had found shoots emerging from three specimens of an exotic bulb called *Ashk-e-Siavash*, the tears of Siavash, that Farhang had sent for from Persia. He'd told her that the nectar that dripped from its flamboyant crown of scarlet flowers was said to show the plant mourning the cruel fate of Prince Siavash.

At the sight – and smell – of her, Farhang raised his eyebrows. 'My lady, since the young duke and duchess may arrive today, I see that you are in need of Tamsin's ministrations to help you change for dinner. Perhaps this is a bad time to take her away.'

'I don't see why,' said Alyce. 'Jack and Bess won't get here until tomorrow. They celebrated Candlemas this morning with the king and queen at Windsor and will surely stay tonight in Henley.' Then she saw Tamsin wrinkling her nose and frowning at her earth-stained fingers and muddy apron. She took the apron off, used it to rub her hands cleaner, and handed it to her.

'Take it to Nan in the laundry on your way to the infirmary. Changing can wait awhile. Farhang, I pulled away the earth a little to see how your bulbs were doing, and they are shooting already, thanks to those glass panels Job Smith fashioned for me. I want to record the date in my garden book. Come back in an hour, Tamsin.' She disappeared into her reading closet, mind already on what she would write. The bulb promised a flower fit for a king. The true king, not this Yorkist upstart.

'It's good news that her grace's family is coming for the Candlemas Hunt,' said Farhang, as they walked towards the God's House infirmary. 'Matters have improved between them. Since Duchess Bess saved your life and packed Sir Robert Harcourt off with his tail between his legs two years ago, they've been fast friends. She's also eager to mend bridges with the young duke after the bad business of her stolen book last summer. Though that may not be easy. He'll still be feeling guilty, and that's no basis for reconciliation. She should trust him more; she still treats him like a refractory child.'

He unlocked the door of the infirmary. Tamsin loved the long, whitewashed room, kept spotlessly clean by her grand-mother Nan Ormesby. She followed Farhang to his inner sanctum at the far end and waited while he unlocked the door. Its walls were lined with shelves, on which stood rows of jars and bottles. Below them, drawers held bandages and surgical tools. Bunches of dried herbs dangled from ceiling hooks. Farhang reached for one of them.

'*Melissa*. Ibn Sina, expert of experts, assures us it makes mind and heart merry. And we'll need beeswax shavings and almond oil. He selected two jars. 'Bring over the smallest pestle and mortar and start pounding. I'll light a candle to melt the beeswax.'

An hour later, holding a small blue and white jar carefully in two hands, Tamsin returned to the palace, and went up to

Alyce's reading closet. Her mistress was at her sloping desk, intent on an open book, but looked up when Tamsin entered.

'What have you got there, child?' She opened the jar and sniffed. 'Lemon balm – my favourite ointment. Sovereign for healing and lingering in the memory. How thoughtful you are! But surely we have none growing at this time of year?'

'Farhang dried long stems of it in the autumn,' said Tamsin eagerly. 'I know just how to make it now. I pounded the leaves and stalks to powder, which I stirred into melted beeswax and almond oil.'

Shouts of welcome sounded from the palace gatehouse. Glancing out of the eastward window, Tamsin saw two harbingers in the blue and gold livery of de la Pole riding through it.

'Your son's outriders are here, my lady.'

Alyce joined her at the window. Her face fell. 'Then they'll arrive today. They must have decided not to overnight at Henley.' She grimaced. 'Young fools. It'll be dark before we've settled them all in. And the children will be impossible. Why on earth did I invite them?'

Tamsin wasn't fooled. She knew that Alyce now adored her grandchildren, particularly eight-year-old John, whom King Edward had just dubbed Earl of Lincoln. She also knew about the hectic events that had preceded the present peaceful state of affairs. Confident these days of her mistress's favour, she dared a comment.

'Seems all told that you are safer with your family as friends than as enemies.'

Her mistress was silent for a long beat. Then she shook her head slowly. 'I'm not safe yet. Bess and I understand each other well enough, but Jack stays reserved. I've forgiven him his foolish plotting against me, but I need to win his loyalty by discovering who was responsible for his father's death. That's the only way to convince him that I didn't betray William. But it's nearly twenty years since the murder. The trail is cold. How in the world am I going to discover who was guilty?'

'Perhaps you could ask Lord Wenlock?' suggested Tamsin. 'You and he are on good terms and my grandmother Nan told me that he was even then at the heart of politics.'

Alyce nodded. 'She has the right of it. Though then as now he was adept at not committing himself. Well, he and Mistress Moulton are going to join us tomorrow for the hunt and the feast. I'll see what I can do. Though he is a hard man to get a straight answer from.'

'Mistress Joan might be able to winkle anything he knows out of him,' said Tamsin. 'He's always ready to dance to her tune.'

'True,' said Alyce with a reminiscent smile as she thought about the redoubtable proprietor of the Sign of the Mole. 'She's a formidable woman. Now, we must ready ourselves for the invasion. Send to the kitchen for hot water and look out my blue velvet gown.'

An hour later, arrayed as befitted the mother-in-law of the king of England's sister, she swept downstairs.

Oxford

Propped up against pillows in the best bedchamber that Oxford's Mitre Inn could offer, Sir John Wenlock smiled at the snores emanating from his bedmate. Joan Moulton lived life to the full, eating, drinking and making love with a gusto that delighted him. He wasn't sure how she would take to the news that he'd married again. But he'd never been more in need of money than he was now.

Joan stirred, farted loudly and yawned as she stretched herself. She shifted closer to Wenlock's well-set, muscled body until she was nestling in the crook of his arm, then looked up at him with a grin that made her look like a satisfied tabby cat.

'That was fun, John. It's been too long. More life in you than in many a young lordling. What have you been up to? I have a feeling that there's something you aren't telling me.'

He looked down at her warily. 'There is. And I hope that it won't make a difference to you and me. I've won myself a fortune. The only drawback is that it was at the price of marrying Agnes Danvers.'

'James's aunt? By the Rood, you'll earn whatever you get from her. She's a gnarling old hussy. Will she be moving into The Royal?'

'No, she has a fancy to get out of London, especially since the return of the pestilence. She'll live at Someries, so The Royal will be all ours. Nor does she have any great desire for my company, only for becoming Lady Agnes, and being able to boast of her rank to other lawyers' wives.'

'But don't you have enough resources of your own? The king has been generous, and you have a retainer from the Earl of Warwick besides.'

He wondered how much he should tell her. It could put her life at risk as well as his own. He resolved, as he generally did, to keep his counsel.

'Can one ever have too much money?' he quipped. 'I have a mind to celebrate with a wedding present to myself of a book that John Doll is saving for me. But how does your god-daughter Kate? Are she and James through the honey-moon stage?'

'They've been married eight months now and are as happy as turtle doves. Kate is expecting a baby, and James is taking to the life of a country squire with a will. He inherited a fine Warwickshire manor from an uncle. And guess who they have as a near neighbour? Lady Elizabeth Malory, Sir Thomas's wife. Weren't you Malory's overlord for a few years until your ward young Mowbray came of age and took up his dukedom? James says that nothing has been heard of him for months. But his son Robert and his wife live nearby at Winwick, and his grandson Nicholas is a promising young lad.'

Wenlock, who knew much of the affairs of Sir Thomas Malory, merely grunted, rose out of bed, and reached for his clothes.

'Time to head for the bookshops, my own. And lovely as Kate Arderne – or rather Danvers – is, I'd rather have you.'

'That's good. Marriage is the last thing that I want, so I don't grudge you a wife. I just think you may live to regret being shackled to that old shrew.'

※

John Doll had changed little since Wenlock had last visited his Catte Street shop. He was still balding and bespectacled, with smears of chalk on his shabby fustian gown. He rose from his high-backed chair beside a grimy lattice window and bowed.

'Welcome, Mistress Moulton. And Sir John, it's been much too long since I had the pleasure of serving you. Not since that unpleasant fracas with Sir Robert Harcourt.'

'Who is presumably still lording it around Oxford with his brother,' said Wenlock.

Doll shook his head. 'Sir Richard is no longer sheriff, though he and Lady Catherine are about, living at Chalgrove. As to Sir Robert, the word is that he's going to join the Earl of Warwick and the royal fleet with his own ship, *The Peacock*. He's gone to Bristol to fit her out. Then he'll sail to Fowey. They are policing the Channel against rebels and pirates – though I suspect that they won't be averse to privateering on their own account.'

'We're on our way to Ewelme,' said Wenlock. 'I'd like to take Princess Alyce a Candlemas gift. You know her tastes, Doll. What do you recommend?'

The bookseller thought for a moment, then crossed the shop to a large oak aumbry. He pulled forward the ring of keys that hung from his belt and unlocked the right-hand door. After groping inside for a few seconds, he pulled out a small octavo book.

'This is Thomas Hoccleve's translation of Christine de Pisan's *Epistle of Othea*. It is, as I'm sure you know, Mistress Moulton, supposedly a letter to Hector of Troy from the goddess of wisdom and prudence. This copy has some very fine illustrations.' Doll opened the book at a marker, and Joan and Wenlock examined the picture of a seductive Circe and a puzzled Odysseus, surrounded by several very meek-looking pigs.

'Alyce would love that,' said Joan. 'Men portrayed as greedy swine, doing what they are told for once.'

'But Odysseus has his wicked way with her in the end,' countered Wenlock with a sardonic smile. 'It's just right, Doll. Please wrap it up and add its cost to my tally.'

Doll nodded and rang a small bell. A boy appeared from the inner recesses of his shop.

'Wrap this up, lad.' The boy retreated, book in hand.

Doll turned to Wenlock and Joan. 'A word of warning.

The pestilence that began in London in Novmeber is heading this way. There has been a case in High Wycombe. It will surely spread to Oxford. Please tell Lady Alyce. Ewelme has rarely been affected by plague, but this seems an especially virulent kind, and the ridge road through Swyncombe goes close to the palace. She would do well to cut off contact with her neighbours as much as she can. I myself am shutting up shop on Friday and retiring to my manor in Wychwood until it passes.'

Joan reached into her pocket and took out a tiny glass bottle. She raised it to her nose and inhaled its spicy scent. Powdered unicorn horn together with cloves, rosemary and wormwood were a sovereign defence against the pestilence, her new herbalist had assured her. She'd asked her to fill a second flask, prettily chased in silver, for Alyce.

'Thanks for the warning, Master Doll. I left London for Charlbury because of plague in the city. I hope it won't follow me there.'

'Where are you bound after Ewelme, my lord?' Doll asked Wenlock.

'I must dare London one more time. Then I need to go to Southampton. I'm commanded by the king to appease the German merchants whose ships were towed there in December by the so-called Gallants of Fowey. After they'd been thoroughly pillaged.'

'The Gallants of Fowey – that name has a fine ring,' said Joan. 'Who are they?'

'Cornish pirates, though they prefer to call themselves privateers, and talk much of being faithful subjects defending England against the French and the Spanish. They're led by local gentry, and the shire court in Lostwithiel is run by justices who are loth to convict their own friends and relations. The Gallants get their name from their base at Golant. It's a fortified haven upriver from Fowey. But the Earl of Warwick is to sail to Cornwall and bring them to heel by indenting them into the royal fleet. King Edward is commandeering every ship he can to confront the French.'

Ewelme

On Monday afternoon Alyce spent a happy hour with her grandchildren. Eight-year-old John was taller than his father had been at the same age, and much better mannered. He proudly showed her the elaborate silver hilt of the short sword that the king had given him when he was knighted at Windsor, and she bit back an admonition about being careful with it. Little Ned was now three, galloping his hobby horse tirelessly up and down the solar. Bess sat by the fire with baby Cecily, rolling soft leather balls for her to crawl after. When Nanny Molly entered to suggest that Bess and the children explore the garden while the sun was out, Alyce waved them away with a smile and headed up to her beloved turret study. If she was going to survive the visit, she knew that she must make some time for herself. Tamsin attended her, happy to be allowed to go on reading a rhyming tale of Tristram and Isolde that Alyce had acquired a week earlier from John Doll.

They had barely had an hour of peace before there was a brisk rat-a-tat at the turret door and the Ewelme steward Ben Bilton strode in. He nodded brusquely at Tamsin as he handed Alyce a packet.

'Looks to be another missive from your former secretary, my lady,' he said. 'He's proving a faithful correspondent at least. Double-sealed this time, too, and sent by king's messenger.'

Bilton had never had much time for Simon Brailles, Tamsin reflected. They were such different kinds of men. Ben was all action, Simon all caution. She turned to the candle box and selected two large ones for the brackets on each side of Alyce's prie-dieu, glad of an excuse to avoid Ben's probing gaze. She had once hero-worshipped him, but he hadn't been interested. Over the past year he had noticed her new poise with admiration, and tried to begin a flirtation, but now it was she who held herself aloof. Ben was baffled by her indifference. He remembered saving her from the drunken advances of Sir Robert Harcourt soon after she first began service in the palace, and how narrowly she had escaped worse from his henchman Hamel Turvey. Perhaps such incidents had turned her against men for good and she'd become one of those weird wenches who preferred their own sex. Or no sex at all. He eyed her graceful figure longingly, then comforted himself a little by thinking of the inviting smiles of Matilda Lovejoy, the new tiring maid. She had started work at the palace after Brailles left for Cornwall and Tamsin replaced him as Alyce's secretary. He gave his mistress a bow, then strode out of the room, crashing the door closed.

Tamsin saw Alyce frown and decided on retreat. 'I'll fetch a glass of malmsey and some sweetmeats from the buttery, my lady,' she said, and left – but not by the door that Ben had taken.

Alyce put the letter from Brailles on her desk and sighed. She was aware of the tension between her two faithful servants, but unsure how to resolve it. Nothing would please her more than their marriage. The handsome timber-framed house she was allowing Bilton to build at the foot of Rabbit Hill would make them a fine home. But she sympathised with Tamsin's determination to stay single until she had seen more of life. She remembered her words when they had first met: 'I want to journey, to see the world.' She had herself once relished travelling. Expeditions to France when she'd been married to Thomas Montagu and William de la Pole. Visits in her widowhood to London and Bruges; pilgrimages to Walsingham and Compostella. Tours of her far-flung estates. But three years ago she'd decided to hand over responsibility for her estates in Suffolk to Jack and had moved back to Ewelme, her heartland. Now her books, her garden and her school were her chief delights.

But was this all there was to life? A dwindling away in a safe haven? Though in her mid-sixties, she was as fit as she had been in her forties, and she enjoyed the chase as much as ever. The thought of hunting and hawking brought to mind her slender golden hound Leo, her faithful companion on so many occasions. Tears rose in her eyes. Last November he had died untimely, as a dog – or of course a person – could. A lump had risen on his shoulder one day after he'd been racing through the Ewelme woods after a deer. Had the deer turned at bay and caught him with an antler? Or had Leo careered into a low branch? For whatever reason, he had suffered some internal injury, a bleeding that couldn't be stemmed. Two days later he had drawn his last breath, patient as ever, his head on her lap. She had other dogs of course, but none that could replace Leo in her heart. She'd directed the men at work on her tomb in the church to recreate him and his thick curly pelt and flamboyant tail in stone around the feet of her own effigy. Were dogs admitted to heaven? she wondered. Shortly after Leo's death, she'd asked John Getour, and he had said comfortingly that God had not pronounced either for or against. 'Then I think Leo will be,' she'd declared. 'There was no beast more faithful and loving – Christian virtues both.' Since his death she had felt acutely lonely.

A brilliant shard of light from the setting sun flashed out of the sullen clouds and lit up the twin hills above Wittenham, as if pointing a pathway to adventure. Then it struck her that retreating into herself was not the answer. Better to venture forth again, so that Tamsin could see something more of the world. It might rid the girl of her foolish fondness for Will Stonor, Alyce's favourite godson, and far above her in rank. Spring was when folk long to go on pilgrimage, her grandfather had written. Perhaps she should plan to do the same, taking Tamsin – and Bilton – with her. To Hailes Abbey, or Pontefract, where the relics of St Thomas, the canonised second Earl of Lancaster, had recently begun to sweat blood.

It would be a seemly way of marking the year when she finally became a vowess, abjuring all possibility of another marriage. But, she wondered, had she altogether given up hope of finding a life companion? A kindred spirit as fond as she was of exploring the literary treasures which were so easy to acquire thanks to her wealth and the miracle of the printing presses of first Germany and now Italy. Someone to accompany her on journeys to Bruges and Venice. A bony face with quizzical eyebrows under a thick tangle of black hair rose up in her mind. Denzil Caerleon had once been her most valued retainer, a man with a mind in tune with her own. But three years ago he had fallen from her favour with a vengeance. She hadn't seen him since. Joan Moulton, his sister-in-law, had written to say that he was now serving in the Earl of Warwick's Channel fleet. He had ever been a wanderer, she remembered wistfully. But perhaps one day he would like a place to call home.

There was a tap on the door and Farhang entered. She had told Tamsin to ask him for something for the dryness in her eyes that was beginning to hamper her ability to read for long periods.

'Here's the eye ointment you asked for, Princess,' he said. 'Made from powdered fennel seeds and *Euphrasia*, which the old wives aptly call eyebright. Place it on your lower eyelids so that it seeps in, then hold a warm flannel to your eyes for a few minutes every night. And why not ask Tamsin to read to you more? She has a lovely voice, and you must cherish your sight.' He stopped, looking appraisingly at her.

'What's on your mind, your grace? You seem preoccupied.'

She sighed. Then, impulsively, she told him the truth. 'I'm lonely, Farhang. And I was wondering about asking Denzil Caerleon to return to Ewelme. And perhaps, if he was minded to, to become more than my man of business. Though I know full well that he's twenty years younger than me and far below me in rank. Do you think it would be madness? After all, Henry V's widow Queen Catherine married her Master of Horse, Owen Tudor.'

Farhang hesitated, knowing that to disagree as adamantly as he felt inclined to would bring out his mistress's innate contrariness. He chose his words carefully.

'Rumi tells us we should be suspicious of what we want. But it might answer, your grace. He's had two failed marriages; perhaps he would welcome a financially secure haven. A May and December match isn't an uncommon option when there's a financial advantage to be gained by the younger party, and comforting companionship for the older.'

He gave a little cough, then went on with a mischievous glint in his eye, 'I believe that the Dowager Duchess of Norfolk feels herself excellently served.'

Alyce grimaced as a vision of 69-year-old Katherine Neville, powdered and rouged and simpering on the arm of her 24-year-old husband John Wydeville came to mind.

Seeing the expression on her face, Farhang felt he could safely hint at his true opinion. 'Though Christine de Pisan's wise words in her book on the Three Virtues do come to mind: "The height of folly is an old woman taking a young man." Owen Tudor and Queen Catherine were much the same age. And it's possible that King Edward would ban the match on grounds of unsuitability. He could, you know, since your son is wed to his sister.'

Alyce winced, walked over to the window and gazed out over her garden. Christine de Pisan had the right of it. Marriage to any man wasn't the answer for her. She was fabulously wealthy and proudly independent; nor did she want to lose control over her Ewelme heartland. Moreover, women friends could be just as kin to one in spirit. Often more. She smiled as the thought of clever, canny Joan Moulton came to mind, successfully running her dead husband's London bookselling business and enjoying her widowhood to the full. She turned back to Farhang.

'Christine is always to be relied on as a guide for women. It was a foolish thought. No sooner had I voiced it than I could see it wouldn't answer. But I need a change of scene. I have it in mind to make a spring pilgrimage. Perhaps to Hailes Abbey, or north to Pontefract. Or do you think I'm too old? Should I keep preparing to become a vowess as I do intend – yet still find myself loth to enter on.'

Farhang shook his head with a smile. 'As to age, you have more energy and acumen than many of half your years,' he said. 'A pilgrimage is an excellent notion. Both an adventure and a fitting prelude to taking your vows, which no doubt you will do when the time feels right. I only wish that I could come with you. But I fear my travelling days are over.' He noticed the packet on her desk.

'Who is your letter from, Princess?'

'Simon Brailles. It's only a month since his last one. I wonder why he's writing so soon.' She sat down in the chair at her desk, broke its wax seals and tried to loosen the knots of the stout twine around the waxed cloth that protected the letter.

'It's tied up as if it contained the Crown jewels,' she grumbled. Reaching impatiently for the small damascene steel scissors that hung on a short chain from her belt, she cut the twine. Then she put on her eyeglasses, unfolded the letter's two closely written pages and began to read. After a few seconds, she gave a gasp.

'No wonder he took such care! Farhang, Simon has found a witness to my husband's murder!'

'In Cornwall?' asked Farhang, astonished. 'Who is he?'

Alyce didn't answer, immersed in the letter. Farhang saw her expression change to horror, then frowning concentration. At last she looked up at him, holding out the letter. He walked over to the window seat and sat down to read.

14th January the eighth year of the reign of King Edward
Most puissant sovereign lady, greetings.

You will be surprised to hear from me so soon. But I pick up my pen with good reason. I have made a discovery that is likely to solve the mystery of your lord's foul murder. As requested in your last letter, I visited your mines at Creddis Creek on the Camel river. On my way back through Wadebridge I saw a battered old ship in the boatyard called the *St John Evangelist*. Her gunwales were being replaced and a new mainmast shipped.

As I was watching it being hoisted into position, its master came up to me. Seeing my Suffolk badge, he thought me in the service of your son. He said that if I made it worth his while he would give me something for which the duke would pay me surpassing well. The old rascal was soused in ale and I waved him away, but he was so persistent that I grew curious, and went with him to the tavern. There he told me that his name was Madoc, and that the ship had once been the *Nicholas of the Tower*, the ship that captured his grace your husband off Dover. He'd been her bosun then, and had watched as John Wyte, the captain of the *Nicholas*, acted as judge at the duke's mockery of a trial, then ordered his execution. No one protested, because the night before Wyte had paid them all well and sworn they wouldn't be punished as he had a parcel of evidences proving who had ordered the murder.

Once the duke's body had been left on Dover Beach, Wyte was even more exultant, telling Madoc that when they'd stripped the duke of his rich attire, he'd taken something that would make his fortune. Madoc distrusted him, and that night, while Wyte and the other ship's officers were carousing in the sterncastle, he crept into the captain's cabin, found the parcel of evidences and hid it away in his own sea chest.

When Wyte discovered its loss next day, he ordered a search, but a squadron of French ships came into view, and the *Nicholas* had to run for Dover Harbour. There the part she played in Suffolk's death came out. Wyte told the court investigating the duke's murder that he had been locked below while it happened. As all the world knows, he was exonerated, though the court was suspicious of him.

Wyte was then required to sail the *Nicholas* to the besieged town of Cherbourg to tell its English garrison that relief was on its way. On her way home she was badly damaged by the French ships blockading the town and Wyte was killed. The *Nicholas* barely managed to reach Portsmouth. A replacement was commissioned, and what was left of the old ship was renamed the *St John Evangelist* and taken to Ireland. Madoc chose to stay with her as master, and later he married an Irish girl.

He has spent the next fifteen years coasting out of Wexford. In December the Earl of Warwick sent word to all ports requisitioning ships for the royal fleet, and the Lord Deputy of Ireland, Lord Tiptoft, told the *St John*'s owners to take her to Wadebridge to be fitted out for war. 'But my wife is dead, and I don't want to fight the Frenchies again,' he told me. 'I want to go home to Wales. So when I saw your Suffolk badge I thought to myself: time to jump ship and sell Wyte's papers to the duke's son.'

It took all the monies I'd collected in Creddis to purchase the evidences, but, as I know how important discovering the truth about Duke William's murder is to you, I was sure that you would not grudge the expense. Although the parcel is securely sealed, I dare not trust it to a courier. Have I your permission to come to Ewelme with it? John Gregory says he can manage without me for a few weeks.

Yours in Christ,
Simon Brailles

Below Simon's signature were three more lines of writing:

My lady, Madoc urged secrecy on me. Not all those concerned in Duke William's murder are dead and gone. Soon after he brought the *St John* into Wadebridge, it was ransacked and he fears he is being watched. For the nonce I have hidden the parcel in a place which will remain a secret between you, me and Our Lady, befall what may. *SB*

Farhang put the letter down, shaking his head over its postscript. 'That loose-mouthed Welsh sailor was taking a great risk in handing the parcel over to Brailles in a tavern. Who knows who could have noticed? Brailles may be in danger. Send a letter by king's messenger advising him to await the arrival of an escort and send an escort straight away.'

'Taking a fortnight to get there and a fortnight to return? That will mean a month's delay before he reaches Ewelme,' said Alyce. 'And if Madoc's story is true, I want to open that parcel as soon as possible.'

Her idea of taking a spring pilgrimage to show Tamsin more of the world came back to her. Simon's earlier letters had made her long to go to Cornwall again. She had been there only once, with her second husband, Thomas Montagu, Earl of Salisbury, in the summer of 1428, shortly before they returned to France, where he was to command the English forces. He'd had judicial matters to attend to in the Cornish capital Lostwithiel; passing judgment on a rascal called Richard Tregoys who had been robbing traders taking tin to Fowey. She and Thomas had inspected her mines near Wadebridge and visited Tintagel. She remembered the dramatic setting of the legendary castle, linked to the mainland only by a high ridge of rock and battered by wild seas throwing up great spumes of foam, the day they had spent there, dreaming.

She shook herself back to the present. 'Farhang, suppose I travelled to Cornwall myself? With a proper company, of course. I would announce it as a pilgrimage to the shrine of the blessed St Materiana of Tintagel preparatory to my becoming a vowess as well as an opportunity to visit my properties there. The Trevelyans of Whalesborough are only half a day's ride from Tintagel. They would help me, I'm sure.'

She smiled reminiscently. *Time Trieth Troth* had been the cryptic motto engraved on the gold cup Sir John Trevelyan had given her fifteen years ago as a thank-you gift for arranging his marriage to her wealthy cousin Elizabeth. Thanks to his good looks and flirtatious ways, John had been a favourite both of Henry VI and of his queen, Margaret of Anjou. After Edward of York was crowned king, Trevelyan had lain low, a closet Lancastrian as were so many of the Cornish, venturing out on the high seas whenever opportunity arose, and sending some of the profits of his piracy to Lorraine, where Queen Margaret was planning her husband's restoration to the throne.

Two and a half years ago he had ventured rather too far, plundering off Essex and getting badly wounded by a crossbow bolt fired from a Yorkist ship. Unbeknownst to Alyce, he had been brought up the Thames from London to Ewelme by Denzil Caerleon and cared for in the God's House by Farhang. He had the narrowest of escapes when the Harcourt brothers came to Ewelme in search of traitors. Ben Bilton had smuggled him away to her neighbours, the Stonors of Stonor Park. She hadn't seen or spoken to him since, but in an earlier letter Simon had said how generously Trevelyan and his wife had welcomed him, even inviting him for Christmas.

Farhang's voice broke in on her thoughts. 'I think it would be most unwise, Princess. Especially at present, when discontent with York is increasing. For all your private loyalties, Jack's marriage made you aunt to the king. Sir John Trevelyan is not a steady man. You'd much better send Bilton and a couple of other men to escort Brailles back.'

But this time his advice fell on deaf ears. Alyce was already planning her adventure. 'I will of course take men with me, led by Ben Bilton. And perhaps some friends as well. Such as Mistress Moulton. She's always wanted to visit Exeter Cathedral's famous library. She's coming for the Candlemas Hunt with Sir John Wenlock. He'd also be a sterling companion.' As she spoke, Lord Wenlock's saturnine face rose up in her mind's eye, inscrutable but, she liked to think, benignly intentioned towards her.

Farhang knew better than to go on arguing. He'd let others declare the impossibility of an expedition west so early in the year. Joan Moulton and John Wenlock would be against it, he was sure. He bowed himself out, leaving his mistress alone.

Alyce's head whirled with ideas. The journey would satisfy both her own restlessness and dear Tamsin's longing to travel. And being so much in Ben Bilton's company might persuade the girl of his merits as a husband. She was sure that Jack and Bess would agree with alacrity to staying on at Ewelme while she was away. They might wonder at her travelling so early in the year, but they would relish the warmth and luxury of the palace in the winter months. So different from chilly Wingfield Castle, blasted by easterly winds.

She looked out of the window to the rooks wheeling over the beech trees on the twin hills above Wittenham. It would be a cold journey. Her grandfather had recommended going on pilgrimage in April 'when sweet showers had pierced the drought of March to the root', but she couldn't wait that long. After all, the roads as far as Exeter were well looked after by the wealthy monasteries along the main highways. Cornwall's remoter roads were notoriously bad, but they were more passable in winter than when muddied by April's often far from sweet showers and rutted by travellers. Winter journeys were also safer. There was less cover for vagrant robbers while the trees and hedgerows were leafless. And spring came earlier to Cornwall than to Oxfordshire.

While she was musing, Tamsin returned from the buttery with a silver cup of Alyce's favourite wine.

'Has Master Brailles written news of moment, my lady?' she asked.

Sipping the malmsey, Alyce eyed her speculatively, and decided to trust her with the truth. 'He has indeed. A sailor who was on the *Nicholas of the Tower* sold him sealed evidences which he says will reveal who was behind the murder of Duke William. Simon asks to come back to Ewelme with them. But I had rather take a company to Tintagel to fetch them myself.' She looked at Tamsin with a twinkle in her eye. 'Do I need to ask if you would like to accompany us?'

Tamsin's cheeks glowed with excitement. 'To Tintagel, my lady? I would love it beyond anything. It's where the story of King Arthur begins.'

'Let us hope that it's also where the mystery of William's death ends. But you must keep the true reason for our journey close. We'll call it part a visit to my properties, part pilgrimage. And I'm going to ask Mistress Moulton and Lord Wenlock to keep us company.'

'Who else will come with us?' asked Tamsin.

'Ben Bilton of course. And grooms and harbingers. And what would you say to my new maid Matilda Lovejoy coming with us? Would she be company for you?'

Tamsin thought for a moment, then nodded. 'She's quick and lively, and she doesn't idle about the way...' She hesitated.

'The way Marlene used to do,' Alyce finished for her. 'Talking of that devious slut, did Matilda say what became of her?'

'She's married to John Yeme. He's one of the Stonor bailiffs and had been sweet on her for years. They've got two babes now. Sir Richard Harcourt still has a soft spot for her, apparently. He's godfather of their first child, little Dicky. The second's a girl called Jeanne, after her mother.'

Alyce sniffed. Dicky indeed. She suspected that the wily Sir Richard might have dispensed with the god part of godfather. Marlene had been the root cause of Caerleon's disgrace and departure. Which he richly deserved for bedding the daughter of her greatest friends. But at least he hadn't been shackled to the girl for life. She wondered how he was getting on in the Earl of Warwick's Channel fleet. Which was, she realised, with a tightening of the muscles of her heart, on its way to Cornwall.

'Good,' she said absently. 'Then I'll ask Matilda if she'd like to come along. But keep an eye on her. Lady Stonor warned me that she was somewhat flighty. Bilton seems quite taken with her, and the last thing we need on a journey is a romance.'

Alyce saw her new secretary's brow crease before she nodded briskly. No doubt at the idea of Bilton being 'taken' with Lovejoy. She smiled to herself, remembering her father Thomas's cynical maxim: rivalry is the spice of love.

TUESDAY 4 FEBRUARY 1469

Ireland

Simon Brailles was wishing he was dead. His terrifying hours in the Tower paled into insignificance beside the wracking agony of his stomach as he was tossed to and fro against the curved wooden ribs of the ship's hold. At least he had been able to end his torture by giving away what little he knew. But there was absolutely nothing he could do to control the wild weather assaulting the ship. He had no idea where he was, or why. He'd come to his senses while he was being trussed up and had heard muttered words from his captors. 'We need to get him away... Duchess of Suffolk mustn't know... Hurleigh said Wexford...' But then he'd made the mistake of opening his eyes and received another crack on the head. When he came to, he found himself tied over the saddle of a horse trailing after a groom on a leading rein. Cautiously, he'd turned his head, but could only see the legs of horses in front and behind. And Morwenna had been expecting him. She'd think he had abandoned her. His chin had caught the curved edge of his silver and blue Suffolk badge, pinned at the neck of his cloak. Seizing the head of its pin between his lips he'd worried at it with his teeth until it came out and the badge dropped to the ground. But then the groom had noticed he was wriggling and dealt his skull another blow.

The next time he opened his eyes was when the horses slowed from a bone-shaking gallop to a trot. In the dawn light he realised they were on a bridge crossing a wide river. The

Camel. It had to be Wadebridge. The riders turned sharply to the right, slowed to a walk, then dismounted on the quayside. He was left in an airless little room in a warehouse trussed like a chicken all day and overnight, then carried on board a sailing cog foul with the smell of fish and shoved into its hold. A flask of water was thrown after him, and a loaf of bread. As the ship worked its way out to sea, he managed to free his hands and find the bread, wet with bilge water. Reasoning that he needed to preserve his strength, he tried to eat it, but threw up. It was now part of the noisome slime that slopped around the bilges. His clothes stank of excrement and urine and he had lost all track of time. Had they been at sea three days or four? Occasionally he was dazzled by light when the hatch to the deck was raised, and more bread and a flask of ale were tossed down.

At long last he heard the rattle of an anchor chain, and felt the motion of the boat change, first slowing, then rocking violently. The hatch was drawn back, and strong arms leant down to haul him upwards. He had to close his eyes against the glare at first, but gradually got his bearings. The fishing boat was at anchor fifty yards or so from a rocky shore. A coracle was lowered over its side, and a securely tied tarred sack tossed into it. Before he could protest, Simon was shoved over the side of the boat, leaving him no option but to leap for the flimsy craft. A sailor threw him a short oar while two others hauled up their anchor and hoisted sail. The man who had thrown the oar shouted a phrase Simon had heard used in Wadebridge by departing Irish fishermen, *slán agus ádh mór*: goodbye and good luck. Then he was alone, bobbing among mercifully gentle waves.

Poking the oar into the water he tried a stroke. The coracle spun in a circle. He tried the other way, and it spun back, tilting

34

perilously. After it steadied, he tried paddling first on one side and then the other. A wave of icy water splashed over him. Think, he told himself. I need to get to land. He summoned up memories of watching the Tintagel locals manoeuvre in similar cockleshells. Slowly, he mastered the art of keeping his balance while kneeling in the centre of the boat, twisting the oar in a figure of eight. Gradually it drew closer to the jagged shore. He steered for an inlet between two rocks. Ahead was a tiny beach. Once the coracle grazed on the shingle, he clambered out, pulling it safely beyond the reach of the waves. Dropping exhausted on the beach, he wondered whether the tide was going in or out. He closed his eyes and slept.

Twenty minutes later an icy wave splashed over his boots and he jumped up. The sea had advanced several feet. So the tide was coming in, which explained why it had been relatively easy to get to the beach. But how high up would it reach? Those heaps of seaweed lying in a low ridge along the shore must be markers of the waterline. He hauled the coracle beyond the seaweed until he came to a stunted hawthorn bush, and tied the rope attached to one side of it around the bush. Then he peered inside the tarred sack. A blanket. Pulling it out, he unwrapped it and found two loaves of bread, a long length of catgut with several hooks tied on at one end, a metal tinder box with a tight-fitting lid containing flints, a steel and tufts of oakum, a short dagger and a leather flask of ale. He wasn't supposed to die, it seemed. Just to disappear. To live off fish and his wits until it suited whoever Mohun served to search him out. He shivered at the prospect.

A huge seabird with wings a yard wide and evil, yellow-circled eyes swooped down and seized one of the loaves in its claws. He swiped at it with the oar, and it dropped the bread, flying off with angry squawks. He grinned. It was a small but satisfying triumph. And birds meant eggs. Though he'd need to defend himself against their savage beaks and talons. He walked up to the crest of the low cliff around the cove and looked about him. A few small trees, bare now of leaves and with their branches windblown eastwards, offered scant shelter. A few hundred yards away there was a low hill. Twenty minutes later he reached its grass-covered summit and turned in a slow circle. As he had guessed, he was on an island. He could see thicker stretches of marram grass on its northern side and further off, across a wild stretch of sea, a second, smaller island. On the horizon beyond it ran a long line of low hills. The mainland of Ireland. Would he be able to reach it in his coracle? First, he had to recover his strength. Then he urgently needed to find fresh water.

He slung the sack containing his paltry possessions over his shoulder and walked downhill towards the other island. Halfway down he saw a small stone building, its marram thatch held down by ropes weighted with stones. People had lived here. They must have had a spring or a stream. Scanning the slope, he made out a low circle of stones. A well. But how could he reach the water? Reaching the building, he tried the latch of the door. It opened. Inside he saw a central cooking hearth, with a blackened iron pot hanging from a tripod. Heavy, but not a bad bucket. On the wall by the door hung a hank of coarse rope. On the wall opposite, an elaborately carved wooden cross. A hermitage, then. He attached the rope to the pot's handle, went to the well, let it down, then gave it a few sharp jerks until its weight told him it was full. He hauled it up. The water sparkled in the sunlight, crystal clear. He scooped some up in a shell and drank eagerly.

He carried the pot back into the hermitage, put it down and emptied out his sack. The blanket was slightly damp, so he took it outside and hung it over a low stone wall to air in the sunshine. Fortunately, the bread was dry, so he placed it on a high shelf near the hearth and hung the fishing line on a wooden peg driven into the wall. Then he remembered the coracle – his only hope of escape. He hurried back to the shore. To his relief, it was still there. He untied the rope around the hawthorn and picked it up. It was light enough to hoist over his head. Negotiating the trees and bushes with care, he walked back to his refuge tortoise-like, the oar under one arm, and took both inside.

His exertions had warmed him up, but as soon as he stopped moving he began to shiver with cold. The next challenge was to light a fire. There was a neat pile of sticks of varying sizes in a corner. He brought them over to the stone hearth and made a nest of the smallest and driest of the sticks. Then he opened the tinder box and put a few of its tarry shreds of oakum on a heap of dry grass and thin twigs in the centre of the nest. He began to strike sparks above them with the flint and steel until first the oakum, then the grass and twigs, caught light. He fed the tiny blaze carefully, then reached for thicker firewood. He picked the sticks up and arranged them criss-cross over the flames. They burnt fiercely, and by the light they gave out he saw more sticks neatly stacked beside a great pile of dried peat turves in the far corner of the hermitage. He realised that though the building might be empty now, whoever had furnished it with the necessaries for survival was planning to return. Perhaps it was a seasonal steading of a monastery on the mainland. The island was fertile enough for livestock to graze here come the summer. He edged up his hard-won flames with the peat turves. Huddled close to the blaze, he grew warmer and his shivering stopped. He looked around the room. It was entirely bare, except for the wooden cross. He bowed his head and said a prayer against perils. Then he returned to the fire. His head drooped.

When he awoke, cramped and stiff, he looked anxiously at the fire. Thank the Lord, it was still glowing. Reviving it with more sticks, he banked it up with more peat. He realised he was starving and tore the end off the driest of the loaves, then swigged from the flask of ale. Hunger assuaged, he began to think. The priority was to gather wood to keep the fire going, the second to find more food, the third to wash himself and his stinking clothes. He went outside and saw the sun low in the western sky. The blanket was almost dry; he brought it inside and draped it over two stools close to the fire. Then he headed for the shore. By the time night had fallen, he had collected two great armfuls of driftwood, which he propped around the inside walls of the hermitage to dry. He had also hurled a rock at an overcurious gull, then picked the dazed bird up by its beak and twisted its neck until it broke. Plucked and gutted, it was now roasting on the spit he'd contrived over a merry little fire. Time to get clean. He took off his doublet, ran to the water's edge and plunged into the icy surf in his filthy shirt and hose. Gasping at the shock, he pulled them off and scrubbed them against a submerged rock. As he raced back to the hermitage an unexpected surge of heat coursed through him. After dipping his undergarments in fresh water, he wrung them out and hung them near the fire. Then he began shivering again, so he wrapped himself in the now dry blanket and sat as close to the flames as he could and waited for the bird to cook.

An hour later, replete after gnawing the tough, salty flesh of the gull and chewing the juicy samphire he'd harvested from the rocks, he couldn't help feeling proud of himself. Two years ago he'd have been dead by now. But after a year among the Tintagel folk, men and women who knew nothing of the luxuries of Ewelme and the privileged state of those who served Princess Alyce, he'd learnt the basics of survival. He didn't fancy another gull, but there was an abundance of shellfish and birds' eggs, to say nothing of any fish he managed to hook, so he wouldn't starve. He pondered his plight. Why had he been attacked? Was it because he had been seen talking to Madoc? But what was that to Sir Reginald Mohun? Had he been one of the *Nicholas*'s owners? If so, why hadn't he had Simon pushed over the cliff edge to his death. Why had he stranded him on an Irish island?

But perhaps his abduction had nothing to do with Madoc and the *Nicholas*. Boats crossed regularly between Wadebridge and Wexford. Perhaps word of his presence in Tintagel had reached his old enemy Sir John Tiptoft, now Lord Deputy of Ireland, and Tiptoft had told Mohun to arrest him and send him there to be questioned. He shuddered as he recalled his interrogation in the Tower after he'd babbled in his cups to Rufus Savernake. Weariness overwhelmed him. He heaped more turves on to the fire. Hopefully, he could revive it in the morning. He wrapped the blanket tightly around his body and lay down beside the hearth on a bed made from a thick pile of marram grass, knees tucked up to his chest and arms clutched around them for warmth. He thought longingly of Morwenna. Had she found the badge he'd dropped on the road to Wadebridge?

Ewelme

The Candlemas Hunt feast that was always a splendid finale to the winter festivities at Ewelme Palace was coming to a close. The minstrels bowed and left the gallery of the great hall to enjoy a meal in the kitchen, and pages carried round plates of sweetmeats for those not already replete. Jack and Bess had retreated to their lodgings. The butler offered Alyce more spiced wine, but her head was aching and she waved him away. Joan Moulton, wearing one of her most revealing gowns, breasts hoicked high by a wide bejewelled band, beckoned to him to refill her own glass. It was a Venetian goblet with a fluted glass bowl supported by a stem of silver vines growing from a gold base, one of a set of two dozen that Alyce's grandfather Geoffrey had brought back from a visit to Italy. Amazingly, all had survived, kept in a stout wooden chest with twenty-four felt-lined slots to secure them.

Alyce's wealth still astonished Joan: gold and silver in abundance, intricately woven wall hangings, and chairs padded with embossed and gilded leather. She looked down the long table. Exhausted by the day's hunt, more than one of the guests had leant forward or backwards and were fast asleep. Alyce gave her a conspiratorial nod: it was time for their promised treat. As they stood to leave, the few guests who noticed rose and bowed. Most didn't see them slip away. But Tamsin, far down at the end of the hall, also rose and followed them, beckoning to Matilda to do the same.

Lord Wenlock watched their exit but knew better than to follow. He turned to Ben Bilton.

'How are you, Ben? Not married yet? If I were you, I'd try courting little Tamsin Ormesby. Not only is she a feisty wench likely to be worth bedding, but she has Princess Alyce as a well-wisher.'

Ben scowled. 'I agree, but I fear she would nay say me. She's got some bee in her bonnet about seeing the world. And she revels in being in Princess Alyce's service even more now she's her grace's secretary.'

'Perhaps this westward pilgrimage that we talked of over supper will be enough to persuade her of the merits of a quiet life here in Ewelme. There are no wilder parts of England than the country south-west of Exeter. I hope Princess Alyce and Mistress Joan adopt my advice to travel modestly rather than in state. Even so, they'll need an armed and resolute company. Will you be leading it?'

'I shall. Might you accompany us, my lord?'

'No. I'm too busy about the king's affairs. I return to London in the morning. The king is beginning to have his doubts about the loyalty of the Earl of Warwick. In December his fleet attacked four Hanseatic League ships. A lucrative venture, but diplomatically dangerous. I've to cross to Calais and assure the League's representative that they'll get compensation. What I won't say is that it will be a long while coming. Edward keeps his purse strings tight.'

How knowledgeable Lord Wenlock was about court politics, Ben reflected. Like a spider at the heart of a web, sensitive to every tremor of its threads. And always to-ing and fro-ing across the Channel. Which reminded him of the previous year's most spectacular event. 'Her grace told me that you and Dame Joan were at the wedding of the king's sister Margaret and the Duke of Burgundy in Bruges last July.'

'We were indeed. Its magnificence was beyond anything I've seen. The young duchess attended her sister – they have always been close – and Duke John quitted himself so well in the jousts that Burgundy made him a knight of his order of the Golden Fleece. I hear he and Bess spent Christmas at Windsor and plan to stay on in Ewelme for a while. Are things going better between him and Princess Alyce?'

'Better than they used to,' said Bilton. 'He's much more attentive to her wishes now. Duchess Elizabeth has been the making of him; she's got brains enough for them both. And she couldn't be a more affectionate daughter-in-law.'

Upstairs, two brawny kitchen maids lifted a last cauldron of hot water off the great fire burning in the hearth of Alyce's chamber and tipped it into a huge wooden tub. Helped by Matilda, Joan shed her finery and stepped in, seating herself plumply down on the wide shelf that ran around its inside. It was cushioned with a large sponge from Greece, imported to London from Venice. The tub was still not full, but when Alyce stepped in opposite Joan and lowered herself down on another sponge, it rose above their breasts. Tamsin placed a plank of wood between them. On it, Matilda put two goblets, a jug of wine and dishes of figs, raisins and almonds. Then the girls closed the tub off with curtains that hung from a large iron ring suspended above the tub, so that Joan and Alyce were sheltered from draughts, and withdrew to the antechamber, out of earshot but within hailing distance.

Joan half-drained her goblet and leant back contentedly. 'This is a splendid way to restore oneself after a day's hunting. But I'm surprised you haven't copied the arrangements at Windsor. They've had piped hot and cold water there for over a hundred years.'

'More for show than anything. Bess says that they rarely use the system. The bathroom is deep in the cellars, and the hot water is tepid by the time it's run all the way from the kitchen. Sometimes traditional ways are the best. But tell me, if I did decide to go to Cornwall, might you really accompany me? We'll be away for a month at least.'

'As I said at supper, I'd like nothing more,' said Joan. 'London's rife with plague and John Doll said to warn you that it has reached High Wycombe. I've brought you a sure preventer of infection, a flask of powdered alicorn and spices, but heading westward may well be wise. Add to that the legendary attractions of Exeter Cathedral's library and of Tintagel, and I'd be minded to go even if you weren't planning to.'

Alyce smiled, but then looked searchingly at her friend. 'Joan, before you decide to come, you need to know that our journey is to be more than a pilgrimage and a tour of my estates. Simon Brailles has written to me saying he's secured evidence that will reveal who ordered the murder of Duke William. I've already sent to let him know I'm coming to get it myself. So I might at last solve the mystery I've been too cowardly to investigate for too long.'

Joan's mouth opened and shut like a surprised fish. She took a swig wine, then smiled.

'And there was I thinking you'd lost your old love of adventure. How exciting: a quest as well as a pilgrimage. I'll certainly come with you. Are you going to tell anyone else about Brailles' letter?'

'Best that as few as possible know of it. I've told Tamsin, but she can keep a still tongue in her head. And Lord Wenlock. He can't come with us and he isn't convinced that my going is a good idea, but he's given me advice as to which route to take.'

Joan soaped her shoulders and neck. 'I wonder where he's off to. He's told me nothing, as usual.' She sighed. 'But we can't choose where our hearts settle. When are you planning to leave?'

'That depends on you. How long do you need to prepare?'

'Three or four days at the most. I don't want to return to the Sign of the Mole until the plague has abated. At Charlbury I have everything I need for a journey, and I can write to my stepson Tom telling him I'll be away for a few weeks. But I need to find a tiring woman. I've lost Monique to Francis Thynne. He's taken her to Edinburgh, where he grew up.'

'The maid who just helped you undress might be suitable. She's called Matilda Lovejoy. Came a fortnight ago, with high praise from Stonor Park. I started her as a laundrymaid, but as I decided to make Tamsin my secretary, Martha Purbeck has trained her as a tiring maid. I've already asked her if she'd like to come to Cornwall with us.'

'That would be excellent. I suspect she's unlettered, but if I need to write, Tamsin can be my scribe. I think you said that she wrote a fair hand.'

Alyce nodded. 'Since Brailles left, she's come on apace. I hadn't realised how nervous Simon made her. Though I must say I miss his scrupulous attention to detail. But he seemed so set on going to Cornwall to study for holy orders that I couldn't refuse him.'

Joan looked thoughtful as she soaped her shoulders. 'What an odd decision that was. The last time he came to London with you he seemed more interested in women than the ministry. Bronwen's attachment to Guy took him aback considerably, as I remember.'

Alyce frowned. 'I knew nothing of that. I'd left for Oxford on John Vere's barge by then. What happened?'

'I don't really know. But I could see that he was deeply shaken when Guy told us that he and Bronwen were all but married. He rallied, though, and was most useful afterwards in establishing what had happened to little Peter Arderne.'

'Well, we'll be able to see for ourselves whether a religious life is suiting him. Hopefully, he'll return to Ewelme. I've no need of a chaplain at present, but John Getour is far from well.'

'When are you planning to set off?' asked Joan, sinking chin-deep into the warm water.

'We could leave in ten days or so. Mid-February is early for a journey, but the weather is milder in the south-west and the roads may be easier to travel on before the spring rains and the summer crowds. Bess says that she and Jack will be happy to stay on at Ewelme and manage my affairs here. My palace is much more comfortable than Wingfield Castle. Suffolk is wild in the winter months.'

'Talking of Jack, have you told him why you're going?'

Alyce shook her head.

'Why not? Wouldn't it improve matters between you if he thought you were looking into his father's death?'

'He's too indiscreet. He'll talk of it to his London friends when they next visit, and it'll be all over court.'

Joan gave her a hard stare. 'Alyce, you underestimate that young man. He's changed, you know.'

'You mean he's found out which side his bread is buttered?'

'Not just that. I've seen the way he looks at you now. With respect. As if he's taken to heart that letter his father sent him before his death. I think you should trust him more. Unless you treat him like the man you want him to be, he'll remain the unreliable child you've made him.'

Alyce's mouth was set in a stubborn line. Joan decided to change the subject.

'What route are you planning to take to Exeter?'

'We'll break our journey at Goring on the first day. Dame Matilda the prioress will give us a meal. Then we'll head south to my manor at Donnington for the night. There are always affairs to settle. Then south again to Andover, where we can join the king's highway to the west. Wenlock says the Angel is a fine tavern with a new-built guest house. Then we can stay at Amesbury Priory. Joanna Arnold is the prioress. Her father Edmund knew mine well, and she's a learned woman after my own heart. The next day we should reach Stourton House, near Mere. Duke William's old friend Sir John died on King Edward's campaign to the North in 1462, but his son ought to make us welcome; he knows how much Stourton owes to my husband's generosity. Then Montacute Priory, then Crewkerne, where my old friends the Paulets live, then Forde Abbey, then Exeter, where it will do us good to have a lengthy stop. Dean Webber will be a congenial host – he was an Oxford contemporary of William Marton, Master of my God's House. We'll have plenty of time to admire the cathedral library.'

'My mind is spinning with names,' said Joan. 'You seem to have a very clear idea of the way.'

'I found an itinerary of routes as far as Exeter among my father's papers. Wenlock looked it over and he says it's still serviceable. It shows places to stay a day's travelling apart.'

'How about after Exeter?'

'The country gets much wilder, and we'll need local guides

to take us across the moors to Bude and Whalesborough, where the Trevelyans are. From there it's only a few hours to Tintagel.'

'Tintagel.' Joan's usually down-to-earth expression grew dreamy. 'A name to conjure with. Where Merlin brought about the birth of Arthur by disguising Uther Pendragon as Igraine's husband. Have you ever been there?' There was a long silence. Then Alyce spoke, her voice high and brittle, with none of its usual clipped confidence.

'Once. I sailed from Southampton to Fowey with my second husband Thomas Montagu on our way to France in August 1428. I inherited the patronage of Tintagel's church as well as the profits from local tin mines from my first husband, Sir John Phelip, and Thomas had a mind to see both them and Tintagel. That summer was the happiest of my entire life. I was pregnant again, and we were both hopeful that this time I'd have a healthy child.' She paused, then continued with icy self-control. 'Two months later Thomas was dead. A fluke of a shot from a bombard at the siege of Orleans. I lost the baby after my return to London.' She drained the wine in her goblet, refilled it from the jug and drained it again.

Joan's heart ached for Alyce, who rarely talked of her past life. Joan was still piecing it together, beginning bit by bit to understand just why her friend had created a prickly carapace round herself, a chilly emotional apartness that discouraged intimate enquiry.

To give her time to recover her composure, she felt for a sponge and dabbed suds over her face and neck before continuing the conversation.

'And whom shall we take with us?'

'I'll bring Tamsin and Ben of course. Joseph Pek insisted

on returning to Ewelme to be at my side after my London troubles, and won't let me leave him behind, I'm sure. And Jem Wingfield, my head groom. He'll make a good harbinger, riding in front to give notice of our arrivings. You'll have a groom of your own and Matilda to dress you.'

'Might Farhang come with us?' asked Joan.

'It'd be good to have a physician with us, but Farhang is too old for such a long journey, I fear. He turned eighty in November. But the larger a company we are, the safer. Is there anyone you'd like to bring?'

'I'll think on it. What about contacting the Trevelyans? And our hoped-for hosts along the way?'

'I'll write to Dean Webber and the Trevelyans first thing tomorrow, and you can take the letters to Oxford and give them to a king's messenger. One rides daily to Exeter, where he can hand my letter to the Trevelyans over to local couriers. Their answer will be waiting for us when we get to Exeter. And tomorrow morning I'll write letters to the Angel at Andover, Amesbury Priory, Sir William Stourton and Forde Abbey, and send my own courier south with them. But we must get to bed.'

Raising her voice, she called to Tamsin and Matilda, who hurried in with two huge linen towels, helped Alyce and Joan out of the tub, patted them dry and handed them their night shifts and caps.

'You girls might like to bathe while the water is yet warm,' said Alyce, as she followed Joan towards the great tapestry-hung bed in the corner of the room.

The girls looked shyly at each other. Matilda's eyes sparkled.

'I've never been in so huge a tub,' she said. 'I'd love to give it a try.'

48

Tamsin thought for a moment, then nodded. It would be a good way of getting to know the girl better. She undressed quickly and stepped in. Matilda followed suit, swishing the now lukewarm water over herself and, after a moment's hesitation, over Tamsin. Tamsin giggled, swishing the water back so that it splashed all over the fireside rug and into the fire, making hissing spouts of steam.

'Were you born in Stonor, Matilda?'

'No, but I've lived there most of my life. My mother came from Stonor and my father from Chinnor. He was a carpenter, making furniture out of beechwood. But he had an accident and lost his right arm. Sir Thomas Stonor took pity on him. He works in the stables, and my mother in the laundry. I left for a year but then I came home. Lady Jeanne gave me work in the laundry too. What about you?'

Tamsin noticed the way Matilda had skated over her year away from home but decided not to probe – yet.

'I was lucky like you. I found something very precious that Lady Alyce had lost, and she took me into her service as a reward.'

'How old are you?'

'Nearly nineteen. And you?'

'Seventeen. Oh, and I'd like you to call me Mattie, not Matilda. I was only called that at home when I'd been bad.' As she got out of the tub and wrapped a towel around herself, she added, with a sly wink, 'Which was quite often. Would you like me to call you "Tammie"?'

'No,' snapped Tamsin, then immediately felt rude. But nobody except her adored brother Dickon had called her that. And he would never do so again. Nor did she want to talk about him to Matilda – or rather Mattie, as she supposed she should now call her. She couldn't help noticing what a supple graceful body the new maid had, with breasts twice the size of her own. She remembered Alyce saying that Ben Bilton seemed taken with her. He's welcome to her, she thought forlornly. Mattie had told her earlier that Will Stonor was still engaged to be married to the daughter of the Stonors' old friends the Golafres. She clenched her jaw and reminded herself that she was going to make her own way in the world and wasn't interested in romance – except reading about it in the old tales.

To make up for her curtness, she offered Mattie some of the attar of rose perfume that Alyce had given her as a New Year gift. Mattie's face lit up as she dabbed it under her ears and on her wrists.

'Thank you, Tamsin. That'll bring the lads flocking. Have you got a swain, by the way? Just so I know who not to flirt with.'

'No, I'm fancy free,' Tamsin replied, taken aback by the girl's confidence, but then thinking ruefully that she had every reason to have faith in her attractions. 'Let's to bed now. We've much to do in the morning.'

WEDNESDAY 5 FEBRUARY 1469

London

Sir John Langstrother, Prior of the English Knights Hospitallers, looked down at the figure kneeling in front of him in travel-worn clothes.

'Sir Thomas. It's good to see you again, but I must warn you that Clerkenwell is not a safe haven for you. Prior Botyll died in September, and though I'm his successor in the eyes of the Grand Master of the Hospitallers and those of the Pope, the queen wants her brother John to be the next prior, and if she can find cause she'll have me arrested. I know for a fact that she has spies among the brethren, though I don't know who they are. And since you were excluded by name from the general pardon issued last July for 'damnable, malicious and most hateful deceptions', you risk arrest as long as you're in England.'

Malory stood up wearily. He was thinner than he had been when Langstrother last saw him. His silver hair needed trimming, and worry lines ran between his grey-green eyes.

'I hope not to trouble you for long, Prior. I sought shelter with my cousin Robert, but he's been dismissed as Lieutenant of the Tower and has left London. I'm planning to follow him, but I want to take two allies with me – Hugh Mill and William Vernon. Hugh is a lawyer, but prone like me to scribble romances. William is a scrivener. They helped us with the printing press that was so nearly discovered here in the priory last September.'

Langstrother frowned. 'Is that wise? Both, like you, were excluded from pardon.'

'They need to get away as much as I do. And I know I can trust them.'

'Are you sure? Two years ago, somebody betrayed us by pointing the finger at Denis Pailton.'

'Surely that must have been the Paul's bookstall keeper Margaret Grafton? Pailton kept his work in their storeroom above the charnel house.'

Langstrother was unconvinced. 'He kept it well locked up. You're altogether too impulsive, Thomas. That's one of the reasons you've been taken to court so often.'

Malory shrugged. 'But I've never been found guilty. Even now, no reason has been given for my exemption from pardon. Just vague accusations. But how does Agnes Quincy?'

'She's ailing. After the priory was searched she sought refuge with the nuns at Syon, and joined the order. Untouchable by earthly law, but vulnerable to the ills of the flesh. She has the shaking sickness. My physician John Crophill attends her and says that she has only weeks to live. She longs to return to Wales to die but she's too ill to travel. Her daughter Bronwen will tell you more. She still keeps house for the vicar of St Giles; you'll find her there.'

Sir Thomas was silent. He had his Arthurian tales with him, but he wanted to recover the manuscript of his history of Britain, which Agnes had undertaken to hide among the books in Syon's splendid library. Would he have time? He needed to head west as soon as he could. He'd heard that his cousin Robert was heading for Fowey to take ship for France in one of the vessels owned by the piratical but loyally Lancastrian Cornishmen known as the Gallants. He hoped to do the same. Then he could play a part in Queen Margaret of Anjou's ripening plans for the triumphant restoration of her husband, his liege lord, King Henry VI.

After bidding Langstrother farewell, he set off for St Giles. Walking along Chequer Lane just east of St Paul's, he stepped aside to avoid a troop of horsemen. Behind them rode a nobleman with a fashionably short doublet slashed to show a scarlet silk lining; he had a scarlet-and-black striped riding turban on his head. Their eyes met, and Lord Wenlock of Someries reined in his horse.

'God's wounds, it's...' He bit off his words and looked over his shoulder. Then he nodded meaningfully towards massive oak double doors that were even then being hauled open for the troop to ride through. Malory hesitated for a moment, then followed the man who had not only been overlord of his family home Newbold Revel for four years but had eased his life immeasurably by recommending him to the new king as an organiser of Arthurian pageants. Edward IV imagined his court as a second Camelot, and often likened his policy of appeasing former Lancastrians to Arthur's appointment of his former enemies as knights of the Round Table. Unfortunately, Queen Elizabeth had not been amused by 'The Wedding of Sir Gawain and Dame Ragnald', a masque that Malory had written for the royal players. The audience had hooted with laughter when the boy playing the Loathly Damsel parodied the queen's notorious hauteur, and his wig of writhing snakes led to nudges between those who knew of Elizabeth's pride in her mother's supposed descent from the serpent fairy Melusine.

He found himself in a spacious courtyard. The Royal was one of the oldest houses in London, and no expense had been spared in making it a luxuriously furnished home. Wenlock dismounted and turned to him.

'Thomas, what are you doing in the city? I thought you'd long ago gone abroad. You should have. You're a wanted man.'

'I'm trying to leave the country and take two friends with me,' Malory replied. 'All the southern and eastern ports are closely watched, but Cornwall has safe havens. So I plan to head west. Fowey is the best place for men of my persuasion. But what of you, my lord? Are you less closely allied to York than you were? I heard rumours that one of your henchmen was put to the torture last July.'

Wenlock pursed his lips. Disillusioned though he was with the increasingly indolent King Edward IV and his avaricious queen, he had never been one to reveal his intentions.

'Just idle gossip. I'm about to leave for Southampton on royal business, but I've an idea that could profit us both. Come upstairs, and we can talk.'

Half an hour later they were sitting on each side of a bright fire in Wenlock's private chamber. Wenlock watched his steward fill Malory's cup and his own with rich red Beaune wine, then dismissed him with a wave. Once they were alone, he leant forward.

'I've just returned from Ewelme Palace. Princess Alyce is also planning a journey west. I warned her that she risked wild weather and ambushes, but she has an urgent reason for setting out. She's long hoped to discover who was behind her husband's murder in order to improve her relations with the young duke. He's been haunted by losing his father all his life. She's received a letter saying that evidence of who was responsible for Suffolk's death has been discovered in Cornwall.'

'Who sent it?'

'Her former secretary Simon Brailles. He's reading for holy orders with the vicar of Tintagel, and he saw the former *Nicholas* in Wadebridge and talked to its master.'

Malory raised his eyebrows. 'Simon Brailles? That timorous fellow I met in London at the time of the theft of the duchess's great book? How did he come to leave the duchess's service?'

'Guilt. He told me why before he left, but he swore me to secrecy. He was arrested by Lord Tiptoft after the failure of the raid on Clerkenwell Priory and taken to the Tower. He knew nothing of the press, fortunately, but when Tiptoft strapped him on the rack and asked him if he knew any of the duchess's secrets, he let slip something he'd seen in a private letter. He didn't tell me what it was; nor does he know its significance. But he felt he'd betrayed her. Going to Tintagel was a penance of his own choosing. A wise one, though. Tiptoft planned to go to Oxford and pursue the matter with him. He was furious when he heard he'd disappeared into Cornwall.'

'But Tiptoft was made Lord Deputy of Ireland last year, wasn't he?'

'He's got a long reach and a longer memory for any hint of treason. Brailles is wise to lie low.'

'I wonder what the evidence consists of,' Malory mused. 'There were a great many rumours going the rounds about the instigators of Duke William's murder. Some more outlandish than others. I suppose the answer must lie in *cui bono?* – who gained most by his death? Did you know the truth of it?'

'I heard the rumours,' said Wenlock cautiously. 'Though nothing definite.'

'But what has Brailles' discovery to do with me?'

'He wrote a sensibly discreet letter asking if he could return to Ewelme and bring the evidence in person. But Princess Alyce, being Princess Alyce, has decided to go to Cornwall herself rather than risk its loss. I warned her of the dangers of such a journey, so she'll take a company and travel modestly as a pilgrim preparing to become a vowess. You and any friends you find would be useful added strength as long as your roads coincide. I know she regards you highly.'

Malory took a long draught of wine before answering. He couldn't imagine a better companion on a journey than Alyce, granddaughter of Geoffrey Chaucer, his favourite poet. He had visited Ewelme twenty-five years ago, bringing with him the greatest heiress in the land, little Anne Beauchamp, Countess of Warwick. Suffolk had won her wardship and intended her to marry his heir. Alyce had shown him the exquisite books in her library and he had talked to her about his passion for Arthurian romances. But now...' He grimaced.

'Wouldn't it be too risky for her? As you well know, I and my friends are outlaws.'

'Indeed. And I heard a few days ago that the new Lord High Constable Sir Richard Wydeville is determined to have you apprehended. You'll need to travel in disguise. I suggest you allow me to retain you. Any man travelling in my livery will pass unhindered. It's well known that I'm engaged on diplomacy for the king and send messengers in all directions.'

Malory hesitated. Could he be sure that Wenlock was not luring him into a trap? And where did Princess Alyce now stand politically? Meekly for York or perilously for Lancaster?

He sat forward and faced Sir John squarely. 'Why are you doing this for me, my lord?'

'Because I believe that you're the finest tale-teller of our age, just as Princess Alyce's grandfather was of his. And I know she'd relish your company. She's curious about the great book about King Arthur you dream of finishing. Moreover, Joan Moulton is travelling with her. The pair of them couldn't be better patrons for seeing it published.'

'Joan Moulton of Paternoster Row? The shrewdest book-seller in London! I've known her for many years. I didn't know that she was close to Princess Alyce.'

'It's an unusual friendship. The much-married daughter of a mercer and one of England's wealthiest noblewomen. But since I introduced them to each other three years ago it has flourished. They share both a love of literature and a love of gardening. They exchange long letters and visit each other with rare books and unusual plants.'

Malory's mind whirled. Though still puzzled as to why Wenlock was helping him escape, he was dazzled by the idea of travelling with such companions. It would be an ideal way of completing his life's work. He could take his unfinished manuscript with him and try passages out on them. The journey could be made as full of storytelling as was Geoffrey Chaucer's Londoners' pilgrimage to Canterbury. 'Nothing ventured, nothing gained,' Alyce's grandfather had written in his *Troilus and Criseyde*.

He made up his mind. 'I thank you, my lord. I'll ride to Ewelme and propose myself. May I say I'm recommended by you?'

'Of course. But it's too late for you to reach her at Ewelme. They're planning to set out before St Valentine's Day, spend a night at Donnington, join the great west highway at Andover, then overnight at Amesbury Priory. I'll send a letter by fast courier to Princess Alyce suggesting that she strengthen her company by joining forces with you either at Andover's main inn, the Angel, or at Amesbury. Her grace is never predictable, but I think you'll be made welcome.'

'I'm indebted to you, my lord. I'll have time to find my friends and to call at Syon Abbey to see Agnes. Perhaps you could ask Princess Alyce to send word to the Angel, either to naysay me or to arrange where to meet. She could address her message to Thomas of Newgate, care of its taverner.'

Wenlock smiled at the pseudonym. Malory had been in and out of Newgate Prison several times.

'A sensible notion. She likes to keep her options open. What you'll also require is money for your journey. You'll need the best horses you can find, as well as warm clothes. It's early in the year for travelling.' He took a key from his belt, walked over to a small chest braced with iron bands, unlocked it and swung the heavy lid upwards. He peered inside and considered. The fuller Sir Thomas's purse, the more hope he had of escaping successfully. He took two leather pouches, both stuffed with coins, and handed them over to Malory, who looked disconcerted.

'I hadn't thought to beg.'

'I know. You never were one to ask for help, but I choose to remain a good lord to you, and a good lord pays his retainers. Also, I'd like you to have the means to send couriers to let me know from time to time how Princess Alyce's quest goes. Now, go and tell my steward to issue you with four sets of my livery – I imagine you'll find a squire. And leave London as soon as you can. The pestilence is rife in the poorer parts of the city. I trust that you won't carry it west. I'll send to Ewelme straight away.'

Malory watched as Wenlock walked over to a desk, took out a piece of paper, and prepared a pen.

'What's happened to your trusted secretary Francis Thynne, my lord?'

Wenlock looked up with a weary smile. 'Lost to a lady. He and Monique de Chinon married in the spring, then removed to Edinburgh, Thynne's home. "We are flitting from this madness," Monique told me. I can't blame them, either. So Mistress Moulton and I are doubly deprived. Still, we have each other.'

After Malory left Wenlock's ancient house, he headed north to the parish of St Giles, just outside Cripplegate. The church was empty of all but a couple of beggars in its porch and a woman in a hooded cloak kneeling at a side altar. Hearing his footsteps slow behind her, she turned her head. He breathed a sigh of relief. What luck. It was Bronwen Pailton, whose family had saved his skin more than once during the perilous time of the smuggling away of the illegal printing press.

She lowered her hood and smiled up at him. 'Sir Thomas. Well met. And I can guess what you want – your writings. My mother has them safe at Syon Abbey but worries that she'll die before she sees you again.'

'I heard she was ailing. I'm planning to visit Syon on my way west. I've decided to take my writings with me.'

'She has her copy of your tales of Arthur safe, if that's what you mean.'

'She also has my history of Britain. Taking them both with me is a risk, but it may be my only chance of finishing them.'

'Are you travelling alone?'

'I'm hoping to escape with William Verdon and Hugh Mill. Like me, they've been exempted from pardon for their part in the making and distributing of handbills and pamphlets.'

'You're too late,' said Bronwen. 'They headed west with your cousin Robert two weeks ago.' Malory frowned.

'I'd like at least one trustworthy companion. Can you suggest anybody?'

Bronwen hesitated. 'How about my son Owen? He's seventeen now, and strong for his age. He dreams of being squire to a knight, thanks to his grandmother forever reading him your *Tales*. And I dread him catching the pestilence or being arrested by the king's intelligencers. I know they've got their eyes on us. I'd leave the city myself if I could, but I must stay with my mother until she makes a good end.'

Malory thought for a moment. 'He showed great resource when the press was almost discovered. If you're happy to trust him to me, I couldn't have a better attendant. But if he comes with me, it may mean that he'll find himself fighting for Lancaster one day.'

'As all loyal subjects should,' said Bronwen. 'Come into the priest's house and you can ask Owen yourself.'

Whalesborough Manor

Denzil Caerleon, Princess Alyce's disgraced steward for Suffolk affairs, now a respected captain in the royal fleet, gazed across the gentle swell as his pinnace approached Bude Haven. It was a relief to be in calm waters after the punishment his ships had received in the stormy waters off Land's End. He had left the four battered vessels to be repaired and revictualled in Wadebridge, explaining to his second in command that he had private business to transact, and would return in good time to sail back to Fowey to await the arrival of the Earl of Warwick and the rest of the royal fleet. He hoped that he was going to find out the truth behind the rumours rife in Wadebridge, rumours of the disappearance of the vicar of Tintagel. Nothing had been seen of him since Candlemas Eve. If anyone knew the truth, it would be the Constable of Tintagel Sir John Trevelyan, who lived twenty miles north near Bude. And Trevelyan owed him a favour. Three years ago he had narrowly escaped capture by the king's men in London, thanks to Denzil smuggling him up the Thames in a barge to Princess Alyce's palace at Ewelme.

Since he had been retained by Princess Alyce for several years before she removed to Oxfordshire, Denzil knew that she held the patronage of Tintagel as part of her jointure from her first marriage. The disappearance of its vicar, who he remembered as being a Balliol don called John Gregory, would cause her concern. Discovering what had happened to him might restore him to her good graces. It was two and a half years since he had left Ewelme under a cloud. He winced as he remembered the deceits practised on him by Marlene Stonor. What a fool he'd been to have believed her. Hopefully by now Princess Alyce knew how he'd been misled. She might even have heard of his fine record as a captain in the royal fleet. If he restored Gregory to Tintagel, it was possible that she would invite him to Ewelme to be thanked. And then perhaps she would once again retain him in some capacity, and their friendship, the most important in the world to him, would resume.

Once the pinnace had been moored beside the harbour wall, Denzil walked into the busy little port, and asked for directions to the Trevelyans' manor. Twenty minutes later he rounded a bend and Whalesborough, a newly built stone house, came into view. Long and low, with four massive chimneys, it was tucked behind a sheltering hill with a fine view east over the valley of the River Bude. As he entered its base court, which was full of children kicking a blown-up pig's bladder around, he saw Trevelyan in the hall porch, talking to a couple of men, a black bird with a red beak and red feet perched on his shoulder. It gave a caw and fluttered away as Denzil approached and Trevelyan glanced round. He stared in amazement.

'Denzil Caerleon, by all that's wonderful!'

He looked far better than when Denzil has last seen him, ashen pale from a gash in his thigh made by a crossbow bolt and barely able to stand. He was fitter and fatter, his sly, handsome face bright with mischief.

'What news of Ewelme and Princess Alyce? I still regret not seeing her two years ago. She has a soft spot for me, I know.'

Denzil shrugged sadly as he dismounted. 'I haven't been to the palace since you were smuggled away to Stonor Park. I lost her favour. A conniving young witch saw me as a way out of being disgraced as a pregnant whore, and I was nearly saddled with her as a wife. Fortunately, I discovered she was pre-contracted, and the marriage could be annulled. But I knew my days at Ewelme had to end. I went on a pilgrimage to Jerusalem, and now...'

He paused, looking warily at Trevelyan. 'And now I am a captain in the royal fleet – under the Earl of Warwick.'

Trevelyan gave a snort of laughter. 'Is that a fact? How the wheel of fortune spins! When we last met I was a pirate and a fugitive. But King Edward has not only pardoned me but made me Controller of the Works of all the royal castles and manors in Cornwall. He's hoping it'll secure my loyalty. He should know better. We Cornish choughs are only interested in feathering our own nests. And we'd prefer a Lancastrian king preoccupied with prayer to this Yorkist busybody. But what are you doing here?'

'My ships were chased down the Channel by a German fleet intent on revenge for some ships captured off Southampton by Warwick. We lost them in a storm off the Lizard, and hopefully they'll be wrecked on the Scillies by now. Our navigator – a Falmouth man, fortunately – took us safely round Land's End. We fetched into Wadebridge to make repairs. That's where I heard the gossip. The vicar of Tintagel disappeared at Candlemas. A few weeks earlier he was seen taking an interest in an old warship moored in Wadebridge harbour, and talking to its master, a feckless old Welsh seaman called Madoc. Soon afterwards Madoc disappeared, and the old warship was sailed away under a jury rig.'

Trevelyan was puzzled. 'But why should all that interest you?'

'Princess Alyce appoints the vicar of Tintagel, and John Gregory was a favourite of hers. She'll be concerned at his disappearance. I'll gain favour with her if I can find out what happened. I heard that you and Lady Trevelyan were wintering at Whalesborough, so I hired a pinnace in Wadebridge and sailed to Bude in the hope that you could help me.'

Trevelyan scratched his head. 'Gregory has been in bed suffering from an ague ever since Christmas, so he couldn't have been in Wadebridge. Perhaps you mean Simon Brailles. He's been standing in for Gregory.'

'But Simon Brailles is the duchess's secretary at Ewelme,' Denzil protested. 'Why was he in Cornwall?'

'He's been in Tintagel for well over a year, taking instruction from Gregory and helping with his turbulent parish of half-pagan tinners. Father John asked Princess Alyce for help as he was finding them hard work. She wrote to Lizzie soon afterwards to say that her secretary had volunteered for the task and asked us to befriend him. When I first met him, I couldn't imagine why such a shy scholarly man should choose to leave the comforts of Ewelme and the clever Oxford minds. Jumpy as a hare too, always looking behind him.'

'And did he say why he wanted to come to Cornwall?'

'Apparently he felt the need to retreat from worldly matters. Frankly, I didn't think he'd last, but he did. Stopped looking so nervous and filled out. Began a village school, which endeared him to the locals. John Gregory is delighted with him. Though whether Brailles will take holy orders now, I don't know. The word is he has a wench – the vicarage laundrymaid. He's got her teaching in his school now. My bailiff was collecting rents in Tintagel one day, and he saw them taking the air along the cliff path – hand in hand.' He winked.

Denzil frowned. None of what Trevelyan said matched what he'd known of Simon at Ewelme two and a half years ago. Thin and pernickety, and so anxious about the Lancastrian fugitives who were smuggled through the God's House that he had nearly given the game away. Times changed men, both for good and for bad, he knew. But what could have caused Brailles to opt for exile so far from his comfortable niche at Ewelme?

'If it's Simon who has gone missing, Princess Alyce will certainly want to know what's happened to him,' he said. 'She valued him highly. Could I borrow a horse to ride to Tintagel? I'd like to talk to the locals.'

'Willingly,' said Trevelyan. 'But why don't I come with you? The locals will be more forthcoming to someone they know and trust. I must sit in court tomorrow. Suppose we ride on Saturday? I'll send a messenger to arrange for us to stay at Bossiney Manor, just west of the village, if we need to overnight. The Bassets are kinsfolk of my wife's. When do you have to get back to your ships?'

'In ten days or so.'

'That gives us plenty of time. Lizzie has gone to Holsworthy market, but she'll be back before nightfall. Tomorrow she could take you otter hunting while I'm in court.'

Denzil was impatient at the prospect of not riding to Tintagel straight away, but he realised it would be churlish to insist on doing so. Just then the bird which had been perched on Trevelyan's shoulder flew down again, circled around them, then settled on a nearby horse trough, eyeing Denzil with malevolence. He flinched and Trevelyan laughed.

'Don't worry. That's Artie. Cleverest chough I've ever

tamed. I named him for King Arthur. Legend says he became a chough.'

'What can he do?'

'He comes at my whistle and carries pennies to whichever child I name. Then they come and find me.' He felt in his pocket, took out a coin and held it out, saying 'Lionel'. Artie blinked, took the penny in his beak, and flew straight for the playing children. Two minutes later, a tall, slim boy came racing towards them, Artie on his shoulder.

'What's your will, father?' he asked with a grin. Trevelyan tousled his hair affectionately.

'I was just showing off Artie's tricks. Denzil, this is my oldest son, Lionel. As the boy bowed courteously, Artie fluttered off his shoulder and back onto Trevelyan's. Trevelyan handed him a fragment of bread from his pocket.

'Artie has fathered two broods already this year and helps to care for them. He's a loyal family man. Just like me these days!' He nodded to Lionel. 'You can go back to your game now.'

Denzil was impressed and became even more so as Trevelyan proudly showed him around the estate.

'Of course, it isn't as civilized as Nettlecombe, Lizzie's manor near Bristol, but the boys love the wildness of it. I've got six of them, you know, one for every day of the week, and a daughter for Sunday. They're all web-footed, just as I am. The sea is so much part of our lives. Annie's thirteen; she's promised to my ward Henry Ash, who'll enter in on a fine inheritance in Suffolk when he comes of age. Lionel's twelve next week; he's determined to live here at Whalesborough. He's named for our family's connection with the old legend of Lyonesse.'

'What's that?' asked Denzil.

'Well, the story goes that after King Arthur died he was taken westward to Lyonesse, the island stronghold of Tristram and Isolde. Many years later it was flooded by the sea. The inhabitants retreated to the highest ground, but one knight, my ancestor John Trevelyan, feared that the island would be entirely submerged. He urged his fellows to take horse and swim to the mainland. They thought him a fool and stayed where they were. So he rode through the surging waters alone – the only person to escape. That's why our coat of arms shows a white horse emerging from the sea.'

Denzil chuckled. 'A fine tale. I know a lover of Arthurian legend who'd enjoy it.' Tamsin's trim little person flashed upon his inward eye, and he found himself wondering where she was now. Busy around Ewelme Palace, no doubt. Then he remembered the little wooden mouse she had wanted to buy for her half-witted friend Wat – and which he had impulsively bought when he passed the woodcarver's stall in Oxford's Cornmarket on his way to Stonor Park, a sulking Marlene on his pillion. He had asked Lord Wenlock to make sure Tamsin got it. Had she? He wondered, remembering her curious eyes, one hazel, one green. A sign of independence, it was said. And independent she had been, he recalled with a smile.

'I'm planning to provide for all the younger boys,' went on Trevelyan. 'John is nine, he'll inherit Nettlecombe. Thomas is seven. He'll get St Veep, our manor in the Fowey estuary. George is five, bright little fellow, loves his letters. He can go into the church – Lizzie has the advowson of Mawnam on the Helford River. Richard's three, but I'll find something for him when the time comes.'

'I envy you your life,' said Denzil, sadly aware of how unfruitful his own was. Thirty-eight, his curly black hair now streaked with grey, with neither wife nor children. And he disliked the uncertainties of serving under Warwick. If only he could be restored to Princess Alyce's favour. He remembered the last time he'd seen her. Upright and proud in the Balliol lodgings, telling Tamsin to lay out her gown for George Neville's feast. She had summoned him to ask if he would like to visit Doll's bookshop with her the next day. 'I'd like to buy you a gift for bringing all my chattels safely from Wingfield,' she'd said. 'I owe you so much.' She had been utterly unaware that he was about to enter service with her greatest enemy.

Swyncombe

After breakfast on Saturday morning, Alyce summoned Tamsin. 'I have a mind to ride up to Swyncombe to tend Sybilla's grave and make my confession, Tamsin. You should too – it's a wise precaution before a journey. Ask Joseph to saddle horses for us, and for himself.'

Tamsin gave a graceful curtsey to her mistress and another to the young duchess, then hurried towards the stables. A few minutes after she disappeared, Jack de la Pole came out of the guest lodgings and saw Alyce sitting on a mounting block waiting for Larkspur to be led out of the stable. On an impulse he strolled up to her.

'Where are you going, mother? I'm in need of some exercise. Can I ride with you?' He waited, a little afraid of a rebuff. He never knew what to expect from her. Not approval. When she wasn't criticising his management of the Suffolk estates, she was absorbed in her books – books that made him feel utterly inadequate. They were quite different from his own collection of rollicking ballads and accounts of notable tournaments. She was even writing a book of her own, Bess had told him, a history of notable women to complete her grandfather Geoffrey's unfinished *Legend of Good Women*.

She looked up, surprised. 'Why yes, Jack, of course. I'm going to Swyncombe to be shriven of sin before our journey. I've asked Tamsin to accompany me, but, if you wish to come, I'd welcome your company. We'll take Pek with us as well.'

They rode in silence up a long rise into the hills above Ewelme. Soon Pek and Tamsin, both on mules, were lagging well behind them. Realising they were out of earshot, Jack summoned up his courage. He cleared his throat and spoke nervously.

'Mother, Bess tells me that I owe you more than I have ever realised.'

Alyce's heart sank. Could Bess have told Jack the truth about his parentage? She'd told her mother Cis Neville, to Alyce's great regret, but Cis knew how to keep a secret, especially one so advantageous to her daughter. To tell Jack, with his taste for drink and unreliable friends, was surely a mistake.

Jack saw her face tighten with disapproval but persevered bravely. 'I know I haven't been a good son to you in the past. The truth is that I've always found you daunting. You're so much cleverer than I am, and so…' – he searched for the right word – 'otherworldly. With your French and Latin books and now your determination to become a vowess.'

Alyce coloured. She was planning to become a vowess for selfish rather than pious reasons. She didn't want to be pressured into a fourth marriage by Queen Elizabeth, as so many other wealthy Lancastrian peeresses had been.

Jack continued. 'I had so much to live up to. But now I know we're not related by blood I can admire you for being what I now realise you always have been: a resolute guardian of my interests. I don't need to feel ashamed of not being like you.'

He looked across at Alyce. To his surprise, her stern expression had softened. She was remembering Joan's words. 'You underestimate that young man. He's changed, you know.' She had never dreamt that Jack's reaction to finding out about his real mother would have been relief rather than fury.

She reined in Larkspur and turned to him. 'But you mustn't breathe a word of this to anybody, Jack. Or the Suffolk estates will be inherited by your cousin Lady Catherine Stapleton, or rather by her new husband Richard Harcourt.'

Slowing his own horse, he shook his head emphatically. 'Of course not. But Bess and I have explored the lineage of the de Burgh family, and I feel prouder than I can say that I have inherited royal blood from them. She was a Mortimer, you know, and, like me, a child of love.' He gave her a shy smile. 'Bess says that it's special to be a child of love.'

Alyce's heart melted. 'And she's right. Your father was delighted when I put you in his arms. He loved Elsbeth very much. Especially as she gave him the son I couldn't.'

'That is generous, mother – for I hope I may still call you that. We also read about my father in the records of the Privy Seal and the King's Council. Dusty old stuff, but Bess got very good at working out the abbreviations. He was reviled for losing France, but it seems to me that keeping it was too great a burden for England. I hope that history will restore his good name.'

Tamsin and Pek drew abreast of them, and she waved them past. Pek was deep in a tale of his service in the French wars, and Tamsin was drinking it in, asking questions, her eyes full of imaginings.

Once they had disappeared into the trees, Jack looked anxiously at Alyce. He was uneasy at her continued silence; she was struggling to find words to express her feelings. At last, he spoke again.

'*May* I still call you mother? For a mother you've always been to me in fact, if not in blood. Though I resented your strictness, in my heart I knew that it was necessary. Every word of that letter my father wrote for me before he set sail for France was true. I always carry a copy with me now, though I have most of it by heart. I keep it by me and read it every day. And from now on I intend to take his advice.' He took a folded paper from the leather wallet tied to his belt, and read aloud:

Remember these words always: to love and worship your lady and mother, and always obey her commandments, and to believe her counsels and advices in all your works. Be assured that she shall be the best and truest to you. And if any other body would steer you to the contrary, to flee their counsel in any wise, for you shall find it nought and evil.

Alyce could only nod as tears rose to her eyes. She was cursing herself for being utterly tongue-tied. She was so used to hiding her real thoughts from Jack that now, when it was vital that she who was so good with words found the right ones to mend matters between them, they eluded her. But at last she thought of a way. Honesty.

'Jack, I've been a fool. I'd be honoured to have you still call me "mother". I hadn't realised that I seemed so daunting to you. I've always assumed that the gulf between us was because I'd failed to discover your father's murderers. For which I deserved your resentment. In truth, I was scared. Scared that your father's enemies would unite against me, and we would lose everything I had managed to persuade King Henry and Queen Margaret to let me keep. After William's death, the Commons accused me of treason, too, you know. It was a perilous year for those the king and queen held dear, and I was foremost among them.'

Jack nodded. 'Dear mother, I do not blame you for your caution. Especially now I know Sir Robert Harcourt for the viper he is. But it's true that the older I got the more I resented the fact that you didn't seem to care who was responsible for my father's murder. I would still dearly love to know. I tried to find out myself but could discover nothing except resentment of his policy of appeasing France.'

'I think that his real crime in the eyes of his ill-wishers was to overreach himself in the matter of your marriage to Lady Margaret Beaufort. She was then talked of as heiress to the throne as King Henry had no children. Your father was accused of having hopes of your becoming king.'

Jack gave a hoot of laughter so loud that it made Tamsin look round. 'Can you imagine that? A duffer like me on the throne of England?'

'You were a very promising proposition at the age of eight, dear boy. But I think that your curiosity is entirely proper. And, in fact…'

She hesitated. Should she tell Jack the real reason for her pilgrimage to Cornwall? Well, if he knew and had kept the secret of his parentage, he could surely keep this one. She took a deep breath.

'In fact, solving the mystery of your father's murder is the real reason I'm going to the west country. Simon Brailles wrote from Tintagel to say that he's purchased evidences of who was behind it from the bosun of the *Nicholas of the Tower*. And I thought the quickest and safest way of getting hold of them was to go there myself rather than let him risk travelling with them.'

Now it was Jack who was lost for words. Far from not caring about his father, Alyce was undertaking a perilous journey in the depths of winter in the hope of discovering the truth about his murder. At last, he spoke.

'I should be the one to go, mother. You cannot risk yourself.'

Alyce shook her head. 'That would mean altogether too grand a progress. And questions would certainly be asked if the Duke of Suffolk set out for Cornwall. Whereas an old lady like me can make a pilgrimage in preparation for becoming a vowess and visit her own estates on the way without raising suspicions. Especially as it is widely assumed that I have put William's death behind me and am loyal to York.'

Jack's face fell, and he looked mulish. Alyce realised that if their reconciliation was to endure, she must trust him, give him responsibility. Make him feel that he himself had a role to play in the securing of his inheritance. And there was, after all, a loose end that had nagged at her for the last two and a half years.

'There's one thing you could pursue,' she said. 'Do you remember the death of a man called Milo just after I left Suffolk and settled back into Ewelme?'

'Yes. The royal spy. Harcourt claimed he had been murdered. But the coroner's jury ruled it an accident.'

'Well, a bundle of letters turned up later. Joseph Pek found them under a floorboard in his lodgings. They showed that Milo had been hired by Harcourt to find evidence of my being a traitor. But there was also one from Dom Robert Hiat, the vicar of Bampton, giving Milo an introduction to Harcourt. It referred to you as the 'false progeny' of the Duke of Suffolk. Fortunately, Harcourt doesn't seem to have thought of that as more than a casual insult, but, as you now know, there is truth in it. I think it'd be a good thing if you went to Bampton and discovered just how much its vicar knows.'

Jack's face lit up with excitement. He couldn't wait to tell Bess about the mission his mother had charged him with. At last he could prove how capable he could be.

Alyce wondered anxiously if she had been wise to suggest he involve himself in what might end with the secret of his birth leaking out to the world. Then she recalled what Joan had said next. 'Unless you treat him like the man you want him to be, he'll remain the unreliable child you've made him.'

They rode on in companionable silence until they reached the simple little church deep in the wooded hills above Ewelme. Tying their horses to the hitching rail, they walked round to the now abandoned anchorite's cell. The turf was ablaze with tiny golden flowers. Alyce looked at them affectionately.

'Winter wolfsbane. Marvellously early, too. Sybilla called them the first sign of spring. That's why they grow so thickly here – she nurtured them. Their blooming now makes me think that those white violets Joan Moulton sent me might do just as well here, sheltered by the church from the north and east. Snowdrops, she calls them, as their heads droop humbly. Could you tell Bess to plant a clump beside Sybilla's gravestone when she next visits?'

Jack nodded. 'I'll bring all the family up and we'll each plant a few and pray for the success of your journey.'

Sybilla's cell was empty now. Beside it there was a slab of stone, carved with a simple cross. They knelt and prayed in silence for her soul. Alyce also prayed for their success in the quest which could finally mend her relations with Jack. And for her goddaughter Meg. Wenlock had told her that the Earl of Oxford had just been released from the Tower after two months of imprisonment. But Meg had been so worried about her husband that she'd lost the baby she had been expecting.

The doctors had said that it was unlikely she would have another child, and she was still desperately ill. Happily, she was being lovingly cared for at Hedingham Castle by her mother-in-law. Alyce grieved deeply for her, remembering the stillborn daughter of her own last pregnancy.

Jack knelt beside Alyce. He felt closer to her than he had ever done, his childish resentment and petulance now entirely dispelled. He prayed for her survival on a dangerous journey into one of the wildest parts of the country. And for her success in discovering the truth about his father. And for his own venture to Bampton.

On the other side of Alyce and a little behind her, Tamsin was recalling the dramatic events surrounding the deaths chosen by Sybilla and Gerard Vespilan soon after she had entered Alyce's service, and of her own narrow escape from death. She thought gratefully of Wat, who had saved her and who was still devoted to her. Working for her grandmother Nan had transformed him from a wild lad who could only make guttural sounds to a competent young man with a real talent for handling horses. On the way up the hill, Pek told her that he had asked Princess Alyce if Wat could come with them on their journey to Cornwall, and that their mistress had agreed. She turned to her now, opening her mouth to thank her, but closed it when she saw her mistress's concentrated gaze and the tears on her cheeks. Instead, she rose quietly to her feet and left the church. She walked over to where the bright yellow flowers were thickest, took a small trowel out of the cloth bag she had brought with her, and began to dig up clumps of them, roots and all, and put them in it.

'Why in God's name are you digging up the flowers, child?' Alyce stood behind her, prayers completed.

Tamsin gave a start of guilt. Perhaps they were sacred. 'I … I'm sorry. Farhang asked me to see if the celandines were out and to dig up as many as I could. He said I'd know them by their yellow flowers and that their roots and leaves make a sovereign ointment – one that offered especial relief to travellers. This is his bag; he asked me to fill it.'

Alyce frowned, thought for a moment, then chuckled. 'Sybilla always called celandine pilewort and swore by their efficacy in easing rumps. But they aren't in flower yet. You're digging up winter wolfsbane, which is as poisonous as its name suggests.' She looked around, then walked over to the east end of the church, beckoning Tamsin to follow her.

'These are celandines – their leaves are dark green and smooth-edged, quite different from the ruffs of wolfsbane. And Farhang is right; we'll need plenty of it. Leaves and roots. Use your knife to dig them up.' She watched approvingly as Tamsin filled Farhang's bag.

'Plundering God's gifts, your grace?'

They whirled around. Sir Brian Fulbert, his wife on his arm, and their children beside them had come out of the manor house.

Alyce smiled. 'Say, rather, gratefully making use of his healing beneficence. Farhang told Tamsin that celandines make a good ointment for those going on a journey. We leave for Cornwall next week.'

Sir Brian was astounded. 'In February? You may get wild weather. How long will you be away?'

Alyce shrugged. 'A month. Maybe more. But Duke John and his family will stay in the palace while I'm gone. Is Father Jerome in the church? Tamsin and I need to be shriven before we leave.'

'He is. And while you're in the church, our children can dig you up some more pilewort. Cornwall? You'll certainly be needing it!'

Tintagel

Huddled to one side of a sulkily smoking fire in the spacious hearth of the Tintagel vicarage's principal chamber, Sir Reginald Mohun broke the Suffolk seal on the letter to Simon Brailles that had just been delivered by the Exeter courier. As he unfolded it, he thought back over the last fortnight's hasty contrivings. A few days before Candlemas he had been summoned to Wadebridge to wait on John Hurleigh, secretary to Lord Tiptoft, Lord Deputy of Ireland. Hurleigh handed him a warrant from Tiptoft, authorising him to use whatever force was necessary to apprehend Simon Brailles, ordinand of the vicar of Tintagel, and to send him to Ireland. Mystified but obedient, Mohun duly abducted Brailles and arranged for him to be taken to Ireland in a fishing boat, A few days later, Hurleigh reappeared, and handed him a heavy purse.

'You're owed an explanation as well as this reward, my lord, but I can't divulge the full story. I can only say that Brailles chanced upon a dangerous secret and had to be silenced. However, some weeks before you took him prisoner, he sent a letter to his mistress, Princess Alyce, Dowager Duchess of Suffolk. So we must both remain in Tintagel to await her reply and discover how much Brailles has disclosed to her.'

Mohun and Hurleigh had taken up residence in the vicarage, to the dismay of Father Gregory, still abed with the ague and mourning the loss of his ordinand. As Mohun scanned the letter from Ewelme, he gave a curse. Whatever Brailles had written had made Princess Alyce decide to travel to Cornwall in person. He sent his page to find Hurleigh, who had taken possession of the vicar's cosy oak-panelled study on the other side of the vicarage's great central chimney. When Hurleigh appeared, he handed him the letter. The secretary read it, frowning, then looked up.

'Princess Alyce will be on her way before we can send a reply to discourage her from setting out. She describes her planned itinerary. Donnington, Andover, Amesbury Priory, Stourton Castle...' He paused for a moment, thinking hard. Then he gave a smile.

'Sir William Stourton is the tenant of several of my lord's Wiltshire manors. Nor is he a lover of Lancastrians. There's ample time to send a messenger to him. Two ladies, one overweight, if I remember Mistress Moulton rightly. Travelling unseasonably early with a couple of maids and a handful of menservants. Anything could happen. Suppose a band of outlaws descended on them and stripped them of their valuables? There must be no loss of life, but the shock and the loss of their baggage will surely be enough to discourage them from continuing westward. Tell your messenger to await the outcome of the attack and, if by any chance they persevere, to engineer other misfortunes until they abandon their journey. Have you a sufficiently enterprising man to hand?'

Mohun's craggy features split into an unpleasant grin. 'I have just the person. A fast rider and as cunning you could wish.' He turned to his page. 'Summon my squire, Guy Despenser.'

Hurleigh felt uneasy on seeing Mohun's look of unholy glee, but knew he had to obey his master's commands. He picked up his cloak and gloves.

'I'll leave you to write to Sir William Stourton, Mohun. Enclose this token from Lord Tiptoft; it will ensure his obedience. But remember, no harm must come to the ladies. Though the odd servant can be risked.' Then he left.

Despenser was a sinewy young man with shrewd eyes and a rakish air. Mohun sent him on his mission with Tiptoft's token and a letter to Stourton nestling among silver coins in his belt pouch. He was settling down to write another letter, this time to an old acquaintance presently in Bristol, when a sharp jangle from the bell announced visitors. A few minutes later his door opened, and his page showed them in. One was familiar, the other a stranger. He rose to greet them.

'Can I help you, gentlemen?'

Trevelyan bowed and stepped forward, quite at his ease. 'Sir Reginald, this is an unexpected pleasure. I had thought you in Lostwithiel.'

Mohun nodded at Trevelyan. 'It's good to see you again, Trevelyan. What brings you to Tintagel? And who's your companion?'

'This is Denzil Caerleon, a captain in the Earl of Warwick's fleet,' said Trevelyan. He turned to Caerleon. 'Denzil, this is Sir Reginald Mohun, deputy sheriff of Cornwall.' Denzil bowed stiffly. He had heard talk of Mohun. None of it flattering.

Trevelyan turned back to Mohun. 'Caerleon arrived in Wadebridge a few days ago as his ships had a battering off Land's End during that storm last week. He's in search of the vicar's ordinand Simon Brailles, an old friend and a valued servant of his former mistress the Duchess of Suffolk. He heard in Wadebridge that he'd disappeared. We're planning to ask around the village, and we thought we'd begin with the vicarage. But what brings you here?'

Mohun's dense black eyebrows met above his hawkish nose as he frowned at them. He disliked accounting for his actions to such a jackanapes as Trevelyan, let alone a minion of Warwick like Caerleon, but realised he'd have to offer an explanation.

'I have an interest in an old hulk in Wadebridge, and when I was there the harbour master told me of the disappearance of the Tintagel clerk. So I rode here to investigate.'

'Have you found any clues to his whereabouts, my lord?'

'He disappeared on Candlemas Eve, always a night of revelry in rural parts like this. He was seen taking a good deal of ale, and it appears that he fell off the cliff on his way home. His body, much-battered by the surf, was washed up a long way down the coast a few days later. Father Gregory saw to his burial.'

Appalled, Denzil crossed himself, and murmured a prayer for Simon's soul.

Trevelyan did the same, shaking his head sadly. Then he gave a sigh. 'Well, that seems to be that, Caerleon. We can go back to Whalesborough, and you can join your ships in Wadebridge. At least you can write to Princess Alyce and tell her that you investigated.'

Mohun gave Trevelyan a warning glance and shook his head. 'No need for that,' he said. 'I'm writing to tell her grace of Suffolk of Brailles's death myself. Gesturing towards his desk, he bowed and sat down again, clearly dismissing them. Trevelyan bowed in return, and walked out of the room, spurs jangling.

Denzil glanced at the books and papers on the desk, then followed him, his mind full of questions. Why had Mohun interested himself in Simon's disappearance? And why had he taken it upon himself to write to Princess Alyce? And why had Trevelyan been so unsurprised by his presence in the vicarage?

As they re-entered the village, he reined in his horse. 'What of Brailles' wench, Trevelyan? She might have a tale to tell.'

'I doubt it,' said Trevelyan easily. 'Or Mohun would know of it. He's a thorough man when it comes to investigations. There's no reason now to spend the night at Bossiney Manor. We can reach Whalesborough before dark if we set off straight away. There's nothing more comfortable than one's own bed. Specially with a willing wife in it.'

As they rode along the coast northwards, Trevelyan pointed up a steep ravine. 'That's the way to St Nectan's hermitage. The old chap had forty-eight brothers and sisters apparently. No wonder he decided to leave Ireland and become a hermit. Lived up the glen for a long time, then ventured north to Hartland. Worshipped the Lord there for a while, but got his head cut off by Irish cattle robbers.'

Denzil was silent. There had been several curious things about the encounter with Mohun, and he hadn't missed the quelling glance Sir Reginald had given Trevelyan. Or Trevelyan's compliant nod.

Trevelyan chattered on. 'Holiness flourishes in our soft south-western air. There's hardly a stone's throw between one saint's shrine and the next along this coast. This is Trevalga. Down that lane is the ancient chapel of St Juliot. He was a friend of Nectan's. He ended up in a hermitage on the island of Tintagel. Your old friend Simon made it a school for the local children.'

A little further on, Trevelyan embarked on a lengthy story about Saint Salom, his wife Saint Wenna, and their son Saint Cybi. Denzil couldn't help wondering if his incessant prattle wasn't intended to stop any discussion of their meeting with Mohun. He was also sure that a letter he had seen poking out from underneath a worn prayer book on the vicarage table was written in Lady Alyce's own elegant script, a hand that he knew well from his service to her in Suffolk. Moreover, the one Mohun was writing was addressed to Sir Robert Harcourt. Why in the world was he writing to Princess Alyce's sworn enemy?

As the chimneys of Whalesborough Manor came into view, Denzil decided to confront his companion directly.

'Trevelyan, why would Sir Reginald concern himself on such a minor matter as Brailles' disappearance if he was only interested in the hulk. And why take it on himself to write to Princess Alyce?'

Trevelyan shrugged. 'I've no idea. But it appears he has. Good of him, really. And saves you doing so. Well – here we are.'

As they rode into the courtyard of the manor, Artie flapped down from the gatehouse turret to Trevelyan's shoulder, nibbling his ear affectionately as Lady Elizabeth, plump and ebullient, came out to greet them. She had a letter in her hand. To Denzil's surprise, it too was in Princess Alyce's handwriting.

'Good news, John,' she called to her husband. 'My cousin Alyce is planning to visit us. She writes that she hopes to be in Exeter by the third week of February. She wants to see how her man Brailles is getting on at Tintagel.'

Trevelyan blinked. 'That's in nine days' time. It's wonderful that she's coming to the west country. But, Lizzie, there's sad news of Simon Brailles. Guess who we met in Tintagel? Mohun himself. Remember me telling you that I met him in Wadebridge just after Christmas? Apparently, he returned there on business, and heard that Brailles had disappeared. He went to Tintagel to investigate and discovered that Simon fell from the cliffs after carousing at Candlemas. He was writing to tell her grace of his death.'

Elizabeth Whalesborough's face fell. 'Poor Simon! And he was so full of plans when he came to stay last Christmas. He told me Tintagel was the first place in which he'd been truly happy.' She turned to Denzil. 'Did you know him well?'

Denzil nodded. 'Yes. I was her grace's steward for Suffolk affairs, and Brailles was her secretary in Ewelme. He always seemed a bundle of nerves, unsure that he was doing the right thing.'

'He was like that when he first came,' said Elizabeth. 'But he'd changed a great deal by Christmastime, when he stayed with us. He was full of his new school, and of Morwenna, the girl he was training to teach there. What a terrible death!'

'At least you'll be able to see your cousin,' said Trevelyan, putting a comforting arm around his wife. 'Nor is there any need for her to come as far west as this now. Why don't we join her in Exeter?'

Elizabeth thought for a minute. 'She says she's planning to make a proper pilgrimage of her journey, to mark her decision to become a vowess. But if she'd like to see more of Cornwall, it would be easiest to take the highway to Bodmin, then follow the River Fowey to the sea. We could entertain her at St Veep. And Fowey itself is convenient for taking ship for Southampton, should she decide to return home by sea.'

Trevelyan thought for a few seconds, then brushed Artie off his shoulder and gave his wife a hug. 'That's an excellent idea, heart of my heart. I can think of nothing better than keeping company with your cousin. I owe her such a lot – not least my marriage to you. Your father thought I was a ne'er-do-well until the duchess vouched for me.'

'Well, you were a ne'er-do-well,' Elizabeth said teasingly. 'I've been the making of you – thanks to all my land and money.'

Denzil was amused at the frank speaking between the two of them. What a redoubtable woman Elizabeth Whalesborough was. He watched with a smile as Trevelyan blithely hoisted her off the ground and whirled her around – with impressive vigour, given her substantial girth.

'And I of you, my dear. Remember that blockheaded ass whom your father wanted you to marry until her grace intervened? You're lucky to have me.'

He gave her a warm hug then, puffing, put her down and turned to Denzil. 'How does this affect your plans, Caerleon?'

Denzil's mind was racing. If Princess Alyce had written to the Trevelyans, then she would surely also have written to Simon Brailles. So in all likelihood that had indeed been her handwriting under the prayer book beside Mohun. So why had he not mentioned it? He looked at the trees, noticing that the wind was blowing steadily from the north-east.

'I'll return to Wadebridge early tomorrow,' he said. 'Might as well take advantage of the fair weather. Could you send word to the harbour to tell my crew that we leave at first light? And when you write to Princess Alyce, please give her my good wishes. Sadly, it seems that our paths are unlikely to cross. My ships will be Fowey-bound as soon as possible.'

'It's just possible we'll see you there,' said Trevelyan. 'With her grace if she likes the idea of travelling with us to Fowey.' Artie, now back on his shoulder, glared at Denzil with beady black eyes.

Next day, Denzil left Bude at dawn, but he had no intention of sailing directly to Wadebridge. As they rode away from Tintagel he'd noticed a small haven just below the castle, and his pinnace fetched into it after a few hours' brisk sailing. Accompanied by his coxswain Dickon, a wiry Falmouth man he knew he could trust in a tight corner, he walked up to the village. The Malthouse Inn was already busily preparing for the new day, and a brawny ostler was opening the doors of the stable. Denzil took a silver groat from his belt pouch and began to twirl it between his fingers. The ostler eyed it for a moment or two, then spoke.

'Can I help you, sir?'

'I don't know,' said Denzil. 'I'm looking for a wench.'

The ostler's face hardened. 'We're an honest house and don't hold with doxies. Get you gone.'

'You mistake me,' said Denzil. 'This girl is the friend of a friend of mine, the fellow who's been standing in for Father Gregory. Her name is Morwenna, and I have a message for her.'

The ostler's eyes became alert with interest. 'For Morwenna? From Simon Brailles? But he's dead, isn't he? They found what the rocks and the crabs had left of him near Port Isaac a week ago and buried him.'

'It isn't from him, but it concerns him,' Denzil said. 'Do you know where she is?'

'This time of day, she'll likely be at the washing ground.' He pointed across the road to a lane running steeply downhill. With a nod, Denzil tossed him the groat, and took his leave. He and Dickon headed down the lane. The washing ground was little more than a shallow pool in the rock through which a stream flowed. Half a dozen women of assorted ages were kneeling around it, banging soaped washing against the stone rim of the pool with short-handled bats to beat the dirt out.

'How about her?' said Dickon, pointing to a lively dark-haired girl who was laughing to an older woman beside her as she thumped at a thick blanket. 'She's a pretty enough lass.'

Denzil raised his voice and called 'Morwenna?'

Startled, the girl looked round and he waved to her. She put down her washing bat and stood up, flexing her shoulders to relieve her aching muscles. He waved again, and she began to walk towards them, looking back at the older woman warily. Perhaps she didn't want to be overheard. He retreated, beckoning her to follow.

'What is it, masters?' she asked, in a soft, musical voice. Denzil could easily imagine Simon finding her attractive.

'I've come in the hope of finding my old friend Simon Brailles. I believe that you knew him. I heard in Wadebridge that he had disappeared, and at the vicarage I was told he had fallen over the cliff celebrating after Candlemas.'

'Who told you that I knew him?' she asked suspiciously. 'And who told you where I was?'

'Sir John Trevelyan told me that Simon had befriended a girl called Morwenna in Tintagel, and the ostler of the Malt House said you might be here. A visitor we met in the vicarage told me Simon had tumbled drunk off the cliff. I wondered what you knew of it.'

Fear showed in her face. 'Was the man at the vicarage Sir Reginald Mohun?' Denzil nodded.

'Then I can tell you nothing. I dare not.' She glanced back again to the washing ground. The women had been joined by a tall man in the gown of a reeve, who was scowling at her and Caerleon.

Denzil lowered his voice. 'I won't betray you to Sir Reginald or any man. But if you know what happened to Simon, please tell me. I'm an old friend of his. From Ewelme, in Oxfordshire. I'll wait down in the harbour for an hour.'

She stared at him, her face expressionless. Then she gave the smallest of nods and went back to the washing ground.

Denzil had almost given up hope, and the crew of the pinnace was readying it for launching when he saw a slender, shawl-wrapped figure descending the steep path to the haven. He hurried towards her, groping in his pouch for coins. But when he offered them to her, she shook her head.

'I don't want payment. I just want Simon back. If you're a friend of his, perhaps you can rescue him.'

'So he didn't fall over the cliff?'

'No. They took him away. Sir Reginald and two men. They came on horses from the south on Candlemas Eve. They were at the very back of the church, but they disappeared when we began the bonfire.'

'How do you know they took him?' asked Denzil.

She blushed. 'Because Simon and I were to have gone to his lodging on the island. I was waiting in our usual meeting place when I heard horses. I ducked down and saw them. Sir Reginald in front, then two more riders, one with Simon's body lying across his horse, tied to the saddlebow. They took the road to Wadebridge.'

'Wasn't it dark? How do you know it was Simon? The ostler said his drowned body was found a week later.'

'I don't know whose body that was, but I don't believe it was Simon's. I found his Suffolk badge on the road south. He must have dropped it deliberately as a sign. It was his most prized possession, given to him by the Dowager Duchess of Suffolk.' She reached into the little leather pouch tied to her girdle and took out a badge.

Denzil recognised the three golden leopards' heads on a blue enamel ground instantly.

'What happened next?' he asked.

'Next day, I walked to Wadebridge to see if I could find him. And a friend of mine said he'd seen Mohun talking to the master of an Irish fishing boat, and his men half-carrying a hooded man on board. The boat was Wexford-bound.'

'Why would Mohun send Simon to Ireland?'

'I've no idea,' said Morwenna. 'Sir Reginald came back to Tintagel a few days ago. He and his men settled themselves in the vicarage, and I decided to go and ask him why Simon had been taken away. He said it was the king's business and I should keep a close tongue in my head or it would be the worse for me and my family. I've got an ailing mother, you see.'

'You've been very brave coming down to the haven,' said Denzil. 'Now go back before you're missed. And worry not: I'll do everything in my power to restore Simon to you.'

She gave him a grateful smile, and hurried away, just as a shout came from Dickon.

'Time to set sail, Master Caerleon. Tide's on the ebb.'

Frowning as he tried to order his thoughts, Denzil stepped on board, wrapping a sheepskin and a tarpaulin around himself as the crew raised sail and the pinnace scudded southwards to Padstow and Wadebridge. Where, he reflected, he might well encounter Mohun again, who would not take kindly to more questions, whether or not he had sent Simon Brailles to Ireland. Looking up at the craggy crest of Tintagel, he saw an ominous, crowlike figure in the long gown of a reeve silhouetted against the sky.

The pinnace reached Wadebridge as the sun was setting. To Denzil's surprise, his ships were nowhere to be seen. He walked along the quay to the customs house to ask the harbour master, a weather-beaten old sailor called Mawgan, what had become of his fleet.

'Sir Reginald Mohun told your shipmaster that they should sail back to Fowey, and finish fitting out there. The French fleet has been seen off the Channel Islands. Warwick is planning to bring the royal fleet down the Channel from Southampton.'

'But I saw Mohun when I was in Tintagel two days ago. He said nothing to me then. I don't see how he could have had news of Warwick – or the French fleet – so quickly.'

'Coasters from Southampton call in at Fowey, and riders come across the moor from Lostwithiel every day,' said Mawgan blandly. 'A letter was waiting for Sir Reginald when he returned from Tintagel, and when he'd read it he sent for your shipmaster.'

'And where is Mohun now?'

'Patrolling the Bodmin road. There's been word of Lancastrians seeking to reach Fowey. He's based his forces at Bodmin.'

'How am I going to join my fleet? Could I get a passage on a ship?'

'Quicker to go overland. The track from here to Fowey is well marked as so many Irish and Welsh drovers use it. The animals don't lose as much weight as they do during a long voyage, and it's far safer than the sea passage around Land's End. Pilgrims take it too – there are so many shrines along it that they call it the Saints' Way. It's barely a two-day ride, much quicker than sailing after your ships. You'll probably arrive in Fowey before them.'

Denzil walked over to the window and considered his options. Ride to Fowey and join his fleet? But then he would be doing nothing to win Alyce's favour. Go to Exeter to meet Alyce? And tell her what? A fantastical tale told by a distraught village girl? Or head to Ireland, in case it had been Brailles in the fishing smack? Preferring as he always did action to inaction, he turned to the harbour master.

'It seems I'll have time to spare while my ships are fitting out for battle in Fowey. I've a mind to look up an old friend in Ireland. Are there any ships bound for Wexford in the harbour?'

'There are always a few. But you need to take care whose craft you ship on. Not all are seaworthy, and not all their masters are honest.'

'Which one would you recommend?'

Mawgan considered. 'The *Bonaventure* is the best ship. Clinker-built cog. She's not long back from Bayonne. Ran into storms off Land's End, though, and is having a new mast made. She'll be ready in a few days.

'I need to leave as soon as possible,' said Denzil. 'Is there another vessel I can get a passage on?'

Mawgan joined him at the window and looked out at the quayside.

'There's the *Maiden Mairi*. Three along from the *Bonaventure*. Setting sail for Kilmore and Wexford at dawn. Sound enough little craft, and if you pay the master well he'll treat you well. Especially if I take you to him, so he knows you have my favour. He's not enamoured of Englishmen though, especially not of the new Lord Deputy. He's a Fitzgerald, and Tiptoft took off the head of his kinsman the Earl of Desmond. Best to make it clear that you're not in his service. And hide your purse.'

'Could we go and ask him now?'

'Let me finish this reckoning. I'll join you on the quayside in ten minutes.'

Thanking him, Denzil went out of the customs house and wandered along the quay. The *Maiden Mairi* seemed well-found; its warps coiled and its sail neatly lashed to the heavy yardarm slung from its single mast. Two sailors were carrying supplies aboard, including a crate of hens and a water barrel. A bearded man in a loose smock of oiled wool sat on a tarred chest lashed to the deck amidships. Seeing Denzil staring, he raised a bronzed forearm.

'Are you seeking a passage, sir?'

Before Denzil could reply, the harbour master appeared at his side.

'That's right, Fergus,' he said. 'Denzil Caerleon's a friend of mine. Wants to be in Wexford as soon as possible.'

'The wind is set fair east nor'east,' said Fitzgerald. 'It should be a quick crossing, reaching all the way. And you won't find a better ship than the *Mairi*. Is it returning you'll be? Or just one way? Is your business in Ireland with the new Lord Deputy?'

Denzil liked the look of Fitzgerald but remembered the harbour master's warning. A Hospitaller knight he'd met in Milan rose to his mind. He'd been returning from a six-month stint in Rhodes to his preceptory in Ireland.

'No. I'm going in search of a friend of mine. I think he's staying with John Kilross. He's a Knight Hospitaller at the Crook preceptory, near Waterford.'

'With the Knights, eh? They are good men. Fairer to the

Irish than that devil Tiptoft, without a doubt. Will you be staying long?'

'I'm not sure,' said Denzil.

'Then I'll charge you just for going. Two groats.'

Mawgan intervened. 'That's robbery, Fergus. One will be plenty. Caerleon is also taking a message to the Kilmore harbour master for me. I'll contribute half a groat towards that.'

Fitzgerald shrugged. 'Then I'll see you tomorrow as soon as it gets light, master. Bring food and water for two days.'

Back in the customs house, the harbour master sat down to write his message for his Kilmore counterpart.

'I also need to send a letter,' said Denzil. 'To Exeter. Can I use your materials?'

'And welcome,' said Mawgan. 'I've a reliable rider who'll take it to Camelford for you and hand it to a courier. He'll be leaving early in the morning.'

Denzil sat down and began to compose a letter to Princess Alyce.

Syon

Sir Thomas Malory and Owen Pailton watched from Syon Abbey's Thames-side wharf as an upstream-bound barge steered towards it. Frost rimed the yellowed grass, and Owen tucked his hands under his arms to keep them out of the icy east wind. Lord Wenlock had provided them with thick cloaks clasped with his own badge and cured leather jerkins to wear over their doublets. Bronwen had supplied warm caps woven from Welsh wool. They were travelling as Sir Thomas ap Gruffydd and his squire. Owen prattled away in Welsh as the master of the barge touched his fur-lined cap respectfully and showed them to a shelter amidships, where they were protected from the chilly weather by thick canvas tilts and quantities of sheepskins. Two friars were already sitting there, one fat and with the red nose of a drinker, one pale and thin, absorbed in murmuring prayers as he passed the wooden beads of a rosary through bony fingers.

Once they were under way, the barge's great square mainsail was hoisted, and they scudded upstream, helped by the rising tide and a brisk easterly.

Owen turned to Malory. 'I have to thank you, my lord. I've had more than enough of London. Anglesey is my family's true home. After my grandmother Agnes dies, my mother says we can return there.'

'Why were you in London?'

'My grandmother came to England with the fifth King

94

Harry's widow Catherine de Valois. She married a Welshman who was a retainer of Owen Tudor.'

'Tudor? The handsome groom who seduced Catherine? I've always enjoyed that love story. Straight out of high romance.'

'Not just a groom. A knight descended from the great Glyndŵr. He was her Master of Horse. But the love was all on his side. According to my grandmother, six years after Henry V's death, the widowed queen needed a husband for the usual reason a woman does. But rumours of her having an affair had led to an Act of Parliament declaring the possessions of anyone she married to be forfeit. Tudor had little to lose, and he worshipped her. After their marriage, they moved to Much Hadham Palace, where Edmund Tudor was born. But their households and their bedrooms were always quite separate.'

Malory was fascinated. 'Who was Edmund's father in truth, then?'

Owen shrugged. 'Rumour had it that he was high-born. Agnes told me that Queen Catherine had many courtly admirers much more to her taste than her driven, conquest-obsessed husband King Henry. She worshipped both the queen and Owen Tudor and was indignant on Owen's behalf when he was imprisoned after the queen's death in 1437. When I was born, she named me for him.'

'I wonder Agnes never told me what she knew or guessed,' said Malory pensively.

Owen shrugged. 'She was never one to gossip. Nor is anyone in our family. Wagging tongues cost lives, my mother always says.'

Malory suddenly realised that the murmured prayers had ceased. He looked across the tilt at the friars and saw that they were listening with interest. But were they friars? Hoods covered their heads, so he couldn't see if they were tonsured. He raised his voice.

'Enough fairy tales, boy. No good comes of talking of the great.'

Two hours later, Kingston Bridge had to be navigated. The helmsman called for the sail to be struck and the mast lowered, and the crew skilfully quanted the barge through its central arch with long poles. By the time they reached Shepperton the wind had dropped, and the tide had lessened, so the helmsman steered to the wharf. Towing horses were hired to haul them the remaining distance to Chertsey Abbey. There, stiff with cold, they disembarked, as did the friars.

'Stop your first night at Chertsey,' Wenlock had told Malory. 'Abbot Angewyn prefers hunting to praying. Give him this letter, and he'll make you welcome and sell you decent mounts and a packmule. He's a great breeder of horses and keeps a fine table.'

Sure enough, after seeing Wenlock's letter, the abbot led them into his own lodgings, calling for food and wine to be brought from the kitchens.

'My lord abbot, before we eat and settle for the night, we'd like to buy two good riding horses,' said Malory. 'Lord Wenlock said that your stock was unusually fine.'

'Where are you bound?' asked Angewyn, as they walked into the vast stone barn in which he stabled his horses. Owen opened his mouth to say Cornwall, but Malory interrupted. The fewer people who knew their intentions the better.

'Pembroke. With letters for the earl.'

Angewyn raised his eyebrows. 'Pembroke? That's a fort-night's riding, more if you run into bad weather in the Welsh hills. But if you are on Lord Wenlock's business then you must go where he sends you. I hope you have warm clothing enough.'

He led the way into the barn. They gazed up at the huge rafters, saw pigeons flitting to and fro. A warm, sweet scent came from bales of straw hoisted high on ropes.

'Keeps them safe from rats,' said the abbot. 'And not having a loft floor lessens the danger of an unseen fire. That's the great enemy. There shouldn't ever be a need to strike a flint in here, but vagabonds slip in occasionally during the winter.'

'What mounts would you recommend, Father?' asked Malory. 'We've a long way to ride, so we need beasts with stamina.'

The abbot looked at Owen, agog with excitement at the prospect of a horse of his own. He led them to the first stall. 'For the boy, I have a spirited pony. She's got his Welsh blood, so she'll keep going as long as he can.'

'We'll be well matched,' said Owen with a grin. He wandered off to peer into the other stalls.

Malory was examining the teeth of a powerful gelding when Owen came quickly back.

'Sir Thomas, come and see. I've found just the right horse for you.'

'Which one do you mean?' asked the abbot.

'The black horse in the end stall. He has a splendidly arched neck and a fine mane.'

Angewyn raised an eyebrow. 'You've an eye for horseflesh, young man. Hades is part Arab, and the fastest horse in my stable. But he's got a will of his own.' They walked down to the last stall.

Malory gazed at the horse. It took him back to his youth in France, to a succession of steeds taken from French castles when the English forces swept unstoppably across Normandy.

He shook his head regretfully. 'No. I need something less showy. That gelding looks strong.'

He began to walk back to it, but to his surprise the abbot stopped him. 'The boy's right, Sir Thomas. I like to think I'm as good a judge of men as I am of horses. You're the right owner for Hades. His last owner was also a knight. He had to sell him as he'd fallen foul of the king. And if you run into trouble, he'll carry you both out of it.' He winked, and Malory wondered just what Wenlock's letter had said.

Over supper he asked about the road to Basing.

'It's a good one,' said Angewyn. 'Forested but cleared for a bowshot on each side of the highway. You could break your journey at the nunnery at Hartley Wintney. I can give you an introduction to the prioress. She's a godly woman and has improved the place a great deal. You'll get simple fare, but good.'

'And where would you suggest staying in Basing?'

'You couldn't do better than the Swan Inn.'

⚜

Next morning Malory strapped his saddle and a couple of packs onto Hades, and Owen did the same to his pony.

'Have you given her a name?' Malory asked.

'Tricksy,' said Owen without hesitation. 'Cos she is.' Malory smiled, but had a twinge of anxiety. The boy was so young. Then he remembered that he'd been even younger when he'd sailed for France to fight.

An hour or two later, they were riding companionably side

by side along the well-maintained highway from London to the west. To Malory's relief, there was no sign of the friars. It was odd, he reflected, that they had not eaten in the hospitable Abbot Angwyn's refectory the night before.

'What is she like, this Princess Alyce we're meeting?' asked Owen as they jogged towards Basing. 'Will she be dressed royally?'

Malory considered. 'In truth, I don't know. It's twenty years since I last saw her, and then she was weighed down with grief. So was I. It was the funeral of little Anne Beauchamp. Her father Harry, the first and only Duke of Warwick, was my liege lord. After he died on the eve of his coming of age, she was sole heiress to one of the greatest inheritances in England. She was contracted to marry the Duke of Suffolk's son John, and I'd taken her to Ewelme three years earlier to live with the Suffolks until they were old enough to marry. Duchess Alyce took her to her heart. She'd always longed for a daughter, she told me. She'd made Ewelme a paradise of beauty and learning, and it couldn't have been a better home for Anne.'

Owen saw a faraway look come into Malory's eyes and heard him sigh before he continued.

'History might have been different had Anne survived to marry the Suffolks' son. Instead, the boy was married to Margaret Beaufort, the closest heir to the throne then, as King Henry still had no child. But there were whispers in high places that he aspired to put his son on the throne, and he was accused of treason. King Henry thought to save him by exiling him abroad, but his enemies caught up with him on the high seas, gave him a mock trial, and left his head stuck on a pole on Dover Beach. Two years later, his son's Beaufort marriage was annulled.'

'Do you have any idea who brought about his murder?' asked Owen.

Malory pursed his lips. 'Duke William had many enemies, both in the House of Commons and among the Lords. One of the most vehement was Humphrey Stafford, Duke of Buckingham, the man I believe responsible for my liege lord Harry's death just as he came of age. I foolishly voiced my suspicions of him, and that brought my own downfall. He persecuted me for a decade. But he was killed at the Battle of Northampton in 1460. Since then my troubles have been of my own making.'

'Like being exempted from pardon for being involved with an illegal printing press that flooded all London with Lancastrian broadsheets?' There was a sharpness in Owen's voice that made Malory realise the boy was angry. He reined in Hades and looked at him.

'What is it, Owen?' Owen slowed his own pony before answering.

'It was the press that brought about the death of my father, wasn't it? They were torturing him to discover its whereabouts.'

Malory nodded slowly. 'Yes. But Denis's involvement was nothing to do with me. He was heart and soul for Lancaster, you know. As of course I am. But neither of us set up the press. That was the work of much more powerful interests.'

'You mean the Earl of Oxford?'

'Did your mother tell you that?'

'Not in so many words. But I know that she had dealings with him.'

'Well, forget she did. He's only lately been released from the Tower, and such a rumour could be the death of him. And of your mother.'

'How did Princess Alyce get to be a princess?'

'During King Henry's illness after France was lost, the Duke of York was Lord Protector. He passed through Ewelme, and took their son John, the Suffolk heir, to Framlingham to be trained in chivalry. The boy fell in love with his daughter Bess. They were married in 1458 to celebrate the Loveday pact between York and Lancaster. Three years later, Bess's brother usurped the throne and became King Edward IV. So Duchess Alyce, his sister's mother-in-law, now has the rank of princess.'

'I suppose she's all for York now.'

'I doubt it. Chaucers have always been loyal to Lancaster, but it would be dangerous for her to declare herself. Especially as...' He hesitated, then remembered Wenlock's counsel of discretion. Better Owen knew nothing of the real reason for Alyce's journey.

'Lord Wenlock told me that she had it in mind to become a vowess, which will take her altogether out of the political arena. This westward journey of hers is a pilgrimage of preparation, apparently. I'm looking forward to getting to know her better. I remember her as unusually learned, and a great lover of books. But she doesn't suffer fools gladly, so watch your tongue.'

Ireland

Simon was getting used to island life, though he was tired of eating fish, apt though it was now that Lent had begun. He'd marked the start of a day with a line each morning, crossing it after saying his prayers each night. He'd survived a whole week now. He was chipping mussels off the rocks exposed by the falling tide when he saw the sail. He leapt to his feet and began to wave wildly. Then he realised the ship, a biggish one, was too far away to see him. But it was getting closer. Perhaps the hermit was returning. Soon the ship was near enough for him to make out the men on the deck. He was about to try waving again when he noticed the flag blowing from its mast. A black cross on a white ground. Bretons, then. Notorious for their raids on coastal villages. He ducked down among the rocks. He didn't fancy the idea of being made a galley slave. He thought quickly. If they did land on the island, they'd easily find the hermitage. What he had to save at all costs was the coracle. Crouching, he dodged through the rocks and up the grassy slope. He looked back at the ship. They seemed to know what they were about – it was heading for the cove where he'd been abandoned by the Irish fishing boat. When he got to his refuge, he stuffed provisions into his sack, slung it over his shoulder and hoisted the coracle over his head. Then, clutching his oar, he headed for the northern end of the island. He'd been practising his paddling skills, but his heart sank as he looked at the roiling waters between it and its smaller neighbour. There was clearly a powerful current. He looked back at the ship. The top of its mast was showing close to the landing cove. There was nothing else for it. He launched the coracle and began to paddle.

Soon he was whirling helplessly, the fragile craft rocking violently from side to side. He clutched its edges with both hands, and to his horror saw the oar and his sack flip overboard. Praying desperately, he shut his eyes. There were shouts from the shore he had just left, and he opened them. Men in dark smocks and red bonnets were waving threateningly. Which way would the current take him? To his relief, the water grew calmer. There was a scrunch. He realised that he had hit a rock. Water began pouring in, at first making the coracle steadier, but soon filling it. There was nothing for it but to swim. But he had never learnt how to. Lips moving in prayer, he launched himself into the water. A wave splashed over his head but his feet struck shingle. Soaked to the skin, he staggered ashore, hauling the wreck of the coracle behind him, and collapsed on the strand. Looking back across the turbulent waters to the other island, he saw the Bretons disperse, baulked of their prey. Hopefully there was no landing place for their ship on his refuge.

After walking around the island, he realised that not only was there no landing place, but there was no shelter of any kind, only wind-stunted trees and rough grass. Perhaps he could repair the coracle. He examined it. There was a gash a foot long in its heavy tarred canvas. Try as he might, he couldn't think of a way of making it watertight. Still, it had the makings of a shelter. He found a place out of the icy wind and propped one end on a rock so that he could crawl underneath it. He had lost everything. He was put in mind of the book of

Job which his mistress had given him a couple of years ago. At the time, he'd longed for an Arthurian tale, but it seemed that Job was better suited to him. 'The Lord giveth, and the Lord taketh away,' he murmured sadly to himself. Just as his life had never seemed better, it had become far worse than it had ever been.

Ewelme

Joan was as good as her word. Seated on a high-backed saddle on a stout ambler, she returned to Ewelme at noon a few days before St Valentine's Day. She was swathed in a fur-lined riding cloak and sported a broad-brimmed green felt hat held in place by a red scarf of soft woollen cloth tied under her chin. Riding beside her on a lop-eared mare with a wicked glint in its eye was a gipsyish woman with the hood of a thick brown cloak pulled over matted grey braids. A knitted scarf muffled the lower half of her face. Behind them came a cart piled with chests and bundles and topped with a spare wheel, all tightly roped down. Astride the lead horse of the two that hauled the cart was a huge dark-skinned man. Tamsin instantly recognised him and grinned with delight. So did Alyce.

'What a good idea, Joan. Cabal will make brigands think twice. And Farhang will enjoy meeting him again, albeit briefly. Where did you find him?'

'He was guarding the stall in front of John Doll's shop. When I told him I was heading to Cornwall with you, he signed that he wanted to come too. He's had enough of snide jeers from unmannerly Oxford students and local louts.'

'Who's your other companion? I thought you said you

lacked a tiring maid. I've told Matilda Lovejoy she's to attend you.'

'And I'm glad of it; I liked the look of her. Godith wouldn't be any good at making me comfortable, but I thought we might need a healer as well as Cabal's muscle. She's my herbalist. She hasn't read Galen or Aristotle. She learnt what she knows from her Moorish mother. But she's rarely lost a patient. And she has the sight. She also has a sister in Camelford, which she says isn't far from Tintagel. Cornwall is where their father came from, and as her husband died just after Christmas she's decided to return there for good.'

Alyce nodded, then looked at the cart doubtfully. It was well made, with iron-bound wheels, but any kind of wagon was a liability on a long journey.

'That's a deal of luggage. And the cart will slow us down, especially after Exeter, when the roads get rougher.'

Joan shrugged. 'Well, let's enjoy its comforts for as long as we can. I'd rather have my own bedding than sleep in bug-ridden sheets. It can carry some of your baggage as well. We'll need plenty of warm clothes.'

Once the cart had been hauled into the stables with the horses, Alyce led everyone into the great chamber to eat. Its walls were hung with tapestries celebrating notable women both pagan and Christian – Medea and Hippolyta, Dido and Cleopatra, Melania and Eudocia. Joan regaled Alyce with news of her latest literary acquisitions, and Godith and Farhang were soon deep in discussion of remedies useful to travellers. Tamsin and Mattie waited on them, their eyes bright with excitement at the prospect of the journey. After the meal was over, Farhang excused himself to tend a patient in the infirmary. Joan, Alyce and Godith retired to the comfort of the solar. Opening the leather wallet in which she had kept Simon's letters, Alyce handed Joan one of them.

'It's from Simon. He wrote it a month or so before the one I showed you. It's rather wordy, like all his letters, but it will give you a feel for Tintagel.' Joan took it and read it aloud.

Sunday, 3rd December the eighth year of the reign of King Edward
Most puissant sovereign lady, greetings. It is now eighteen months since I left Ewelme and living here has been an inspiration. John Gregory was sorely in need of support, and I think I have succeeded in helping him. He has made me responsible for the much-neglected chapel on the Castle island, and I have a lodging next to it. Knowing your devotion to Our Lady of Fontrevault, I suggested to Father Gregory that the chapel have a shrine dedicated to her, as Tintagel was once under that abbey's sway. The services I hold there celebrate the lives of such notable patrons of Fontrevault as Elizabeth of Anjou and Eleanor of Aquitaine. From the chapel I can see St Materiana, your own church, high on the mainland. It is as if a spirit path stretches between them.

The parishioners are uncouth in their habits, but they are improving in godliness. I warn them of damnation from the pulpit and have established a school on the island similar to your own in Ewelme. With the help of a very intelligent village girl, I have had some success in persuading local children to abjure the superstitions that are rife here.

It is a daily joy to pace the island, and gaze out on the ocean. I relish both the wild seas that pound the headland in stormy weather and the God-given calm that descends on land and sea when the gales pass. It brings to mind the wonderful tales of King Arthur which Sir Thomas Malory is penning. I wonder what has become of him. I imagine he has taken refuge in Lorraine with Queen Margaret.

I spent a week in September at Whalesborough Manor with your cousin Lady Elizabeth and her husband Sir John Trevelyan. He has a marvellously tame bird called a chough which comes at his call. Legend has it that its red beak and red feet are inherited from a crow which paddled in the blood of St Thomas à Becket in Canterbury Cathedral. Make what you will of that; I myself am doubtful.

While I was staying there I met Sir Reginald Mohun, the deputy sheriff of Cornwall – he is the most powerful royal servant in the West Country. The Trevelyans have elected to hold Christmas in Whalesborough rather than at St Veep, their Fowey manor. They invited me to stay with them for the festivities, but my place is in my parish. They commend themselves to you and ask me to send their hopes that all is well with you. As of course do I.

Your servant in Christ,
Simon Brailles

'It seems that Simon has at last decided on his vocation,' said Joan as she handed it back to Alyce. 'When do you think he'll take orders?'

'It must wait on Bishop Booth's next visit to the diocese. When we get to Exeter we could ask Dean Webber when that is likely to be.'

Godith gave a cackle, and they turned towards her in surprise. 'I wonder. Listening to the thought behind your servant's written words, I suspect he has other things on his mind.'

Alyce was taken aback. 'What do you mean?'

Godith just smiled, picked up the wallet and began to study Simon's other letters.

Alyce stared at her, unsure that she was going to enjoy Godith as a travelling companion. Then she turned back to Joan.

'It's an odd chance that Simon should have mentioned Sir Thomas Malory. He isn't in France. I got a letter from John Wenlock a couple of days ago. He says that if we would like Malory's company, he's also heading west.

'I'd welcome riding at Sir Thomas's side,' said Joan. 'Will he be alone?'

'He told Wenlock that he hoped to find at least one companion. It's never wise to travel alone.'

'The more the merrier. Any friend of his will be congenial.'

'There's a problem,' said Alyce. 'Because he was suspected of being involved in the printing of treasonous broadsheets he was outlawed. So he's going to travel in Wenlock's livery. At the Angel, he'll make himself known as Thomas of Newgate.'

'That's apt enough,' said Joan with a grin. 'He knows it all too well.' Then she looked pensive.

'But isn't Wenlock taking a risk in protecting him? That's not like him. I wonder what he's hatching now.'

'He's always had a soft spot for Malory,' said Alyce. 'He had him reading aloud to his wards in The Royal at the time of that Pailton business. And the chances of his being recognised are few. I've only met him briefly, but I've enjoyed what I've read of his stories of King Arthur. I'd be very happy for him to join us, if he doesn't mind being bossed about by two opinionated women.'

'Three,' put in Godith.

'From what I've heard, he's used to that,' said Joan. 'His wife rules the roost in Warwickshire. Which is why he preferred lying low in London.'

'No wonder there are so many dominant women in his tales,' said Alyce. She thought for a moment, then stood up. 'I'll leave you and Godith to settle in. Mattie will show you where your chamber is. I need to sign the new will my attorney has drawn up for me.'

The next day dawned cold but bright. By the time the sun had risen, Joseph Pek, Jem and Wat had tied the saddled horses to a rail in the stable yard, and Cabal had trundled the cart out of the tack room and backed a horse between its shafts. Then he harnessed the lead horse in front of it. Ben Bilton watched the preparations critically. His own horse Bayard, named after the magical steed in a book Princess Alyce had lent him to read, was a magnificent beast with eyes full of flickering fire. Ben prided himself on his horsemanship; once he had saved enough to acquire Bayard, he had spent every spare penny of his wages on handsome harness. He attached a large pack behind his Cordoban leather saddle.

Mattie Lovejoy, still hardly able to believe her rapid promotion from the Ewelme laundry to tiring maid to the formidable Joan Moulton, watched him admiringly. She handed her pack to Wat, who strapped it behind the saddle of her pony. He was beaming with excitement, cheeks rosy and hair still wet from the dousing under icy water from the well that Nan Ormesby had insisted he underwent early that morning.

'Happen it will be a while before he washes again,' she'd said to Tamsin. 'At least he'll start clean.' Tamsin grinned, then noticed that Ben was handing Mattie a bunch of snowdrops from the clumps that Alyce had established in the shelter of a rosemary hedge in the drying green, and that she was looking flirtatiously up at him. Martha followed her gaze. 'Blows the wind in that quarter?' she said. 'I seem to remember you were given Ben's Valentine violets last year. Men are a fickle breed.'

Tamsin tossed her head impatiently.

'I gave them back to him last year, and I'd give them back to him now. Mattie is welcome to him.' But two lines gathered between her eyebrows as she marched away to the solar to see how she could help her mistress.

She found Alyce dithering over which books to take with her. Her grandfather's *House of Fame* was the first to be put in the stout little oak chest that she used as a travelling library; the second simplified extracts from Bartholomew the Englishman's encyclopaedic *On the Properties of Things*, amusingly illustrated for children. She thought Simon would find it useful for the school he had established. Now she was trying to choose between her other treasures. She looked up as Tamsin came in.

'It's so hard to decide what I'll want to read,' she said in despair. Tamsin, used by now to Alyce's insistence on taking too much of everything with her, looked over her shoulder at the titles.

'Well, my lady, as Mistress Joan is with you, take *The Epistle of Othea* she and Sir John gave you. And you've been wanting to read those Thomas Hoccleve verses that you found last week at Doll's. And it might be as well to ask Mistress Joan what she has with her, so you don't bring the same books.'

'That's a sensible notion, child. Where is she?'

'Still in the hall, eating a hearty breakfast.'

'Wise woman,' said Alyce. 'I'll do the same and ask her what she'd like me to bring.'

Half an hour later, an English telling of Boccaccio's

Decameron, Geoffrey of Monmouth's *History of the Kings of Britain* and a rhyming *Sir Gawain and the Green Knight* had been wrapped in fustian, fitted into the book chest and locked up safely.

'No need for more tales of Arthur if Malory is joining us,' Joan had said. 'Monmouth's *History* is well suited to our Cornish wanderings. And Boccaccio's stories will keep us amused. I've got Pisan's *Treasure of the City of Ladies* and a book of riddles which the young ones will enjoy trying to guess. And Godith has a very practical little book by a German monk about the laying out of a herb garden. She's planning to give it to her sister, but you can read it on the journey.'

'How about *Reynard the Fox*?' suggested Tamsin. 'We can pass the book round, and each read separate parts. It's good for that, what with all the different animals. And God.'

'Who'll be God?' asked Joan, hopefully.

'My lady, of course,' said Tamsin firmly.

🦊

The church clock chimed for terce as they mounted up. Joan grimaced.

'I was hoping we'd have been on our way by eight. Getting a company this size on the move is a much slower business than I'd expected. Where Godith is, I've no idea.'

'Things will speed up after a while,' said Alyce. 'Leaving home is the hardest part of a journey. One has so many afterthoughts.'

Just then a little procession emerged from the great hall. It was led by the newly dubbed Earl of Lincoln and his three-year-old brother Ned. Then came Bess and Jack, followed by Nanny Molly with baby Cecily in her arms. Little Earl John handed his grandmother a short sharp knife in a stout leather sheath.

'It's from Ned and me and Cecily, Grandmother. For fighting off robbers,' he told her solemnly. 'Molly says you'll be... be... besieged by them.'

Molly gave an indignant snort. 'I did nothing of the kind, Master John. I said it would come in useful. That's all.'

Bending down from her saddle, Alyce took it from him with a smile. 'And so it will. I'll treasure it. It will never leave my pocket and it will remind me of you.'

He beamed, then led Ned away to inspect Bayard's harness.

Jack stepped forward. 'Bess and I have got a present for you too, mother,' he said. He handed up a small book with a long tail of leather extending from its binding and tied in an elegant knot. 'It's a psalter. You twist this knot round your belt, so you can read as you go along. God speed you and bring you back to us safely.'

'Thank you, Jack,' said Alyce. 'I've long wished for a girdle book.' She extended her hand for him to kiss. 'And may your own mission succeed.'

Finally, she turned to Bess. 'Take care of yourself, daughter.' Their eyes met in affectionate understanding.

Joan's voice rang across the courtyard. 'But where are Godith and Cabal?' As if in answer to her call, they came through the gatehouse, Godith deep in conversation with Farhang, Cabal laden with small parcels.

'Put those into my saddlebag, Cabal,' said Godith. She looked up at Joan and Alyce mischievously. 'I've been in the infirmary storeroom. Farhang has provided for every ill under the sun and a few more.'

As Godith mounted her mare, Farhang came over to Alyce's

side. He handed her a silver phial with a cork stopper. 'Here's a new eye ointment, my lady. Godith advised me on its making. I've added chamomile to the fennel and the eyebright. And be sure to return in time to see your new bulbs in flower. They'll astound you.'

His rheumy old eyes, calm and wise, dwelt on her for a moment or two. 'You have a good addition to your company in Godith. Bear with her oddness. You can trust her.' He stepped back and raised a shaky arm in farewell.

❧

After the company had ridden up Rabbit Hill, their road wound gently downwards, running parallel with the Thames until they reached the priory of Augustinian nuns at Goring. They had sent Ben and Joseph ahead, so the gates were wide open. The prioress was standing in the courtyard to greet them, her white habit drawn in at the waist by a black leather belt, from which hung her rosary and a bunch of keys. The bells of sext were ringing as grooms took their horses into the priory's stables, and the prioress led the way into the great hall, where a long table had been placed running the length of the hall.

'You wrote that you'd welcome a meal but didn't want to stay long, so I've arranged it like a breakfast rather than a dinner,' she said as they sat down. Spread down the centre of the table were bowls of soused herrings, boiled eggs and a huge ham, carved into slices. Wat's face lit up, and he began to squirrel hunks of bread, eggs and ham into the pocket that Nan had sewn into his cloak. Tamsin was about to remonstrate with him, but Godith held her back.

'He's a wise lad,' she said. 'Riding is hungry work and

finding good food when travelling uncertain. You might well be asking to share it with him. Which he'll do before you even ask. I can see that he worships you.'

They crossed the Thames on Goring's long and rickety wooden bridge, rode through the hamlet of Streatley and up a steep hill to Basildon. The road west gave them wide views over the Berkshire Downs and a blustery wind forced them to secure their cloaks, hats and hoods tightly. As they approached Yattendon Castle they heard the clatter of hoofs, and a tow-haired young knight and his squire overtook their cavalcade.

'Your grace of Suffolk, by all that's wonderful. I caught sight of you from the smithy in Basildon and followed as soon as my horse was shod. Why didn't you send me word you were passing? You must come and greet Jane. She's only lately been churched and has been starved of company.'

'Willingly, Sir William,' said Alyce. 'How good to see you. I'd have sent a messenger, but I'd heard you were waiting on your stepmother at Ockwells. I was delighted to hear that you are made sheriff of Oxfordshire. The office has for too long been held by villains. So how many children do you now have?'

Joan's heart sank as they turned from the inviting road winding away to the south-west and dismounted in the castle's outer garth. Alyce saw her disapproving frown.

'Worry not, Joan,' she called. 'We won't stay for long. But William's wife Lady Jane Norreys is a great friend of my god-daughter Meg. I'm hoping she has news of her.'

Drawing closer, she whispered, 'As you can imagine, they are far from friends of York, though they submit just as we do. William's father John Norreys died three years ago. He was very close to Queen Margaret. I wish I'd asked him about my husband's enemies at court before he died.'

They all dismounted, and Sir William sent servants to tell his wife they had visitors, and to lay out refreshments in the hall. It was two o'clock before they set off again.

'At this rate, we won't be at Donnington before nightfall,' said Joan drily as they slowed again behind a flock of sheep being led to market. 'You seem to know every soul along the way.'

'Yattendon had its uses,' said Alyce. 'I asked William if his father had ever talked of my lord's murder. Apparently, he used to say that foremost among his enemies was Humphrey Stafford, the Duke of Buckingham. It seems Stafford always doubted Jack's legitimacy as he was born twelve years after we married, and when my husband got King Henry's permission to wed the boy to Margaret Beaufort he frothed at the mouth with rage. He was ever a choleric man. He threatened the French witch Jehanne d'Arc with his knife, you know, when she was being questioned by the English at Rouen. And he treated Cecily of York abominably while she was imprisoned at Maxstoke after the rout at Ludford eighteen years ago.'

'Was he in London when King Henry sent your husband into exile?'

'Yes, but not for long. He accompanied the king to Wales to put down the insurrections there. He might have known of a plot to intercept William but couldn't have been directly involved.'

'Perhaps travelling to Wales was a tactical move to avoid suspicion,' said Joan. 'But isn't Buckingham dead now?'

'Yes. He was killed nine years ago at Northampton by Kentish soldiers who'd suffered his brutality when he was cleaning up after Jack Cade's rebellion. I wish I could talk to his widow. He might have spoken to her about William's murder. But she married Lord Mountjoy two years ago and lives far away in Derbyshire.'

Alyce's memory for genealogical connections was astonishing, thought Joan. But it was typical of the great families, who always had an eye for the possibilities of spousing a family member to a ward or netting a sideways shifting inheritance.

The sun was low in the sky as they wound along the Lambourn brook and up the hill from which Donnington Castle commanded a view in all directions. The castellan Sir Rafe Arches hurried out to welcome them as they rode through the gatehouse. He escorted the women through the chilly great hall to Princess Alyce's usual apartments, and a yeoman showed the rest of the company to the men's quarters. When they'd settled in, they gathered in a small room off the hall for supper, a delicious meal of spiced mutton pies, spit-roasted hens, braised leeks, cheeses and plum pudding, which they ate sitting at two trestle tables placed close to the huge log fire. Arches, a descendant of the Abberbury family who had built Donnington at the end of the last century, was a talkative man who lost no time in telling Alyce about the iniquities of John de la Beche, from whom Alyce had acquired the neighbouring manor of Chieveley three years earlier.

'He's cutting down timber in your woods, poaching fish from your fishponds and filching your sheep from the downs. I complained to the sheriff Sir Richard Harcourt last year, but he gave me short shrift. I suspect Beche paid him handsomely to lose my petitions.'

'Try Sir William Norreys, the new sheriff,' said Alyce. 'He'll see justice done. And how are my bedesmen and women?'

'Thriving, Princess. The extra allowance of firewood and

the thick quilts you ordered for their beds are much appreciated.' Alyce turned to Joan.

'It was the Donnington almshouses that inspired our Ewelme God's House, you know. They were built by Rafe's great-grandparents a few years after the castle was completed. My father acquired both after their son died at Agincourt, and he left them to me in his will. I was married to William by then, and I persuaded him to attach a similar foundation to the new church we were building at Ewelme.'

Bored, Mattie tugged at Tamsin's arm. 'Shall we slip away and watch the sun setting from the gatehouse? It's so high – we'll be able to see for miles.'

Tamsin nodded, and the two girls stood up. Alyce looked across at Tamsin, a query in her eyes.

'Mattie wants to climb the gatehouse tower and watch the sun set, my lady,' she said.

'Take Ben with you, then,' said Alyce, wishing she too could break away from her steward's grumblings. 'And wrap up warmly.'

The three young people bowed and left the hall. As they did, Wat rose from the second table and followed them. Joan winked at Alyce. 'Sticks to her like a shadow, doesn't he?'

Alyce nodded. 'And it's been the saving of her more than once.'

The outlook from the top of Donnington's five-storey tower was magnificent. Ben pointed to the south. 'There's the great tower of High Clere, one of Bishop Wayneflete's palaces. No flag, so he isn't in residence. We'll get our midday meal there tomorrow and reach Andover by nightfall.'

Tamsin looked down and over the dense forest that skirted Donnington. Weary though she was from the ride, she was thrilled to be journeying to new places. Mattie edged closer to Ben.

'Icy cold up here,' she said with a shiver.

Ben looked down at her and smiled. 'I'll soon warm you up,' he said. Spreading his cloak around her, he pulled her closer. Tamsin felt a stab of jealousy. Annoyed with herself, she called to Wat and headed for the narrow stone spiral of the stairs.

'Let's go down and explore, Wat. Race you to the kitchen.'

Andover

Few words were spoken as Malory and Owen trotted briskly westward. Although there was a cold wind, it was at their backs, and they made good speed. They stopped at Hartley Wintney Priory for ham and peas pottage served on trenchers of rough brown bread.

'Make the most of this,' said Sir Thomas. 'Lent begins on Wednesday.'

Owen grimaced. 'Don't travellers get a special dispensation?'

'Travellers have to eat what they're offered.'

They reached Basing as dusk was falling. There were several taverns. Owen pointed to the White Hart, attractively positioned on the banks of the Loddon, but Malory shook his head.

'A tavern called the White Hart is likely to be a haunt of Yorkists. Let's go to the Swan as the abbot suggested. I can see its sign further down the high street.' He spurred Hades forward.

The host of the Swan made them doubly welcome when he heard that the Abbot of Chertsey had recommended him, and after a welcome meal of roast beef and turnips, washed down with a fine ale, they were soon snoring in the men's dormitory over the stables. Next day they rode on through Oakley, Overton and Whitchurch.

They reached Andover at dusk. The Angel had a long frontage onto the high street, close to the crossing of the road from London to Bristol and the road from Newbury to Southampton. It looked new-built and prosperous as they rode through the arch between its hall and its parlour into a spacious courtyard. On each side long wings stretched back, with kitchens and stables below and guest chambers and communal dormitory above. The stables were being extended along one side of the gate in the west wall; on the other was a guest parlour with a chamber above it. In the centre of the courtyard was a baggage wagon. A one-armed man sat high on the bench across its front, a stout truncheon across his knees.

'I wonder if that belongs to the Duchess of Suffolk,' said Malory in a loud voice. The head of the one-armed man whipped round and, after an assessing glance, he raised his club in greeting.

'Might you be Thomas of Newgate?' he called.

Malory smiled. 'I'm known by that name. Might you be in the service of Princess Alyce?'

'I am – and have been for more than thirty-five years. Before that I was an archer under her husband the Earl of Salisbury. I lost my arm during the siege of Orléans a year later, just after my Lord Salisbury was killed. I travelled back to England with Lady Alyce and a barrel holding his bones for burial in Bisham Priory with his ancestors.'

Malory gave a respectful salute. 'We'll have tales to tell, you and I. What's your name?'

'Plain Joseph Pek. And you and your companion are most

welcome. I've been worrying about keeping my ladies safe in these troubled times.'

'We'll do our best.'

As they dismounted, a voice rang from an open window. 'Thomas of Newgate?'

Malory looked at the plump, red-nosed man leaning out of the casement, and nodded. 'I am.'

'I was told to expect you. I'm the taverner, John Waterman. Welcome to the Angel.'

Waterman put two fingers into his mouth and gave a shrill whistle. Two boys ran out of the tack room at the end of the stable block and took care of their horses. Malory and Owen went into the inn. It was crowded with travellers, and the evening meal was being served. Malory looked around, searching for Princess Alyce or Joan Moulton, but could see neither of them. The room was full of men, who crowded around a dark-skinned woman with matted grey braids. She sat by the great hearth with a pack of cards face up on a low table, her skirts pulled up to her knees to warm her spindly shanks. Owen turned away, embarrassed at how much the woman was revealing. She looked keenly at them, then beckoned them over.

'I'm thinking you're to be our fellow travellers,' she said.

'If you're with Mistress Moulton, you think right,' said Malory. 'Can you take us to her?'

'Not without you introduce yourselves properly,' said the woman tartly as, to Owen's relief, she pulled up her stockings, tied garters around their tops, and lowered her skirts.

Malory was amused. 'You know who we are already, mistress, I'll be bound. But you're right to be cautious. Who knows whose ears are wagging even now?' He reached into the capacious leather wallet he wore over one shoulder and took out a small slate and a piece of chalk. He thought for a moment, then scratched a few words, initialled it with a flourish and handed it to her. The woman scanned it, gave a grin that revealed jagged stumps of blackened teeth, spat on it and wiped the words away. She signalled to a brawny young man sitting on the end of a nearby bench.

'Wat, tell Tamsin that our friends have arrived.'

He nodded obediently, gave Owen a grin, and left the taproom.

'Can we know your name, goodwife?' said Malory respectfully.

'I'm known as Godith,' she snapped. 'But I'm nobody's good wife.' Owen quailed.

When Wat returned he was followed by a remarkably pretty girl. She had a direct, confident gaze, and her tawny hair was held away from her face by a blue silk caul. On seeing them she gave a wide smile. Then she looked around the tavern. No one seemed interested in them, but she spoke in a cautious whisper.

'I remember you both from September twelvemonth. We were hiding in Malachi Fryse's pharmacy while Sir Robert Harcourt's men hunted for Agnes and the printing press. And you and Owen came in.'

'I remember too,' said Owen. 'And you thought I was Spanish.'

Malory looked at her with admiration. 'I recall a tousled-haired chit, but you've grown into a fair maiden. Tamsin, isn't it? Good to see you again. I was told you liked my tales of Arthur. I've some new ones to tell you.'

Tamsin's eyes lit up. 'And we're on a quest of our own now.' Then she put her hand to her mouth. 'Oh, I forgot. It's a secret.'

'Never to be told, then,' said Malory teasingly. 'Say no more.'

Tamsin led them across the courtyard, nodding to Pek and waving to a girl who was rubbing smallclothes clean in the washing cistern in the centre of the courtyard.

'That's Mattie,' she explained. 'And the men over there brushing mud off our riding cloaks are Jem Wingfield and Cabal of… of I don't know where.'

Malory chuckled. 'But I do.' He gave Cabal a wave, and Tamsin saw the huge man's face light up in recognition.

'So how many are there in your company altogether?' he asked her.

'Nine. Four of us women,' she answered as she rapped at the door of the west parlour. After a moment, she opened it, and stood back for them to enter. Alyce and Joan looked up from their books. They were sitting on opposite ends of a long window seat with their backs against its end walls, their feet up and their bodies wrapped in furs. Through the window Malory could see a kitchen garden stretching down to a stream. Bedraggled kale stalks and a few forlorn leeks poked out from a thick layer of manure.

Alyce smiled a welcome. 'Sir Thomas. It has been far too long. It must be twenty years since you came to Ewelme. I fear you see me sadly aged.'

She held out her hand, and Malory advanced to kiss it.

'Undertaking this journey shows you have lost none of your spirit, my lady,' he said as he straightened up. 'As for ageing, I fear I'm much more worn by time.'

She smiled. 'You were ever graceful with compliments. But I now know you are a notable wordsmith. I've read several of your tales of King Arthur, thanks to John Doll. And you have another admirer in Joan Moulton here.'

'I know her and her bookshop in Paternoster Row well,' said

Malory, bowing again. 'I'd welcome both of your opinions on the new stories I've brought with me. I'm hoping that together we can improve them.'

Alyce looked at Owen. 'And who is this young man?'

'Young, but a veteran secret-keeper and adventurer,' Joan put in. 'His name is Owen Pailton. You solved the mystery of his father's death last year, Alyce.'

'Then he's doubly welcome,' said Alyce. 'Tamsin, take Owen to meet the others.'

'Shall I take your cloak to be brushed?' Owen asked Malory.

Sir Thomas nodded. 'Thank you,' he said, swinging it off his shoulders. 'And don't forget your own.' He turned back to Alyce and Joan. 'What are you reading?'

'Joan is deep in a little treatise on gardening her herbalist brought. And I'm reading my grandfather's *House of Fame*. I wish he'd finished it; its conceits are enchanting.'

Joan Moulton eyed him and Alyce and decided that it would be a good idea to leave them alone to talk books. And perhaps much else. It was a shame, she reflected as she heaved herself off the window seat, that their paths had not crossed more often. She could imagine no one better suited to her friend. Muttering something about sorting out their bedding, she followed Tamsin and Owen out of the room.

Once the door had closed behind them, Alyce smiled at Malory. She noticed that though he still held himself proudly upright, there was a grim wariness in his eyes.

'Lord Wenlock wrote in his letter that you've had troubles aplenty recently,' she said.

He gave a weary smile. 'I've weathered worse. But I'm sorry that you were caught up in the matter of the printing press.'

She shrugged. 'That was no fault of yours, I know. Sir

Robert Harcourt has long been making wild accusations against me. Nor, I fear, will he ever stop trying to disgrace me. Happily, he's unlikely to cross my path on my journey to Tintagel.' She saw his eyes light up at the name and smiled. 'You must surely have been there.'

'Just once long ago, soon after I returned from fighting in France after King Harry the Fifth's death. My cousin John Chetwynd was its constable, and he showed me round when my father and I visited him. It was he who first told me of the old legends of Arthur. I never forgot that journey.'

He gazed dreamily out of the window, watching a heron rising from the bank beside the stream, huge grey wings slowly flapping, disappearing behind the starkly bare branches of the great willow trees that overhung the water. Watching it too, Alyce thought how like the bird he was, spare and thin but with a coiled strength about him. She silently blessed Wenlock for suggesting he ride with them.

Ireland

John Tiptoft, Earl of Worcester and now Lord Deputy of Ireland, stirred in his comfortable four-poster bed in Wexford Castle and looked affectionately down at his new wife, Lisbet. Widowed in her late twenties, she was now heavily pregnant, her second baby since their lightning courtship in Ludlow two years ago. He remembered the drawn-out deaths in childbirth of both his previous wives and thanked God that Lisbet took pregnancy in her stride, as she did everything else. She was pragmatic and lively, and, though she did not have much interest in the library of classical literature he had brought with him from England, her upbringing in Bristol had given her a shrewd insight into the thinking of the Irish merchants and lawyers who were proving more loyal to him than the conniving English and Irish gentry. She was also an utterly reliable confidante.

Her eyes opened and met his. 'Good morning, my lord. Are you able to tell me now why we are in this godforsaken place? Much as I love you, I'd rather be in Dublin.'

'I don't blame you,' he said with a smile. 'But I've some business to complete.'

'In Wexford?'

'No, but not far away. In Kilmore.'

'Is that somewhere I'd like?'

'I think not. It's a very primitive fishing haven twelve miles to the west. There's a man recently arrived from Cornwall whom I need to question. Then we can sail home.'

'Is it anything to do with the troubles over the death of Earl Desmond?'

Sir John frowned, recalling the disastrous execution a year ago that had all but cost him the favour of King Edward. He'd been misled by a forged letter into thinking that the king wanted Desmond dead. Not just the earl but any of his sons who were with him. He'd been loth to kill the two boys, who were mere children. But he had obeyed the royal command without question, as he always did. It had cost him all the credit that careful diplomacy had won him in the first year of his rule in Ireland. It was only recently that he had discovered that the letter had been the work of the queen, not the king. Five years ago she had been deeply affronted when Edward teasingly told her what Desmond had said to him about their marriage. 'He said I had much abased my princely estate by marrying a lady of so mean a house and parentage.' Pretending to laugh the insult off carelessly, she had waited for an opportunity to revenge herself, and last year she had found it. She borrowed the privy seal while Edward was away and used it to seal a letter to Tiptoft containing Desmond's death warrant.

'Fortunately I've no fear of the queen's intervention this time. It's a matter of old history, concerning William de la Pole, the first Duke of Suffolk.'

'Who was murdered off Dover two decades ago?'

'Quite so. I was in charge of the commission set up to investigate it, but only the sailors who'd been paid to behead him came up before the court. Most of those really responsible for his death are dead now.'

126

'Do you know who they were?'

Tiptoft paused, wondering if it was wise to open his mind so fully. But he found it useful to think aloud to Lisbet; it gave him a sense of how the world would judge him, as it surely someday would. So he answered her honestly.

'Of course. But it wouldn't be politic for his widow to discover their identities.'

'Why not? You told me you thought highly of her.'

'And I do. But one person who was part of the conspiracy is someone she believes to be her friend. And it is useful to me that she should continue to believe that.'

Lisbet thought for a minute, then asked another question.

'Why is she interesting herself in the matter after so long?'

'For the sake of her son, the young duke. He has long blamed her for his father's death, which has led him into some ill-judged behaviour with her enemies. She's doubtless hoping that solving the mystery will mend matters between them once and for all. And I heard yesterday that she's even now on her way to Cornwall in search of the truth.'

'How are you going to stop her?'

'By finding out how much the man I've had brought over from Cornwall learnt from a garrulous Welshman who was master of the ship I sent to Wadebridge to be refitted just before Christmas. It was the vessel that intercepted the duke. Madoc was then its bosun and knew more of the truth of the business than I realised. My captive is a servant of the widowed duchess. He was being prepared for ordination by the vicar of Tintagel. He was seen giving money to Madoc in exchange for a parcel, and then sending a letter to Ewelme, home of Princess Alyce, as she's now known – though Suffolk was not of royal blood, their son is married to King Edward's sister.

I need to know what the bosun told him, and if he gave him anything. After that he can be disposed of. That won't be a problem because he's assumed to be dead. But it was Madoc who lay in his coffin. Sir Reginald Mohun can be overzealous on occasion.'

He saw Lisbet shiver. 'What is it, my love?'

'It all sounds rather cold-blooded.'

He smiled grimly. 'As politics often has to be. But I won't need to kill the duchess's servant. He'll be found a new though distant home and warned to stay there. I'm not a murderer – unless death is decreed by the king.'

'Or the queen,' thought Lisbet to herself.

⚜

Denzil was enjoying the third day of his passage. He had slept well, lulled by the slapping of the waves on the hull of the *Mairi*. Fitzgerald was an excellent seaman, the weather was clement for the time of year, and they were scudding towards the Irish coast.

'What are those islands?' he asked.

'The Saltees. Great and Little. They belong to the monks of Tintern Abbey, who bring livestock to graze on them in the summer. There's good grazing on both, and a well and a sound enough stone shelter on Great Saltee. It's often used by French and Breton sailors of fortune, who find the island a useful shelter in winter. In fact, there's a ship in its haven now.' He stared into the distance.

'Yes, that's the Breton flag for sure. Let's hope they don't chase us.'

'It looks as if most of the crew are ashore,' said Denzil, pointing to a crowd of figures at the northern end of the island.

128

'Thank Jesu for that. I've no mind to be taken for a slave.'

They were coasting past the smaller island, when Denzil gave a gasp of surprise.

'I can see a man on Little Saltee. He's waving as if his life depended on it. But I thought you said it was barren. Perhaps he needs help. Can we sail closer?'

'Afraid not. It's far too shallow for a safe mooring. Nor does he need saving. When the tide is out there's a causeway to the mainland. We call it St Patrick's Bridge.'

They sailed on to Kilmore Quay, and tied up among an assortment of fishing boats and rowing gigs. Denzil looked back towards Little Saltee. The man, now ant-sized, was still waving. Could it possibly be Brailles?

'What time is low tide?' he asked Fitzgerald.

'In about two hours. He can cross easily in an hour or so. At full low water, the water's only about a foot deep, apart from a bit of a dip in the middle.'

But what if he were a stranger who had no idea that the water was shallow enough to wade through at low tide? Denzil decided to follow his hunch.

'How long are you staying here, Fitzgerald?'

'I've got cargo to unload. And the crew need dinner. About three hours. Then I'm for Wexford. Which is where I thought you wanted to be.'

'I did. But the man on Little Saltee could be the person I'm looking for. Could you wait for me to find out? There'll be a rich reward in it for you.' Fitzgerald's eyes strayed towards the leather bag hanging at Denzil's belt. Remembering the harbour master's warning, Denzil continued smoothly.

'I left my monies in Wadebridge for safety. But if that's Simon, I don't need to go to the Crook preceptory. I'll pay you well to take us both back to Cornwall when you've finished in Wexford.'

Fitzgerald pursed his lips, then nodded. 'We made good speed. I've time in hand. Take one of my men with you. They're locals, and it's no bad thing to have a guide over the causeway. The footing's slippery.'

He beckoned to a nut-brown seaman. 'Angus, could you get our friend here onto Little Saltee? He thinks that waving loon is the man he's in search of.'

Angus nodded, and Denzil followed as he set off briskly along the shore from Kilmore Quay to a tapering outcrop of shingle. Little Saltee looked a long way off.

'Surely we can't wade that far in time?' he asked the sailor.

'Tide's not out yet. We've a while to wait. Angus sat down, took a lump of wood from his belt purse and settled down to whittle with his knife.

'What are you making?'

'A St Patrick cross from holly wood. They sell well to visitors.' Denzil watched admiringly as the point of the man's knife carved an intricate pattern above a simply executed human figure.

'I'd like to buy that from you when it's done. It'll make a good keepsake.'

Half an hour later, Angus stood up, stretched his arms, took off his smock and, holding it over his head, began to wade into the sea. Denzil did the same with his doublet and shirt, and followed him, shuddering as icy water lapped his shins. At first the shingle was slippery with seaweed, but as the water got deeper it made surprisingly steady footing. A breeze got up, and soon they were wet to their waists, then to their chests.

It was an hour before they found the shingle rising beneath

them as they reached the shore. Denzil put his clothes on thankfully. There was no sign of the man he had seen. Perhaps he was scared. As they walked towards the centre of the island, Denzil began calling out Simon's name. But there was no reply.

'We need to head back in half an hour,' said Angus. 'Unless you want to swim.'

Denzil gave one last despairing cry. 'Brailles! Are you here? It's Denzil Caerleon!'

He heard a rustling in the gorse on the central knoll of the island and saw a familiar head poke up.

'Caerleon! By the Holy Rood, how did you come to be here?'

Two hours later Denzil and Simon, warmly dressed in borrowed clothes, sat on the poop of the *Mairi*, enjoying seeing the Irish coast pass by on their way to Wexford. Fitzgerald came up to them, and pointed inland at a troop of riders heading west.

'Looks as if Kilmore is to have eminent visitors. Those horsemen are flying the banners of the Lord Deputy Sir John Tiptoft on their spears.'

Simon gasped. 'Then *he*'s behind all this. He thinks to find me on the Saltees. God be praised you rescued me when you did.'

'What does he want with you?'

'I'm not sure,' Simon said, glancing at the seaman at the helm of the *Mairi*. Denzil could tell he was holding something back but realised that now was not the time to press him.

Fergus was shouting to the crew. They were nearing Wexford's harbour, and soon the sail was rattling down and the great oars were bringing the ship alongside the quay. Seamen tossed warps down to lads eager to earn a farthing or two.

Fergus turned to them. 'We'll offload our cargo and bring

the stuff bound for Wadebridge aboard. Then we'll eat and set off again. Does that suit you both?'

Denzil nodded. 'Is there a tavern you recommend? Nothing fancy. I've no wish to come across such gentlefolk as those.' At the far end of the quay, a party of well-dressed men and women were watching the arrival of the *Mairi* with interest.

Fergus pointed down the beach to an alehouse close to the fishermen's shacks.

'You'll find none but locals at Iscar's Teach. And they've a fine home brew to warm you up.'

'That'll be welcome,' said Denzil, and led Simon towards the alehouse.

'So how did you come to be on that barren little island?' he asked once they had ordered bowls of the day's pottage and cups of a fiery spirit.

'And how did you come to be aboard that obliging Irish boat?' parried Simon.

After they had exchanged their stories, Brailles shook his head in despair.

'This is going to make it difficult to return to Tintagel. But unless I do, I won't be able to take Madoc's evidences to Ewelme.'

'As to going to Ewelme, there's no need for you to do that,' said Denzil. 'While I was staying with the Trevelyans, Lady Elizabeth had a letter from Princess Alyce asking if she could stay with them in Whalesborough so she could visit you in Tintagel. She has no idea you're thought dead, and she's on her way west already. We could go to Bude, but I'm feeling rather doubtful about Trevelyan. I'm sure he's hiding something. The best thing would be to seek out her grace in Exeter, but the Trevelyans are also planning to go there.'

Simon shook his head. 'I need to return to Tintagel for the evidences. I could hide on the island or up in the hills. Morwenna would help me, I know.'

'Tintagel will be the first place searched when Tiptoft finds you've escaped from Great Saltee. That's the island you were on at first. The one I rescued you from is Little Saltee.'

'I don't care what their names are, Caerleon,' snapped Simon. 'I'm never going back to them if I can help it. We'll be safer with my own people. I can trust them not to betray me.'

Denzil blinked. Decisive, sure of his friends, evidently greatly loved by a very taking young woman, this wasn't the Brailles he'd known in Oxfordshire. He looked at him with new respect.

Amesbury

The Angel bustled with activity as the new day dawned. Alyce was woken by the shouts of the stable boys getting horses saddled and bridled for a party of pilgrims who were leaving early. She stretched each of her limbs experimentally. The cramps that gripped her legs every morning were easing somewhat as her muscles strengthened. She looked around the bedchamber. Joan and Godith were both fast asleep, as was Mattie. But Tamsin's bed was empty. She frowned, but then the latch of the door lifted, and Tamsin came in, carrying a two-handled wooden bucket. Seeing Alyce's eyes on her, she grinned.

'Hot from the kitchen fire, my lady. I thought we would all welcome a wash.'

'I certainly would,' said Alyce, turning on her side and

raising herself from the sagging straw mattress that had given her an altogether new ache in the centre of her back. As she got up and crossed to the table where Tamsin had put the hot water, Joan groaned and opened one eye.

'Surely it isn't morning already? What's that din outside?'

'The pilgrims are on their way,' said Tamsin. 'They said last night that they'd be leaving early to take ship from Southampton. They're sailing for Compostela.' Alyce saw Tamsin's mouth move as she repeated the musical lilt of the word to herself. She sighed. Perhaps Cornwall wouldn't prove enough to satisfy her secretary's wanderer spirit.

An hour later, their newly formed company had breakfasted, and they set off in a long cavalcade in pale wintry sunshine. Joan was as flamboyantly rigged out as ever, since she was travelling as herself, but Alyce had decided to dress modestly in a grey gown and a black cloak. She had a large ebony cross hung around her neck on a leather thong. Her beloved rosary was securely looped around her belt, as was her new girdle book.

There was still frost in the air and the going was hard below their horses' hoofs. After half an hour or so, Malory noticed that Owen was trailing behind them. Then he saw him stop, dismount and examine his horse's right fetlock. He turned Hades, and rode back to join him.

'Something wrong, Owen?'

Owen signed to him to dismount. 'No, Tricksy is fine. I just wanted to make sure we weren't being followed. I thought I saw those friars who were on our barge in the inn. But I could have been mistaken. Perhaps they were with those pilgrims who left earlier.'

'Just as well to check,' said Malory, pleased with his new

squire's resourcefulness. They waited for ten minutes, but there was no sign of pursuit. Spurring on their horses, they caught up with the rest of the company.

Noon found them approaching Amesbury. They trooped along its main street to the priory, which was contained in a great loop of the River Avon in the west of the town, its church crowned by a tapering octagonal steeple.

'Ring the gatehouse bell, Bilton,' Alyce said to Ben. He pricked Bayard's flanks lightly with his spurs and trotted towards the iron-bound oak doors of the priory. Dismounting, he took the worn handle of the bell pull and tugged at it. A discordant jangle sounded, and a peephole opened in the right-hand door. Then both doors were swung back. A lay brother in a coarse brown gown motioned them inside. They found themselves in a courtyard, and two grooms bustled forwards to take their horses as they dismounted.

'The prioress told me to take you to the guest lodgings,' said the lay brother. He gestured towards a long two-storey building at a right angle to the stables. 'She'll join you in its hall shortly.' He looked at their swords with a frown.

'You must leave your weapons in the gatehouse.'

When they'd done so, Sir Thomas looked around the court-yard with a faraway look in his eyes. Only Tamsin heard the words he murmured under his breath. 'Here Guinevere worked to gain her soul's heal.'

'We've made good speed,' said Alyce. 'How about riding out to see the Giants' Dance after we've eaten? It's less than two miles away. And we've plenty of time, as we're overnighting here at the priory.'

'What is the Giants' Dance?' asked Tamsin.

'A circle of huge and ancient stones,' said Alyce. 'Some have other stones balanced over them. How they were raised no one knows.'

'Geoffrey of Monmouth has it that Merlin summoned giants to bring them over from Ireland by magic for Uther Pendragon, so that his brother King Aurelius could make a worthy memorial for the British kings who died in battle against the Saxons,' said Malory. 'That's why it's called the Giants' Dance. Both Uther and Aurelius are said to be buried in the circle. Aurelius's first name was Ambrosius, and the French books say that Amesbury takes its name from him.'

Owen's eyes shone with excitement. 'We could search for his grave. Perhaps his sword is buried with him.'

Godith looked stern. 'It's a place to respect, Owen, not to plunder. It was holy to the Druids before the Pendragons arrived. Bones in their thousands lie in the long graves around the circle. And wights haunt it.'

Tamsin shivered. She hadn't decided what she thought about Godith. She felt as if the shrewd, sharp-eyed herbalist could read her thoughts.

Alyce saw her secretary quail. 'But it's a holy place to Christians now,' she said firmly. 'Chapels encircle it like the beads of a rosary.'

Joan eased herself off her horse. 'I've had more than enough of riding. You go to the Giants' Dance. I want to see Prioress Joanna's library. Especially the famous Amesbury Psalter.'

The porter showed them to the guest lodgings where two chambers, one for the women and one for the men, had been prepared for them. They had just gathered together again in the guest hall when an elegant nun in the white wimple and black habit of the Benedictines entered. A rosary of polished quartz beads hung from her intricately woven silk girdle. She held both arms out to them in a general blessing. 'Welcome, all. But especially to you, your grace. It is far too long since we spent time together. That was when you stayed the night on your way to your Dorset manor of Newton Montagu twenty-five years ago.'

Alyce was shaken by the unexpected exactness of the prioress's recall, but she managed to maintain her composure.

'I had all but forgotten that occasion,' she said casually. 'And I'm indebted to you for offering hospitality to our company today. I look forward to hearing over dinner how the priory does. Then I think most of us will make an expedition to the Giants' Dance, though my friend Mistress Moulton – she indicated Joan with a nod of her head – would like to see your library. She owns a notable London bookshop in Paternoster Row.'

The prioress gave Joan an appraising glance. Alyce could easily imagine her thoughts. Joan, worldly, buxom and bold-eyed was not most people's idea of a bookseller. Then she nodded.

'I'd be happy to show her our books, though none of them are for sale. The library is one of Amesbury's proudest possessions.'

'And I've brought a gift for it,' said Joan. 'A life of your patron saint, St Melor. I came across it in a bundle I bought in Bruges from a Breton merchant. It is much damaged, but I thought your scriptorium could restore it suitably and rebind it.'

Dame Joanna's eyes widened. 'That is generous indeed. We have a sacred relic of his right thumb, embalmed, and set in gold, but no chronicle of his life.'

Dinner in the priory's refectory was a silent meal, eaten

while listening to a reading from *The Mirror of The Blessed Virgin*. It was a particularly gory passage from the book of Judges, praising Jael, wife of Heber the Kenite, for hammering a nail through the head of the sleeping Canaanite general Sisera, after his defeat by the Israelites on Mount Tabor.

Joan bent towards Alyce. 'It just goes to show that women can play as active a role as men in war.' Alyce stifled a smile and looked around to see if anyone was frowning at such irreverence. But few of the nuns were listening to the reader, let alone Joan; most were discreetly conversing in sign language. Alyce noticed that their numbers had shrunk since her last visit. As had their quality. Previously there had been several sumptuously dressed corrodians, great ladies who had retired from the world to prepare their souls for the next. Now there was only one, sitting on a chair of state on the other side of the prioress. She wore a miniver-edged black velvet mantle over her long-sleeved gown of patterned purple and black silk, and her hair was drawn tightly back in a jewelled net under a brocade coif. Alyce frowned. Surely she knew that face, though it had been deeply etched by unhappiness since they last met. She leant forward to look more closely, and saw recognition flood the woman's eyes and her lips part in delight.

'Duchess Alyce!' she exclaimed. 'By all that's wonderful! I hardly knew you in such sombre guise. We haven't met since your son and his bride walked at the head of the Loveday procession a decade ago. Did I ever tell you that your foundation of a God's House at Ewelme inspired me to do the same? At Heytesbury we have an almshouse for twelve worthy men and women and a thriving school.'

Dredging into her memory, Alyce found the name she searched for.

'Lady Margaret! I have long wondered what became of you since... since...'

She hesitated. The Hungerfords had been loyal to Lancaster ever since Henry IV seized the throne in 1399. Until his death in 1459, Margaret's husband Robert had been a close friend of King Henry VI. Their son, another Robert, had fought with the famous Earl of Shrewsbury John Talbot at Castillon, the last stand made by the English in France. Captured and only released six years later for the ruinously high ransom of £6,000, he'd returned just in time to fight for Lancaster against Edward of York and the Earl of Warwick at Towton. He'd fled to Scotland with Margaret of Anjou but had been captured at Hexham five years ago and beheaded. Margaret's grandson Thomas, as loyal as his sires had been, had been executed at Salisbury only a month ago for plotting rebellion with Henry Courtenay, brother of the Earl of Devon.

Lady Margaret gave a wistful smile. 'A grandson still remains to me. Walter has been cannier than his brother and his father. He made his peace with Edward of York, and he holds at Heytesbury. It's only seventeen miles away. His prospects are good, though his Moleyns inheritance is presently still in the hands of his mother's second husband, and part of our Hungerford estates have been inherited by his brother Thomas's wife's family, the Hastings. They are as loyal to York as the Hungerfords have always been to Lancaster.'

Joan Moulton leant forward from the other side of the long table. 'Lady Hungerford, it is a pleasure to meet you. Sir John Wenlock has spoken to me of your doughty fight to preserve your family estates for the benefit of your heirs.'

Lady Margaret turned to Joan with interest tinged with anxiety. 'Do you know Lord Wenlock well, then?'

Alyce sensed anxiety in her question and remembered that Wenlock had a reputation for profiting from the wardship of Lancastrian widows and heirs. But she had also heard that the estates he held in trust were well managed and not wasted for quick profits.

'I do,' said Joan. 'I believe you were his ward in London for a while. Not that he talked about your affairs.'

Alyce saw relief in Lady Hungerford's eyes.

'Yes. I lived at The Royal with Walter for a few years after the death of my father Lord Botreaux in 1462. He died of injuries fighting against the Yorkists at St Albans, so my inheritance was forfeit. If the attainder is ever lifted, however, it could return to Walter. It includes our manor of Bampton in Oxfordshire, of which I'm especially fond. Like my other estates, it's held at present by Wenlock, but he always dealt fairly with me. In fact, I've often wondered where his true sympathies lie.'

'As do we all,' said Joan. 'Have you seen Lord Wenlock recently?'

'He stays here on occasion,' said Lady Hungerford. 'We're on the road from Someries to Southampton.'

Alyce had not known that Wenlock held Bampton. She wondered uneasily how direct his connection with it was. She also hoped that when he stayed at Amesbury, Dame Joanna had not mentioned her long-ago overnight stay at the priory with Elsbeth de Burgh and Sybilla. Surely, though, the prioress would not have connected her brief stay with the birth of the Suffolk heir. They had eaten alone in their guest chamber on the grounds that Elsbeth had contracted a fever and had remained swaddled in thick cloaks throughout their visit. She had returned from Newton Montagu to Ewelme a different way, not wanting to account for the absence of Elsbeth and the presence of a baby and a wet nurse. Nor had the birth of an heir been announced to the world until William had returned from France five months later.

After the nuns had filed out towards the church, Prioress Joanna rose.

'If you are going to see the Henge by daylight, you'd best ride to the Great Down now. Mistress Moulton, shall we make our way to the library?'

Joan brightened. Nothing delighted her more than browsing among books. She was pleased to see that Malory also stood up. 'I know the Henge well, and I would also welcome being shown round the library. Do you have any French legends of King Arthur, Dame Joanna?'

'The only book we have about King Arthur is a Welsh telling. It came as part of the dowry of a novice many years ago. It is called the *Brut y Brenhinedd*, which is to say the History of the Kings. It is embellished with finely worked initials – one shows Arthur himself, sceptre in hand. The novice made a copy of it in English.'

Alyce saw Sir Thomas's face light up, and part of her wished that she was staying with them. But she wanted to avoid conversation with the prioress as much as possible. Moreover, the Giants' Dance had haunted her ever since she and Sybilla and Elsbeth had paused among its looming stones on that fateful journey, and she was curious to see how she felt about it now.

The ride was a short one, just over two miles. A race developed between Ben and Owen, easily won by Ben, though Owen was not far behind. He and Tricksy took shortcuts across rough ground pitted with ruins where Ben hesitated to risk Bayard. The little pony was impressively sure-footed and sensitive to the slightest twitch of its rein. Wat tagged along with Tamsin and Mattie, and Cabal and Godith rode beside Alyce. Last came Jem, watchful as always.

As the huge stones came into sight, they slowed. Smoke rose from cooking hearths in the disordered group of thatched shacks that had been built north of the Henge, but there was no one in sight, just sheep lazily cropping the grass. The vast slabs of rock were silhouetted against the western sky. Some were erect, some flat on the ground, some hoisted across others to create what must once have been a continuous circle of flat-topped arches. The closer they got, the more immense the stones seemed. Cabal dismounted and walked through one complete arch; tall though he was, he was dwarfed by it. The youngsters followed him.

Alyce sat down on a fallen stone and looked around her. Inside the outer circle were the remains of a smaller one, and inside this central ring there were a few smaller fingers of rock. A huge slab lying on its side had red-brown stains on its flat top. She shuddered, wondering what was sacrificed.

'Just the odd sheep these days, Princess,' said a voice behind her. It was Godith. A mind-reader, it seemed, as well as a herbalist.

The sun was sinking in the sky, and slanting shadows alternated with rays of golden light. Suddenly a black-cloaked figure stood proudly erect on the lintel across one of the biggest monoliths. Arms spread wide, it began to declaim.

'Taliesin and Morrigan, Myrddin and Aneirin: a finer bard than any of you is singing the old legends of Britain.'

Alyce was startled at first, then smiled as she recognised Owen. Bronwen had evidently taught him all about his own country's lore as well as reading him Malory's tales. As he bowed, and disappeared, another shape rose up on another lintel. Slim and supple, and dressed only in a shift tucked into woollen hose, it hesitated a moment, then performed a series of leaps and back handsprings that took it from one lintel to the next and then on to a third and back with astonishing grace. Then it too slid from view.

Alyce gaped in amazement. From behind her Godith gave a cackle of laughter. 'Matilda. Little daredevil. She told me she was an acrobat.'

'I thought she was Stonor born and bred,' said Alyce.

'She grew up there. But when she was fourteen she ran away with some travelling minstrels. They'd seen her dancing and thought that with a bit of training she'd pull in audiences. Which she did – until two of the company started arguing about who should have her favours. The master minstrel decided to send her home before they fell out over her.'

'How do you know all this?' said Alyce. 'All Jeanne said was that she might be a little flighty.'

'I suspect she is. We gossiped when we shared a bed at the Angel. She asked me if I could make her a love potion. I asked her who it was for, but she just giggled. I mixed up a stimulating simple from chervil seeds and dried southernwood, and wished her luck.'

Mattie, now decently clad in a kirtle and woollen shawl, came out from behind the stones and walked towards them, unsure of her reception. Behind her came Cabal and the others.

Alyce shook her head reprovingly but couldn't repress a smile.

'Wretches. It's fortunate there was nobody to witness your pagan antics. But your handsprings were prettily executed,

Mattie, if at an alarming height. How did you and Owen get up get up on to the lintel?

'I stood on Cabal's shoulders, and they climbed up us,' said Ben, who was clutching his right hand. 'Mattie trod on my fingers. I think she's broken at least three of them.'

'Let me see,' said Godith. Expertly she felt along each of his fingers. He winced when she got to the smallest.

'That'll need binding up. The others are just bruised. Keep rubbing them, that'll help. And when we're back at the priory I'll give you a cream that works wonders.'

Listening, Alyce smiled. She had a sense that the motley collection of individuals she'd gathered for her expedition was settling into a true company. She signed to Jem to bring Larkspur over, and, using his cupped hands as a step, swung onto her saddle.

'Come on, everybody: we must head back to the priory. I don't want to miss vespers.'

Chattering merrily, the young people disappeared to find their mounts, and soon overtook their elders. Alyce looked round for Cabal, but there was no sign of him.

'He'll find his way back when he's ready,' said Godith. 'Though he might spend the night here. He'll want to wash in water from the spring that runs east of the stones. He loves places like this – that shimmer between past and present. I'm hoping he'll stay with us in Cornwall.'

⚜

After vespers, at which the priest asked them to pray for Guinevere and all queenly women, Dame Joanna said that she had to visit the infirmary, but that they were welcome to spend the evening in her parlour. In it, they found Lady

Margaret Hungerford ensconced in a high-backed chair beside a cheerful fire. She smiled, and gestured Alyce to a chair on its other side. Malory and Joan sat on a cushioned settle, and Tamsin perched on a footstool beside the hearth.

'Sir Thomas has kindly agreed to read us what he has written so far of the last battle,' Lady Hungerford said. 'The murderous clash of Mordred and King Arthur near Dover and the death of Gawain. And the tale of Queen Guinevere's last days.'

Startled, Alyce looked at Sir Thomas. He nodded reassuringly.

'Lady Hungerford recognised me. We met when she was living at The Royal and Lord Wenlock had me reading to his wards. But she will tell no one. We've been talking over old times. And more recent happenings.'

'Does Dame Joanna also know who you are?' asked Alyce, wondering as she spoke what Malory meant by 'recent happenings'.

'No. She knows me only as a bookish knight writing his own version of Arthurian tales. She showed me the Welsh telling they hold here. It was curious – making Caerleon Camelot. How did you find the Henge?'

'Much as before, though there are more cottars' dwellings near it than there used to be. No doubt there are profits to be made from guiding summer visitors.'

'Likely there are. There's so much interest these days in ancient times, and in tales of Brutus and Merlin. Jumped-up kings hope to borrow nobility from pretended ancestors. But I want to make people remember the high ideals of the old days of chivalry, when truth and honour came first; nor was might always in the right.'

Alyce was struck by the fire in his eyes, his intensity. She was now regretting not having taken the opportunity of talking to him at The Royal two years ago. But she'd have plenty of opportunities of getting to know him better on the journey to Exeter. And of asking him more about the events that preceded Duke William's flight from London. She knew that he'd been summoned to the turbulent Parliament of 1449, which had called so vociferously for William's trial for treason.

The door opened, and Dame Joanna entered, followed by three servants, each carrying a large tray laden with dishes of sweetmeats, bowls of fruit and cups for wine and ale. Mattie and Owen advanced on them eagerly, but a cough from Alyce reminded them of their manners, and they began to pass them round. Once everyone was served, they settled down to listen to Malory's reading.

He stood up and pulled a sheaf of paper from his leather shoulder wallet. 'As we rode from Andover, I told the tale of Lancelot's flight from the realm of Logres, and of Gawain urging Arthur to invade Lancelot's French lands, leaving Mordred as regent,' he reminded them. 'And of the great battle between Lancelot and Gawain, and of Gawain's wounding. Now, as we are at Amesbury, I will tell of the regent Mordred's perfidy.' He shuffled through the pages until he found the right one. Then he cleared his throat and began to read:

No sooner was Sir Mordred made regent than he spread
false tidings that Arthur had been killed by Sir Lancelot,
and proclaiming himself king was crowned at Canterbury.
Then he went to Winchester and ordered Guinevere to
become his wife...

His voice was spellbinding, his words more formal than everyday speech, but aptly chosen for the expression of high romance. From time to time he hesitated, and Alyce realised that he was thinking of improvements to the story as he read. She looked around at the circle of entranced faces and realised that they were witnessing the making of a masterpiece.

Then fled Queen Guinevere to Amesbury, to a nunnery, and there she clothed herself in sackcloth, and spent her time in praying for the king and in good deeds and in fasting. And in that manner evermore she lived, sorely repenting and mourning for her sin, and for the ruin she had brought on all the realm. At Amesbury she worked to gain her soul's heal. And there anon she died. She was a true lover and therefore she had a good end.'

He looked around at their rapt faces and smiled with satisfaction. 'Enough. Reading aloud always makes me aware of better fashionings. I'll retire to the library if I may, Prioress, and make some changes to my copy.'

He bowed to Dame Joanna and left the room. She looked after him with interest, and Alyce wondered if the canny nun had recognised him.

Joan yawned. 'I'm for bed,' she said as she rose.

The rest of the company followed her out of the room until only Lady Hungerford and Alyce were left to gaze into the embers of the fire. Alyce decided to ask her old friend what she remembered of the terrible early months of 1450.

'I wasn't at court myself,' said Lady Hungerford. 'But my son Robert talked of the conspiracy against Suffolk. He said it was hatched not by his enemies but by those he thought his friends.

In truth, Alyce, your husband went too far in persuading King Henry to allow your son Jack to marry Margaret Beaufort, the niece of Edmund, Duke of Somerset. Until Queen Margaret managed to have a child, she was the Lancastrian heir to the throne. Robert said he was surprised Somerset agreed to it.'

Alyce nodded sadly. 'I did advise William against the match, but he rarely listened to me.'

'What happened to Margaret Beaufort?' asked Tamsin. 'Did she die young too?'

Alyce shook her head. 'After William's death, Edmund Beaufort replaced him as chief royal adviser. A papal dispensation declared Jack's marriage null in 1453 and two years later Margaret was married to the king's half-brother Edmund Tudor. Henry liked the idea of his mother's grandchildren having a claim to the throne.' She turned back to Lady Hungerford.

'Did your husband mention any other names?'

'Robert had his doubts about Sir John Trevelyan. He was a charming young man, a great favourite of the king after Harry Beauchamp, the young Duke of Warwick, died untimely. And Duke William had contrived handsome rewards for him, such as the constableship of Hadleigh Castle on the death of the king's uncle Duke Humfrey. But Robert said he was out for nothing but his own gain, and that your husband was a fool to trust him.'

Alyce felt a chill in her heart. 'Any others?' she asked. But Lady Hungerford's head had drooped. Alyce realised that she was falling asleep. 'Your pardon, Margaret, I've kept you too late. Shall I call for your tiring maid?'

The old lady jerked awake, yawning. 'That would be kind,

my dear. I'm sorry not to have been able to help you. So many are dead now. As I will be before long.'

Sensing dismissal, Alyce rose, bestowed an affectionate kiss on her forehead, and swept out of the chamber. Lady Hungerford's maid was dozing in the anteroom.

'Attend to your mistress,' Alyce said crisply. 'It's time for bed for us all.'

Ewelme

Three sets of eyes, all the same deep blue, watched intently as Bess's long, delicate fingers untied the velvet ribbon and unfolded the silk around her birthday gift. Then her own hazel ones widened in delight, as she held up the long strand of alternately milk-white and coal-black pearls, closed with an intricate gold clasp.

'They are truly beautiful, Jack,' Bess said as she looped them twice around her neck and went over to her looking glass to admire her reflection. Her husband and their eldest son John smiled with satisfaction, and little Ned stretched up a hand to feel their silky smoothness.

'I went with father to a jeweller in Foster Lane by the Goldsmiths' Hall, and we chose them,' said John proudly. 'One for each year of your life. Then he strung them with a knot and a tiny bead of gold between each one while we watched. When I grow up and marry, I'll have one made just like it for my wife.'

'First you must attend to your studies,' said Nanny Molly tartly, 'or you'll be diddled out of your inheritance as many another has been.'

She glanced at Jack, then, wrinkling her nose, gathered up baby Cecily from her cradle. 'Time for a change for this little princess and for you boys to go over to study with Master Greene in the school, and for your parents to have some peace.' Herding John and Ned in front of her, she gave Jack and Bess as much of a curtsey as she could with Cecily in her arms and headed for the door.

Jack raised his eyebrows. 'That was rather pointed, wasn't it?' he said to Bess. 'Was the old beldam talking about me? She needs to mind her manners.'

'She's spoken bluntly for all the years she's been in our service,' Bess replied. 'I remember her ticking off my mother when I was a child and Mama fed me sweetmeats before I went to bed. There's no changing her now.'

Jack sighed. 'Well, at least she's loyal to us. Unlike my old London cronies.'

'And unlike the Harcourts. Marton says Sir Richard is appealing the court judgment against his wife over Marsh Gibbon. But don't worry. He says there's no possibility of it being rescinded.'

'What about Sir Robert? He's a good deal less law-abiding than his brother.'

'He's far away in Bristol overseeing the fitting out of his ship, the *Peacock.*'

'Thank the Lord for that, at least. I'd rather he knew nothing of my journey to Bampton. Are you sure you wouldn't like to come with me? To make sure I don't mess things up.'

Bess shook her head firmly. 'No, this is your business, and I have every faith in you. Belle-mère trusts you to find out what the vicar knew about your father, and so you will. The Yates, our tenants in Buckland Manor, have been alerted to your coming for the night. From there it's only an hour to Bampton.'

It was mid-morning when Jack and his squire Dick Quartermain, the seventeen-year-old son of Alyce's neighbours in Rycot, rode into Bampton-in-the-Bush, still a thriving wool town but now overtaken by the prosperity of Witney and Burford, more conveniently situated on the Gloucester-to-London road. The absence in France of its overlord Sir John Talbot for the best part of two decades had done it no favours.

He and Dick left their horses in the stables of the Swan Inn and walked to the vicarage. Its door was opened by a slovenly manservant, who said that Dom Robert was at prayer, then gave them a broad wink. What he meant by the wink was explained after they had entered the church. Hiat was in the chancel close to the altar, slumped in the chair of state reserved for the bishop's visitations, a chalice brimful of wine in his fist. He raised his head and peered at them.

'Wha' mi' you fine gennelmen want?' he asked, slurring his words together. ''Fess your sins, eh?' Jack hesitated, but Dick stepped forward boldly.

'This is his grace the Duke of Suffolk. He has questions for you concerning one Milo of Bampton, about whom you wrote to Sir Robert Harcourt three years since.'

A cunning look spread over Hiat's face. 'Answers'll cost him. As they did Sir Robert.' He turned on Dick. 'And he mi' not wan' you lis'ning to them.' He gave a cackle of laughter.

Jack motioned Dick to wait at the west end of the church. Hiat heaved himself up, took another slurp of wine, and beckoned Jack to follow him through a nearby door. It turned out to be the vestry, hung about with surplices and robes for the various Christian seasons, but smelling dank and musty. Hiat pulled out a key hung round his neck on a long string and walked over to a cupboard set high in the wall. Once he had unlocked it, he felt inside, and took out a bundle of letters.

'If you just want to read them, it'll cost you a noble. If you want to keep them, as I'm sure you will, I want five. I di'n tell Harcourt I had 'em, 'cos I knew one of these days a Pole would happen along in search of them and pay me more than that stingy rogue.'

Jack took the bundle, sat down at a table, and undid the twine that bound it. He spread the letters over the table. Each was headed Wootton Glanville and they were meticulously dated, beginning in 1440 and ending in 1443. They were from Oliver Roos, the rector of Newton Montagu's church. He was an assiduous correspondent, writing twice a year at Easter and in September. After toiling through several tedious accounts of the state of the weather and the misdoings of parishioners, he looked up at the grinning Hiat.

'Why should these interest me?' he demanded.

'Just you wait,' jeered Hiat. 'You're nearly there. Keep going.'

Jack gave a sigh and began the next one.

Thursday, 2nd day of September, 1442.
Dear brother in God Robert,

Today we had strange doings. The Countess of Suffolk, who I knew to be staying in her manor of Newton Montagu, asked me to baptise a boychild John Mortimer de la Pole. He was a scrawny imp, screaming lustily until the holy water drove the devil out of him, when he became meek as a lamb. The countess told me that the Earl was away in France, that the boy was his bastard and that his mother had died giving birth to him. She also begged for my discretion, reminding me how much I owed her. It struck me that in time it might prove profitable to have this occasion set down, so I am writing of it to you in case by chance or by mischief my own notes on church happenings are destroyed. They are, however, well-concealed from prying eyes, behind the third panel

153

from the left on the back of the rood screen; just press the knot in its front face.

Yours in Christ, Oliver Roos

Jack looked up to see Hiat's bloodshot eyes fixed on him shrewdly. He no longer looked drunk.

'Happen you're the right age for that scrawny imp to be you. And I know from what your man said who you pretend to be. Son of the man who drove poor Milo's father off his holding at Kelmscott, but not of his high and mighty wife. You can have the letter for five nobles. But I want another five every year to keep my mouth shut. This will cost you, cost you now and till the day of my death, lordling.'

Jack considered for a moment, then decided his only option was to agree.

'Why did Father Roos write to you?' he asked as he handed over five nobles.

'We were ordained together in Oxford thirty years and more ago. We both stayed in Oxfordshire and saw a good deal of each other until...' He hesitated, then hiccupped and continued. 'Well, it doesn't matter now. There were rumours we saw too much of each other. That hypocritical swine your father the Earl – this was before he won himself a marquisate and then a dukedom – was for having us both defrocked, but Countess Alyce persuaded him otherwise, and sent Oliver to be priest at Wootton Glanville. As she held at Newton Montagu, she had the right to appoint its vicar.'

Jack was puzzled. 'Why do you call my father hypocritical? Surely, he was in the right? The law of Holy Church...'

'Our 'Holy Church' is rife with such friendships. So is the royal court – as your father well knew. He was something of a Ganymede himself. Truth was, he was jealous. Liked the look of Oliver.'

Jack drew his sword in fury, but Hiat just laughed and shook his head.

'Temper, temper,' he sneered. 'Killing me would be a mortal sin much worse than your father's venial ones. You're lucky I'm settling for a few nobles a year. The grudge I bear you Suffolks will never lessen.'

Jack and Dick Quartermain left Buckland Manor at dawn the next day and reached Ewelme before darkness fell. Bess hurried out to welcome them home. After supper, once Dick had gone to bed and Bess had settled down with a tiny jacket she was embroidering with brightly coloured silks for baby Cecily, Jack related their adventures. Bess looked thoughtful.

'So Hiat has guessed the truth. But he won't be able to prove it, especially as you have the vicar of Wootton Glanville's letters. Unless he made a copy. And from what you say of his sodden state, he may not survive long.'

'We could give him a helping hand towards meeting his Maker,' said Jack angrily, stabbing at the fire with a poker.

Bess was shocked. 'Jack, remember the sixth commandment.'

'Of course I will,' Jack sighed, putting down the poker and going over to sit beside her as she embroidered. 'What I do need to do is journey to Newton Montagu and find out what happened to Father Roos's records. His letters to Hiat stopped in 1454. I asked if that was because he had died, but Hiat said it was because they had fallen out over the rights and wrongs of the war between York and Lancaster. He held to Lancaster, and Roos to York.'

'Which could work in our favour if he's loyal to my brother.' said Bess. 'And if he's dead, you know from that letter where he hid his notes on church happenings. If you set off on Monday, how long will it take you to reach Newton Montagu?'

'Riding the fine horse that you gave me for my birthday and with equally well-horsed companions, we could overnight at Amesbury and reach it on Tuesday evening. And Bess, I want to take little John with me. He can ride in front of me.'

Bess frowned. 'He's too young for such a journey, Jack.'

'He's rising nine. Older than I was when my father was murdered. And he needs to understand how the world works better than I did at that age. I realise now that my father spoiled me, made me arrogant and unnoticing. My mother intends to make Newton Montagu and all the west-country properties she inherited from the Earl of Salisbury over to little John for the rest of her lifetime, and I want him to learn that he has duties to those who owe him fealty.'

'But we can't trust a child with the secret of your parentage.'

'There's no need for him to know my business with Roos. Dick can stay with him when I go to the church. There's no time to be lost. We'll leave tomorrow.'

Stourton Castle

The battlemented walls of Stourton Castle looked down over a great mere bordered by gaunt, leafless trees. Alyce gazed across at it from the highway, Malory at her side.

'The Stourtons profited mightily from the wars in France,' she said thoughtfully. 'And Sir John wheedled a dozen or more profitable holdings out of my husband Duke William.

He was also steward of the Duke of Buckingham's estates in Wiltshire.'

Malory frowned. 'I'm glad I didn't know that when I rode north with him in 1462 in King Edward's army. Humphrey Stafford was the bane of my life for a decade.'

'I didn't know that you fought for the Yorkists.'

Malory grimaced. 'Like you agreeing to your son's marriage, I had no choice. Those who didn't rally to the Yorkist cause were declared traitors. Warwick besieged Dunstanburgh and then Bamburgh, where Sir John Stourton was wounded. I was at his deathbed in Durham.'

'Do you know anything of his son William's loyalties?'

'I suspect he's as much of a time-server as his father was. So Owen and I will take leave of you here. Sir William might recognise me – I stayed in the castle in his father's time. I've taken our weapons from the cart, and we'll get lodgings in the tavern in South Cadbury. It's only ten miles further on.'

Alyce nodded. 'That's a wise precaution. We'll meet you there tomorrow for a midday meal. Around noon?'

'Yes. That'll give us time to climb up to the ruins of Cadbury Castle in the morning. Some say it was King Arthur's Camelot, though I believe that to be Winchester, where even now the Round Table hangs. We'll watch the road from Wincanton from the summit and come down to join you in the village.' He paused, then spoke again.

'Princess Alyce, I hope you realise how much your welcoming myself and Owen into your company means to me. Not just because of the protection you provide, but because of our conversations. I've been starved of like-minded friends with whom I can think aloud and be sincere, and Joan and you – especially you – are among the best I've ever known.'

Before Alyce could reply, Malory waved an arm in farewell and wheeled Hades around, calling to Owen to follow. She watched him go, gratified but confused. 'Especially you,' she repeated under her breath, then looked round nervously in case she'd been overheard. But Joan was talking to Godith as usual, and no one else was in earshot.

The rest of the Ewelme company wound its way down the hill and along the border of a huge lake to Stourton Castle and rode over its drawbridge into its base court. As grooms and stable boys took their mounts, a tall nobleman dressed in a showily slashed murrey doublet with puffy upper sleeves emerged onto a balcony above the porch of the hall. He waved a welcome with exaggerated courtesy.

Alyce took in his lank hair and the humourless cast of his thin features and shivered.

'Sir William is a chip off the old block, I fear,' she said to Joan. 'No more trustworthy than his father. But he might let slip some useful information after dinner. He's rumoured to be something of a drunkard.'

Joan nodded. 'I'll do my best to lead him on.'

The wave was all they saw of Sir William until dinner time. It was the castle steward who escorted them to the guest lodgings, explaining apologetically that his master was in the middle of business dealings. Curling her lip at such discourtesy, Alyce nodded, but reflected philosophically that they could all do with an opportunity of washing and changing their clothes.

Dinner was excellent: fresh fish from the lake, venison and plum puddings. Markedly tense at first, Sir William tossed back a great many goblets of wine and became more and more genial. Alyce waited until he was beginning to slump in his chair before she brought up the subject of her husband's gruesome death. Had his father ever talked about it?

Stourton stared at her glassy-eyed, then nodded his head.

'He did indeed. I'm afraid he was pleased about it. I was a mere boy then and didn't properly understand why at the time. It was a terrible way to die. Executed with a rusty axe and dumped on Dover beach with his head on a pole. A cruel pun on his name.'

A snigger sounded beside her. Alyce turned her head quickly and was chilled to see Stourton's son John stifling the noise by swilling more wine. Sir William gave him a warning look before going on.

'The truth is my father blamed your husband for the loss of France. It was profits from the French wars that built this castle, and when Caen was surrendered because Suffolk failed to supply troops to relieve it, my father lost all the estates he'd been granted in Normandy. As did many others.'

'Did your father say anything about how my husband's murder came about?'

Sir William hesitated. 'Well, not to me directly. But I did overhear him and the Duke of Buckingham talking about Suffolk just before he was arraigned for treason. Sir Humphrey was saying that – begging your pardon, your grace – a jacka-napes from Hull had no business to be heading the royal council. And my father said, "especially not one in the pocket of the French".'

Joan Moulton leant forward. 'And what did Buckingham say?'

'That one of the greatest lords in England was even then engaged in ensuring his downfall.'

'And whom did he mean?' asked Alyce.

'I don't know, your grace. I was but seventeen at the time, and more interested in celebrating the knighthood that Buckingham gave me. I wanted to lead my own troop to the defence of Aquitaine. But the chance never came. After Talbot and his younger son died at Castillon, France was utterly lost.'

'Talbot. The English Achilles,' murmured Joan. 'Who greater than he?'

'A legend, indeed,' mused Alyce. 'And the most quarrelsome man in England. I remember him joining us in Anjou and travelling back with us as we escorted Queen Margaret to England. He swore at my husband for days on end.'

'Could Talbot have been involved in Suffolk's death?' asked Joan.

Sir William shook his head vigorously. 'He was far away. He gave himself up to the French as a hostage when Rouen fell in 1449 and made the pilgrimage to Rome required of him by the terms of his ransom. He didn't return to England until well after Suffolk's death.' He belched, then raised his goblet to Joan, and took another generous swig of the heavy red wine. 'Moreover, there was no subtlety about Talbot, and the duke's downfall was most cunningly contrived. The commission to investigate was headed by the whiter than white paragon of virtue Sir John Tiptoft, who unaccountably didn't manage to find anybody of rank to hold responsible. The *Nicholas* sailed off down channel and was all but sunk off Cherbourg.'

He sniggered as he drained his goblet. 'But enough of the past. Would you like my steward to show you round the garden before it gets dark? I've heard that you are both accomplished plantswomen.'

'I'd welcome it, Sir William,' said Alyce. 'Your fountains and your great lake are famed far and wide.'

Joan shook her head. She had allowed Sir William to refill her goblet several times and was nodding with fatigue. Alyce looked down the hall to where Tamsin and Mattie were sitting with Godith and beckoned to them.

'Matilda, please escort Dame Joan to our lodgings. Tamsin, you'll accompany me. And you, Godith?'

The herbalist shook her head. 'I'll stay by the fire. Sir William asked to have his fortune told.'

After the tour of the castle gardens, Alyce and Tamsin joined Godith and Mattie by the fire. On the table lay half a dozen curiously painted cards, evidently turned up from a pack in Godith's hand. There was no sign of Sir William.

'He's retired for the night,' Mattie told them. 'After hearing his fortune. Godith whispered it low, so I don't know what she said. But he didn't look best pleased by it.'

Godith gave a knowing grin. 'The cards never lie. I can only say what they show. Shall I tell yours, my lady?'

Alyce shook her head firmly. 'What will be, will be. I'll enjoy the ups when they come, and I'd rather not know about the downs beforehand. Bedtime for me. It's been a very long day.'

Tamsin followed Alyce upstairs to their bedchamber. Joan was snoring in the great bed, but there was no sign of Mattie. Tamsin livened up the fire and hung Princess Alyce's winter nightshift in front of it. Then she undid the lacing of her mistress's gown. Where was Mattie? she wondered as she helped Alyce climb up into the great bed, already warmed by Joan's slumbering body. Had she slipped away with Ben? As she pulled heavy drapes across the windows, she realised how brilliantly the stars were shining now that most of the lights in the house had been doused.

'It's a wonderfully clear night, my lady, and there's no moon,' she said as she handed Alyce her nightcap. 'Might I go star-gazing?'

Alyce thought for a moment. Surely no danger would threaten Tamsin here?

'Well, don't go further than the fishing lodge we admired on the edge of the lake. It'll be icy cold. Borrow my cloak. It's warmer than yours.'

Tamsin went down the servants' stair into the empty kitchen, unbolted the back door and went outside, enjoying the sharp, clean air after the stuffiness of the bedchamber. She followed a path down to the fishing lodge, sat on its steps and gazed up at the sky, Mattie and Ben forgotten. She could recognise some of the patterns in the stars, thanks to Denzil Caerleon's teaching at Ewelme long ago. She imagined him in a ship far out at sea, using the constellations as guides.

As she became more accustomed to the darkness around her, a movement further along the shore caught her eye. She shrank back into the shadow of the little building and watched. Two hooded men, one short and fat, one tall and thin, were pushing a small boat into the water. The taller man held it steady while the plump one clambered in and took up an oar. Then, pushing off from the shore with a well-placed shove with his leg, the thin man took up a second oar. Their progress was eerily silent. Sacking round their shafts, Tamsin guessed, to muffle scrapes in the rowlocks. Poachers, perhaps. Sir William had mentioned how much game he lost because of the camp of outlaws in Castle Woods. Though they had had neither rods nor nets.

When the boat reached the far shore, the men clambered out and disappeared into the trees. Were they going somewhere or returning? She shivered. Even wrapped in Alyce's fur-lined cloak, she was cold.

Leaving the fishing lodge, she began to walk back to the castle. She paused beside an elaborate fountain, enjoying the brilliance of the night sky and the reflection of the stars in its pool. Suddenly a dark shape rose out from the shadows, and she felt herself being heaved towards the water. With a shriek of alarm, she twisted round and kicked her attacker in the groin as viciously as she could, glad of the lessons in self-defence that Ben Bilton had given her after her ordeal at the hands of Hamel Turvey. There was a surprised grunt, and she was released. She heard feet running away, and then a shout of 'Who goes there?' from the castle porch. Two watchmen came hurrying towards her. When she told them what had happened, and of the boat she had seen just before she was attacked, the older shook his head.

'It isn't wise to be out alone in the dark, little lady. You were fortunate we heard your scream and frightened the churl away.' They escorted her back into the castle where, after thanking them gratefully, she put her head round the door of the great chamber. It was empty except for Godith. She had heaped a wide stone seat at the side of the deep hearth with cushions and blankets and was clearly planning to spend the night there.

'Any handsome strangers by the lake?' the herbalist asked, teasingly.

'As a matter of fact, there were strangers, though I don't know if they were handsome,' said Tamsin. 'Two hooded men. They had a boat, and muffled oars. And a man attacked me from behind on my way back. Luckily the watchmen heard me cry out and he ran away.'

Godith sat up, startled. 'Christ's wounds, what strange doings!'

'Should I rouse Sir William?' asked Tamsin.

Godith thought for a moment, then shook her head. 'No. He's been abed for a while. The men have doubtless gone for good. It's too late to catch them now. Tell Lady Alyce in the morning.'

Alyce was fast asleep when Tamsin crept into her truckle bed beside the fourposter. Mattie's still lay empty.

Just before dawn next morning, she heard light footsteps and the creak of the other truckle bed. Guessing that Mattie had been with Ben, she was relieved but annoyed, then annoyed at herself for being annoyed. Then she fell asleep again.

Next morning, Tamsin told her mistress what she had seen by the lake and of the attack by the fountain.

Alyce paled. 'I should never have let you wander alone. What a knack you have for running into danger.'

At breakfast, she told Sir William about the attack on Tamsin and the men she saw leaving in a boat. All he did was give a resigned sigh.

'The outlaws in Castle Woods get overbold. They've settled themselves in an old hill fort they call Jack's Castle after their leader Jack Reynard and raised brushwood palisades all around it. They count on not being too much of a nuisance, and the truth is that it isn't worth my while attacking them. Their coming so close to the castle is strange – they usually stay at the far side of the lake. I wonder what they were doing. You say that Tamsin was wearing your own cloak? Perhaps they thought they were winning a greater prize than a mere maid.'

Alyce considered. Surely the attack on Tamsin could not have been intended for her. She was after all well within her rights to be journeying to visit her western estates, even if it was unusual to travel so early in the year and with so little pomp. No, it was mere chance. But she was glad that Malory and his company had not risked recognition by staying in the castle. She played his last words over in her mind and smiled. When she got the chance, if she had the courage, she would tell him how well they matched her own feelings. There was something deeply reassuring about him. He'd been sorely tried by life, risked death in war and spent far too much time in prisons. Yet he'd risen above it all, staying true to the work he saw as his mission in life: to inspire future generations with retellings of tales of the greatest, most magnanimous ruler Britain had ever – perhaps, she conceded with a private smile, never – had.

It was a fine sunny day with a hint of frost in the air. The Stourtons' servants loaded their baggage onto the cart, and Cabal mounted the lead horse. Jem trotted beside it. As Bilton, Pek and Wat led the horses out of the stables, Sir William rode up to them.

'Which road are you taking, your grace? If it's the highway to the west, I'd be delighted to ride with you for the first six miles. It's market day in Wincanton and I have business there. My son John and his groom will be with us too. It would be as well to be many as we pass Jack's Castle.'

'We'd welcome your company,' said Alyce. 'We have it in mind to stop for our midday meal at South Cadbury. The young people want to climb the castle and imagine King Arthur's Camelot.'

Sir William gave a thin-lipped smile. 'So the old legends have it. Locals claim to have heard ghostly horseman galloping down through what's left of its gateway on Midsummer's Eve.

Romantic nonsense, of course. More likely Reynard and his men. But the tavern in the village below it serves good food.'

Alyce and Sir William led the little company. Joan and Godith rode side by side, Joan raucously recounting a ribald joke which Mattie giggled at while Tamsin blushed. Cabal whispered encouraging words to the horse hauling the cart, and Ben Bilton, Jem and Pek brought up the rear. Young John Stourton loosed his kestrel at a pigeon, then he and his groom clapped spurs to their horses to follow the flight of the hawk as it soared in circles above its prey. Sir William watched with a frown.

'I hope they don't go too deep into the greenwood. That's Jack's Castle up above the trees.'

Alyce screwed up her eyes, trying to see what he was pointing at. Just a blurry crag of rock, above the trees. Smoke was rising above it.

'Roasting deer poached in my woods, no doubt,' grumbled Sir William. 'I'm trying to persuade the sheriff to lead a force against them, but he's strangely averse. I think they have the protection of some great lord.'

'Who's got more power in the county than you, Sir William?' asked Alyce.

'The Earl of Worcester.'

'Lord Tiptoft? But I thought he held at Shrewsbury.'

'So he does, for the main part. But he has three manors adjoining Stourton that I rent from him.'

Twenty minutes later John Stourton, hawk now hooded on his wrist and a dead pigeon tied to his groom's saddle, returned. The road, the main highway to Honiton, was a good one. They passed farmers on their way to Wincanton market, and a band of travelling players with a rickety wagon piled high with theatrical lumber: gilded helms made from straw-padded linen, wooden spears and swords, heaps of robes sewn with coloured glass gewgaws. Godith nudged Cabal as they passed them, and pointed to a gaily clad harlequin, his face painted with exaggeratedly pointed eyebrows.

'Isn't that Nero?' she said. Cabal nodded, and gave a wave, which the harlequin acknowledged with broad smile.

'Where are you bound?' Godith called to him.

'To Exeter. But we'll play along the road at Crewkerne and Yeovil and Honiton.'

'Then, God willing, we'll meet again,' she shouted.' We're also Exeter-bound.'

'Who's your friend?' Joan asked her.

'Nero Farthing. A Witney man as adept at acrobatics as at juggling. Cabal worked with his troupe for a while. I knew his mother, but I couldn't cure her of the bloody flux. Good to see he's making a living.'

In Wincanton they waved farewell to Sir William and his son and rode out of the town through throngs of farmers and their families. Sir William had told them to turn off the main highway when they saw the tall steeple of Compton Pauncefoot on their left and follow the road through it towards South Cadbury. Half an hour later they saw the looming green bulk of a hill topped by the ruins of a castle and could smell smoke from the chimneys of South Cadbury village. They paused at a fork in the road. Right to South Cadbury, left to the hill. High on its rocky summit, they could see two tiny figures waving at them. Two others stood beside a tree a few hundred yards to their left.

'That'll be Malory and Owen,' said Alyce. 'I wonder who the other men are.'

167

'I'm more than ready for dinner,' said Joan. 'Let's go on to the tavern.'

'I'll take the girls and Wat and tell them to come down,' said Bilton.

'Take Jem too,' said Alyce. 'Just in case you run into trouble. We'll be fine with Cabal and Pek. We're nearly at the village. Ben nodded, and the four of them turned their horses into the steep-sided lane leading up to the castle. Cabal, who was astride the cart's lead horse, headed right, and they ambled on behind him.

Barely ten minutes later, there was the sound of riders approaching fast from the village. Soon they came into sight: half a dozen hooded horsemen with kerchiefs tied over the lower half of their faces.

'Brigands!' exclaimed Joan. 'What an ill chance that they should happen upon us when we are so few.'

'They must be the outlaws from Jack's Castle that Sir William talked of,' said Alyce. 'They must have seen us pass and outridden us along the ridge road.'

With an agile leap, Cabal jumped off the lead horse and strode in front to confront the approaching men, his quarterstaff held ready. Joseph followed him, stubby sword drawn. The leader of the band reined in his horse and signalled the other riders to stop. He looked down at Cabal and Pek and shook his head slowly from side to side.

'A painted savage and a one-armed ancient. You are outnumbered, churls. Drop that stave and that toy of a sword and stand back. And ladies, to save yourselves from insult, get off your horses and throw any valuables on your persons to the ground.' Without bothering to see if his orders had been obeyed, he turned to his henchmen.

'Jerrid, Roger, turn the cart. We'll take it back to our camp.'

But none of his men moved. They were staring past him at Godith, who had given an unearthly scream and thrown back her deep hood to reveal wild eyes and grizzled braids. In a sibilant whisper, she uttered a stream of curses, her silver-tipped hazel staff pointing towards them. They looked at each other in consternation.

'A witch!' shouted one of them. 'Let's begone, Reynard. We have no quarrel with women. This was an ill plan of yours.'

Reynard scowled. 'You'll do as you're bid, Roger. Turn the cart.'

Unwillingly, Roger and two other men began to urge the cart's horses around. Suddenly there was a terrified whinny. A throwing knife had pierced the rump of the lead horse, turning it from a calm plodder to a wild beast. It reared in its traces and the cart began to topple over. Furious, Reynard turned to Alyce, Joan and Godith, none of whom had moved.

'Dismount, I said, Or...'

Hoofs sounded on the track from the castle. Bilton, Malory, and Jem galloped into sight, swords raised menacingly. Owen burst out of the bushes, retrieved his knife, and joined the attack. Reynard found himself alone, as the rest of the band turned their mounts and rode off. Cabal advanced on him and dealt him a resounding blow with his quarterstaff. He fell to the ground and lay still. Owen stood over him triumphantly.

'*Cachadur*! Attacking women. You'll go before the justices for this.' Then he felt his ankle seized and tumbled to his knees. Like an eel, Reynard rose up, a long dagger in his hand. He pulled Owen in front of him and held it to the boy's neck.

'Step back unless you want to see this pretty lad's throat slit,' he snarled.

They watched helplessly as Reynard retreated with his captive to where his horse was grazing a few yards away down the road. He took a cudgel from its saddlebag and cracked Owen over the head with it. Then he vaulted into his saddle and galloped away.

'After him!' shouted Bilton, but Malory shook his head. 'Too dangerous. His men could be regrouping round the corner.'

He dismounted and strode over to his fallen squire. As he bent over him, Owen groaned and opened his eyes.

'Bold, but rash. Youth incarnate,' murmured Joan. 'But the lad certainly has spirit. Throwing his knife at the horse turned the tables.'

She looked around the company. 'Where are Tamsin and Mattie?'

'Here,' came a call, and Tamsin and Mattie, followed by Wat, emerged from the trees. 'Ben told us to stay back and set Wat to guard us.'

'Quite right too,' said Alyce, relieved that they were safe. She turned to Malory.

'Sir Thomas, did you meet anyone up on the castle?'

Malory shook his head. 'Why?'

'When you were waving to us, I saw two other men among the trees below the summit. They started downhill as I watched.'

'Do you think the outlaws posted lookouts up there?'

'They could have. In which case it wasn't chance that made us so vulnerable to attack, but a well-laid plan.'

'But why attack such an unpromising company?' said Joan. 'Three old ladies and a couple of servants.'

'Perhaps the cart enticed them,' said Alyce. 'Their leader was intent on capturing it.' But she was remembering Tamsin's tale of the men with muffled oars on the lake the night before. And of the attack on her when she was swathed in Alyce's own cloak. Had they been targeted from the time of their arrival in Stourton?

They left Cabal and Jem to watch over the broken cart and set off for the alehouse. Once they'd told the taverner what had happened, he sent two stable lads to strengthen the guard on their belongings, taking with them a large pie for Cabal and Jem. While they were waiting for their own food, Godith applied a poultice to the lump that had risen like a pigeon's egg from Owen's head.

'Will he be all right?' Malory asked her anxiously. 'I'll have to answer to his mother and his grandmother if he isn't.'

'No lasting harm, Jesu be thanked. He's lucky to have a thick Welsh skull.'

'What are we going to do about our luggage?' said Joan. 'The cart is beyond repair. Two wheels and an axle smashed, and the frame a splintered wreck.'

'It was never a good idea,' said Alyce. 'It has slowed us up already and would have been ill-suited to the rough roads beyond Exeter. When they've eaten, Bilton and Jem can ride back to Wincanton and acquire two mules to carry what the cart's two horses can't.'

Joan looked sulky. 'But what about my feather bed? I don't want to toss all night on bug-ridden heaps of straw?'

'Well, you'll have to,' said Alyce unfeelingly. 'It's too bulky to go on a horse.' Joan glared at her.

Two hours later, Ben and Jem returned with two mules and the groom who had attended John Stourton.

'We met Sir William and his son in Wincanton,' said Ben. 'They were shocked to hear of the ambush. Sir William insisted on buying the mules and sending his son's groom Guy Despenser to ride with us as far as Exeter. He thinks we needed more protection. He says Guy is a handy man in a fight and knows the road well.'

'That was uncommonly good of him,' said Alyce, taking the measure of the wiry young man. He certainly looked competent. Perhaps she had been unfair to Stourton. The thought persisted as she heard Guy talking cheerfully as he rode in front of her between Ben and Mattie, pointing out features in the landscape for their benefit. Having an experienced fighting man who knew the country was an unlooked-for boon, and they would make far better speed without the cart. But she winced as she relived the ambush, remembering Owen prostrate on the ground.

Malory drew level with her, leaving Joan ambling in the rear, grumbling to Godith about the loss of her feather bed, Pek and Jem watchful behind them.

'We seem to have gained a valuable ally,' Alyce said to him, pointing to Guy. 'He'll prove useful if we need to divide the company again.'

'Time will tell,' he said. 'I'm always doubtful of a gift horse, even one so seemingly obliging.'

They rode on in silent harmony. The road rose over the Blackdown Hills, then wound down to the Parrett River valley. Malory cleared his throat nervously.

'I hope you're not regretting my travelling with you,' he said. 'It may have been the price on my head that occasioned the attack at Cadbury. I fear we were followed from London. Two men dressed as friars travelled with us to Chertsey, and Owen thought he saw them again at the Angel.'

'I doubt it,' said Alyce. 'You weren't even with us when we were attacked. We just seemed easy game for the outlaws from Jack's Castle. And I relish hearing your tales. There's a directness about them that keeps me hungry for more. What are you planning for this evening?'

Reassured, he smiled. 'The Tale of Balin and Balan. I thought that Ben and Owen would enjoy it, brothers-in-arms as they are fast becoming.'

'I hope that Guy doesn't succeed Owen in Ben's favour,' said Alyce. Malory raised an eyebrow and shook his head. 'Small chance of that,' he said. 'It's Mattie who interests Guy. Look at the way she's simpering up at him, hanging on his every word. Ben is looking rather grim.'

'Where's Tamsin?' asked Alyce.

'She and Wat are with Owen acting vanguard in case there's another ambush.'

'Eager for another adventure, as young people should be. But we'll reach Montacute Priory before dark.'

They rode in silence for a while, winding along the banks of the Parrett. Alyce remembered Tamsin saying that Malory might remember something of matters at court before William's downfall, and was wondering how to raise the subject. Then Sir Thomas did it for her.

'Your grace, Lord Wenlock told me that your journey had more than one purpose. I believe you have hopes that your former secretary has discovered new evidence concerning the murder of your husband.'

Alyce looked around nervously, but no one was within earshot. 'So he's told you about our quest. And that I thought it quickest and safest to go to Tintagel myself to see what

Simon has acquired. From what he wrote, secrecy is vital. The guilty who survive will be determined to prevent the truth coming out.'

'Do you have any idea who they are?' Malory asked. 'I've long wondered myself why no one of rank was brought to book for the crime. Or for the murders of Bishop Ayscough and Lord Moleyns, your husband's closest allies. Or, for that matter, of the King's own uncle, Humfrey Duke of Gloucester, three years earlier.'

'Do you think that was murder too?' Alyce asked.

'Undoubtedly. Though it was passed off as apoplexy. And in the scramble for his lands, it was Buckingham who picked out the plum: Penshurst Castle.' Sir Thomas hesitated before continuing. 'I may not be an unprejudiced judge, as I was beset at the time. The Duke of Buckingham trumped up all sorts of accusations against me, and when I wasn't in gaol I was a fugitive. He thought, rightly in fact, that I was in love with his wife and that my affection was returned. Which it was,' he said sadly. 'Until false accusations of rape were laid against me by a creature of her husband, God rot him.'

Alyce was startled by his intensity. 'But surely no one could believe that of you, given the message of your tales of King Arthur? That true knights should protect women of whatever degree and never force them?' Then she remembered what William Norreys had said about Buckingham when they visited Yattendon Castle.

'Buckingham's name keeps recurring,' she said slowly. 'At dinner last night Stourton told me that Buckingham was hot against William's low birth. And that he spoke of a great lord who was devising his downfall. We wondered if Buckingham meant Talbot, but Stourton reminded us that both were far

174

away at the time of his death, Buckingham putting down rebels in Wales and Talbot in France. But I think he knew more that he was telling. He gave an unholy giggle as he remarked on the subtlety of the plot.'

'Well, neither Buckingham nor Talbot had subtle minds. Though they may have had allies who did.'

'When Buckingham returned from Wales, he and Lord Tiptoft, the Earl of Worcester, led the investigation into William's death,' Alyce mused. 'But the results were inconclusive. Rebels were blamed – as they were for the deaths of Ayscough and Moleyns.'

'I wouldn't put anything past Buckingham. But I'm prejudiced against him. And unless the evidences your secretary has acquired reveal his involvement, there's no proof.'

Wadebridge

Lord Tiptoft stared coldly at the harbour master. He was finding it hard to suppress his fury. Although Medoc the bosun had apparently been dealt with, nothing else had happened as he had intended. Brailles had somehow escaped from Great Saltee and questions asked in Kilmore and Wexford had received contradictory, perhaps deliberately misleading, answers. The locals were Fitzgeralds and hated him. When he arrived in Wadebridge, Mawgan told him about Caerleon's visits, and handed him the letter Denzil thought was on its way to Alyce. Tiptoft opened it, read it through, and cursed.

'I thought it best not to give it to the courier, my lord, knowing of your interest in this affair,' Mawgan said nervously.

'You did right,' said Tiptoft. 'So this Denzil Caerleon went to Wexford in Fergus Fitzgerald's boat the *Mairi* and returned yesterday with Simon Brailles. Where did they go?'

'They didn't tell me. But they were seen on the road to St Petroc Minor. That's the overland way to Fowey. I told Caerleon that it was the quickest way to rejoin his ships.'

Tiptoft considered. Irish affairs demanded his immediate attention. He could not afford to remain in Cornwall. There was nothing for it but to leave the whole business to Sir Reginald Mohun. Mohun was a ruthless man, but he had been sternly warned not to harm Princess Alyce in any way if she was not deterred by the ambush arranged by Stourton or later setbacks. He cursed inwardly. If she did get as far as Cornwall, she would visit Trevelyan, and Trevelyan, impulsive and unpredictable, was the weakest part of the cloak of secrecy veiling Suffolk's murder. But perhaps there was a way of ensuring Trevelyan's obedience.

He stuffed Caerleon's letter into his belt pouch and returned to his ship, where he instructed four of his retainers to hire horses and ride to Fowey in search of Caerleon and Brailles. As he watched them disappear, another thought struck him. Though Caerleon would surely head for Fowey to find his ships, Brailles might want to return to Tintagel and his wench. He walked back to the harbour master's office and found Mawgan sitting outside with a huge beef pasty and a jug of ale.

'Do you know of a local without many scruples who could ride to Tintagel with a gang of henchmen and keep a watch out for Brailles? Just in case he has parted company with Caerleon.'

Mawgan thought for a long minute. 'You couldn't do better than my cousin Sir Patrick Tregoys. He knows Brailles. He had a row with him before Christmas over the takings from the Duchess of Suffolk's mines. And he's in town for the market today.'

An hour later, Tiptoft had written a letter to Mohun and come to an understanding with Tregoys. He told him to get descriptions of Brailles and Caerleon from the harbour master and promised him a fat purse if he succeeded in finding either. He also told him that from now on he was to answer to Sir Reginald Mohun. Tregoys grimaced – all Cornishmen resented Mohun's bullying ways – but agreed. Tiptoft returned to his ship and directed the master to sail for Bude.

༄

John Trevelyan was in the stable yard, Artie on his shoulder, watching the grooms checking the harness of the horses they'd be taking with them to Exeter. The chough squawked crossly and fluttered away, and Trevelyan looked round to see a band of riders approaching the house from the direction of Bude. With a deep sense of unease, he realised that they were headed by the Earl of Worcester and his secretary. He called to his oldest son, who was kicking a football around the courtyard with two of his brothers. 'Lionel, go and tell your mother that we have guests.'

He managed a welcoming smile as the visitors drew closer. 'My lord, I thought you to be in Ireland. You're lucky to find us here. We leave for Exeter at dawn to meet Princess Alyce. Elizabeth is packing our bags.'

'Have you had word from her grace?'

'Not since her letter of Candlemas, asking if she could stay with us. But today a courier came from the Dean of Exeter. Princess Alyce sent him a letter from Forde Abbey. It said that they were attacked by outlaws near Cadbury Castle and that a fire had broken out while they were staying with friends in Crewkerne, but she hoped that her company would arrive in Exeter sometime on Wednesday. Lizzie and I are removing to our manor close by the city. We'll be there to greet her.'

Tiptoft's face remained a mask, but Trevelyan could sense that the news disturbed him.

'Does she still intend to visit Tintagel?'

'I imagine so. I don't think she knows that Brailles is dead.'

'Then make sure you tell her immediately. And discourage her from visiting Tintagel. I'll reward you well if you manage to dissuade her.'

His ice-blue eyes strayed to Trevelyan's oldest son, who had returned and was standing shyly by his father's side.

'I have to return to Ireland without delay,' he said. 'The country is on the brink of rebellion, and I'm concerned for the safety of my wife and the child she's expecting. We'll remove to Dublin as soon as we can. But I must ensure that Brailles and Princess Alyce don't meet.'

Trevelyan was puzzled. 'But you told us Brailles was dead.'

'I had him removed to Ireland,' said Tiptoft curtly. 'Unfortunately, he managed to escape, and return to Padstow, aided by a maverick called Denzil Caerleon, a former servant of Princess Alyce. But that isn't something I want noised abroad. Tell no one. And if you get a chance to apprehend them, do so. I must get back to Wexford, so I need you to act for me in this matter.'

'Of course, my lord,' said Trevelyan, relieved that Tiptoft did not know of his own connection with Caerleon.

'You'll be answerable to Sir Reginald Mohun, the Constable of Lostwithiel,' Tiptoft continued curtly. 'I've told him that he can rely on your support.'

'I will be honoured to be of assistance,' said Trevelyan, intending to be nothing of the sort. He had a visceral dislike of Mohun, who leered lasciviously at Elizabeth whenever they met. And he owed Denzil his life. But then Tiptoft spoke again, nodding at Lionel. 'Is this boy the oldest of your sons?'

Trevelyan nodded, suddenly anxious.

'To show my gratitude, I'm going to give him a splendid opportunity. I'll take him to Ireland with me as my page and in time perhaps my squire. Tell him to get his necessaries together. Meanwhile, you will relay any news through Oswald Marrack, the reeve of Tintagel. Mohun says he can be relied on.'

Trevelyan's heart sank. A mere Cornish knight could not refuse a lord as eminent as the Earl of Worcester. Little Lionel was to be a hostage to ensure his obedience. What Elizabeth would say when he told her, he dreaded to think.

Tintagel

After they disembarked in Wadebridge, Denzil and Simon spent some time arguing about what to do next. Flee to Fowey or head for Exeter? Simon wanted to do neither.

'We'll be safest in Tintagel,' he insisted. 'People know me well there and won't betray our presence. It's where Princess Alyce will come, I'm sure, even if the Trevelyans tell her I'm dead. She'll want to inspect the parish, but she also loves the place. She was always telling Tamsin tales about it. And I need the parcel Madoc gave me. It and everything I've saved are on the island.'

'But Tintagel will be the first place Tiptoft will have searched when he finds you have escaped.'

'He may search. But that doesn't mean he'll find. Morwenna has relatives all over the place. She'll think of a safe refuge for us. She's a wonderful woman.'

Denzil gave in but insisted that in case they were being watched they head eastwards as if they were going to Fowey, before casting back to the road north. It took them two days to get to Tintagel. An obliging carter took them part of the way; otherwise they walked, ducking out of sight when they heard riders. Dusk had fallen by the time they reached the church, set alone high above the village. Simon led Denzil along a track that ran downhill towards the mainland castle, then took a narrow path round its west wall to the narrow ridge that was the promontory's only link to the land. Towards its end, several tree trunks had been put over a deep gap. Denzil shuddered as he looked down at the huge slabs of stone that had tumbled down at each side, surf thrashing against them. But Simon strode across without hesitation, though damp mists whirled around them and gulls swooped down aggressively. As soon as they entered the courtyard of the island castle, Denzil relaxed, enchanted by Tintagel's brooding timelessness. He went over to where a barred gate led down steep steps to a stone quay, twenty foot above a sandy beach.

'No escape that way except at high tide,' Simon called. 'Follow me.' He led Denzil up a steep track to a chapel on the broad summit of the island. Several low stone buildings stood nearby. One had a new oak door with iron hinges. Simon reached up to its lintel, took out a key and unlocked it. Inside, Denzil saw a narrow bed, a dresser with a few basic utensils on it and a cupboard above, and a chest.

'Untouched, praise the Lord,' said Brailles triumphantly. 'I told you it would be. We're safe enough here for tonight. Let's eat and get some rest. There are sheepskins in the chest.'

He opened the latticed doors of the cupboard and took out a flagon of ale, a smoked leg of mutton and a tinder box. He struck sparks to fire shreds of oakum, then lit a candle stub set on a scallop shell on the windowsill. Taking out his knife, he cut off some thin slices of meat, and offered them to Denzil.

'It lasts an age and is very good eating. Tomorrow we'll find Morwenna.'

'Will she know someone who would take a letter to Exeter? I need to let Lady Alyce know that you're safe, but a fugitive. And that Tiptoft is involved in the matter of the *Nicholas*. And that she can't trust Trevelyan.'

Simon thought for a moment. 'Jim Perrin, the ostler at the Malthouse Inn, is her uncle. He has a son with a good horse. And he can be relied on for discretion.'

'Have you paper and pen?'

'Of course. And ink and twine and wax to seal it. While you write, I'll check that the evidences are still where I put them, under the sill of the chapel's east window.' He groped between the bedhead and the mattress, extracted a key, and left the lodging.

High on the cliff on the mainland side of the chasm between the ruined castle and the mainland the gaunt figure of the reeve watched as a light glimmered from the island's summit. Perhaps the fugitives Sir Patrick Tregoys was seeking were hiding there. Marrack considered going to the vicarage and rousing him. Then he decided against it, imagining Tregoys' wrath if it turned out to be only village lads and their lasses making the most of Brailles' disappearance. Tomorrow would be soon enough. He turned back and retraced his steps to his house in the village.

Someone else saw the light. Coming back from the outside privy in her mother's yard, Morwenna stood stock still, heart in mouth. Could it be Simon? She went back to the house, stuffed bread and ale in a bag, wrapped a warm cloak around herself and set off for the island. She knew every twist and turn of the steep track up to the island from the haven below.

Exeter

The journey from Cadbury to Exeter was for Tamsin a blur of new experiences. Montacute Priory made them comfortable, but not especially welcome. Prior John Dove was a dyed-in-the-wool Lancastrian who greeted Alyce civilly enough, but later confided to Joan that he had no time for the turncoat dowager, as he gruffly termed her. At Crewkerne they divided into male and female companies. Alyce, Joan, Godith and the girls stayed with Alyce's childhood friend Elizabeth Denebaud and her husband William Paulet, and the men in the White Hart tavern. In the middle of the night, fire broke out in the Paulets' stables. If Godith hadn't smelt the smoke, they would have lost their mounts and possibly their own lives. But she raised the alarm, and Tamsin and Mattie ran to the tavern to summon help. Cabal led the rescue of the horses, sneezing and snorting with fear, and a human chain carrying buckets from the well prevented the flames spreading to the thatched roof of the manor house.

The next night was spent at Forde Abbey, where Abbot Elias proved a kindly host; he had a deep respect for Chaucer's writings, and was delighted to be able to spend an evening with the poet's granddaughter and to talk about books with her and her companions. The evening meal was meagre, and it was evident that the size of the company was a strain on the abbey's scant resources. Alyce pressed a purse of silver and a jewelled reliquary she had intended for Exeter Cathedral into the abbot's grateful hands as they left.

The day Tamsin remembered best was the last. They had stopped for their midday meal in Honiton, where the busy market offered stall after stall of the local speciality: finely woven serges, colourfully embroidered. Mattie had gone off with Guy Despenser to explore, so it was Ben who squired Tamsin around the stalls, cursing Mattie the while as a faithless flirt. The players that they had last seen in Wincanton had set up their wagon as a stage in the marketplace, and they enjoyed watching the jugglers. Ben had insisted on buying her a kerchief. She had hesitated before accepting it, but he had urged it on her, saying that Dickon would have bought it for her if he had been alive. Which made tears start in her eyes and gave him an excuse to put a comforting arm around her. For once she didn't resist. It was unmistakably a brotherly arm. She knew he had fallen heavily for Mattie and resented the fact that since Guy had joined their company the girl had taken to disappearing with him whenever the chance offered. Knowing all about hopeless love, Tamsin did her best to cheer him up.

At midday they reached Ottery St Mary, and Alyce had sent Ben and Jem ahead to Exeter to give the dean notice of their coming. Later that afternoon they trooped wearily into the city. Malory and Owen bid them farewell outside St Nicholas's Priory, where they'd arranged to lodge. Then Guy Despenser blew Mattie a kiss and turned his horse back towards the east.

Alyce, now in an ermine-trimmed purple gown befitting her rank, led her company up the steep hill to Broad Gate, the main entrance to the cathedral close. The wardens hauled its great doors open, bowing a welcome, and they passed under the elms that ringed the graveyard surrounding St Peter's Cathedral. A throng of clerics were assembled on its paved forecourt to greet them.

Tamsin was struck dumb by the splendour of the great church's broad façade of pale golden stone. There were three tiers of stone statues: apostles, prophets, kings and queens, colourfully painted, each with individual character. Buttresses stretched away along the cathedral's sides to where its twin towers, topped with tall spires, soared towards heaven. Balanced and orderly, it was utterly different from the huge, rambling edifice of St Paul's, scene of her misadventures in London. It put her in mind of a great ark, battlemented and pinnacled and eternal.

A stooped, cadaverously thin man in a white surplice and a short black cloak stepped forward and bowed. 'Princess Alyce, you are most welcome. I'm Canon Jerome Stevens, steward of the cathedral. We decided to wait vespers on your arrival. Dean Webber sent me to take you to your places.'

He turned and led the way to the cathedral's great west doors. As they entered, Tamsin gasped. It was as if they were in a petrified forest flooded with colour by huge stained-glass windows. On each side of the nave, slim pillars circled a succession of columns. From their capitals, branching ribs of stone fanned out, meeting their counterparts along a long central stem punctuated by gilded bosses. The view down the aisle was interrupted in front of the chancel by an elaborate rood screen. Across it, ranks of wooden statues echoed those on the outside of the cathedral, and a gigantic cross towered above it. Beyond it, more slender stone fans rose into dusky mystery.

She followed Alyce past the townsfolk assembled in the nave and through an arched doorway in the centre of the rood screen. There a different glory met them. The flames of countless candles wavered from sconces along choir stalls filled with men and boys. Behind them the cathedral dignitaries bent their heads in prayer. Canon Stevens took them beyond the stalls to where benches had been put out for them, then led Alyce to a chair of state beside the bishop's throne, above which a wooden canopy rose fifty feet or more in a fragile fretwork. Tamsin stood in attendance on her, dumb with awe. Musicians struck up from the gallery halfway along the north wall of the nave, and the choir began to chant.

An hour later, vespers was over. The choristers and the clerics processed away, holding lit candles and chanting as they disappeared through the arch in the rood screen, and walked down the nave. Tamsin had to shake herself out of a trance as their voices died away. Stevens left his seat and approached Alyce.

'We can go directly into the cloister through the south door,' he said. 'Dean Webber is looking forward to welcoming you.' He pointed towards an arch just beyond three stone sedilia with elaborate canopies rising above them. Just inside it a black-clad figure beckoned. Stevens led Alyce towards him. After them came Joan and Godith, heads bent together and grinning as if sharing a joke. Tamsin looked back to see Mattie and Ben following hand in hand – since Guy had departed, she had taken him back into her favour. She paused in front of a statue of the Virgin glowing golden to the left of the high altar. Bowing her head, she murmured an Ave Maria.

Stevens escorted Alyce across the south choir aisle, and into a chapel dedicated to St James. The door in its south wall led to a cloister which was closed in on the north side and open on the other three. The canon nodded to the long windows of the closed section.

''That is where we keep our books.'

'I look forward to seeing them,' said Alyce. 'And I have brought a contribution to your library. A Life of St Margaret of Antioch, whose skull I believe you have among your relics. We have a celebrated place of healing at Binsey, near Oxford, which is dedicated to her.'

Joan had caught them up. 'Ah yes, a spirited lady. Swallowed by a dragon, but the cross she was carrying pricked his stomach so much that he threw her up.'

Stevens's nostrils flared in disapproval at such irreverence. Hiding her amusement, Alyce introduced Joan to him.

'Mistress Joan Moulton is a London bookseller. She's very widely read and comes across all manner of apocryphal tales. But she means no disrespect.'

'Then her levity can perhaps be excused,' said Stevens, though he looked dubious.

Dusk had fallen by the time they arrived at the gatehouse of the deanery. Stevens tugged on a rope and a bell clanged noisily. The gates swung open to admit them. Once in the courtyard they could see four tall arched windows framing flickering candles hoisted high on cartwheels. They followed Stevens inside and found themselves in a large wainscoted room. They gathered gratefully around the brightly burning logs heaped in its fireplace.

'That's better,' said Godith, 'During the service I was wishing I had a lambskin-lined cassock like yours, Canon.'

Stevens's eyes bulged as he wondered how to react to such an intimate observation, but a booming voice from the far end of the hall saved him.

'Princess Alyce, I'm delighted to welcome you to Exeter. How long is it since we met? It's all of twenty-five years since I left Oxford and came west. Never regretted it, either. Though there are those in the Close who wish I'd never come.' Dean Webber guffawed, and held out his hand for the duchess to kiss his elaborate ring.

Alyce performed the customary ritual gracefully. Webber was huge, with a high forehead and short-cut black hair brushed forward as if he was a Roman emperor. His eyes were large and liquid and brown beneath shapely black brows. Silky grey fur lined his shoulder cloak, and embroidered daggings edged his exaggeratedly deep sleeves. The pointed leather shoes beneath his cassock were embroidered with gold and silver thread.

'Come this way, your grace. Your cousin of Whalesborough and her husband arrived in Exeter this morning, and they're eager to greet you.'

Alyce was taken aback. 'The Trevelyans are in Exeter? I hadn't expected them to come here.'

She followed the dean as he bustled towards the far end of the hall, where a round table was set in a curved alcove formed by a semicircle of armorial windows. A man and a woman rose from their chairs and came forward. Alyce smiled. There was no mistaking her cousin. Lady Elizabeth Trevelyan was all smiles and double chins, her chubby fingers heavy with rings, and an elaborate necklace adorning her generous bosom.

'Cousin Alyce, what a pleasure,' she said, and curtseyed. Her husband, who had been half hidden by her substantial figure, now stepped forward and bowed. He was older of course, thought Alyce, but otherwise just as she remembered him at court long ago: tall and broad-shouldered, with dancing eyes and a mouth made for laughter.

'At last I can thank you for saving me, your grace. But for Denzil Caerleon taking me up the Thames to Ewelme I'd have been taken to the Tower and not seen again.'

'It's him you need to thank, not me,' quipped Alyce, her eyes softening at the sight of him. 'I knew nothing of what my disobedient servants had been up to until you were safely removed to Stonor Park.' She paused, then added 'Though I regretted not seeing you.'

They smiled at each other, and Mattie nudged Tamsin.

'What's the story between our mistress and that lordly rascal?' she hissed. 'I've never seen her look cow-eyed before.'

'Ask Ben later,' Tamsin whispered back.

Alyce turned back to Elizabeth. 'You must meet my companions. This is Mistress Joan Moulton, a notable London bookseller. And this is Godith Hawksmoor of Woodstock. She's skilled in leechcraft and a great frightener of rogues.'

Lady Elizabeth looked a question.

'She cursed a band of outlaws who attacked us near Cadbury Castle with such witchy menace that they were stopped in their tracks,' said Joan. 'Which was just as well. Most of our company had gone up the hill to explore the castle. Fortunately, they returned in time to frighten them away.'

The dean raised his eyebrows. 'You were lucky to find outlaws so superstitious. And I'm delighted to meet you all. Time now to dine. Your servants will eat with my household in the great hall, but we'll be served in my private chamber.'

He clapped his hands, and a bevy of pages appeared bearing bowls of scented water and towels. Once his guests had washed and dried their hands, he led the way through another door to his own quarters.

Stevens ushered Tamsin, Mattie, Ben, Cabal and Wat back into the great hall, now busy with preparations for the meal.

They sat down at the far end of the hall, and Mattie turned to Ben with an arch look.

'So, what is Sir John Trevelyan to Lady Alyce?'

Happy to be back in Mattie's favour now Guy had left, Ben grinned. 'She's known him since long before her husband's murder. Never anything unseemly between them, but she's always had a fondness for him. After Duke William's death he lost all the patronage the Suffolks had acquired for him, but she arranged his marriage to her cousin. Lady Elizabeth is very wealthy.'

Mattie's eyes gleamed with mischief. 'Seems to me that for all her age her grace has a weakness for a pretty face and a shapely leg.'

Tamsin was about to object to her impudence when a tall young man in the livery of the dean's household came over to them. Her eyes widened, and her stomach lurched. What was Will Stonor doing in Exeter?

He nodded at Ben and sat down beside Tamsin with a broad smile. 'When the dean told me that Princess Alyce was going to spend a few days in Exeter, I wondered if you'd be with her. It's good to see you again.' Tamsin was silent, heart thumping.

'What are you doing here, Will?' asked Ben in amazement. 'I thought you were working for James Danvers in London.'

'James has all but given up the law since he married Lady Arderne,' said Will. 'And who can blame him? Fortunately for me, the king's uncle Archbishop Neville – he used to be Exeter's bishop – recommended me to the dean; I'm advising him on legal matters.' Then he saw Mattie and gave her a mocking grimace.

'But here's a surprise. Why are you so far from home, Matilda? Did my mother become weary of your naughty ways? Surely Princess Alyce has no need of a maid when she has Tamsin.'

'Tamsin is a tiring maid no longer,' said Ben. 'Since Simon Brailles left, she has been promoted to acting as Lady Alyce's secretary.'

Will pretended astonishment but relented at the sight of Tamsin's indignant frown. 'A well deserved promotion. And are you still reading legends of Arthur?'

Placated, heart singing, Tamsin nodded. 'Not only that, Will,' she said eagerly. 'We've actually had Sir Thomas Malory himself with us, and…'

'Hush, you fool,' Ben interrupted angrily. He looked around, but to his relief no one seemed to have heard her words. He leant closer to Will.

'He's in disguise. After he was excluded from the royal pardon he decided that he needed to escape to France. Princess Alyce agreed to let him and his squire join our company. They wear Lord Wenlock's livery and are lodging at St Nicolas's Priory.'

Will nodded. 'Worry not. I'll stay mum. But what brings Princess Alyce to Exeter?'

'She got a letter from her former secretary Simon Brailles. You'll remember him from Ewelme, no doubt.'

'I do. Thin and twitchy.'

'He's been reading for ordination with John Gregory, the vicar of Tintagel, for over a year now. Princess Alyce is patron of the parish, and when Gregory wrote requesting an assistant, Brailles asked if he could go. Said he'd decided to become ordained. A few weeks ago he wrote to her grace to say he'd found the ship that intercepted Duke William. She decided to go to Tintagel and hear what he had to say.'

Now it was Tamsin's turn to grow angry. 'Ben – who told you about Simon's letter? Lady Alyce swore me to secrecy.'

Ben reddened. 'Mattie overheard Joan talking to Godith about it,' he said defensively. 'And she asked me who Simon was. So I explained. I didn't know we weren't supposed to know.'

Tamsin glared at him. 'Why do you think Lady Alyce didn't tell you at the start of our journey?' she snapped.

Ben shrugged. 'I supposed it wasn't that important. I thought the main point of our journey was to go on pilgrimage before our mistress took her vows.'

'Well, I certainly won't spread it further,' said Will. 'Though travelling so far at such an unseasonable time of year must seem odd to many.'

'Lady Alyce isn't one to be deterred by weather,' said Tamsin. 'She hopes that discovering who was behind her husband's murder will resolve the young duke's bitterness towards her.'

'My parents told me about that. A year or so ago he came near to having her arraigned for treason, didn't he?'

Bilton nodded. 'Yes. And if it hadn't been for your father she'd have been found in possession of quantities of banned books.'

Will grinned. 'So my father said. He kept one or two for himself, too – but don't tell her grace that.'

Tamsin felt excluded as the two young men chatted. She wondered how well Will had known Mattie. And whether he had married Elinor Golafre yet. But she was determined not to ask him.

At last Will turned to her again. 'What of you, Tammie? Are you courting?'

Before she could reply, Ben interrupted.

'Turned against men,' he said brusquely. 'Won't give any of us the time of day since the duchess made her her secretary. Book learning is all she's interested in.'

'Maybe it depends on the man in question,' Will said teasingly. As he gazed at her, she could feel a blush rising in her cheeks. He winked at her, then turned back to Ben.

'But you're fortunate indeed to have Sir Thomas as a travelling companion. I wish I could come with you. Still, we'll be able to spend some time together before you go. I'd love to show you something of the city. There's a good bookseller who Joan will want to meet. Not so good as Doll's of course.'

He glanced at Tamsin meaningfully, and she lowered her eyes, heart beating so loudly that she was afraid both young men would hear it. Then he stood up.

'I must pay my respects to my godmother.' And with a lingering look at Tamsin, he walked away.

※

After the best meal they had had since Stourton Castle, Dean Webber invited his guests to join him for sweetmeats and wine in his privy chamber. Tapestries of biblical scenes lined the walls, and cushioned benches provided comfortable seating. Alyce adroitly managed to sit next to Elizabeth Trevelyan, and once they had both been served turned to her.

'In his letters, my servant Simon Brailles told me how hospitably you welcomed him to Whalesborough, cousin. I must thank you.'

Alyce saw Elizabeth's merry face fall. 'What is it? Has something happened to him?'

'Have you not heard, Alyce?' she asked.

'Nothing since his last letter to Ewelme. Which came – let me think – almost a month ago.'

John Trevelyan broke off from his conversation with the dean.

'I'm sorry to have to tell you that Brailles is dead, my lady,' he said. 'He fell from the cliffs of Tintagel after the Candlemas Eve celebrations.'

Alyce paled with shock. Had her journey been pointless? Then she frowned.

'That sounds most unlike Brailles. He was never one to take risks.'

Trevelyan shrugged. 'Not when he first arrived, but we soon taught him to enjoy himself. He became close to a local girl and confided to me that he was changing his mind about becoming a priest. The villagers are a pagan bunch, who always drink more than they should around their Imbolc bonfire after the Candlemas Eve service, and it appears that on this occasion Brailles joined in with too good a will. Denzil Caerleon and I heard the sad tale when we went to Tintagel.'

Alyce froze. 'Denzil Caerleon? I thought him to be with the Earl of Warwick's fleet.'

'Warwick's fleet is still in Southampton, but it's going to be based in Fowey to deal with enemy ships raiding from the Channel Islands. Caerleon's squadron was acting vanguard, but it was chased down channel by German ships. He came close to being wrecked off Land's End and had to put in at Wadebridge for repairs. He heard there that Tintagel's vicar had disappeared. He knew that as patron of Tintagel you would be concerned, and so while the boat yard set about repairing his ships he sailed to Bude to ask me what I knew of the matter. Not that he knew that it was Brailles who'd vanished. He thought it was Father Gregory.'

'So you took him to Tintagel?' asked Alyce, her brain spinning.

'Yes, he and I rode there ten days ago. We found Sir Reginald Mohun, the deputy sheriff of Cornwall, taking charge of the matter. He told me that he was writing to tell you about Brailles' death. I dare say that his letter awaits you at Ewelme.' Trevelyan gave his wife a warning glance before continuing. 'We returned to Bude, and Caerleon sets sail for Wadebridge the next day. He'll be back with his ships in Fowey by now, I imagine.'

Dean Webber, his face flushed with wine, broke in on their conversation. 'Is there anything you'd particularly like to see in Exeter, your grace? I'll arrange a tour of our library, of course. Perhaps on Thursday? We have more than three hundred books.'

Alyce stared at him unseeingly. She was imagining poor Simon plunging to his death – just as he had discovered how to enjoy his life. And Denzil Caerleon sailing from Fowey before she had a chance to see him again. But why had Trevelyan given Elizabeth such a look? The kind of glance from husband to wife that meant 'say nothing', she reflected, and wondered what lay behind it.

It was Joan who answered the dean. 'We'd like that beyond anything, Dean. Do you have any printed books in your collection?'

'We do,' said Webber. 'A bible imprinted at Mainz by Johann Gutenberg himself.'

Trevelyan coughed to reclaim Alyce's attention. 'Since a visit to Tintagel would now be fruitless, perhaps you should take this opportunity to visit our most famous shrine, St Michael's Mount. Lizzie and I would happily escort you to Fowey. You could stay in our manor of St Veep, and then travel by sea to Penzance. It's a far easier journey than venturing into the wilds of western Cornwall. You might even encounter Caerleon in Fowey.' He had not missed Alyce's loss of colour at his first mention of Caerleon. What lay behind that? he wondered.

Alyce had the sense of a play being acted out. A play with a particular purpose: to prevent her from going to Tintagel. She nodded slowly, then gave a yawn, and rose from her seat.

'I must thank you for your hospitality, Dean, and look forward to admiring the library tomorrow. But now I must quit your company. Fatigue is overtaking me. Our weeks of travelling have punished my ageing bones.'

Webber rose and bowed. 'Of course.' He beckoned to an attendant. 'Show our guests to their chambers.'

The Trevelyans also rose. 'So that's settled,' said Sir John. 'When you've had enough of the splendours of Exeter, we'll return and escort you to Fowey.'

'That's a most generous offer,' said Alyce. 'I'll let you know my plans as soon as I have decided what to do. But now I'm desperately in need of sleep. You must excuse me.'

She saw a frown of displeasure cross Trevelyan's face, quickly veiled by a smile. She remembered how he had hated to be crossed when he proposed a scheme to William, and reflected sadly that his evident admiration for her then had been such a welcome contrast to William's neglect that she had entirely suspended her critical faculties. She also recalled what Lady Margaret Hungerford had said about his involvement in the conspiracy to murder Duke William. She had dismissed it at the time as an old woman's memory being awry, but sometimes the distant past grew clearer as one aged.

When she and Joan entered the bedchamber they had been allotted, Mattie and Tamsin had already busied themselves unpacking their baggage. A curtained bed of state filled a quarter of the room. Two pallets had been provided for the girls. A feather bed on a wide bench was already occupied by Godith, who had excused herself straight after their meal on the grounds of fatigue. She opened a sleepy eye as Alyce and Joan entered.

'You survived the worthy clerics' conversation better than I did. Did they say anything of interest over the wine?'

'A great deal,' said Alyce miserably. 'Shock on shock. My former secretary Simon Brailles, who wrote to me of the *Nicholas of the Tower*, is apparently dead in somewhat shameful circumstances. Whatever he discovered about the owner of the ship has presumably died with him. And my former man of business Denzil Caerleon, who left Ewelme in disgrace two years ago, has turned up in Cornwall.'

As usual, Joan rallied to the defence of her brother-in-law.

'Denzil's disgrace was none of his fault,' she objected. 'That hussy Marlene...'

A giggle came from Mattie's pallet.

'That's enough, Matilda,' snapped Alyce. 'You are altogether too impudent.' She stared into the glowing red logs of the dying fire.

Just then Godith sat up, pulling the coverlet up over her thin shoulders. 'Did you bring with you the letters that Brailles sent you, your grace? The last one he sent struck me as curiously phrased. As if he wanted to say something in a way that only someone who knew him well would understand.'

Alyce remembered how Godith had cackled with laughter when she listened to Simon's Christmas letter. And how long she had spent reading his final one. She walked over to the travelling bag that Tamsin had unpacked, felt inside and took out a leather wallet. Leafing through, she found the one in which Simon had written of the discovery of the *Nicholas*.

'What was it that puzzled you?' she asked Godith. The herbalist held out her hand. A little unwillingly, Alyce handed it over. Godith ran her eyes across Simon's elegant secretary script. Then she pointed a claw-like finger at the end of the last paragraph.

'He mentioned the establishing of a shrine to Our Lady of Fontrevault in the castle chapel in the other letter you read out to me. And in this one, after writing that he dared not set down the name of the person involved with the ship, he writes that he'd hidden the evidences in 'a place which will remain a secret between you, me and Our Lady'. It struck me as strange phrasing at the time. I wonder if it meant that he had concealed them somewhere in the castle chapel he'd dedicated to Fontrevault. In case anything happened to him.'

Alyce stared at her. It was exactly the sort of precaution that the cautious Brailles might take. Especially if convinced of the incendiary nature of his discovery.

'Thank you, Godith. You've decided me. Tomorrow I'll tell the Trevelyans that we'll continue to Tintagel.'

'What, I wonder, will they do then?' asked Joan. 'My money would be on Sir John changing their plans and coming with us.'

'In which case we'll need to part company with Sir Thomas and Owen. I wouldn't trust Trevelyan not to betray them.'

'I hope you can trust him not to interfere in our own quest,' said Joan.

Newton Montagu

It took Jack, Dick, little John and their picked company four days of riding from dawn to dusk to reach the Vale of Blackmore, where Wootton Glanville lay under the scarp of the Dorset Downs. They stayed Sunday night at Amesbury, where Joanna Arnold the prioress made them welcome.

'It's barely a week since we had the pleasure of your mother's company, your grace,' she said as they sat at dinner. 'Are you following in her footsteps?'

Jack shook his head. 'No, we're on our way to Newton Montagu. It's a manor which she intends to be held by my son in her lifetime, and I'm taking him to see it.'

Prioress Joanna raised an eyebrow. She remembered Princess Alyce's evident embarrassment at being reminded of her visit almost three decades ago. And the obviously pregnant companion with her on that visit. A companion who had been hustled into the guest quarters by Alyce's attendant Sybilla as soon as they arrived.

'Does your mother know of your journey?' she asked.

Jack hesitated. 'No, but I'm sure she'd approve it. As well as showing John his future estates, I am seeking word of a cleric she sent there many years ago, and who was important to her.'

Joanna looked at him thoughtfully. 'And how old are you now, your grace? – if you don't mind my asking.'

'Twenty-seven in September,' Jack replied uneasily. Why should the prioress interest herself in his age?

Joanna sensed that it was time to change the subject. 'I suggest that tomorrow you make a small detour in the morning, and ride past the Giants' Dance. It's a place your son ought to see. Ancient and profoundly holy. It's a reminder of mankind's beginnings.'

Next morning both father and son were awed by the sight of the colossal monoliths, made the more dramatic by the thin veiling of snow that had fallen overnight.

'How did they get there?' little John asked.

'Magicked by Merlin, if your grandmother's favourite taleteller Sir Thomas Malory is to be believed,' quipped his father. 'I prefer to think they show what impossible things men can do, if they set their minds to them. And help each other.'

When they reached Newton Montagu on Tuesday afternoon, they were greeted by dropped jaws from the tenant, a prosperous local farmer called Jon Downton. Jack explained that he had decided to show his son the Dorset estates which he would inherit and asked if they could stay the night.

'Of course, my lord,' said Downton. 'I wish we'd had notice of your coming so we could have made you properly welcome. As it is, we're at sixes and sevens. But we're only too happy to provide for you.'

There was a flurry of activity as beds were aired and a smoked haunch of bacon unhooked from inside the hearth. Downton's wife brought cheeses out of the dairy, and children chased chickens into the kitchen courtyard to be killed, plucked and spitted.

'Would your grace be wanting to survey the whole estate?' Downton asked anxiously. Jack shook his head. 'No. Just to give little John an idea of its size. We won't disturb you for longer than tonight and the next.'

Soon they were seated in the manor's hall enjoying a remarkably good meal, considering how little time the Downtons had been given to prepare it.

'This is very fine cider,' said Jack, as Mistress Downton refilled his cup. 'In the morning I must pay my respects in the church. Incidentally, is the rector still Oliver Roos?'

Downton shook his head. 'No. Father Roos died soon after coming here. We've had four rectors since then. One caught the plague, one disappeared with our greatest treasure, the gold pyx that held the consecrated host, and one died of old age.'

'Who's the incumbent now?'

'John Lugge. He's from a local family but was educated in Sherborne Abbey. He's been a breath of fresh air. Cleared out all the rubbish in the church cupboards and the rectory. Not to speak ill of the dead, Father Roos had little interest in ministry. Always deep in old writings. Father Lugge made a bonfire of them. He's all for sticking to the word of the Gospels. So is the chantrist, John Browne.'

Jack nodded. 'Very wise. Now, tell me about the estate.' He was relieved to hear that Roos had died and his papers destroyed. But the perilous evidence of his baptism might still be in the hiding place that his letter to Hiat had described.

Next morning, he announced that he was going to say prayers in Wootton Glanville's church. He told his men to take a well-earned rest and left little John fishing in the great pond in front of the manor house with Downton's son Francis, a mischievous-looking ten-year-old. He and Dick Quartermain reached the village soon after terce. The church door was unlocked, and inside they saw a wagon-roofed nave. Through a huge arch on its right-hand side was a square chantry chapel, with an octagonal font in pride of place. The walls between the richly coloured stained-glass windows were painted with figures from Christian legend, including an imposing St George. The candles on its altar were lit, and they could hear a mass being sung by an elderly priest. Once it ended, and he was dousing the candles, Jack approached him.

'Are you the chantrist, John Browne?' The priest nodded.

'I'm John de la Pole, Duke of Suffolk. I'm visiting my mother's manor of Newton Montagu and I've come to pray for Sybilla de Glanville. A particular friend of my mother's was descended from her. I'd appreciate solitude.' Browne bowed respectfully, and retreated. Jack turned to his squire. Though he knew Dick was loyal as the day, he didn't want anyone to witness his search.

'Follow him. Ask him about those tombs in the graveyard. Something that will keep him out of the church until I've finished my private prayers.' Quartermain caught Browne up, and soon Jack heard the heavy door of the church scrape closed. He walked through the rood screen and studied the back of its oak panelling. Just as Roos's letter had described, there was a knot in the wood of the third panel from the left. He pressed it, and there was a click as the whole panel fell outwards. He peered into the dark space behind it, then put his arm inside and groped around. Nothing but gritty dust and cobwebs. His journey had been in vain. He sat back on his heels wearily.

'What's inside?' He jerked round to find Dick behind him. Annoyed at being discovered, he stood up, dusted off his doublet and stood up.

'Why are you still here? I told you to distract the priest and give me some time to myself.'

'There was no need to distract him. He told me he was off to tend his lambs. The local farmer gives him the ones rejected by their mothers, and he brings them up. How did you know there was a secret panel? And what were you hoping to find inside it? The stolen chantry treasure?'

'No. Papers of no value to anyone but me and my mother. But there's nothing inside.'

'Are you sure? Let me have a try.'

Before Jack could stop him, Dick knelt down, stretched his arm into the panelling right up to his shoulder and groped upwards and to the right. Then he swept his arm to the left, over the inner faces of the neighbouring panels. He gave a satisfied grunt.

'There's a piece of leather fastened to the back of the wood of the next panel but one. And it feels as if there's something in it.' Shoving his shoulder even further inside, he felt up to the top of the leather and reached in. Jack watched, heart in mouth.

'Got it!' Dick pulled his arm out and handed Jack a tightly rolled scroll of parchment. Jack took it from him, hand trembling.

Dick looked at him searchingly. 'Sir John, you can trust me, you know. I swore on my father's sword that I'd serve you with my life.'

There was a scraping sound as the church door opened. Jack hurriedly put back the fallen panel, relieved to hear it click into place. Then he tucked the scroll inside his doublet and turned. It was Jon Downton, with little John and Francis.

'It never rains but it pours. We have another visitor. Come in search of you, my lord.'

A tall, well-set man in a scarlet cloak entered the church, three turbaned moors' heads on the badge that secured his scarlet and black riding turban. To his astonishment, Jack recognised Lord Wenlock.

'Sir John, what business do you have here? My mother said you were sailing to Calais.'

'Your servant, your grace,' Wenlock said with a bow. 'I was Calais bound, but on my way to Southampton I stayed overnight at Amesbury Priory, and a royal messenger reached me to say that the matter of the Hanseatic League's ships has been settled satisfactorily. Prioress Joanna told me that I might catch up with you here. Have you found what you sought?'

John was bewildered. Though he had told the prioress he was on his way to Newton Montagu, he had not said he was searching for anything. Seeing his confusion, Wenlock realised he had said too much. Time for a distraction. He took a letter out of his doublet pocket.

'I have had a letter sending intelligence of numerous mishaps that have impeded your mother's journey. And I fear from what I've heard at Westminster that her grace is in great danger. For which I hold myself in part responsible. We need to make a plan.'

Exeter

On Wednesday morning Godith announced that the troupe of players they had seen both in Wincanton and Honiton had arrived in Exeter, and that she and Cabal were going to visit some acquaintances among them. Ben told Alyce that Will Stonor had offered to show him and the girls around the city. Alyce, glad to have Joan to herself and longing to feast her eyes on Exeter's many literary treasures, assented absentmindedly.

The dean explained apologetically that he would be busy with cathedral matters in the chapter house, but that Canon Stevens would accompany them to the library.

Stevens bowed, and led them up a spiral stair in a corner of the cloister to the door of the library. In his arms he was holding two sheepskin-lined cloaks.

'Unless it's a sunny day, the library strikes very chill in winter,' he said. 'We light pans of charcoal on the windowsills, but they don't have a great effect.'

Once warmly cloaked, they entered. Built over the length of the north side of the cloister, the library was a long, narrow room with light flooding in from the south-facing windows. It was regularly divided by the great buttresses that soared up against the wall of the cathedral, and sloped desks with shelves underneath them were fitted into each of its five bays. There were books everywhere, leaning on the slopes of the desks, flat on the shelves and locked away in chests and aumbries. As they gazed around in awe, a bent old man with shrewd blue eyes and a sheepskin draped over his shoulders rose from his desk by the door and bowed a welcome.

'This is Father Joachim,' said Stevens. 'He's been librarian for eight years now, and we haven't lost a single volume in all that time.'

'You succeed better than Oxford's university does, then,' said Alyce. 'Books constantly go missing there.'

'Ah, but we've installed a thief-proof way of keeping them safe,' said the librarian, and gestured to the book bays. Alyce and Joan saw that all the books were attached by chains to long metal rods that ran the length of each desk between its slope and the shelf beneath. The rods were locked into place at the end of each bay.

Joan studied the series of twin keyholes admiringly. 'Your Oxford friends would have no more trouble with thieves if they fitted these,' she said to Alyce. 'I've a mind to fit them in my own showroom at the Sign of the Mole.'

There was a polite cough from Father Joachim. 'The dean told me that you'd be visiting this afternoon, your grace,' he said. 'Is there anything that you would be especially interested in seeing? I can recommend a psalter made by the nuns of St Helen's for the quality of its illuminated initials.'

'I believe that you have a book of riddles,' said Alyce. 'I remember my father challenging me to solve the one about a bookworm.'

'And a printed bible,' said Joan. 'It's the future, I'm sure, if only those hidebound self-servers in the Scriveners' Guild would relax their strictures against printing presses in London.'

'You are well-versed in our treasures,' said Joachim. 'The book of riddles, which also has some elegies and lives of the saints, was acquired by Bishop Leofric over four hundred years ago. The Bible was donated by his grace George Neville on his departure. Both are locked in chests. But I'll have to help you make sense of the book of riddles. It's written in the oldest form of our English tongue.'

'I have a small acquaintance with that,' said Joan. Father Joachim looked at her doubtfully. She was not his idea of a learned scholar. Unperturbed, Joan continued.

'Many years ago my husband Thomas Moulton and I visited Canterbury to see if a copy might be made of the ancient English chronicle they held there. It was written with a Latin translation. We decided it was too great an undertaking, but our scrivener copied a few pages of the two versions, which I kept as a curiosity.'

Father Joachim raised his eyebrows, impressed. 'Then you'll enjoy our book. The script is very beautiful indeed, and one can make guesses at the puzzling meaning of the words. I am told that the answer to some of the riddles is contained in the initial letters of the lines, an ingenious conceit.'

He turned to the man sitting at the closest of the reading desks. 'Brother Jacques, could you go to the treasury and request the keys needed to open the great chest and the iron chest.'

Jacques rose, bowed, and left the room. Joan wandered over to look at the book he had been copying.

'He has a graceful hand,' she said admiringly.

'Jacques is our best copyist,' said Father Joachim. 'He came to us from Fontrevault, in Anjou.'

'Indeed, said Alyce. 'The home of Queen Eleanor, and the burial place of King Richard called Lionheart. It fell on hard times during the French wars.'

'It did indeed. That was the reason that Brother Jacques left.'

Once the two chests had been unlocked, and the books they had requested reverently taken out, Joan sat at one of the library desks, admiring the astonishing regularity of the printed letters in the Mainz Bible. Alyce sat at a second desk, and Joachim placed the book of riddles in front of her, standing quietly by to help decipher its ancient spellings.

After an hour, they changed places, and another hour passed in silence.

A clock chimed, and Canon Stevens rose from the desk by the door.

'We must go now, Princess Alyce. The books have to be locked safely away and the key returned.'

'A machine-printed book is a miraculous invention, but

there's a dullness to it,' Alyce said as they waited for the books to be locked up again. 'I prefer the individuality of a scribe's lettering. And the decorations with which they embellish their pages.'

'Printed pages can be decorated as easily as handwritten ones,' said Joan. 'Imagine countless copies, plain and cheap or coloured and costly, of everything. Learning made possible for everyone, not just the gentry.'

They were strolling across the south cloister bickering amiably when they saw Sir John Trevelyan advancing purposefully from the direction of the deanery.

'Ah, here you are, cousin. I came to tell you of the arrangements for our journey. I suggest that we set off on Friday if the weather has improved. We'll go by the high road to Newton Abbot and Plymouth, and then take ship to Fowey. The less time spent on Cornish roads, the safer.'

Alyce shook her head. 'Thank you, John, but I've decided to continue to Tintagel as I planned. I want to inspect my Cornish holdings. I regret very much that we won't travel in company, but I hope that we'll be able to stay a night at Whalesborough on our way. Elizabeth has sung the praises of your children, and I'd love to see them. Perhaps you could also send word to the Bassets of Bossiney Manor and ask if we could lodge there for a few days.'

She saw Trevelyan's eyes narrow in anger. Why was he so intent on keeping her away from Tintagel? After a moment's silence, he rallied.

'No need for that, Lady Alyce,' he said with an easy smile. 'Elizabeth and I wouldn't hear of you travelling alone across the moors. We'll change our plans and take you to Whalesborough, then go to Tintagel with you. When your business is completed, we can travel with you on the overland route to Fowey.'

Joan's eyes met Alyce's. Alyce gave her a discreet wink as she turned to Sir John.

'That is kindness itself, Sir John. I'm more than happy to leave on Friday, as you suggest. But now I must make haste. Mistress Moulton and I are going to Powderham Castle to visit Lady Bonville.'

Trevelyan watched them disappear uneasily. How on earth was he going to halt their determined progress to Tintagel? He imagined Lionel in Ireland, a hostage to his father's obedience. Now perhaps never to return.

⚜

Early that afternoon, Joan, Alyce and Godith, attended by Tamsin, Jem and Pek, rode across the many-arched bridge across the Exe to Powderham Castle, where the widowed Lady Elizabeth Bonville lived.

'Is Lady Bonville also a relative?' asked Joan, preparing herself for another of Alyce's complicated accounts of cousinage.

Alyce chuckled. 'No, but we became good friends when she and her husband came to France with us in 1444 to take part in the ceremonies by which Margaret of Anjou was betrothed to King Henry by proxy. We all returned with Margaret in the spring, and my husband saw to it that the king made Bonville Baron of Chewton as a reward. They stayed at court for several years, but after William's murder they returned to the west country. When Lady Elizabeth heard I was in Exeter, she sent a message inviting me to visit her.'

Lady Elizabeth came into the castle's base court to greet them as they rode in, and Alyce was shocked to see how she had aged. Stick-thin and dressed in black relieved only by a snowy miniver edging inside the high collar of her gown, she walked with a silver cane. Beside her was a girl of about nine or ten.

'That will be her great-granddaughter Cecily,' Alyce said to Joan and Godith. 'As Elizabeth's only son was killed six years ago at the battle of Wakefield, she'll inherit all the Bonville estates.'

'Quite a prize, then,' said Joan, watching as the child skipped away from her grandmother towards the great stone conduit at the centre of the courtyard. Tamsin went over and joined her.

'Has the child been found a husband yet?' asked Godith.

Alyce shook her head. 'She's the ward of Sir William Hastings, King Edward's boon companion. He'll have the choosing of her husband. Who will no doubt be to the liking of King Edward's avaricious wife.'

Now close enough to hear Alyce's words, Lady Elizabeth grimaced as she gave her an affectionate embrace.

'I'm praying that Fortune's wheel will spin once again before she's taken from me,' she said, looking around warily as she did so.

'And what makes you think it might?' said Godith bluntly.

Lady Elizabeth looked at her as if inspecting something she had stepped on.

'Who is this?' she asked Alyce, her voice chill with disdain.

'A discourteous herbalist from Oxford,' Alyce replied, glaring at Godith. 'She should mind her manners when speaking to her betters.'

Godith shrugged and wandered across the courtyard to join Mattie, Tamsin and Cicely at the conduit. Joan followed her, and Alyce prayed without much hope that she would caution her outspoken familiar. She was missing the meandering, unpredictable but always illuminating conversations she and her old friend used to have in Ewelme and in London. Godith's sardonic presence inhibited her; worse, time and again Joan chose to ride beside the herbalist rather than beside her.

Once they were out of earshot, Lady Elizabeth spoke again. 'I've had word from London. The queen over the water has a new ally.'

Alyce stared at the bird-like old lady. 'Who is...?'

'None other than the great Earl himself.'

'Warwick?' Lady Elizabeth nodded.

And Caerleon is now in his service, reflected Alyce. The possibilities were endless.

'Who told you of this?'

'King Henry's own gaoler. Now a fugitive, as he was discovered admitting messengers from Lorraine to his majesty. He's on his way there now himself.'

'You mean Robert Malory?'

'The same.'

'How long ago did he pass through Exeter?'

'Two days since. He and his companions are hoping to take ship from Fowey.'

'This is a happy chance, Lady Elizabeth. His cousin Sir Thomas has been in our company for the last two weeks. He'll be delighted to hear word of Robert. He was denied a pardon, and also hopes to flee the country from Fowey. He and his squire are staying in St Nicholas's Priory rather than the deanery, where Sir Thomas would be recognised. He'll want to make haste after them. And since I'm going to Bude in company with the Trevelyans, we'll need to part company, dearly as I'd love him to join me in Tintagel. Might you be able to help them on their way?'

Lady Elizabeth nodded. 'Robert Malory was planning to overnight with the Hospitallers at Temple, their preceptory on the moor near Bodmin. He may still be there; if not, the preceptor will know what his plans were. Six of my men are taking a load of dressed fleeces and bales of wool on pack horses to Bodmin early tomorrow morning. If you send Sir Thomas and his squire here this evening, they could travel with them as far as Temple. Such a substantial company need have no fear of attack by ill-wishers.'

'Thank you,' said Alyce. 'I'll call at the priory on the way back to the city. You will, I promise, find him a most congenial guest.'

As she spoke, she realised how much she would miss his company. They had not only talked of books. Over the days they had journeyed together she had found him as interested in her as she was interested in him. Prompted by his gentle questioning, she had told him of her childhood, her three very different marriages, and the recent plottings of Sir Robert Harcourt against her. She had seen things more clearly as she had talked. He was, she now knew, well acquainted with the malice of great ones, having suffered ruthless persecution by the Duke of Buckingham for eight years. That had only been ended by Buckingham's death. 'I fear Harcourt's death will be the only way for you to be free of him,' Malory had said. 'But you've done well in becoming reconciled with your son. In old age, the support of one's children is the greatest of blessings.'

Snow was falling thickly as they entered the city through the West Gate. They were riding cautiously up the steep and icy Stepcote Hill when they heard frantic shouts. A horse was charging down the hill towards them, a driverless cart swaying wildly behind it. There were houses on each side, and no way of escape. Alyce and Joan stared, rigid with shock. Without a thought for himself, Joseph Pek urged his horse in front of them and made a wild grab at the runaway's flapping reins with his single arm. He caught hold of them, but the force of the horse's hectic rush dragged him out of his saddle, and he crashed to the ground. Tamsin blenched and, heart in mouth, spurred her own horse forward. As she did so, Godith gave a strange variation of the shriek with which she had terrified the men who ambushed them at Cadbury Castle. It rose, then fell, tailing away in a series of fluting cries.

The maddened horse pricked up its ears, then slowed, and Tamsin managed to grasp its reins and bring it to a halt. The cart skidded sideways and knocked over a baker's stall, sending loaves of bread cascading to the ground. There was a moment of shocked silence, then a babble of voices as townsfolk rushed to help. Pek lay still as stone, his body at an unnatural angle, snow flecking his cloak. As she dismounted, Tamsin looked up the hill down which the horse had careered and saw a familiar figure duck into the entrance to the cathedral close. Guy Despenser. She frowned. Why hadn't he returned to Stourton?

Half an hour later, the unconscious Pek had been settled in a bed in the infirmary, a long hall between the deanery and the precentor's house. It was comfortably warm, thanks to three small hearths along its inner wall. There were eight beds, all empty except for the one on which Pek was lying. As Alyce and Joan entered, attended by Tamsin and Wat, they saw the infirmarer stooping over him, running his hands gently over his inert body.

Alyce fumbled for words. 'Is he…? Is there…?'

The infirmarer shook his head. 'He's still alive, just. But I fear his back is broken. And there's internal bleeding. To say nothing of a crack on his skull. I'll do what I can – but I don't hold out much hope for him. Come back in an hour.'

'Let's go into the cathedral and pray for him,' said Joan, taking Alyce's arm gently and leading her away. They found a side chapel in which a Mass was being sung by a priest and his acolyte. Kneeling on its icy stone floor with bowed heads, they prayed for Joseph's recovery, heedless of discomfort.

When the service was over, they returned to the infirmary. As they walked towards Pek's bed, they saw a nurse bending over him. She had placed a coin on each of his closed eyelids and was about to draw a sheet over his head. Tears streaming from her eyes, Alyce hurried forward and stopped her covering his weatherworn face. Joseph, her oldest and most faithful servant. Always outspoken. Always so hot in her defence. She stroked his forehead, and smoothed his hair, and touched a finger to his lips as she murmured prayers.

At last, she turned to the nurse. 'Did he recover consciousness?' The nurse shook her head.

Joan put her arm round her friend. 'Happen he would have chosen to die as he did, protecting you, Alyce, rather than withering away by a fireside,' she said, holding out a kerchief.

Dabbing her eyes with it, Alyce nodded sadly. 'Happen he would. He certainly made the most of his three score years and ten.' She took out her rosary, and once again they knelt in prayer.

Tintagel

Wrapped in a thick cloak, in the shelter of a farmhouse's deep stone porch, Denzil Caerleon gazed westward across the snow-covered slopes below to the river of silver light cast by a huge moon on the smooth swell of the sea. The day before yesterday he and Simon had left the castle before dawn and followed Morwenna back to the mainland and up a steep pasture to an old steading called Trehane, a mile or so north of the village. It was the home of her uncle Philip, a taciturn farmer who lived alone. 'Safer than Tintagel itself,' Morwenna had said. 'No one will think to look for you here. I've told my uncle that you're fugitives from English justice. He'll see you safe.' She'd left them there, taking Denzil's letter for Alyce, and promising to return as soon as she could.

'They call the February full moon the Chaste Moon,' said Simon Brailles, emerging from the house to give Denzil the leg joint of the scraggy hen they'd roasted two hours ago. 'Perhaps because it comes at a time when it's too chilly to...' He grinned.

Denzil chuckled. He liked the resourceful new Brailles with his ribald humour much more than the old one. He liked Morwenna too, a confident and competent girl who evidently adored Simon. If only he could find somebody as well suited to him. Though his wanderer life wouldn't appeal to many women.

'From here we've a fine view of travellers on the road between Tintagel and Bude,' Simon added, sitting down beside him. 'If Lady Alyce does come to Tintagel, we might be able to intercept her.'

'But what if she doesn't get my letter warning her that

Trevelyan is in league with Lord Tiptoft?' said Denzil. 'And Trevelyan is with her?'

'Trevelyan serves primarily himself,' said Simon. 'Princess Alyce could probably buy his loyalty if she needs to. Time for bed now, at any rate. It's past midnight.'

Just as they stood up to go back into the farmhouse, they heard hoofs on the steep track up to the old stone farmhouse.

'Who can that be?'

'Whoever it is must have ridden from Tintagel on the back road. Only locals know that road.'

'Pray heaven it's Morwenna then.'

It was. She tied her horse to the oak tree beside the house and dumped a lumpy sack beside them.

'More provisions. And you must be extra careful. Someone besides me saw your light on the castle island last night, and Sir Patrick Tregoys and his henchmen are searching it and every house. The villagers have no time for such ruffians, but Tregoys has a warrant from Sir Reginald Mohun and is throwing offers of money around, so...'

She froze as Philip's shaggy old dog Loki gave a low growl.

'What...?' began Simon, but Morwenna signed to him to stop speaking. They listened and heard the cautious crunch of footsteps coming from the direction of the barn. Denzil began to retreat into the house, beckoning them to follow. Once they were safely inside, he slid into place the beam that kept the door shut and turned to Philip, a dark silhouette hunched beside the dying embers of the fire.

'Seems we've got trouble, Philip. Morwenna has been followed from Tintagel. Have you any weapons?'

A heavy staff struck the outside of the door.

Philip gave an obscene curse and rose from his stool.

Opening a door set into the wall to the right of the hearth, he pulled out two pitchforks and a billhook.

'Morwenna, up the ladder. And Simon, you go with her. Take this.' He handed Simon one of the pitchforks, and he and Morwenna scrambled up into the loft, pulling the ladder after them.

Philip turned to Denzil. 'Take this pitchfork and stand behind the door.'

He slid open a small hatch set in the door at eye level and peered out. 'What's your business?' he called. 'Rousing honest men at midnight.'

'We're Sir Patrick Tregoys's men. He says you're housing outlaws.'

'He lies. There's only my niece, come to keep me company. And she's in bed.'

'Then she's been quick about it. We followed her up the hill. And two men were seen riding this way earlier this afternoon. And in the barn there are horses too fine for a farmer like you. Open up, or we'll burn the house down.'

Philip looked at Denzil, who took a firm hold of his pitchfork, and signed him to open the door. Two well-set men in the padded doublets of soldiers shouldered their way into the low-ceilinged room and looked around. One glanced up at the open trap door to the loft.

'Where's the ladder?' he asked Philip.

'My niece hauled it up after her.'

'Then tell her to let it down again.'

'And let you villains have at her? That I won't!'

The taller of the two men gave a leap towards the roof and managed to grasp the edges of the trap with his fingers. He swung his feet up to lever himself through it, then he gave a scream, and fell back, the tines of Simon's pitchfork driven deep into his chest. His companion gave a curse, and drew his sword, but Denzil stepped out from behind the door and sank his own pitchfork into the man's back just as Philip scythed forward with his billhook. Before they could stop him, the old man had slashed both men's throats as if he was slaughtering sheep.

'Christ's wounds,' said Denzil. 'What are we going to do with their bodies?'

Philip shrugged, kicking straw into the gore on the floor. 'Pigs'll make short work of them. Help me haul their bodies to their pen.'

He looked up and saw Morwenna and Simon staring down in horror from the loft.

'You two can clear up in here,' he said. 'Throw the soiled straw onto the fire. There's a mop in the bucket in the corner, and a cauldron of hot water by the hearth.'

By the time he and Denzil had returned from dragging the stripped bodies of the men into the eager maws of the pigs and burying their weapons, Simon and Morwenna had set the house to rights. Fresh straw lay on the floor and the fire burned merrily.

The four of them huddled round the hearth gulping down hot water enlivened with an ardent brew of Philip's own making.

'The sooner we leave the better,' said Denzil. 'Someone must have betrayed us in Tintagel, so we can't go back there. I think we'd better head for Fowey early in the morning. My men and my ships will be there by then.'

'That makes sense,' said Philip. 'Take the lane up into the hills heading east, and you'll get to the highway from Exeter to Bodmin. And Morwenna had better go with you. If they knew to follow her, then she won't be safe.'

Simon and Denzil looked at each other. Denzil shrugged. 'He's right. We'd best take her with us.'

'What about you, Uncle?' asked Morwenna.

'I'll be alright. I'm known to be an old curmudgeon. I'll just deny everything.' He gave a crooked grin. 'There won't be much left of our friends by morning. I'll sink anything uncrunched up into the pond.'

'I'll get my things together,' said Morwenna, and scrambled back up into the loft.

'You could break your journey with Ruari Maclean at Hendraburnick. It's a stone's throw from the highway,' said Philip. 'He's my late wife's brother-in-law. Tell him I sent you. And to keep a still tongue in his head.'

'How far away is Hendraburnick?'

'About eighteen miles. A long ride, but you should reach it by nightfall.'

Morwenna hugged her uncle gratefully. He hugged her back, his weather-beaten old face creased into a smile.

'And mind you two look after her well,' he said to Denzil and Simon. 'She's a girl in a thousand.'

'I know,' said Simon.

At first light, they trooped away, Morwenna mounted one of the dead men's horses and Denzil led the other, laden with their packs. A flurry of snow whipped into their faces. They pulled their cloaks tightly around themselves, grateful for their thick hoods.

'I hope another storm doesn't hit in while we're high on the moor,' said Morwenna. 'It's easy to lose the way.'

'The sunrise will guide us,' said Denzil. He was wondering

whether Alyce would get his second letter. If she did, she would know of Trevelyan's perfidy. Though not that he and Simon had had to flee from Tintagel. He could risk sending word to her at Whalesborough, but what would she be able to do, ringed as she was by pretended friends? And his letter might go astray – as his earlier ones might also have done. What an uncertain world this was.

Exeter

Joseph Pek's funeral was held on Thursday morning in the cathedral's Lady chapel. A grave had been dug for him, and a single deep bell tolled nine times, then once for each of his seventy-two years. His coffin was carried to the grave on the shoulders of Ben, Wat, Jem and Will. Alyce, Joan and Godith, attended by Tamsin and Mattie, walked behind it and Canon Stevens intoned the customary prayers. Holy water was sprinkled into the grave, and Pek's body, wrapped in a snowy white shroud and topped with his stubby battle-scarred sword, was lowered into it, Alyce threw the first handful of earth, mingled with white ashes. Then she turned and walked silently away on her own. Casting about for a refuge in which she could mourn in peace, she glanced up the spiral stair to the library and noticed that its door was open. She walked up it, and went in. Father Joachim and Brother Jacques were both sitting at their desks, Joachim reading and Jacques writing. They looked up, then hastily rose.

'Please do sit down,' said Alyce. 'I don't want to disturb you. I just wondered if I could work here for a while on some writing of my own. A record of a most faithful servant and friend.' She pulled a small leather-bound book out of her pocket. 'I just need pen and ink.'

Dinner at the deanery was delicious as usual; the centrepiece was a joint of pork seasoned with caraway and coriander seeds, served with spiced clarrey wine. But Alyce had no appetite for it. The terrible scene on Stepcote Hill kept replaying itself in her head. It had been a miracle that Tamsin hadn't suffered the same fate as Joseph. Godith had pronounced her only a little bruised, but in need of rest, and had packed her off to bed.

She was about to leave the table to go on with her record of Pek's life when her godson Will Stonor came in. He hesitated when he saw her, but she beckoned to him to sit beside her.

'How are you, Will?' she said. 'Enjoying the West Country?' He nodded apathetically, but avoided meeting her eye. She tried a new subject.

'What of your marriage? Elinor is quite lovely, I believe. And the Golafre holdings march with your parents' Fyfield lands. Has a date been set for your wedding?'

He shook his head. 'Only that it won't be until I've served my six months here with the dean's lawyers. Elinor is some years older than I am, you know. And it was my father's idea that we should marry. Not mine. But I'll have to do my duty, of course.' He hung his head gloomily.

Alyce felt a surge of sympathy for her godson. She knew all about marital duty. A very miserable business it was, too. Then an uneasy suspicion rose into her mind. She recalled that yesterday when Ben and Mattie had eagerly told her about the play they had seen performed outside the cathedral, Tamsin had been unusually silent, picking at her food and excusing herself from the table early.

'And did you and Tamsin also enjoy the play yesterday?' She saw his cheeks redden, and her heart sank. What, she wondered, had they been up to?

'Time to get back to your studies, Will.' The booming voice of the dean ended her inquisition, to her godson's evident relief. He stood up, bowed, and hurried away. Alyce looked over to the table where Tamsin was sitting with Ben, Wat and Mattie, and saw her eyes follow him mournfully. She sighed. How hard life was when love and duty clashed! She looked across at Joan and Godith, deep in conversation with Elizabeth Whalesborough, and decided not to return to her writing but to have an early night. She caught Tamsin's eye, and gave a nod towards the door.

Half an hour later, she watched from her own high bed as Tamsin folded up her discarded clothes and lit the wick of the shallow oil lamp they kept burning all night. Then she stripped to her under-shift and slipped into her pallet bed. Alyce saw her curl up into a tight ball, hugging herself with her arms, eyes staring into the distance. Clearly the girl had something on her mind. What was it? she wondered. Thwarted love?

'You seem worried, child,' she ventured. 'Would it help to talk to me about it?' Tamsin hesitated, then sat up. A flood of words poured from her – but they did not concern Will Stonor.

'It's Guy Despenser. When our journeying began, Mattie was so happy and cheerful, and she and Ben got on so well. But then Guy joined us, and she didn't have any time for Ben after that. She told me that Guy said he'd marry her when he'd saved enough money, but that he needed to return to his lord. Now she's frightened that she may be bearing his child. It's too early to be sure, of course, but she's missed her courses. I saw her talking to Godith, and I'm worried she'll do herself damage the way… the way poor Sarah did. And Guy is still in Exeter. I saw him at the top of Stepcote Hill after the accident with the runaway horse. Watching.'

Alyce was shaken. 'Then, as well as seducing Mattie, he could have been responsible for Joseph's death. Malory told me not to trust him. But he was so charming. So helpful.'

'I never liked him,' said Tamsin. 'He smiled too much, and he was always asking questions. And at Crewkerne I saw him hanging around the manor kitchen when he should have been with the other menservants in the tavern. Do you think he had something to do with the fire in the stables' roof?'

🙣

Next morning, they visited Canon Stevens's almshouse, tiny cells on two storeys arranged around a courtyard and a small chapel. Only its common room, where the poor men ate and talked together, had a hearth. Overshadowing all was Stevens's own grandiose canonry.

'Seems to me rather hard on the bedesmen to shiver while the canon lives in state across the way,' whispered Joan as Stevens showed them round the canonry, boasting of its comforts. 'I prefer your provisions at Ewelme's God's House and at Donnington.'

Soon after they returned to the deanery, a shabby horseman brought a letter to Alyce's lodgings. It turned everything she thought she knew topsy-turvy. Denzil Caerleon was not in Fowey, but with Simon Brailles, who was not dead but had been rescued by Denzil from an Irish island where he'd been marooned awaiting questioning by Lord Tiptoft. Now they were back in Cornwall but were being hunted by Sir Reginald Mohun's men. John Trevelyan was in league with Mohun, and both were conspiring to prevent her finding out what Brailles had discovered. And Denzil and Simon were hiding in a farm high above Tintagel, watching for her arrival.

She turned to the man who had brought it. 'When did you set out from Tintagel?'

'Tuesday, your grace,' he said. 'I made the best speed I could, as Master Brailles said that the matter was urgent. But there was wild weather high on the moor, and I had to take shelter in Okehampton for a day and a night.'

'You've done well,' she said, and handed him a silver groat. Then she sat down beside the fire to think. So he had taken three days to reach Exeter. Depending on the weather, their slower-moving company would take at least that long to get to Bude, and another half day to reach Tintagel. Would Denzil and Simon still be there? And what had been in what Caerleon referred to as 'my first letter'? A letter she had never received. But perhaps someone else had...

Joan glanced up from playing cards with Godith and saw the look on Alyce's face as she read, then reread, the letter. She came over to her. 'Who's your letter from?' she asked. 'And why are you scowling?'

'With good reason,' said Alyce. 'It's from your brother-in-law. And he writes that Simon isn't dead. They're both fugitives in Tintagel after Denzil plucked Brailles from Lord Tiptoft's clutches.'

'Denzil! In Tintagel? But surely Tiptoft is in Ireland, quelling rebels?'

'So he is. But it seems he had Simon abducted by Sir Reginald Mohun and marooned on an Irish island until he had time to question him. Presumably about what he'd heard from the bosun of the *Nicholas*. Though why that should interest Tiptoft, I don't know. Anyway, Denzil discovered what had happened, got a passage to Ireland and rescued Simon from the island before Lord Tiptoft got there. And he says we can't trust Trevelyan. He's hand in glove with Mohun and Tiptoft.'

'But I thought Trevelyan was so fond of you,' said Joan.

'He's always seemed to be. But he's evidently even more fond of feathering his own nest. My affection for him has been misplaced.' Her heart sank as she remembered again what Lady Hungerford had said about Trevelyan's loyalties at the time of William's death.

'Where are Denzil and Simon now?' asked Joan.

'Hiding in the hills above Tintagel. How we'll get in touch with them when Trevelyan is intent on not letting us out of his sight, I don't know.'

Godith, who had been listening with fierce concentration, interrupted.

'Why not let me and Cabal leave you when we reach Okehampton? The players told us that they are on their way to Bodmin. We'll join them as soon as we can, and pass as entertainers. Cabal can show off his muscle and I'll tell fortunes. We could take Mattie to show off her acrobatic tricks, and Wat as a messenger. We can travel with them to Camelford, where my sister lives. It's very close to Tintagel. As soon as we have news of Denzil and Simon, we'll send Wat to Whalesborough. If you've been able to set out for Tintagel yourself, he'll meet you. There's only one road.'

'That has the makings of a plan,' said Joan. 'No one'll take much notice of a beggarly crew of players.'

'Less of the beggarly,' protested Godith. 'They earn their keep honestly enough. The world would be a sadder place without them.'

Well content though she was at the prospect of having Joan to herself once again, Alyce frowned. 'I'm not sure that it's a good idea for you to take Mattie,' she said. 'Tamsin tells me that she had been pining ever since Guy Despenser left. It seems that she may have been too generous with her favours.'

Joan groaned. 'Foolish chit. Will these girls never learn?'

'I wondered who she wanted that love philtre for,' said Godith. 'Not that she needed any such thing.' She sighed. 'But we'll need a pretty wench to attract an audience. How about Tamsin? She has a sweet singing voice.'

Alyce hesitated. She had grown so used to Tamsin's deft, intelligent service that she was loth to do without her. But she supposed she could make do with Mattie. Indeed, it might be an opportunity to find out more about what had happened between her and Guy Despenser. Had he probed for secrets? And, as Tamsin was showing absolutely no sign of interest in Ben, he might be just the comfort Mattie needed.

Bodmin Moor

The journey to Hendraburnick had been slow and perilous, with dense snow sweeping in from the west as darkness fell and night descended. But Morwenna knew the way, and as the sky grew lighter it became easier to see ahead. At last, they saw the outline of farm buildings and, most cheering of all, a lamp lit in the window of a barn.

'That'll be Ruari Maclean milking his cow,' said Morwenna. 'She's his pride and joy.'

Maclean was a gaunt Scot who'd fallen for a Cornishwoman in the household of his liege lord Sir Hugh Courtenay. When he was too old to serve Courtenay in arms, they had settled on a steading she had inherited from her father. After he heard their story, he insisted on their sheltering there until the weather improved. There was creamy milk to drink for breakfast and rough oatcakes slathered in bilberry jam to eat. Then they drowsed by the hearth until the snow had stopped falling and a pallid sun showed itself. They readied themselves to ride on.

'Keep to the moor tracks, Morwenna,' Maclean said, as he handed Simon a bag of provisions. 'And shelter in barns, not farms. There are far more sheriff's men than usual patrolling the Bodmin road. With sleuth hounds canny to follow a scent. They almost caught three Lancastrian fugitives a few days ago thanks to their dogs sniffing a cloak one of them left at a tavern in Okehampton. But they lost them at the edge of Dozmary Pool. It's a huge mere high on the moor. They must have found a boat. Mohun's offering a big reward for news of them, they say.' He looked at Caerleon. 'You're not Cornish, are you? Where do you hail from?'

'Mohun always offers more than he gives,' said Morwenna quickly. 'Denzil is Simon's cousin. Simon and I need to be married by the priest at Temple and Denzil is to stand witness.' She placed a hand on her belly as she spoke, and a smile spread across Maclean's craggy face.

Pretending embarrassment, she gave him a nod. 'Though I'd be grateful if you didn't tell my uncle. He thinks I'm just showing Simon and his friend the way across the moor.'

Maclean grinned. 'I won't say a word.'

'How clever,' Denzil whispered to Simon. 'She's distracted his attention from the thought of a reward and made him feel like a generous man of the world.' Simon, paralysed with a combination of shock and joy at the idea that Morwenna could be carrying his child, didn't answer.

Though the snow was falling less heavily, great drifts had piled up, making it hard to find the moorland track that wound erratically to Temple. They stayed a night in a barn and crossed the highway the next day as dusk fell. Temple lay deep in a sheltered combe a mile south-east of the highway. Owned by the Knights Templar until the Order was dissolved in 1312, it was now an important Knights Hospitaller preceptory. It was especially popular locally because Hospitaller chaplains were allowed to marry couples who could or would not ask their own priest to do so. They approached it cautiously, dismounting a hundred yards away and concealing their horses in a copse of holly trees.

'Wait there,' Denzil said. 'I'll go and see how many horses there are in the stables.'

As soon as he disappeared, Simon turned to Morwenna. 'Is it true about… about…' All his old nervousness had returned. He stopped speaking and looked at her stomach shyly.

'What if I was?' she said with an impish smile. Then she nodded shyly.

'Then I'll ask the preceptor to marry us here and now,' said Simon, and pulled her into his arms.

'What's this?' Denzil had returned, his approach muffled by the snow. 'This is no time for dalliance. We're not Temple's only visitors.' Blushing, they jumped apart.

'What did you find in the stables?' asked Simon.

'A fine black horse and a Welsh pony. Neither of them in warlike harness. I think it's safe to go in.'

He knocked at the door, and after a few moments the cover of a barred peephole slid open. Then the door was opened by a grizzled old man in a black gown bearing the white cross of the Knights Hospitaller. He looked at them warily but relaxed when he saw Morwenna. 'Runaways, are you? Needing your elopement sanctified?' Heart thumping, Simon put his arm round her and nodded.

'I'm Father Solomon. As chaplain of the preceptory of Temple, I have the authority of the Pope to do so. Far better to marry than to burn. Your friend here is doubtless to stand as witness.'

Denzil looked at Simon's and Morwenna's expectant faces and rose to the occasion. 'I am indeed,' he said. Then he added casually, 'Father, I saw two horses in your stable. Do you have other visitors?'

The old man turned his head to the shadowy interior of the preceptory as if asking a question. A distinguished-looking man stepped forward, attended by a lad dressed as a squire.

Simon looked with interest at the cloak badges they wore. Three moors' heads on a white ground. 'Isn't that Lord Wenlock's device?' he asked.

'Do you know him?' said the older man.

'He's a friend of my mistress, Princess Alyce, Dowager Duchess of Suffolk,' said Simon. 'Until a fortnight ago, I was an ordinand at her church at Tintagel.'

Malory's jaw dropped. 'Then you are Simon Brailles. She's on her way to talk to you. I am Sir Thomas Malory of Newbold Revel, and until Exeter Owen and I travelled in her company.'

Now it was Simon's turn to look amazed. 'Malory! King Arthur's chronicler! How her grace must have relished your company. And was Tamsin, her secretary with her? She has long been a great lover of your stories.'

'I liked Tamsin very much. A quick and perceptive girl. I'm surprised she hasn't been spoken for.'

He turned to Denzil. 'And you are?'

'Denzil Caerleon. I was once in her grace's service, but foolishly forfeited her trust. I'd dearly love to win her favour again.'

'Which you will when she hears that you rescued me,' said Simon. He peered at Owen, who was standing in the shadows.

'But surely I know you – aren't you the son of Bronwen Pailton?'

Owen stepped forward with a grin. 'Yes – who once offered to guard your horse outside St Giles. Which you refused.'

Simon grimaced. 'To my eternal shame. How does your mother? And Guy of Yarnton?'

'Well. They only remain in London to see the last days of my grandmother Agnes.'

'She's someone else I misjudged badly.' Simon turned back to Malory.

'What are you planning to do now, Sir Thomas?'

'I'm suspected of treason. The truth is that there isn't evidence to convict me, but I'll be thrown into Newgate or even the Tower if I'm found. Owen and I seek to take ship for France from Fowey. Have you come from Bodmin, by any chance? I'm hoping to catch up with my cousin Robert and some friends of mine. Father Solomon told me that they left here for Fowey yesterday morning.'

'We've come from Hendraburnick,' said Morwenna. 'It's a steading just west of the high road. The farmer is Ruari Maclean, my uncle's brother-in-law. He told us that the Bodmin road is being patrolled by Sir Reginald Mohun's men with sleuth hounds. They almost caught three fugitives a few days ago.'

'They must have been my friends. Father Solomon told me that they'd only escaped capture by chance: they stole a fishing punt at the edge of Dozmary Pool and poled it across so the hounds lost the scent. Though I'm sorry to miss them, I hope they've found a ship for France by now.'

'They should have,' said Solomon. 'Since war with France is more and more likely, there's a lot of coming and going in the Channel for all the winter weather. Now – what about this marriage? We have witnesses aplenty, and we can make supper something of a feast. Follow me to the chapel.'

🜨

Wild dreams raced through Denzil's head that night, some of tossing about on the high seas, some of riding blindly through the snow, all threaded with panic. In the last, he was battering at the locked door of a bakery – until he realised that the noise was real. So was the smell of freshly baked bread. He opened his eyes to see Solomon peering through the peephole in the preceptory's outer door. He saw a look of relief come over his face as he opened it. A lad came in, shaking snow off his cloak as he entered.

'Welcome, Barney,' said Solomon. 'What news?'

'Nothing good,' said Barney. 'A dozen of the sheriff's men will be demanding you conceal them about Temple in an hour's time. They have come from Bodmin and stayed in my father's tavern last night, and I heard them saying they expected some Lancastrian fugitives to seek shelter here soon.' He looked round at the sleepy faces of Malory, Owen and Denzil. 'But perhaps they already have.'

'Then we've no time to lose.' said Malory. 'What do you suggest, Father Solomon?'

'Your best chance of evading them would be to do the unexpected. Don't head for Bodmin or Fowey. Ride west for Camelford, taking the paths over the high moor. When you get there, ask for Gwennol, the wise woman. She's no friend of York. Barney, will you be their guide?'

Barney nodded with alacrity. 'Anything to spite Mohun,' he said. 'His men half-wrecked the inn last night. Have you good mounts?'

As he spoke, Morwenna and Simon came in, she alight with happiness, he full of pride. When she saw Barney, she looked anxious.

'What are you doing here, Barney? Is something wrong at the Fourways?'

'He's ridden to warn us that the sheriff's men are on their way,' said Denzil. 'Father Solomon says we must ride with him at once. To Camelford. We'll stay there until the hunt is over.'

They gathered up their possessions, and Solomon handed Barney a sack stuffed with sweet-scented loaves of bread. They bowed their heads as he made the sign of the cross and said a farewell prayer. Then they raced to the stable for their horses.

Exeter

At ten o'clock next morning, the Trevelyans and a dozen men met up with Alyce's company and they set off westward. 'We'll stay at Teignton Drewe,' said Sir John. 'There's a good inn there.'

'How did Teignton Drewe come by its name?' asked Godith.

'Teignton because of its position on the river Teign, of course,' said Trevelyan. 'As to Drewe, some say it was once the seat of the Archdruid of the West. Our road passes four great stones, one propped up by the other three. Local legend has it that they form a portal to the underworld, and the great lake beside it is said to be sacred. More down-to-earth souls point out that before the manor was held by the Dabernons it belonged to the Drewes, the first of whom was a Norman baron called Drogo.'

'Any legend of druids will interest Cabal,' said Godith, and reined back her mare so that she was beside him and the train of packhorses. That left Joan riding beside Trevelyan, and Alyce with Lady Elizabeth. Mattie and Ben were riding side by side, whispering together.

Tamsin, unusually morose, rode next to Wat. She was glad that Ben and Mattie had made up their quarrel, but her own mind was in a turmoil. Yesterday, while the others had gone to watch the players, Will Stonor had taken her to walk along the ramparts of Rougemont Castle, high on a hill above the cathedral. He'd taken her hand in his as they negotiated the narrow walkway that led to the top of its gatehouse. As they gazed out past the cathedral's spires to the river winding its way towards the sea, he had put his arm around her shoulders and turned her to face him.

'Heart of my heart, it's been wonderful to be with you again. I want to see your lovely hair loose about your shoulders. Can I?' Without waiting for her answer, he had drawn her close and pulled off the caul into which her silky chestnut hair was coiled. Running his fingers through it gently, so that tremors of pleasure ran through her, he had bent to kiss her. She'd shivered, torn between longing and guilt. After he had drawn back, eyes alight with love, she'd heard herself saying in a small, stilted voice: 'What are you about, Will? Mattie says that you're still promised to Elinor Golafre.'

He had hesitated a moment, then shrugged. 'I am, and of course I'll have to marry her once I return to Oxfordshire. She's well-born enough to grace the royal court, and Stonor Park needs her fortune and heirs of good lineage. But she hasn't got your daring, adventurous spirit, your love of romance. She's dull as ditchwater and all she's interested in is making Stonor Park as grand as Ewelme and bringing up babies. I'll have to do my duty by her, but you're my true love. I've known that ever since our wild ride to Swyncombe four years ago. We're meant for each other just as Tristram and Isolde were in the story Sir Thomas wrote, even though Isolde was promised to King Mark.'

'Will, they're not real people,' she'd said, pulling away from him. 'And things didn't end well for them, anyway.'

Will had laughed, pulling her close again. 'Trust you to argue, Tammie. Your honesty is one of the things I love about you. Alright, then how about Joan Moulton and Lord

Wenlock? He's just married Agnes Danvers for her money, and Joan hasn't turned a hair. We'll be like them, enjoying each other's company – and each other's bodies – as often as we can.'

He had showered kisses on her hair and pressed her against the rough stones of the gatehouse turret, stroking her breasts with one hand and running the other down to her thighs, whispering her name again and again. Then he had pulled up her skirt. She'd trembled with longing, then ugly memories flashed into her mind. Sir Robert Harcourt drunkenly assaulting her on the stairs of Ewelme Palace. Hamel Turvey's vicious, probing fingers as she lay bound across his saddle. She had given a wail of despair, shrieked 'Don't you dare call me Tammie!' and twisted away from him, fleeing along the walkway as if the devil was following her and creeping tousled and tearful into her pallet bed in the women's shared chamber in the deanery.

So much for Arthurian romance and knights honouring their ladies, she thought sadly as she jogged along the rough track towards Teignton Drewe. Other images rose up. Sarah, whose death after aborting her child had led to Tamsin being taken into Princess Alyce's service. Amice, bruised and broken, desperately stabbing Rufus Savernake. Mattie, anxious at missing her courses. Women seemed always to have the worst of things. A tear trickled down her cheek. Wat saw it as she brushed it hastily away and gave her a worried look. He felt in his pocket and took out the little carved mouse she had given him three years ago, pushing it into her hand in the hope that it would comfort her. Which it did. Not least because it reminded her of Denzil Caerleon's long-ago words. 'You'll go far if you keep that resolve. Hold to your truth.'

Next day, although the road was rutted and wound steeply up and down hills, they made good speed, and reached Okehampton by noon. Alyce couldn't resist pointing out to Joan how much better off they were without the cart.

'Better during the day, but not at night,' grumbled Joan, reaching under her cloak to scratch an armpit. 'I was all but eaten alive by the fleas in the inn's bedding.'

'You'll be made much more comfortable at Whalesborough,' Lady Elizabeth assured her. 'We air everything thoroughly in the winds that blow from the sea. And burn dried fleabane in all the bedchambers.'

Godith came over to Alyce. 'This is where Cabal and I leave to join the players. Is it alright for us to take Wat and Tamsin?'

Alyce began to nod, then shook her head. 'Maybe Jem rather than Wat. Wat's grown up a lot, but he hasn't Jem's common sense.'

Cabal frowned and began to sign rapidly to Godith. Once he finished, she turned to Alyce.

'Cabal thinks Wat would be best. If we need to send a messenger back, a lad like him will be less noticeable than a well set-up horseman like Jem.'

Alyce agreed, a little unwillingly. What was left of their company rode on. The Trevelyans led, Ben squired Mattie, and Joan rode beside Alyce. Trevelyan's retainers and Jem followed behind.

'Lady Elizabeth seems unhappy,' Joan observed. 'She's spoken barely a word since we left Exeter. I wonder what's upset her.'

'Trevelyan also seems morose,' said Alyce. 'Denzil wrote in his letter that he was hand in glove with Mohun and Tiptoft.

Perhaps they ordered him to keep me away from Tintagel. What perplexes me is why he would agree to act against me, his wife's cousin and the source of all his good fortune.'

'Maybe they have some sort of hold over him,' said Joan. 'But enough of gloomy surmises. I'm looking forward to seeing Tintagel. It's a shame Malory isn't with us. I'd love to hear him read of Arthur's birth there.'

She glanced at Alyce, a question in her eyes. 'I hope the two of you had plenty of time to talk of Arthur. And of other things. I left you together as much as I could, knowing that you'd have much to say to each other. I've never seen anyone better suited to you. It's a shame that he has to go abroad.'

Alyce suddenly appreciated Joan's selflessness in absenting herself from just the sort of literary conversation she revelled in, so that Alyce could deepen her new friendship. And there she had been resenting the way Joan had seemed to prefer Godith's company to her own.

That night they stayed at Solden Manor, near Holsworthy, with friends of the Trevelyans called Prideaux. Sir John announced that he had business to transact with Terence Prideaux, and the two men disappeared, leaving Alyce and Joan with their wives. Stefania Prideaux, an exile from London, was eager to hear of the latest fashions, and Joan regaled her with descriptions of plunging frontals and pointed hennins. Lady Elizabeth remained silent, her thoughts clearly far away. In half an hour Trevelyan returned, followed by a servant who served them all with spiced gotobeds and cups of mulled ale. As Alyce listened to Stefania and Joan gossiping, she heard a horse's hoofs and wondered uneasily about Trevelyan's loyalties.

Whalesborough

At midday on Monday they sighted smoke rising from the chimneys of Whalesborough Manor. Trevelyan had sent an outrider ahead, and as they approached the house a jostling gang of children on rough-coated ponies trotted towards them, a black bird fluttering above them.

'Welcome home, Mother! Welcome home, Father!' Trevelyan's daughter Annie called. 'Cook has slaughtered a pig for us to feast on. We've so many visitors already that he may have to kill a cow. Sir Reginald Mohun and eight of his men have been here for ages, First they searched the house, then they sent a search party out over the moor. He says there are two n–n–notorious traitors at large. What does "at large" mean? Nicholas says "very big". We told him there were no giants around here, but he wouldn't listen.'

Chattering nonstop, the children dragged Lady Elizabeth towards the house, and Artie settled possessively on Trevelyan's shoulder, He turned to Alyce with an ingratiating smile.

'Your grace, I should have warned you. Sir Reginald Mohun sent word to me that he'd been told by Lord Tiptoft to watch over you while you were in Cornwall. But I hadn't expected him to come to Whalesborough so soon.'

He had barely finished speaking when Mohun emerged from the house. Artie fluttered away with an angry caw as the burly deputy sheriff strode up to them.

'Good day, John,' he said, ignoring Alyce entirely, 'My apologies for intruding in your absence, but we received intelligence that some notorious Lancastrians were seeking to escape by sea. We nearly caught three last week, and we're on the trail of two more. There was no word of them seeking a ship in

Bude, so they're probably heading for Fowey. I've sent my men to conceal themselves in the preceptory at Temple, a notorious refuge for such fugitives. When they've been captured, we will head for Lostwithiel.'

He turned to Alyce and gave her a cursory bow. 'Princess Alyce, I presume. This is a fortunate chance. I'd thought you and the Trevelyans to be on your way to Fowey rather than visiting Whalesborough, but now I can escort you to Fowey myself. Restormel Castle is well furnished and spacious, and you will do well to make it your base for the remainder of your stay in Cornwall.'

His fierce black eyes met her grey ones in unspoken challenge, and she realised that the slight to her rank dealt by his speaking first to Trevelyan was quite deliberate, and that he did not intend to be refused. What did he know of Brailles? she wondered. And were the Lancastrians he was pursuing Sir Thomas Malory and Owen?

His next words left her no wiser: 'As the Trevelyans will have told you in Exeter, the servant you planned to visit in Tintagel fell from its cliffs. I'm surprised that Sir John has allowed you to waste your time continuing westward. I told him to take you and your companions directly to Fowey, a much more suitable place for pilgrims than this pagan coast.' He glared at their quivering host. Trevelyan opened his mouth to explain, but before he could say a word Alyce drew herself up to her full height.

'I do not choose to be taken hither or thither like a chattel, Sir Reginald. I am a princess of the realm and I make my own decisions. As patron of Tintagel, it is my responsibility to make sure that the parish is properly furnished with clerks, especially if, as you say, Simon Brailles is dead. As to suitable places of pilgrimage, my memory is that the north coast of Cornwall is generously endowed with saintly memorials. Tintagel itself may have druidical connections, but its fascination to most right-thinking English folk is as the place where our greatest Christian king was conceived: Arthur, son of Uther Pendragon and Igraine.'

'A fanciful romance,' said Sir Reginald. 'Don't forget that you're far from home, and at the limits of the reach of the king's writ. As his proxy in this county, I reserve my right to advise and protect you.'

Heavy footsteps sounded in the screens passage and two men entered the hall. Sir Reginald looked past Alyce and smiled a welcome.

'Cousin! This is an unexpected pleasure. How come you to Whalesborough?'

Alyce turned and received the worst shock of the whole journey. Sir Robert Harcourt stood smiling sardonically at her.

'Princess Alyce!' he exclaimed. 'What a pleasant surprise! I knew of course of your journey west; my wife wrote in her last letter that all Oxfordshire is full of it. No doubt you are surprised to see me – you won't have heard that for the last few weeks I have been in Bristol fitting out my new ship, the *Peacock*. The king's men are scouring the country for vessels to fight the French, and I'm on my way to join the Earl of Warwick. When we called in to Bude for provisions, I heard that Sir Reginald was at Whalesborough, so I decided to come and find him. His wife is my cousin, just as Trevelyan's wife is yours.'

Alyce suspected that neither Mohun nor Harcourt was in the least surprised to see her. She remembered Trevelyan disappearing with his friend Sir Terence Prideaux at Solden and the sound of galloping hoofs soon after. Again, she sensed a play being acted for her benefit, or rather to engineer her downfall. And then another all-too-familiar figure entered the room and she realised that the performance had begun much earlier. Guy Despenser, now dressed in Sir Reginald's livery, strode in, and gave her an exaggerated bow before wandering over to where Sir Reginald's other retainers were playing dice.

'And is this the whole of your company?' Mohun asked with a touch of a sneer. 'I had heard that there were others travelling with you. A knight and his squire. Not to mention a witch and a tattooed savage.'

'Two of Lord Wenlock's men rode with us for a while,' Alyce replied coolly, brain racing as she realised that they had been harbouring Mohun's spy ever since they left Cadbury. 'We came across them in Andover and they proved doughty in our defence when we were attacked by rogues near Cadbury Castle. But they left us in Exeter. Why are you interested in them?'

'My servant Guy Despenser who rode with you from Stourton discovered that one of them was the traitor Sir Thomas Malory. No doubt you were unaware of the fact. Did they say where they planned to go after Exeter?'

Alyce thought hard. Despenser had left them on the outskirts of Exeter. But he would have seen Malory and Owen go into St Nicholas's Priory. And Tamsin said she had seen him at the top of Stepcote Hill. He must surely have contrived the murderous runaway cart. And perhaps the fire at Crewkerne Manor. But she needed to be careful. The less she said about her suspicions the better.

'They told us that they were taking a pilgrimage to

Compostella,' she said with dignity. 'I've no idea what route they planned to take.'

'If they were heading for Fowey, they would have taken the highway over the moor to Bodmin,' said Mohun. 'Malory's family were Hospitallers, so they'll doubtless rest at the Knights' preceptory at Temple. My men are already on their way there.'

He gave her another piercing stare, and to her horror she felt a blush rising as she wondered what other secrets Guy Despenser had overheard, or coaxed Mattie into telling him?

Harcourt took up the inquisition. 'I'm surprised you didn't recognise Malory, Princess Alyce. He was retained by Lord Wenlock when you visited London two years ago. It was his connection to an illegal printing press housed in the Hospitallers' Priory in Clerkenwell that marked him as a traitor and was the cause of his being exempted from the general pardon last July.' He looked searchingly at her.

Joan Moulton had been watching and listening. Seeing Alyce utterly lost for words, she bustled forward and placed a plump hand affectionately on Harcourt's arm.

'Sir Robert. What a pleasure to see you again! I haven't forgotten the interest in *litterae esotericae* you mentioned to me the last time you visited the Sign of the Mole. Indeed, I have a couple of volumes in one of my packs which might well appeal. Why don't you come to the guest lodgings?'

Harcourt turned away from Alyce and looked appreciatively at Joan, dressed as always to impress.

'I'm always open to temptation, Mistress Moulton. Especially by you. Let's go indoors, and you can show me what you have to offer.' He winked at Mohun as he took Joan's arm and led her into the house. Muttering something about arranging a meal, Trevelyan followed them. Mohun turned to Alyce again.

'Our priority now is to pursue Malory and his squire. We'll ride at once for Temple. Once we've taken them, I'll come to Tintagel, and when your business there is done I'll escort you to Fowey.' He gave an insolent bow, made a sign to Despenser and followed Trevelyan indoors.

Camelford

Chilled to the bone, Godith knocked on the low door of her sister's house in Camelford. Gwennol opened it wide and gave her a lingering hug. Godith introduced Tamsin, Cabal and Wat, and Gwennol directed them to sit on the benches on either side of a long table. She could have been Godith's twin, her eyes as beady, her hair as haystack-hectic. She poured a pale gold liquid into five glazed clay beakers. A single mouthful made Tamsin cough and splutter and sent Wat's eyes rolling upwards before he slumped onto a stone seat deep in the hearth. Cabal sipped, then put his beaker down on the table with a shake of his head. Godith, who had already tossed hers back, picked it up and drained it, smacking her lips.

'I've missed that brew of yours, sister. As potent as ever, I'm glad to say.'

Gwennol gave a pleased nod, then began filling bowls of spiced barley soup from the great iron pot that hung over the fire. She set them down on the table. The travellers took out their spoons and ate gratefully.

'How did you know we were coming today?' asked Tamsin. 'Or do you always have food ready for travellers?'

'How could she not know that her own sister, her second self, was approaching?' said Godith teasingly. 'She knew because when we reached Okehampton I sent a rider to tell her we were on our way, though I couldn't be sure when we'd arrive.'

Gwennol turned to the man sitting chopping kindling in a dark corner of the room. 'Garth, wasn't I just saying that it would be today they'd be here?' she said, beaming with satisfaction. 'I read it in the cards.' She gestured to the five images she had turned up.

'The Magician (nodding at Cabal), the Fool (nodding at Wat), the Star (nodding at Tamsin), and of course the High Priestess.' She bowed to Godith.

'But you must beware.' She pointed to a fifth card, a grisly skeleton with an hourglass in one corner and a candle in another. 'There's danger of death. And it's connected somehow with where you said you were going. Tintagel.'

Tamsin shivered, but Godith gave a derisive chuckle. 'Save your tricks for credulous strangers, dear,' she said to her sister. 'Now, what do you know of real threats?'

Gwennol shrugged her shoulders and changed from fey prophet to practical plotter. 'Tintagel is occupied by Sir Patrick Tregoys and his men. They're working for Sir Reginald Mohun, the deputy sheriff. As you're strangers, they'll arrest you on sight.'

'We've planned for that,' said Godith. 'We're travelling with a company of players and I've persuaded them to stage a performance in Tintagel. It's market day tomorrow. We're part of the entertainment. I'll tell fortunes, Cabal will perform feats of strength, Tamsin will sing, and Wat will collect the takings. Tregoys's men won't give us a second glance. When it gets dark we'll slip over to the chapel on the island. I'm sure that's where we'll find what we're looking for. Just where Simon Brailles hinted it would be.'

Gwennol looked unconvinced. 'Are you wise to risk your life for this spoilt, wealthy woman, sister?'

'She isn't spoilt!' Head spinning from Gwennol's cordial, Tamsin swept the brightly coloured cards to the floor. 'My Nan told me all about her. She's had years of misery – made to marry far too young, watching the only husband she loved die in agony, and going through twenty years of neglect and insult from her third and last one. Now she's free to do so, she looks out for her people. She makes sure that the old are comfortable and the young taught and settled in life. And now she's risking her own life to discover the truth about her husband's murder, not because she cares, but to give her son peace of mind.'

Cabal and Wat gaped at her sudden fury. Godith considered her through narrowed eyes. She hadn't understood the depth of Tamsin's feeling for her mistress. Or was there some other cause for her rage?

Gwennol smirked and added fuel to the flames. 'If he is indeed her son,' she said caustically. 'There have been rumours that he was of noble-get but bastard-born ever since he came into the world, her first child after a decade of marriage to his father.'

'What good there is in him is all of her doing,' yelled Tamsin, picking up a long-handled saucepan and swinging it at Gwennol's head.

Garth sprang to his feet, but before he could intervene Cabal stretched out a huge hand and stalled the pan in mid-air. Tamsin collapsed next to Wat and wept. Wat put a comforting arm around her, rocking her gently and dabbing at her eyes with a grimy kerchief.

There was a sharp rat-a-tat-tat on the door. Gwennol looked startled. Godith motioned Cabal to move behind it as Garth went to open it. Five cloaked figures stood outside. 'Is Gwennol there?' asked the tallest of them. 'Father Solomon of Temple told us that she would give us refuge. We are fleeing Sir Reginald Mohun's men.'

'Any friends of Father Solomon are friends of mine,' called Gwennol. 'And I suspect that I have with me friends of yours.'

Wiping away her tears, Tamsin watched with amazement as Sir Thomas Malory entered, followed by Owen and a girl with sea-green eyes, high cheek bones and sun-browned face. Holding the girl's hand possessively was Simon Brailles, as sun-browned as she was, confident and upright. Finally, wonder of wonders, in came Denzil Caerleon. He put his hand on his sword hilt apprehensively as a tattooed giant emerged from behind the door.

'None of that,' said Gwennol. 'You're among friends. Cabal, slide the bar across the door.' She motioned the newcomers to warm themselves at the fire and refilled the beakers on the table. 'Here you are, Morwenna,' she said, handing one to the girl. 'A loving cup for you to share with your husband. Or do I misread the signs?' Tamsin saw the girl shake her head and give Simon a proud smile as she sipped the spirit, then passed it to him.

'How far behind you are Mohun's men?' Godith asked Denzil.

'We hid in the woods around Temple until they arrived and settled themselves in, not realising their birds had already flown. Then a boy from Fourways Inn led us across the moor to Camelford.'

'Barney, no doubt,' said Gwennol. 'He knows the moors like the back of his hand. Where is he now?'

'He pointed us to your house, then set off back to his father,' said Owen. 'They've a deal of work to do mending it after Mohun's ruffians wrecked it.'

Denzil looked wonderingly at Cabal, then turned to Godith. 'And who might you two be? And this giant?'

'I'm Gwennol's sister,' Godith replied. 'I travelled to Exeter with Princess Alyce and Mistress Moulton from Ewelme, Cabal came with us as a bodyguard. He's worth three men in a fight.'

'Princess Alyce and Joan Moulton! Are they in Camelford too?'

'No,' said Godith. 'They're still at Whalesborough. But they're planning to ride to Tintagel as soon as they can.'

Just then Denzil noticed Tamsin and Wat half-hidden at the side of the hearth. He gave a broad grin.

'Tamsin! How do you and Wat come to be here?'

She smiled back tremulously. 'We came with Godith and Cabal and the players. Princess Alyce will be at Whalesborough Manor by now, with the Trevelyans. But she's hoping to travel to Tintagel as soon as she can.'

She turned to see Simon advancing on her, arms out-stretched. He folded her into a warm hug, then turned to Morwenna.

'Morwenna, this is Tamsin Ormesby. I've known her since she was my most disobedient pupil in Princess Alyce's school in Ewelme. Now she's her grace's secretary in my place.'

'And has grown up most gracefully since we last met three years ago,' put in Denzil. 'Are you still dedicated to independence and adventuring, Tammie?' he asked, his eyes twinkling. She opened her mouth to object to his calling her Tammie. But then she discovered she did not mind it in the least and closed it. It was such a relief to have someone she had always liked and trusted joining them.

'So, what now? Are we all going to travel to Tintagel with

the players and search out the evidences you hid in the castle chapel, Simon?' said Godith.

Simon's jaw dropped. 'How did you know that?'

'Princess Alyce showed me your letters. That's why she's heading for Tintagel.'

Denzil stepped forward. 'Did she get a letter from me? Does she know Simon is still alive and that he and I are fugitives?'

'Yes,' said Godith. 'And she's eager to see you both again. But she's travelling with the Trevelyans, and your letter warned her not to trust them. We thought it best for some of us to go to Tintagel and get the evidences ourselves. Will you come with us?'

Simon shook his head. 'Morwenna and I would be recognised straight away. We'd best take refuge with her uncle at Trehane again. That would be safest for Sir Thomas and Owen too. And we can see comings and goings on the road between Bude and Tintagel from there.'

'Well, there's nothing to stop the rest of us going into Tintagel with the players and seeing how the land lies,' said Godith.

'I'd like to come with you,' said Denzil. 'No one is likely to recognise me if I'm not with Simon. And I know where the evidences are hidden.'

Godith looked at him consideringly. 'You might well be useful, but I can't see you passing for a player.'

'Suppose I accompany him?' said Gwennol. 'We could arrive later than the players. I'll say he's my nephew from Exeter.'

'So you're coming too?' said Godith.

'You're going to need local knowledge,' said Gwennol. 'Who to trust and who to avoid. And now I've got you back, I'm not going to risk losing you.'

Whalesborough

Alyce sat on a window seat in her bedchamber, tapping her foot impatiently. She was longing to set off for Tintagel, but there was no sign of Joan or the Trevelyans. Mattie had disappeared, and so had Ben Bilton. Presumably Jem was in the stables. Racked by doubts and frustrated by forced inactivity, she was feeling desperately alone. At last, she heard a horseman arriving, and rough male voices in the courtyard. Then there was the sound of many horses riding away. Pray heaven that both Mohun and Harcourt had left. Though if they had all set off in pursuit of Sir Thomas... Her heart sank.

There was a shy knock on her door, and Elizabeth Whalesborough entered, looking pale and anxious.

'Cousin, I have a confession to make,' she began. But before she could start speaking, she broke down in tears. Alyce hurried over to her and made to put a comforting arm around her shoulder. Elizabeth pushed it away, sobbing. Bewildered, Alyce stood back, unsure what to do. At last Elizabeth straightened, sniffed and recovered herself enough to continue.

'John and I have lied to you. But we didn't have a choice. You see, Lord Tiptoft has taken our oldest son to Ireland to ensure that we did what he told us to do.'

Alyce felt as if she had been punched in the stomach. What had all this to do with Tiptoft?

'And what was that?' she asked icily.

'To tell you that Simon Brailles was dead. And prevent you from reaching Tintagel.'

'As to Simon being alive, I know that already,' said Alyce. 'I received a letter from a former servant of mine whom I once doubted, but who I now realise has always been steadfast and loyal. He rescued Simon. He also told me not to trust your husband.'

'You mean Denzil Caerleon?' said Elizabeth. 'Yes, he made it clear when he came here that he valued your goodwill above everything. But we told him Simon was dead. I wonder how he discovered the truth. Do you know where he and Simon are now?'

'No,' said Alyce. 'Nor would I tell you if I did. But I'd like you to tell me why it is so important to Lord Tiptoft that I don't go to Tintagel.'

Elizabeth sighed. 'Simon had a parcel Tiptoft desperately wanted destroyed. His abductors searched him but found nothing. Lord Tiptoft fears that Simon told you in his letter where he had hidden it; that's why he wanted you kept away from Tintagel. At the minute the church, the vicarage and the village are being ransacked by Mohun's cousin Sir Patrick Tregoys – he's a ruffian who'll do anything for money. Mohun told John to keep you here while they searched. Tregoys has just sent a messenger to say he found nothing, and Mohun has told us to escort you to Tintagel, in the hope that Simon did tell you where the parcel is, and that you'll lead us to it. He's going to join us there when he's caught the fugitives he's hunting.'

The church, the vicarage and the village, Alyce thought to herself, but not the island. They did not know what Simon's letters had told her and Joan and Godith: that his favourite place was its chapel. And she remembered again the phrase he had used, the phrase that had so struck Godith: 'a secret between you, me and Our Lady'.

'And why are you telling me this now?' she asked Elizabeth, unable to stop herself sounding bitter. She saw Elizabeth's shoulders droop in misery as she answered.

'Because John thinks that the only hope of getting our son back is for me to appeal to you as a mother. If we go to Tintagel together, and you know where the evidences are, he thought that you could read them and then hand them over to him to give to Lord Tiptoft. And we could get Lionel back.'

As a mother. The words stung. Alyce looked out of the window to where the Trevelyan children were joyfully kicking a football around the courtyard. She watched as John Trevelyan joined his children, picking up the smallest and taking the hand of another. Anger flared up in her at the sight of him, but then flickered out. She thought of how fine a family he and Elizabeth had raised in this remote, lawless corner of the country and how barren and hedged around with formal duties her own life had been. She'd made a cultured paradise at Ewelme and had done what she could to increase the well-being of those around her. But what after all were material things and charity compared with bringing up those who were flesh of one's flesh, bone of one's bone? Any mother, any father, would move heaven and earth to get a lost child restored to them. What wouldn't she do for Jack, the child she had only chosen to call her own? She remembered his anxious face as he asked if he could still call her Mother.

She turned to Elizabeth. 'Go and tell your husband that he's an arrant coward not to speak to me himself. Tell him that I will do anything in my power to help you get your son back, but that I also intend to discover who was behind my husband's murder, and I expect you both to do what you can to help me.' Elizabeth began to stutter her thanks, but Alyce waved her away, her mind still in confusion. She heard the door close and gazed out of the window again at the merry band of young Trevelyans.

Five minutes later, the door opened again. Alyce braced herself to confront John Trevelyan, but it was Joan who bustled in, chuckling.

'You won't believe this, Alyce,' she crowed. 'That old goat Harcourt actually had the nerve to propose that I accompany him across country to Fowey, then spend some time with him on his ship. Pigs might fly. Thank the Lord he's gone with Mohun.' Then she saw her friend's pale, drawn face.

'What's happened, Alyce? Have you had bad news?' Alyce nodded wordlessly.

Joan sat down beside her. 'What is it?'

'Lord Tiptoft was behind Simon's abduction. He must have an interest in the *Nicholas*. And the Trevelyans are in his pocket. He's taken their oldest son hostage to ensure they do as he says. Elizabeth has just begged me to find Simon's parcel for them so that they can use it to bargain for the return of their son. We're to ride there with them tomorrow at first light. At least Sir Reginald and Harcourt won't be with us. They'll still be on their way to Temple.' She saw concern replace Joan's smile. Then calculation. Then the smile returned.

'Tomorrow is Wednesday. That means we'll reach Tintagel on the same day as the players. Godith and Cabal and Tamsin and Wat will have joined them by now. Worry not, Alyce. Between ourselves and Godith we will contrive.'

Alyce looked at her old friend doubtfully. 'Three old hags against the world?'

'Four with Godith's sister Gwennol. From what Godith has told me of her, she'll make all the difference. By the way, Godith also told me that that godson of yours has been trying to seduce your little maid.'

'Will Stonor?' asked Alyce, shaken.

'Yes. In Exeter. In a corner of the battlements of Rougemont Castle. Godith was in a nearby turret, watching the sun set.'

'And?' demanded Alyce, heart in mouth.

'She ran away in tears, poor mite. Godith told me that he'd used both Tristram and Isolde and me and Lord Wenlock as examples of true love having its way. So I had a word with Tamsin later myself. I pointed out that she's at the start of her life, not making the best of its twilight as I do. And that Isolde was a character in a romance who came to a bad end. And that she'd lose your favour for ever if she gave way to his blandishments. I think she was persuaded, though she'll be heartsore for a long while. Nor will Master Stonor be approaching her again after the scolding Godith gave him. Except perhaps to say he's sorry.'

'Thank you, Joan. I feared that something was troubling her. I wish she'd confided in me. Why can't she fall in love with Ben Bilton? He couldn't be more suitable.'

'Alyce, that's exactly why she didn't confide in you. You know as well as I do that hearts have a mind all their own. Consider yourself.' Alyce turned away abruptly.

Joan decided to change the subject. 'Have you had any word from Ewelme?'

Alyce nodded. 'Bess sent a letter to Exeter by king's messenger that reached me just before we left. They're all well, but they were worried by my letter telling them of the ambush at Cadbury. Jack visited Bampton. Robert Hiat knows far too much, but he's on his last legs, sodden with strong liquor and willing to do anything for money. Jack acquired letters sent to him long ago by Oliver Roos, the rector of Wootton Glanville – that's the church in which Sybilla and I had Jack baptised. I had good reasons for thinking I could count on

Roos's discretion, but it seems that I was wrong. Hiat thought Roos was still rector. He easily could be; he was only thirty or so when we visited.'

'Was Jack going to Newton Montagu?'

'Yes. He left the day before Bess wrote. Taking with him little John, and a strong company. He thought it was a good opportunity to introduce him to the tenants, as I told him it was one of the manors I planned to make over to the boy for my lifetime. But I hadn't expected him to take the child on such a long journey. It's typically thoughtless and foolish. Perhaps dangerous.'

'I disagree. Taking little John with him was a good idea. If the rector has any heart, he might be moved by the sight of the boy. It sounds to me as if Jack's fulfilling your trust in him. As to danger, it's nothing like the peril you've put yourself in.'

Alyce coloured. Was Joan right? Had Jack's behaviour been a reflection of her own frequently voiced lack of confidence in him? But this was not the time or place for doubts. She was so near to the end of her quest for William's murderers. Discovering the truth of that awful crime would, she was sure, mend bridges between them for good.

There was a sharp tap on the door and Mattie came in, carrying a tray on which were two goblets and a bottle of canary wine.

'A happy thought, Mattie,' said Joan, eagerly reaching for a goblet. Ignoring her, Mattie filled the other and handed it to Alyce, then filled the bookseller's rather less full before going to make up the fire. Joan chuckled.

'I can see you're becoming as devoted to your mistress as Tamsin is. Rightly so. She's someone who'll stand by you through thick and thin.'

Mattie peeped mischievously round at her. 'Sorry, Mistress Joan, but I'm no Tamsin. I serve Princess Alyce just as I should do. But only for as long as it suits me. I was born fickle.' She scampered away before she could be berated. But Alyce only smiled wearily.

'At least she's honest. I've had enough of people seeming true.'

Tintagel

Wild weather swept over the company of players as they rode towards Tintagel early on Thursday morning. Wrapped in sheepskins, Godith and Tamsin wedged themselves among the stage properties in one of the gaily painted carts, and Wat perched on one of the horses hauling it, felted cap pulled down and hood raised. Cabal strode ahead, listening with a smile and total lack of comprehension to the animated chatter of Toby, a tiny Cornish juggler he was carrying on his shoulders. Nero Farthing, the master of the players, thought the contrast between their sizes would raise smiles and bring in spectators. Toby was holding a cloak over them both, shaking it occasionally to shed snowflakes.

At last, the snow stopped falling and the clouds parted to reveal a watery sun. Wat gave a whoop and pointed into the distance. Tamsin gasped. Spread before them in all its vastness was the sea. Something they'd both heard of but never seen. Long waves with curling white crests rolled in towards the land, and the air was full of the shrieks of gulls. And silhouetted on a craggy spur of land that jutted out beyond the village was a castle – semi-ruined but still formidable. The opening lines of the story Tamsin had begun to read three years ago in Doll's Oxford bookshop leapt to her mind:

> It befell in the days of Uther Pendragon, when he was king of all England and so reigned, that there was a mighty

duke in Cornwall that held war against him long time.
And the duke was called the Duke of Tintagel.

Tamsin stayed lost in dreams of hurtling knights and wily sorcerers and ships setting out to sail to Lyonesse until the cart in front of them slowed to a halt in the village. They had arrived at the Malthouse Inn. Its ostler came out to greet them.

'You've done well to reach us!' he exclaimed cheerfully. 'I'm Jim Perrin.' He showed them to a barn half full of bundles of straw. 'Let me know if you need anything. You can warm yourselves in the inn and get food from our kitchen. The pump is by its door. And no fires in the barn.'

'Where's the best place to put up our stage?' asked Nero. 'We'd like to give a performance this afternoon.'

'The troupe before you put theirs up over there, beside the market cross,' said Perrin. 'I told the stallholders to leave a space for you. Not that many of them are braving this weather. What are you playing? A legend of Cornwall? Something to make them laugh or weep will go down better than a holy mystery preaching pieties. Tintagel folk have a hard life; they prefer to be entertained rather than urged to mend their ways.'

'I can't blame them,' said Nero. 'This is the furthest west we've ever come, and I've never seen wilder country.'

'You were lucky to get here when you did.' Perrin nodded eastwards, where black clouds were massing ominously. 'We can be cut off for days here.'

A tall man in a hooded black cloak came up and scowled at Nero.

'I'm Oswald Marrack, reeve of Tintagel. 'I'll be keeping an eye on you and your thieving friends, so no picking of pockets or creeping into empty houses while folk are watching your pagan antics.' He began to walk away, then turned. 'Have you come from Camelford?' When Nero nodded, he went on. 'Did you see any other travellers on the road?'

Nero shook his head. 'We could hardly see the tail of the horse ahead. I pity anyone who's still on their way.' He turned to his players. 'Unload the cart and wheel it over to the market cross. Then fold out the stage sides and put the roof on as quickly as you can. The sooner folk see we're going to entertain them, the better.'

Marrack gave a grunt of disapproval and walked off towards the castle.

'Seems a mean-spirited fellow,' said Nero to Perrin, who nodded.

'But he's not a man to cross. Has the favour of the deputy sheriff Sir Reginald Mohun and Sir Patrick Tregoys, whose men are stationed up there, in the outer bailey of the castle.' He gestured to a castellated wall that towered above the track leading to the sea. 'It's the soundest part of the castle, except for the chapel out on what we call the castle island. Though it isn't quite cut off from the mainland.'

Tamsin listened with interest. 'Will Tregoys and his men be coming to the performance?' she asked.

'Sure to,' Perrin replied. 'Downing ale and throwing their weight about. We're thoroughly weary of their bullying ways.'

'How many of them are there?' It was Denzil. He and Gwennol had ridden unobtrusively into the village on a path known only to locals. Tamsin felt her heart lift.

'Half a dozen. And Tregoys and his squire. I must go and tell the taverner to prepare for a busy afternoon.' As he walked away, two voices chorused.

'Then that's our chance to...'

'Then we could go across...'

Denzil's and Tamsin's eyes met as both stopped speaking.

'You're of one mind, it seems,' said Gwennol. 'A sure sign you'll succeed.'

'I must go, as I know the way and where Brailles's evidences are,' said Denzil. 'But not with Tamsin. I need a fighting man at my back.' Wat stepped eagerly forward, but Gwennol shook her head.

'Better just Tamsin,' she said firmly. 'If they've left a guard there, you can pretend to be lovers, and will have a chance of bribing him to let you pass.'

Tamsin opened her mouth to protest, but Godith nodded her agreement. So, a little uncertainly, did Denzil. Sulkily, Wat retreated into the barn. There was another gust of sleety snow and they hastened after him into shelter. After unloading the cart, they took advantage of a break in the weather to drag it out and transform it into a gaily painted stage. Then they headed for the inn, where a rich-smelling fish stew bobbing with dumplings awaited them. They fell to eagerly, then returned to the barn to plan the afternoon's entertainment.

Rough voices sounded outside. Tamsin looked through the gap at the hinge of the barn door and saw half a dozen men in mailed doublets coming up the path from the castle's outer bailey. They disappeared into the inn.

'Shall we go now?' asked Tamsin, nervously.

Godith shook her head. 'No. Wait until the players start their performance. If they decide the weather's too bad, the guards might get bored and return.'

'I doubt they will,' said Denzil. 'The inn will be much

more welcoming than their chilly quarters. They'll stay there awhile whether the players perform or not. I think we should go straight away.'

'You're right,' said Gwennol. 'Tamsin, wrap this sealskin cloak of mine around you. The snow's lessening, but the castle island will be wet and windy. And good luck.' She raised her staff and sketched a complicated figure in the air. Godith watched them slip down the lane that led to the castle. She murmured a prayer under her breath and crossed herself. No harm in appeasing all the available powers that be.

Tamsin looked around to bid Wat farewell, but he was nowhere to be seen. Her father's motto 'Grab a chance and you won't be sorry for a might-have-been' beat in her brain as she followed Denzil, who led the way confidently, turning occasionally to make sure that she was close behind him. The path wound downhill at first, then climbed steeply up to a high walled passage with a gatehouse at its far end. One door gaped open.

'Looks as if they've all gone down to the inn,' Denzil whispered. 'But in case there's a sentry inside, I'm going to knock on that door. Get out of sight.'

Tamsin ducked into a coign in the wall as Denzil rapped his sword hilt on the door. Silence. He waited a few seconds, then gave another triple rap. After half a minute, he beckoned to Tamsin, and disappeared inside. She followed. They found themselves in a courtyard with a battlemented wall on three of its sides and a turret lookout in the north-west corner. There was a gate at the far end that must lead to the island. A stair immediately on their left led up to the soldiers' lodgings. Denzil went up cautiously and disappeared inside. After a few minutes, he returned.

'It all seems to be empty. We're in luck.' He headed for the gate at the far end. 'The island's this way.'

But when he turned its heavy iron handle and tried to open it, nothing happened.

'Locked, damn their eyes. And they'll have taken the key with them.' He looked at her appraisingly.

'How's your head for heights?' he asked. 'We'll have to take the cliff path that Simon took me along.' He led her out of the castle's outer ward and turned right to reach the narrow track close to its stone wall on the seaward side. She could hear surf crashing against the rocks far below. As they edged their way along it, Denzil took her hand. Instinctively, she withdrew it and almost immediately stumbled. He grabbed her just in time and gave her a shake.

'Have some sense, girl. I know the path. You don't. And I'd rather not lose you.' He took her hand again, and this time she left it in his until they reached the paved ridge that led across to the island castle.

'Mind you don't miss your footing,' he said. 'Would you like me to hold your hand as we cross?'

For answer, she set off alone. She'd show him that she wasn't a helpless ninny. But she'd gone barely twenty yards before her foot slipped, and she found herself face down on the ground. He helped her up, shaking his head but grinning broadly.

'Same old Tamsin. When will you learn to look before you leap?'

She brushed stones and sandy grit off her kirtle and smiled at him ruefully. But she set off on her own again, treading more carefully now.

He was about to follow when he heard a small sound. He froze. Silence. He looked back. There was nothing to be seen.

263

Probably just the scuffle of a rabbit retreating to its burrow. Treading warily and making as little noise as possible, he set out after Tamsin. At last they reached the arched entrance to the castle proper. Its door was also locked, but Denzil had seen where Simon Brailles hid the key. Counting three stones up and three to the left of the door, he found a crevice and felt the cold iron of a key.

As they let themselves inside, closing but not locking the door behind them, a dark shape rose out of the turret lookout on the wall of the mainland castle. Marrack the reeve stepped out from his hiding place and turned down towards the village. The last time he'd seen a light on the castle island, he'd waited until the morning to report it, and the birds had flown. This time he'd get the guards to return straight away.

Only steely determination kept Alyce riding through the snowstorm that blasted into their faces from the south-west. John Trevelyan and his men rode ahead. Beside her, Joan muttered profanities. Close behind them was Mattie, hunched miserably on a mule. Ben and Jem brought up the rear. Then, as suddenly as it had begun, the wind dropped and the snow lessened. A wintry sun appeared ahead of them, and in the distance they saw the high ragged outline of Tintagel Castle jutting into the sea. Alyce's heart sang. She had returned at last to the scene of the happiest, most hopeful days of her marriage to Thomas Montagu. The place where, nursing the joy of the child stirring inside her, she had asked him whether, if it was a boy, they could call him Arthur. She remembered him putting his arms around her and agreeing. 'Though I'd be as happy if it were a girl. This is only the first of the many children we'll have together, and there's nothing like an older sister to keep a man in order.'

Trevelyan's voice broke into her reverie. 'Just another couple of miles,' he called. 'That's Trevalga Manor down there.' He signed to his men to stop and pointed to the west. Half a mile away they saw a handsome two-storey stone house with short wings jutting forward at each side and a roof of stone slates. 'Do you want to rest for a while?'

'No,' Alyce called back. 'Let's make the most of this break in the weather. There may well be another storm on its way.'

Trevelyan sighed, and motioned his men forward. An hour later they reached Bossiney Manor. Sir John Basset and his wife Lady Emma had left a week earlier to spend the rest of winter in the milder climate of their winter home in the Fowey estuary, but the chamberlain had been given notice of their coming by a messenger sent the day before by Trevelyan. Every hearth in the thick-walled house held a well banked-up fire, and its low ceilings and small windows ensured much welcome warmth.

After a heartening noon meal of game stew, Alyce rested beside Joan on a thick feather bed under heaps of furs, hot bricks wrapped in flannel clutched to their chests. Her thoughts turned again to the past, to her first visit to Bossiney and the plans she and Thomas had made for a future that never happened. Now Joan rather than Thomas lay beside her, snoring contentedly. Alyce wished she shared her friend's exuberant acceptance of whatever life threw at her. And what, she wondered, were Tamsin and Godith and Cabal and Wat up to? If all had gone well, they would have reached Camelford a day or two ago. They might even be in Tintagel already. With a determined effort, she got out of the warm bed, and went to the window. The snow had stopped, and a watery afternoon sun shone through the ragged grey clouds. Then she heard trumpets blare and drums beat.

'Seems we're just in time,' said Joan, rising out of bed. She pulled on her boots and wound her riding turban around her head. 'Nero's players must be beginning a performance. Let's go and watch it.' They wrapped fur-lined cloaks around them, pushed their feet into high wooden pattens to hold their boots above the snow, and walked the short distance from the manor house to the market square, escorted by Trevelyan and his men. The first thing they saw was Cabal, with a tiny man standing on his massive shoulders juggling five brightly coloured balls. Distracted by their appearance, the dwarf missed a catch, and a red ball rolled to Alyce's feet. She picked it up, walked forward and handed it to Cabal, whose gaze met hers impassively, not even risking a wink. Before she returned to Joan's side, she scanned the faces of the other entertainers. No sign of Tamsin or Wat. But surely that was Godith sitting on the end of the cart, with a woman who must be her sister Gwennol beside her. Their eyes met, again without a flicker. Trevelyan and his men disappeared into the alehouse, and Alyce and Joan casually made their way towards the cart, followed by Ben and Mattie. Stools were hastily found for them and they settled down to watch the play. It was a knockabout farce, involving a puny St George screeching as he was trampled underfoot by three pairs of heavy boots sticking out from underneath the body of a much-patched green dragon, its hideous head belching clouds of flour.

🜚

Tamsin looked around the walled courtyard in which she and Denzil found themselves once they'd climbed to the summit of the island. On one side was a small chapel, and adjoining it was an even smaller building.

'That's Simon's lodging,' said Denzil, nodding towards it. 'He keeps the key to the chapel inside it. And its key should be...' He reached up above the lintel of the lodging's door and felt along it. 'Here!' he said triumphantly. He unlocked the door and they both stepped inside. It held only a narrow bed, an oak chest and a chair padded with a sheepskin. Tamsin thought of Simon's comfortable room in Ewelme Palace. Why on earth had he retreated to Cornwall?

Denzil saw the amazement in her eyes and chuckled. 'You're wondering why Simon gave Ewelme up for this. As I did when I heard. But, as you saw in Camelford, he's a changed man. Changed for the better, too.'

He bent down, felt between the head of the bed and its straw mattress, and pulled out another key. 'Now for the chapel – and the evidences.'

He led the way across the courtyard, unlocked the chapel door, and went inside. It was quite substantial, a church in miniature, with a short nave, a rood screen and a chancel. There were no windows on the north and west walls, where the worst of the weather came from. Light came from a slit on the south wall of the chancel and a narrow double-arched window on the south wall of the nave. A skilfully carved and painted wooden statue of the Virgin stood inside an arched wall shrine on the right-hand side of the altar. He went confidently to the small window above the shrine and tugged at its sill. The long flat stone slid out, revealing a hollow space. Which was completely empty. Denzil gave an angry curse.

'This is where he told me he kept them. But they're gone. Someone must have taken them. Saw him checking them one day, perhaps, and when he disappeared, came and took them. Only he and Morwenna knew where they were. Perhaps she told somebody...' He broke off, head cocked. 'What's that?'

Tamsin wasn't listening. She stared first at the sill, then at the little shrine, remembering the letter that Godith had been so interested in. What had Simon written? 'A secret between you, me and Our Lady.' What could he have meant by that? Surely somewhere that Alyce could guess at. Not a window sill – that must have been a false trail in case Caerleon couldn't be relied on. And he'd rededicated the chapel to Our Lady of Fontrevault. She walked over to the shrine and carefully lifted out the statue. She turned it upside down. It was hollow, and stuffed inside was a small, leather-wrapped parcel, bound with strong cord, its knots sealed. She drew it out and turned to hand it to Denzil.

He wasn't there. She tucked the parcel deep inside her bodice so that her belt gripped it, replaced the statue and pushed the sill back into place, then went out into the court- yard. A tall thin man with his back to her was shouting commands, and she could hear stumbling feet and angry oaths from men on the rough hillside. What to do? Then she remembered Godith's words. Thinking fast, she ducked into Simon's lodging, pushed her shift off one shoulder, lay down on the bed and pulled its coverlet over her just as the door opened and the man who had introduced himself to them that morning as Oswald Marrack came in.

'What are you doing on the island?' he demanded. Then his eyes narrowed. 'You're one of the players who came this morning aren't you? I remember your hair. I saw you and a man crossing onto the island. Planning a bit of nug-a-nug, were you? Was it Brailles or the other recreant? Where is he now?'

Tamsin pulled her shift back over her bare shoulder, let her lower lip wobble and stared at him vacantly, hoping to seem a simpleton. He gave an exasperated sigh and went out of the lodging.

'He's left his wench and gone,' she heard him shout. 'He must have heard us coming and taken the steep path down to the cove. Ten marks for the man who catches him.'

Tamsin peeped out of the door and heard the guards swearing as they slid and slipped down the precipitously steep cliff. Marrack watched them but did not follow. She wondered if she could make her escape, but he turned back towards her. She cringed away from him as he took off his corded belt. Seeing the fear in her eyes, he smiled unpleasantly, shaking his head.

'No need to fear me. Sluts like you are not to my taste.' He used his belt to tie her hands together behind her back, then took her arm and led her back through the castle bailey and down the track that led to the village.

The players had finished their performance and were enjoying the Malthouse's excellent ale. Tamsin looked around hopefully for her friends, but there was no sign of them. She felt very alone. Would Denzil be caught? she wondered. Where was the reeve taking her? And what on earth was she going to do with the parcel tucked into her bodice?

Then a voice called to her from the door of the tavern. 'Tamsin, what's going on?'

She turned and saw Sir John Trevelyan advancing on them. 'Marrack, you fool, why have you bound this girl's hands? She's Princess Alyce's personal servant.'

The reeve was unrepentant. 'I found her on the island with

one of the recreants Sir Reginald told us to look out for. It was either Brailles or the man who rescued him. Planning to have unlawful congress, they were. He ran away, but I'm thinking she can be persuaded to tell us where he's gone.'

Trevelyan looked at Tamsin. 'Is this true, girl? Who were you with?'

Unsure whether she was doing the right thing but recalling that Denzil had said he'd ridden to Tintagel with Trevelyan, she decided to tell the truth. 'With Denzil Caerleon, whom I think you know. He used to be Princess Alyce's man of business at Ewelme until...' She trailed away into silence as she realised that Marrack has spoken to Trevelyan as if he was confident that they were on the same side. Not Princess Alyce's side, or Denzil's, but that of Sir Reginald Mohun, who was hunting Sir Thomas Malory and Owen.

Trevelyan winked knowingly and began to untie her hands. 'I suppose you and Caerleon crept off alone to renew an old friendship, did you?'

She thought fast, then nodded, managing to look shame-faced and guilty.

He gave a laugh, elbowing Marrack in the ribs. 'But Marrack here barged in and spoilt your fun. Well, behave yourself in future. Or be more careful.' His eyes twinkled as he looked at her, and she remembered her mistress's fondness for him. And her recent doubts.

'And do you know where Caerleon went?' She shook her head. 'Then I'll take you to your mistress, who I'm sure will deliver the appropriate correction.'

'But Sir John, she might know where he and Brailles are hiding,' objected the reeve. 'Surely we should question her more severely.'

'Nonsense,' said Trevelyan. 'She's just a foolish girl. It's getting late. Too dark to hunt fugitives now. I'll take her back to Bossiney Manor.'

Newton Montagu

Jon Downton beamed at the distinguished company seated around his table, enjoying the venison roasted in their honour and a mighty boiled ham studded with cloves and soused in a sharp cherry sauce. The Duke of Suffolk himself and Lord Wenlock of Someries, one of the king's most trusted diplomats, were lodged in his house. Old John Newburgh, the squire of Glanville Wootton and his wife Isobel, the vicar John Legge, and the chantrist John Browne had been invited to dine with them. His son Francis sat proudly beside his new friend the young Earl of Lincoln, and Downton imagined Francis serving as his squire in a few years' time, just as that handsome young man Dick Quartermain was serving Duke John. Though, as his wife Edith had warned when he aired this dream to her before dinner, the de la Poles were a notably unlucky family, wealthy as the duke's mother was.

'Does your lady mother keep well?' Squire Newburgh asked Jack. 'I was away from home when she last visited – that was more than twenty years ago. A sad time for her, I fear. One of her companions fell sick of the ague and died. But that must have been before you were born.'

Jack glanced across at Wenlock, but he was deep in conversation with Edith Downton.

'Yes, it must have been,' he answered casually. 'This is my first visit to her Dorset estates.' He nodded towards little John. 'She has willed them to her grandson when he comes of age.'

'I trust he'll visit them more often than she has done,' said Newburgh. 'Fortunately, she has a good tenant in Jon Downton. He's done much to improve both land and manor house, and he's hoping that his own son will be allowed to continue in the tenancy after his own death.'

'I see no reason why he shouldn't,' Jack answered pleasantly. 'Little John has taken to him already. And Downton tells me that there's excellent hunting to be had in the Blackmore Forest.'

Towards sunset, the guests took their departure, and the retained men headed for the nearby tavern. Jon Downton and Edith disappeared with their children and the young earl. Jack and Wenlock were left by the great hearth in the solar, alone at last.

There was a pregnant silence. Then Jack spoke. 'Now, my lord, how did you know I was in search of anything?'

'As to that,' Wenlock temporised, 'when Dame Joanna told me that you were going to Newton Montagu to show your son his future inheritance...'

Jack interrupted him impatiently. 'My lord, I sense that you are not being honest with me. Very few people know the details of my birth, but one of them is Mistress Moulton. With whom I know you have long been intimate. But enough of that. I have accomplished what I came for. It is my business alone, and I trust and believe that you are my mother's well-wisher. Tell me about the dangers that have assailed her. Are they connected with her search for the truth about the death of my father?'

Wenlock swallowed. 'I fear that they are. Powerful interests want to prevent her getting the evidences that Simon Brailles purchased from the errant bosun of the *Nicholas of the Tower*.

My men and I were staying the night with the prioress of Amesbury, Dame Joanna, on our way to Southampton when letters reached me. One was from the king cancelling my mission to Calais, the other was sent from Exeter by Mistress Moulton and told of the misfortunes your mother's company has suffered. They were ambushed after visiting Stourton Park, and their cart wrecked. The stables of the Crewkerne manor house in which they were staying caught fire, and if it hadn't been for Joan's herbalist Godith's sharp nose they could have died. And in Exeter a runaway horse and cart careered down a steep Exeter street towards them, killing your mother's doughty old servant Joseph Pek.'

Jack felt horribly helpless. 'Who's behind this persecution?'

Wenlock hesitated. How much was it wise to disclose to Jack? He looked at him, considering. It was over a year since they'd met, and the young duke had changed remarkably. Fitter, slimmer and dressed much more soberly than he had once done at court, he showed every sign of turning into a redoubtable successor to his ill-starred father.

As he pondered the best course of action to take, Jack spoke again, unexpectedly shrewd eyes boring into Wenlock's. 'Tell me the truth, my lord. I've had enough of your diplomatic shilly-shallying. Who is behind it all?'

Wenlock decided to be uncharacteristically frank. 'Chief among them is the Earl of Worcester, Lord Tiptoft.'

Jack paled. 'But he headed the commission looking into my father's murder! Was he behind it? No wonder the recreants weren't found.'

'Tiptoft wasn't responsible for it, but he's intent on protecting the identity of those who were. And, though in Ireland, he's taken steps to do so.'

'How do you know all this?' said Jack suspiciously. 'Are you involved as well?'

Wenlock shook his head. 'I know your mother is in peril because Tiptoft sent word to me as soon as he heard that Brailles had seen the *Nicholas of the Tower* and bought information from its bosun. His letter said that he had put the matter in the hands of the deputy sheriff of Cornwall, Sir Reginald Mohun. A man with no scruples, who does whatever profits him most. His cousin is your mother's worst enemy, Sir Robert Harcourt. By ill chance, he too is in Cornwall. And I've placed your mother in further jeopardy by suggesting that Sir Thomas Malory accompany her. I knew that they would relish each other's company, but Malory was excluded from the king's general pardon. Sir Thomas is riding in disguise, but if his identity is discovered Mohun would be justified in arresting her.'

'So what do you suggest?'

Wenlock hesitated again. If he followed the course his heart advised, it was the end of sitting on the fence between York and Lancaster. He thought of the wine-sodden, overweight, philandering king that Edward of York had become, and of his devious and calculating queen, the serpent of division whose avarice had brought about the downfall of so many honest men. Then of King Henry, mild-mannered and pious, patiently enduring his imprisonment in the Tower of London. And his lively French queen and promisingly valiant young son, in exile in Lorraine. Henry of Lancaster now had a male heir to the throne, whereas Edward of York had as yet sired only daughters. Moreover, Lancaster was now backed by the mightiest noble in the land: Richard, Earl of Warwick, the Kingmaker, as he had been dubbed by foreign diplomatists. He made up his mind.

Tintagel

High above Tintagel on a bench in front of the old steading of Trehane, Malory, Simon and Owen were laughing over a game of knucklebones while Morwenna's uncle Philip sharpened a small armoury of axes, billhooks and knives in readiness for unwanted visitors. Suddenly Loki rose to his feet and gave three sharp barks. He stared seaward, stiff-legged and snarling. Simon selected a knife and braced himself for action – only to lower it in relief when he realised that it was Denzil who came stumbling towards them, soaking wet, clothes torn and flesh severely grazed.

'What happened to you, Denzil?' he said, taking his arm. 'Where have you come from?'

'The castle island,' panted Denzil, collapsing on the bench. 'Pray God I've not been followed.'

Alerted by Loki's barks, Morwenna came out of the house. She winced as she saw Denzil's cuts and grazes and went back inside. Malory followed her.

'Why were you on the castle island?' demanded Simon. 'Did you go to the chapel to get the evidences? I'm afraid you won't have been able to find them. They weren't where I told you. I... I wasn't sure that I could trust you.'

'No – I couldn't find them,' said Denzil. 'But if they were in the little statue of Our Lady beside the altar, I think Tamsin may have. She was with me in the chapel, and she had just picked it up when I heard voices and went outside. There were soldiers surging up the hill, led by a surly-looking man in a black gown. He ordered the men to arrest me, but I ran for the cliff and slid down it into the water. It was only chest deep, and by the time the men had made their way down a deal more cautiously, I'd reached the beach and scrambled up into the scrubland to hide. I lay low all night, then made my way across to Trevalga and back here.'

Morwenna came out of the house, carrying a bowl of water, a cake of soap and strips of cloth to bind up his wounds. What a practical young woman she was, Denzil reflected. No questions. Just action. Malory was behind her, with a hunk of bread and a cup of ale for Denzil.

'You were lucky the tide was in,' said Simon. 'Or you'd have broken your neck. The black-gowned man must have been Marrack the reeve. And, yes, the evidences were in the statue. I'd hinted at that in the letter I sent to Princess Alyce, which Tamsin would have read.' He groaned. 'If Marrack gets his hands on them, he'll give them to Mohun and they'll be destroyed.' He looked wanly at Morwenna, busily binding up a long gash on Denzil's arm. 'So much for all my hopes for our future together.'

'Let's not despair yet,' said Malory. 'I wouldn't be surprised if Tamsin managed to conceal them. She's a quick-witted young lady.'

'I wonder what's happened to her,' said Denzil.

'It's more than likely that her captors will have taken her to Sir John Trevelyan, as he's Constable of Tintagel,' said Simon.

'If he takes her to Lady Alyce, she'll be safe enough,' said Denzil. 'Whatever story Marrack trumps up against her.'

Suddenly Loki raced away from them. Owen ran after the dog as it loped towards the rough unmade road above the steading. Then he stopped, wagging his tail. Riding towards them were Godith and Gwennol. Behind them came Cabal and then Wat, leading a pack mule and looking utterly miserable.

'What news?' Owen called out. Loki was nuzzling Cabal's leggings hopefully. Cabal felt in his pocket, took out a lump of cheese, and broke a piece off for him. Then he sat down in the ground cross-legged and scratched him behind the ears in the spot that makes a friend for life of any dog.

Godith shook her head. 'Nothing good. Tregoys and his men are still quartered in the Tintagel outer ward, and we've no idea where Denzil is. Or whether he found the evidences. Though at least Tamsin is safe. From the tavern we saw Sir John Trevelyan free her from that death's head of a reeve's clutches and take her to Bossiney Manor to account for herself to Princess Alyce.'

'I'm here,' said Denzil, who had followed Owen and Loki. 'But I haven't got the evidences. We're hoping that Tamsin has.'

'I'm sure of it,' said Gwennol. 'The cards said she'd save the day. Who else is with you?'

'Sir Thomas, Simon Brailles and Morwenna. And Morwenna's uncle of course. But you look ready to drop. Come inside and warm yourselves and have something to eat. There's venison stew seething over the fire. Plenty for everyone.'

'We'd welcome something to eat,' said Godith. 'But we won't stay long. My sister and I are going back to Camelford. We've done all we can to help you. As for Cabal, he's so taken with his little friend Toby that he's decided to join the players for a while. Nero's eager to have him. They're going to put on a final entertainment in Bodmin, then return to Exeter for the Easter revels. But Wat insisted on being brought up here. He won't be content until he's with Tamsin.'

Denzil led them into the farmhouse, leaving Owen and Loki outside to keep guard. An hour later, warm and well fed, Godith, Gwennol and Cabal set off for Camelford. The rest of the company sat round the hearth, tucked into the venison stew in their turn, and made plans.

'Owen and I need to head across the moor to Lostwithiel,' said Sir Thomas. 'But first, as I'm so close to it, I'd like to walk the heights of Tintagel Castle again. It's likely to be the last time I ever do. Can we leave our horses here with you, Philip?'

Just then the door opened and Owen put his head round it. 'Come and see,' he said excitedly. 'Travellers on the road.' They followed him outside, careful to keep low so that they wouldn't be seen. Sure enough, a troop of horsemen could be seen far below, heading north.

'It's the Trevelyans,' said Denzil. 'There's Sir John. And Lady Elizabeth is at his side. And their retainers are with them.'

'But Princess Alyce and her company aren't,' said Malory. 'They must be staying in Bossiney. My guess is that she'll have refused to leave until she's visited the island, whether she has the evidences or not.'

'In that case we can all go to Bossiney,' said Denzil. 'I'm for setting off straight away.'

'Would that I could,' said Malory. 'But Sir Reginald Mohun could be there. He'll arrest me.'

'Suppose you and Owen go on foot to the castle island?' said Simon. 'With Morwenna as your guide. There's an old hermitage on its western slope. I rebuilt it and made it weathertight and fitted it out as a school. If you set off at dusk the tide will be low, and you'll be able to go up the steps to the island quay. From there you can get to the hermitage without being seen.

There's provender there too, as I also use it to store food. And the well isn't far away.'

'What about you?' asked Morwenna.

'It's time I paid my respects to my mistress,' said Simon. 'If Tamsin did manage to rescue the evidences, I'm eager to know whether they're all Madoc promised. So I'll go to Bossiney with Denzil. We'll take Sir Thomas's and Owen's horses with us and leave them in the stable of the Malthouse Inn for you to collect later.' A brawny young arm seized his, and he turned to see Wat's beseeching face.

He gave a grin. 'Wat will come with us, of course, and tomorrow, if we can, we'll bring Princess Alyce over to the island so that I can show her the school. And Sir Thomas can say farewell to her.'

'And...?' Morwenna asked in a shaky voice. Simon realised how anxious she must be. Was he going to acknowledge her? He took her in his arms. 'And I'll introduce you to her grace as the wife of my dreams,' he said, holding her close. Her face lit up, and she hugged him back. He turned to Malory.

'When we get to the island chapel, I'll blow my horn three times and Owen can come and find us. If you hear four blasts, stay in the school. It'll mean it isn't safe for you.'

Malory nodded. Owen and Morwenna gathered what they needed for the journey and they set off towards the coast in the light of the setting sun.

�֍

It was almost dark when Simon, Denzil and Wat reached Bossiney Manor. A tall man rose from his seat in the porch, raised a quarterstaff and called to them to halt.

'It's me, Jem,' called Wat. 'And Simon Brailles, back from the dead. And Denzil Caerleon, turned up like a bad penny.'

Jem Wingfield grinned. 'Good to see you again, lad. And you, sirs. You come at a time when we need every friend we can muster.'

They followed him into the manor, Wat and Simon eagerly, Denzil trailing behind anxiously. All his happy years of service with his former mistress and their easy-going comradeship rushed into his memory. So too did the terrible night when he had betrayed her trust and eloped with Marlene.

Alyce was seated on a settle by the hearth, Joan Moulton beside her. The scent of apples, cloves, ginger and cinnamon rose from the steaming cups on the low table in front of them, and an iron pan containing more of the mulled cider hung from the chimney crane. Alyce's face lit up at the sight of Simon, and she rose to greet him, holding out her hand for him to kiss.

'Simon! Praise God you're still alive for me to thank you for what you discovered – and your foresight in concealing it so cunningly.' She gestured to the parcel next to the cups on the table. 'Tamsin rescued it, and we're just about to open it. But where's Denzil? I have to thank him too, both for saving your life and for his letter alerting me to the Trevelyans' treachery.'

Simon bowed deeply, glowing with happiness at his welcome. He turned and waved Denzil forward. Alyce smiled a welcome, but quailed inwardly. She had longed to see him for so long that she had magnified him in her mind as a hero. Now here he was in the flesh, shabbily dressed, face tanned by sun and weathered by wind. He was smaller than she remembered, and thinner than he had been. But there was no mistaking the alertness of his carriage, the flash of joy in his deep-set brown eyes as he raised one eyebrow quizzically before he bent his head to bow.

She took a deep breath and managed a smile. 'Returned to the fold, have you, stranger?'

Straightening up, he gave her a similarly shaky smile.

'It is my greatest wish that you should never again consider me one,' he said. They stood in silence for a long minute. Then he turned to Joan.

'It's good to see you again, belle-soeur. And thank you for defending me against the world. Lord Wenlock has told me how stoutly you did so at the time of my disgrace.'

Joan rose and hugged him. 'We soon discovered that you were more sinned against than sinning. And you've performed adequate penance, to say nothing of finding a way of life that seems to suit you well.'

Denzil looked round the room. 'But where's Tamsin? We heard that Trevelyan brought her here. Wat is longing to see her again.'

'She's in front of the kitchen fire, bathing herself clean after her adventures,' said Alyce. 'When she comes back, we're going to open the parcel. I wish Sir Thomas were here too. He was in London at the time – a member of the Commons when William was accused of treason.'

'Malory was with us until lately,' said Denzil. 'But he thought it too dangerous to come to Bossiney. We saw the Trevelyans leave, but Tregoys and Mohun could still have been with you. He isn't far away, though – he had a mind to walk the heights of Tintagel again before he takes ship from Fowey. Simon's wife Morwenna has taken him there. And he's hoping that you'll be able to join them tomorrow.'

'Simon's wife?' gasped Alyce. She turned to her former

secretary in shock. Simon blushed, briefly thrown back to his old anxious self. Denzil grinned broadly.

'There's a lot about Simon that is going to surprise you, your grace. Cornwall has been the making of him. Hear him out.'

Simon squared his shoulders. 'Yes, my lady,' he said resolutely. 'My wife. Nor could I have found a truer soulmate.'

Alyce studied him more closely. Gone was his habitual uncertainty, his preference for not meeting her eyes. He had filled out and stood more upright. He looked in balance, comfortable with himself. But married?

'A *wife*?' she said in bemusement. 'But, Simon, you were to be ordained. Why have you ruined your life's chances by marrying? What will I do for a chaplain?'

Simon opened his mouth, then shut it helplessly. Nothing was working out as he'd hoped.

'Who is she?' Alyce continued. 'A connection of the Bassets of Bossiney? If she's of respectable birth, I look forward to meeting her, and to welcoming her at Ewelme when we all return. I'll give you a lay position in my household and a house of your own as a reward for finding the evidences.'

Simon hesitated. How was he going to tell his mistress that Morwenna was a village washerwoman who didn't know who her father was? And that she was already expecting his baby. Nor would she want to leave her beloved Cornwall. Nor, he suddenly knew for certain, would he.

Just then the door opened and Tamsin came in, her long chestnut hair left loose around her shoulders to dry, her face scrubbed and rosy. She gasped when she saw Simon, Denzil and Wat, then ran to Wat and hugged him. A rapturous grin spread over his face.

'So, you survived, Tammie?' said Denzil, smiling. 'And

here's your faithful squire to take better care of you than I did. Did your captors fall for your fine performance as my trollop?'

Still shaken by the idea of Simon having married, Alyce frowned. Tamsin had not gone into her adventure on the island in detail. How far had her trolloping gone? And since when had Caerleon called her Tammie, the pet name she said her brother had given her and that no one else was to use? Her heart sank as she realised, looking at them together, how well matched they were. Denzil was a soldier of fortune, not required to make a great marriage. And, after three years of Alyce's tutelage, Tamsin was a young woman of poise and character. Disillusioned about Will Stonor and with a love of adventure as great as Denzil's. If only she could have time alone to think over these unexpected developments.

Seeing Alyce doubly discomfited, Joan tugged at her friend's sleeve. 'Enough of greetings and revelations,' she said firmly. 'Let's open the parcel.'

She picked it up and handed it to Alyce, who took out her eyeglasses and put them on, then unwrapped the tarred cloth which had protected the evidences for so long. She unfolded a large piece of parchment that had been wrapped around a small scroll, a folded sheet of paper and a velvet drawstring bag. Carefully, she laid them out on the large table in the centre of the room. Tamsin, Simon and Denzil joined them, and Joan gave Jem and Wat a wave of dismissal, gesturing to the door of the buttery.

Jem gave her a grateful nod and tapped Wat on the arm. 'Time to wet our whistles, lad. Letters aren't our business. Let's join Ben and Mattie.' Wat gave Tamsin a last lingering glance and followed him out of the room.

The five of them bent over the parchment. It was a family

tree showing the children of King Edward III but the descendants of only three of them: his second son Lionel of Clarence, his third son John of Gaunt and his fourth son Edmund of York. The names of Gaunt's oldest son Henry IV, his son Henry V and Henry V's son Henry VI had red circles topped with crowns drawn around them, just as that of Edward III did. Three of Gaunt's descendants by his third wife Katherine Swynford had red squares drawn round them: thin squares around that of the oldest, John Beaufort, Earl of Somerset and that of Somerset's son John Beaufort, Duke of Somerset; a thicker red square round the name of the duke's only heir, his daughter Margaret Beaufort. Thin black squares were drawn around the names of Philippa, daughter of Lionel, Duke of Clarence, Anne Mortimer, Philippa's daughter by Roger Mortimer, and Anne's husband Richard, Earl of Cambridge, son of Edmund, Duke of York. There was a thicker black square around the name of Richard, Duke of York, son of Anne Mortimer and Richard, Earl of Cambridge.

'This has the look of old John Hardyng's work,' Alyce said. 'It reminds me of the simplified pedigree he made me of the Neville family. It shows Margaret of Anjou as King Henry VI's wife but doesn't show their son Edward, Prince of Wales. It must have been made before his birth in 1453.'

'And well before the death of Richard, Duke of York, in 1460,' said Joan, 'as it doesn't include his son, King Edward.'

'And before Margaret Beaufort married Edmund Tudor and had a son, Henry Tudor, in 1457.'

'What do the squares and circles and their colours signify?' asked Denzil.

Alyce studied them for a while. 'Circles signify crowned kings. Edward III and the three Henrys, all legitimate descendants of Gaunt. The red squares show the descent of the Crown via the Beauforts, but their claim is dubious. Though legitimised after John of Gaunt married their mother, they were barred from inheriting the throne. The black squares show the claim to the Crown through the daughter of Edward III's second son Lionel and the descendants of his fifth son Edmund of York. Lancastrians deem that inferior to that of Beauforts; Yorkists disagree.'

'It's all very speculative,' said Joan. 'How odd that despite Edward III having five vigorous sons, the choice of an heir to Henry VI before he had a son was between a female descendant from a bastard line married to his half-brother and a descendant via a woman and Edward III's youngest son. But it's no sort of clue to Suffolk's murderers. The Duke of York was in Ireland when William was killed and Margaret Beaufort was only eight years old.'

'But it is one of the evidences given to the *Nicholas*'s captain,' said Simon. 'We shouldn't dismiss it.'

Joan picked up a small scroll wound tightly around a wooden rod, then sealed. 'Whose device is this?' she asked, stroking the crest indented into the wax. Alyce examined the grid of tiny squares. 'A portcullis. That's Beaufort. Undifferenced, so it's the seal of the head of the family. Though which one, I wonder?' She turned back to the family tree and ran her finger down the descendants of John of Gaunt and his third wife Katherine, all surnamed Beaufort.

'The first Beaufort to adopt it was Gaunt's grandson John Beaufort, third Earl of Somerset. He was captured in France in 1421 and imprisoned for the next seventeen years. Hence the portcullis, the sort of grim joke heralds enjoy. When released, he fought in France again, was paid indecently well and given a dukedom. But he never had much success in the field. He made blunder after blunder, then returned to England in 1444. He was killed by a bull – or so the story ran. Some say he killed himself for shame. Suffolk was granted the wardship of his daughter, Margaret Beaufort…'

Joan broke in. 'Which led to all your troubles, Alyce, didn't it? William married her to Jack and boasted that their children would have a claim to the throne if King Henry died childless. My rascally husband Walter Caerleon told me that Suffolk was cock-a-hoop over it. He had the marriage formally celebrated, young as they were. And the most serious of the Commons' accusations against him was that he sought the throne for his son.'

Simon could see his mistress's distress and intervened. 'What happened to the Beaufort inheritance?'

'The estates and the Beaufort claim to the throne were inherited by little Margaret; the title by her uncle Edmund,' Alyce replied, relieved to return to safer ground. 'That's why her square is thicker.'

'Ah yes, Edmund,' said Joan reminiscently. 'A great man for the ladies. The word was he had an affair with Henry V's widow Catherine of Valois. Whose eldest son, supposedly by Owen Tudor, was christened Edmund.' She raised her eyebrows suggestively.

'But that was because Edmund Beaufort was his godfather,' protested Alyce. Then she thought of Marlene. Whose oldest son had been christened Richard, after Richard Harcourt, who had stood godfather to him. But who had also, she suspected, fathered him.

'After William's murder and the annulment of Jack's marriage to Margaret, Edmund Beaufort went to great lengths to get Edmund Tudor married to her,' Joan continued obstinately. 'What better match could he win for his bastard while King Henry was still childless? And, though Queen Margaret gave birth to a son in 1453, Margaret and Edmund Tudor's child Henry, quite possibly Edmund Beaufort's grandson, is now second in line to the Lancastrian throne.'

'And did Walter hear Beaufort boasting about that?' asked Alyce tartly.

'Of course not!' chuckled Joan. 'Edmund was far too canny to intimate that King Henry's mother had been his lover. Catherine's long dead now, of course. And Edmund Tudor died of plague before his son Henry Tudor was born.'

Alyce sniffed. 'Rumours were running riot in those days. Wasn't there one that said Edmund Beaufort sired Queen Margaret's son Edward?'

'They were certainly close,' retorted the irrepressible Joan, pouring all that was left of the mulled wine into her cup. 'Walter said that when King Henry heard that his queen was pregnant, he couldn't believe it. He muttered that it was a miracle and that the Holy Ghost must have been responsible. Then he fell into a trance for a year and half.'

'Anyway, all that happened after William's death,' said Alyce impatiently. 'It can't have had anything to do with his murder.'

She picked up the scroll, prised off the seal and unrolled a long narrow parchment screed. 'It looks like verse,' she said, moving a candle to shed light on the closely written lines.

'Tamsin, fetch some more candles,' said Joan. 'And then read it to us. Your young eyes will make sense of it.'

Tamsin brought over two sconces, each with three candles, and placed them on the table. She ran her eyes down the scroll. When she got to the end, she looked up, puzzled.

'It makes no sense.'

'Read it to us anyway,' said Joan. Tamsin began to read aloud, stumbling occasionally over ink-smudged words.

The Root is dead, the Swan is gone,
The fiery Cresset has lost his light.
Therefore England may make great moan
Without the help of God Almight.
The castle is won where care begone,
The Portcullis is laid down.
Enclosed we have our velvet hat
That delivered us from many storms brown.
The White Lion is laid to sleep
Through the envy of the Ape Clog,
And he is bounden that once our door should keep,
That is Talbot, our good dog.
The Bear is bound that was so wild,
For he has lost his ragged staff.
The Cart now is spokeless,
For the counsel that he gave.
The Lily is both fair and green,
The Conduit runneth not, as I ween.
The Cornish Chough oft with his train
Hath made our Eagle blind.
The Falcon flieth, and has no rest,
Till he wit where to build his nest.
RR

Joan blew out her cheeks and sighed, mystified. But Alyce looked thoughtful. 'It's the sort of thing that Sir Richard Roos enjoys composing.'

'You mean the sort of thing that nearly cost you and the Earl of Oxford your heads,' said Joan, irritated. 'The man's a menace. I remember him at court constantly making snide coded allusions to people's love affairs. Including Walter's with Monique.'

'This is rather different,' said Alyce. 'It's a list of those in and out of favour with King Henry. It begins by mourning the death of his old advisers. The Root and the Swan were Henry V's uncles: John, Duke of Bedford, and Humfrey, Duke of Gloucester. The Cresset was John Holland, the former Duke of Exeter. I think the castle "where care begone" is a reference to the fall to the French of Chateau Gaillard, Richard the Lionheart's beloved "saucy castle". "The Portcullis is laid down" is either a reference to John, the second Duke of Somerset, losing battle after battle or to his brother Edmund, the next Duke of Somerset surrendering Rouen, and giving up all of Normandy.'

'I can guess the "velvet hat",' said Joan. 'Cardinal Beaufort, his uncle. The ablest and wealthiest of them all. He bailed out King Henry time and again. Enclosed in his grave by the time Normandy was lost. "Talbot, our good dog" who was "bounden" is of course the Earl of Shrewsbury, taken hostage at Rouen in 1449. The "Ape Clog" is the device of your own husband, the Duke of Suffolk, always on the make. But who was "the White Lion"?'

'The Duke of Norfolk. The most violent and treacherous man I ever encountered,' said Alyce. 'He and William were ever at odds. But he left England on pilgrimage in 1449 to appease the king after he was accused of murdering one of our servants. He died in 1461 and left his son, a minor, in the care of John Wenlock. "The Bear" who "lost his ragged staff" is of course the Earl of Warwick, out of favour by then and soon to go over to the Duke of York's party. The "Cart"...'

Denzil intervened. '...is the device of the Duke of Buckingham, a vicious bully as I remember. Why is it called "spokeless"? And what was the "counsel" he gave?'

'Malory might know,' said Alyce. 'He was all but at war with Buckingham in Warwickshire in 1450.'

'Go on,' said Simon. 'Who does the "Lily" signify?'

'It's the device of Thomas Daniel of Cheshire,' said Alyce. 'He was a squire of the body, and a crony of John Trevelyan. There was much talk of his being corrupt, and he was an intimate of my husband. The "Conduit" is Sir William Norreys' father John, who was Queen Margaret's treasurer. What "runneth not" means I have no idea.'

'Perhaps it means that, unlike Daniel, he wasn't cheating the king and queen,' Simon suggested.

'Or that he was failing to do his duty,' put in Joan. 'Didn't he have special responsibility for the queen's jewels?'

'Put next to "The Cornish Chough hath made our Eagle blind", that sounds all too likely,' said Joan. 'Our "Eagle" must mean King Henry, And the chough is Trevelyan.'

'Yes,' said Alyce. 'I fear I was mistaken in Trevelyan. There were always rumours that he rifled the royal treasury.'

'What of the Falcon?' asked Tamsin.

'Cecily Neville's husband, Richard, Duke of York,' said Denzil. 'Sent to Ireland in 1447 to keep him away from the king. He returned in 1450 and was made Protector when King Henry collapsed in 1453. Then he went on to claim the throne. He'd have become king himself if he hadn't made a rash sortie from Sandal Castle in 1460 and been surrounded like a stag in a buckstall by Lancastrian forces. He died bravely but was cruelly defiled. His head was put on a spike over Micklegate

Bar wearing a paper crown. But his son avenged him and became King Edward IV.'

Alyce unfolded the third document. It turned out to be a bill of sale for the *Nicholas of the Tower*, dated Rochester, September 1450. It described it and its pinnaces, and the price paid by its new owners: Robert Wennington and John Jay of Wexford, merchants, and Sir Thomas Neville of Guernsey. The waxed seal hanging from it was indented with an *X*, overlaid from lower left to upper right with a wide groove.

'That cross is the Neville saltire,' said Denzil.

'Overlaid with a baton sinister,' said Alyce. 'Sir Thomas Neville is the bastard of William Neville, Baron Fauconberg. A great one for the sea and commander of his own fleet, harrying all the foreign ships he can. And occasionally English ones.' She gave a wistful smile. 'He came to our castle at Wingfield once. A very dashing young man.'

'What about that?' asked Mattie, pointing to the small drawstring velvet bag that had been at the heart of the parcel. Alyce loosened the drawstring and felt inside. She took out a chunky ring and a badge, both made of gold. On the badge was a beautifully etched dog, the crest of the Talbots. They all stared at it. 'Talbot again,' said Alyce. 'Does it mean the Earl of Shrewsbury was at the heart of the plot?'

'None greater than he,' said Joan, remembering their evening at Stourton Castle. She picked up the ring and studied it. 'This ring has a seal with a leopard mask inset.'

Alyce frowned. 'Great heavens,' she said, fumbling for her eyeglasses. 'Give it to me.'

She stared at the tiny snarling face. 'This is the ring William always wore on his forefinger. He never took it off. It was missing from his body when his remains were handed over to me for… for…' Her voice broke, and Joan put a sustaining arm around her. Recovering herself, she continued. '…for burial in his birthplace, in Hull.'

They gazed down at the curious collection. Alyce sighed. 'The answer must be here somewhere, but it isn't obvious.'

'Perhaps Malory will be able to shed more light on them,' said Joan. 'He's as well versed in noble connections as you are. And was in London at the time.'

Alyce brightened. 'So he was. And we can consult him tomorrow.'

Tintagel

Once they had broken their fasts, the little company assembled in front of the manor. The men carried swords or quarterstaffs taken from the manor's armoury. To override objections from Tregoys or his minions, Joan and Alyce had dressed to emphasise their station, Joan in a particularly richly embroidered crimson velvet gown, Alyce regal in a midnight-blue ermine-trimmed gown under her beaver-fur cloak and a ruby-studded gold coronet over her snowy white wimple.

'We can ride as far as the outer bailey, but it's only possible to cross to the castle island on foot,' Simon explained. They trooped off, led by Wat and Jem, each holding upright staves from which fluttered long pennants in Alyce's red and gold colours. Behind them, Denzil rode at Alyce's side, then Tamsin with Joan and Mattie. Ben and Simon brought up the rear. A quarter of an hour later they were at the entrance to the outer ward. Denzil slipped down from his horse and rapped the hilt of his sword against the door. It was opened by a wrinkled ancient with a broadsword hanging from his belt.

'What's your business?' he growled, then made a belated attempt at a bow when he caught sight of the pennants and of Alyce and Joan.

'We're crossing to the castle island,' said Denzil.

'Do you have permission from Sir Patrick Tregoys?' the gatekeeper demanded.

'I have no need of that,' Alyce declared in an assured voice.

'I'm Princess Alyce, aunt of the king and Dowager Duchess of Suffolk. I intend to pray in the island chapel.'

'I know nothing of you English or your here-today-and-gone-tomorrow kings,' countered the gatekeeper. 'Do you carry a token from Sir Patrick?' Denzil stepped forward, feeling in the purse on his belt as he did so.

'We would have brought one if we had seen him,' he said. 'As we didn't, perhaps this will prove our credentials. He handed the man a gold angel.

The gatekeeper's eyes narrowed, and he bit into the coin. Satisfied by its softness, he nodded his head.

'It does indeed, my lord,' he said with a gap-toothed grimace. 'I'll watch over your horses while you cross over. You can rely on me.'

Denzil rather doubted it, but at least they had gained access to the island. The wind whipped at their cloaks as they began to cross the narrow ridge, and spume tossed up from the surging waves below made them feel as if they were making their way through a cloud.

He waved Jem and Ben ahead in case they met resistance on the other side of the chasm; Mattie pranced after them, careless of risk, and Denzil turned to Alyce. 'Can I offer a steadying arm, your grace?'

Having seen how confidently Mattie was crossing, Alyce shook her head. But, after a few paces, her foot slipped on a smooth slab of rock wet with sea spray and she staggered, only just saving herself from falling. Like maid, like mistress, thought Denzil. He knew better than to offer his arm again unless she asked for it – which, to his relief, she did a moment later. He looked round to see Wat protectively close to Tamsin and Simon escorting Joan. Had they been foolish in bringing all these women? he wondered briefly. Still, it was too late to turn back. When they reached the heavy oak door of the island castle, Jem unlatched it, peered inside to make sure there were no guards, then motioned them onwards. Denzil waited until everyone was inside, then followed himself. No one saw a ragged urchin leave the mainland bailey and run down the hill to the village as fast as his legs could carry him.

Simon pointed uphill and led them up to the chapel on the highest point of the goat-grazed pastureland that topped the rocky headland. Its door hung crookedly open, one of its hinges smashed. Alyce walked down the nave to the tiny chancel. She stopped at the sight of an exquisitely carved wooden statue painted in a semblance of Our Lady of Fontrevault. Underneath it was the bold red shield and three lions passant of Eleanor of Aquitaine, Fontrevault Abbey's patron. So this was where Madoc's parcel had been hidden. Bowing her head, she murmured a prayer of thanks for its preservation. When she turned round, she saw Denzil waiting patiently, a look of affectionate respect on his face – or was it more than that? She remembered again how in tune his mind had always been with her own. Could she bear to lose him to Tamsin?

Blithely unaware of Alyce's thoughts, Denzil only saw that she had finished her prayer. 'Shall we sound the horn for Owen to take us to Sir Thomas?'

She nodded and followed him out of the chapel. The wind had strengthened even more as Denzil set his lips to his horn and blew three times. A few minutes later, Owen came hurrying eagerly towards them.

He gave Alyce a bow and nodded to Denzil and Simon. 'Glad you got here safely. We've seen no sign of anyone, only rabbits and goats.' He led the way past a well and a walled garden to a stone building, evidently recently rebuilt. Opening its door, he stood back so that they could go inside. It was divided into two rooms. The one they had entered had four small windows. Peering through one of them, Alyce saw a breathtaking view southwards along the coast. A long sloping shelf of wood ran under them, with six hornbooks neatly lined up along it and six stools tucked under it. On the walls were large whitewashed boards with the letters of the alphabet and the numbers from one to twenty carefully inked onto them. Another listed the seven deadly sins, and another the paternoster. Alyce smiled; it was a miniature version of the classroom in her school at Ewelme. She turned to Simon.

'You've returned to your old job of school-mastering, Simon. I recognise your careful lettering on the hornbooks.'

Simon shook his head. 'It isn't mine, your grace. It's my wife Morwenna's hand. She's been an apt pupil.' He walked across the room to another door. 'I expect she and Sir Thomas will be in here.'

The second room of the little building had been wainscoted and thick matting made of plaited rushes lay on its floor. A brazier of charcoal on the sill of its single window took the chill off its interior, but even so its two occupants kept thick rugs over their shoulders as they stood up to greet the newcomers. Alyce's pleasure at seeing Malory again was diminished by the sight of the girl beside him. Handsome enough to look at, but wearing a coarsely woven kirtle of blue serge and with hands red and raw from the harsh lyes used by washerwomen. It was instantly clear that she was no relation of the Bossineys. What a scrape Simon had got himself into, seduced by a young harpy on the make. He was as much of a fool as Denzil had been.

Joan also inspected Morwenna with interest, but she came to a different conclusion. She approved of Simon's choice. Despite her shabby gown and work-worn hands, the girl had an air of distinction about her, with a high forehead and bright, hopeful eyes. She held a stylus in one hand and a wax tablet in the other.

Malory stepped forward and bowed first to Alyce, then to Joan. 'I never thought that this would come to pass, ladies. Three lovers of the tales of Arthur together in his birthplace.' He looked past them and saw Tamsin. He gave a welcoming smile. 'More, in fact, for I know Tamsin also loves the tales, and so too does Morwenna here. I've been suggesting the best ones to teach her pupils when classes begin again at Easter.'

Simon looked proudly at Morwenna, then hopefully at Alyce. His mistress remained stony-faced. She realised that if Morwenna was planning to stay in Tintagel, Simon would be planning to stay with her, wasting all the scholarly talents he had acquired at Ewelme. She decided to change the subject.

'But where are Ben and Mattie?'

Simon was taken aback. 'I thought they were just behind us.'

Jem went outside. After a few minutes he returned. 'There's no sign of them. They must have lost us in the morning mist.'

'Queer shapes shift and shimmer in it,' said Morwenna. 'We call it *an Tullor*, the Deceiver.'

'I'll go and look for them,' said Simon. 'I'll take Wat. Jem, you stand guard.'

Malory turned to Alyce. 'Shall we go out as well, your grace? I'd dearly love to walk the heights of the island with you.' She nodded, and they followed Simon and Wat into the open air.

'Take that path, your grace,' said Simon, pointing westward. 'It leads to the best view.'

Malory offered his arm to Alyce, and they walked up to the smooth rock plateau at the highest point of the island. After gazing out to sea, they turned and took in the view to the east, past the tiny island chapel and across the water to the church of St Materiana, standing proud and visible for miles around. Alyce sighed.

'This is just where I stood forty years ago with my own Thomas, my second husband the Earl of Salisbury.'

'And where I first conceived the idea of writing a history of King Arthur when I was came here with my cousin,' said Malory. 'That too was some forty years ago. I planned for my history of Arthur to end here, where it began.'

'Why should it not?'

He shrugged. 'Some duty of observance to the old legends has made me have him taken not here but to Avalon, where a barge hung in black full of mourning queens takes him aboard and vanishes.'

'Perhaps they take him to Tintagel. Or Lyonesse. Isn't that one of the legends?'

'So's the idea that he turns into a bird. A Cornish chough.' He chuckled.

Looking up at Malory's lined, austere face, alight with amusement, Alyce recalled how much she had enjoyed his company on their journey. Joan had the right of it. She and Sir Thomas were well suited. But now he was planning to take ship from Fowey for France, and the chances were that she would never see him again. What a strange matter life was, she reflected. Full of the unexpected. Like Simon's marriage.

They stood a long while, lost in thoughts of bad choices

made, of roads not taken. Then Alyce shivered. 'It's time we returned to the school. As soon as Simon gets back with the wanderers, we should return to the mainland.'

Oswald Marrack watched with interest from behind a rock as the young man he had seen ride confidently into the village ahead of the Dowager Duchess of Suffolk and the Trevelyans two days ago led a slight figure muffled in a thick cloak along one of the maze of tracks made by the goats that grazed over the castle island. Where were they going? he wondered. Surely that was a wench with him? And what had happened to the rest of the company he had seen cross from the mainland and ascend to the chapel high above the castle? Perhaps these two had missed their way. He saw them reach a fork in the track, then hesitate. Then they set off southwards. Well, there was no escape that way, he knew. He turned back and saw a squad of armed men trudging up from the castle. After the gatekeeper's boy had brought news of the visitors to the island down to the village, Sir Patrick Tregoys had sent him ahead to reconnoitre while he took word to Sir Reginald Mohun, who had returned the day before from Bodmin with Sir Robert Harcourt and Guy Despenser. Mohun had evidently wasted no time in organising a pursuit. Marrack hurried down to meet them.

'Where are they?' shouted Mohun as he approached, his words torn away by the wind.

'They headed for the school Brailles runs on the west side of the island,' Marrack shouted, and pointed to the track past the walled garden.

'You'll be rewarded for this,' said Mohun, puffing from the uphill climb. 'How many were there?'

'Eight, but only six went to the school. Three of them women.'

Mohun smiled grimly. 'One of them no doubt her high and mighty grace of Suffolk. Where did the other two go?'

'They'd lagged behind. Looked like servants. One was a girl. I think they may have lost their way in the morning mist. They went off to the south. But there's nothing but sheer drops that way.'

'Perhaps they wanted privacy,' said Guy Despenser, giving his hips a suggestive thrust.

Mohun looked round at his men.

'Who else knows the way to the school?' Tregoys raised a hand.

'Good. You can lead us to it. We'll catch them like rats in a trap. Guy, you and Marrack go after the lovebirds.'

Despenser and Marrack set off southwards. The ten remaining men followed Tregoys, Mohun and Harcourt towards the school.

⁂

Malory and Alyce returned to the school to find Jem outside on guard and Denzil, Owen, Tamsin and Joan in the classroom sitting in a circle around Morwenna. Joan looked up.

'Come and join in. Morwenna's telling our fortunes.'

'Excellent,' said Malory. 'I'm eager to know mine.' He pulled out the last two stools and made way for Alyce to sit down.

She shook her head, frowning. 'Where are Simon and Wat? Did they find Ben and Mattie?'

'They aren't back yet,' said Joan. 'Come on, Alyce. Forget your high horse and sit down. You need to get to know Morwenna. She's sharp as a new-honed knife. I wouldn't be at

300

all surprised if she wasn't gotten by John Trevelyan before he married your cousin. She's got a remarkable look of him when she smiles. Clever of Simon to wed her. And even cleverer of Godith to have foreseen she'd taken his fancy when she read through his letters to you.'

Alyce had an irrational urge to snap back that she knew what was best for Simon, and it wasn't throwing himself away on a fatherless village girl, but she stifled it and sat down between Denzil and Malory.

Sensing her disapproval, Morwenna cleared her throat nervously. 'Hold out your hands, palms downwards.'

Alyce had always been proud of her slim fingers, and her hands were as shapely and graceful as ever. But she was sharply aware of the contrast between their prominent veins and wrinkled knuckles and Tamsin's unlined hands, a little roughened by hard work but small and strong and practical. Denzil's were burnt brown by the sun and scarred. Malory's had long sensitive fingers. Joan's flesh bulged out between her rings.

'Now turn them over,' commanded Morwenna. They were presenting their palms to be read when there was a commotion above them and shouts. They froze. The door crashed open and the triumphant faces of Mohun and Harcourt peered in at them. Mohun raised his eyebrows in mock surprise.

'Your grace!' he said with a sneer. 'We seek traitors to York. I did not expect to find you. Though Harcourt insists to me that you are numbered among them, when proof is found.' A few minutes later, the room was packed with jostling bodies. One man held Jem's limp form.

'Leave that churl outside to recover his wits,' Mohun said, looking around the room. He nodded at Joan. 'We meet again,

Mistress Moulton. Sir Robert has told me that you are not averse to dealing in illicit literature. Can it be that you are also guilty of treason?'

Joan drew herself up haughtily. 'Perhaps you should ask my patrons that. Among them are Queen Elizabeth's brother Sir Anthony Wydeville, the king's brother the Duke of Clarence and indeed King Edward himself.'

Mohun grunted and turned away. He stared searchingly at Malory and Denzil, then addressed Alyce again.

'Why don't you introduce me to these men, your grace?'

Before she could reply, Harcourt spoke. 'No need for introductions, Sir Reginald. I know exactly who these men are.' He pointed to Denzil. 'This is Princess Alyce's former steward Denzil Caerleon, a villain and a seducer.' Then he turned to Malory. 'And this is the Lancastrian traitor Sir Thomas Malory.'

Mohun grinned in triumph. 'Is he indeed? I trust that you had no idea of this, Princess Alyce?'

Harcourt snorted. 'Of course she knows who he is. Your squire Guy Despenser told us that they travelled together to Exeter, telling tales of Arthur every night.'

Malory stepped forward. 'I'm certainly Malory of Newbold Revel, and proud to be him. But you're mistaken in thinking Princess Alyce in the wrong.' He tapped his cloak badge. 'My squire and I are retainers of Lord Wenlock, who has always been a good lord to me. He is doing what he can to get my plea for pardon accepted, but in the meantime suggested I join Princess Alyce on her Cornish journey. Nor have the charges against me been proven.'

Mohun hesitated, knowing of Harcourt's hot-headedness and aware that in accusing Princess Alyce of treason he was acting well beyond Tiptoft's instructions. He decided to prevaricate. 'We'll wait on Guy's return. Doubtless he'll be able to clear the matter up.'

'First I'd like you to clear up the matter of your abduction of my servant Simon Brailles on Candlemas Eve.' It was Alyce's voice, authoritative and angry. 'On whose orders was it done?'

Mohun hesitated again. 'I have no knowledge of your servant's whereabouts,' he said at last. 'I heard he was dead.'

'Far from it,' said Alyce crisply. 'He was rescued from an Irish island by Denzil Caerleon after your men hit him over the head and stranded him there.'

Mohun resorted to bluster. 'Madame, these matters need to be considered by men of greater authority than myself. I'm concerned for your well-being, as I am sure your royal nephew would be if he knew that you and this bookseller who claims him as a patron were roaming the Cornish wilderness with such a small company. As I said at Whalesborough, I'll escort you to Restormel, where you will be safe and comfortable and the justices can be consulted in the court sessions at Lostwithiel. We'll overnight at Bodmin, and I'll keep Sir Thomas under close guard until we reach Restormel.'

Joan saw Sir Thomas stiffen, and decided to cause a distraction. With a sigh, she slid off her stool and onto the floor. Tamsin rushed to her side, bent over her and felt her neck for a pulse as Farhang had taught her. Then she looked up.

'She's fainted.'

'No wonder, with such a crowd of people around her,' said Alyce, realising that this was a time for tactical capitulation. 'Sir Reginald, it suits us well to go to Lostwithiel and consult the proper authorities. I've nothing to fear, and I welcome the additional security that your men will provide.

Perhaps they could begin their service to us by carrying Mistress Moulton up into the fresh air. I'm sure that will revive her.'

Mohun counted them out as they surfaced. 'One, two, three, four, five, six. And when Marrack and Guy return with the lovebirds, we'll have eight of you. Just as Marrack said.'

Tamsin was puzzled for a minute, then realised that Mohun had known nothing of the two members of their company already on the island, or of Morwenna's presence there. She walked beside Joan, who was being half carried, half dragged, between the two strongest of Mohun's men. Joan's eyes had flickered open once they were in the open, and she had given Tamsin the ghost of a wink before closing them again. As the dispirited company slowly made their way back to the mainland, the clouds thinned, the wind dithered to a breeze and the sun shone brilliantly.

Malory walked by Alyce's side. 'I fear I have imperilled you,' he murmured. 'Harcourt has the right of it. As a wanted man, I should never have joined your company.'

'I understood the danger,' she replied in a low voice. 'And I'll never regret a moment of the time we've been able to spend together. I've thwarted Harcourt before, and I'll do so again.'

He chuckled. 'Bravely spoken.' Looking around the crest of the island, he sighed. 'I wish we'd had more time here. To linger and dream.'

'What are you whispering about?' growled Mohun.

Before either could answer, a distant scream sounded from the far south of the island. Everyone froze.

'Who was that?' demanded Mohun.

'Only seabirds,' said Tregoys. But then came a series of shrieks fading horribly into silence.

'That was no seabird,' said Mohun. 'And where's that girl going?'

Alyce looked round to see Morwenna racing away, fleet-footed as one of the island's goats.

Harcourt shrugged. 'She's not important. Just a village girl by the look of her. Let's keep moving.'

❀

Blinded by the mist, Ben and Mattie stumbled on across the uneven pasture, pitted with rabbit burrows and stone rubble. The goat track they were following was so narrow that he walked in front, leading her by her hand. The sound of the crashing waves grew louder, and he slowed cautiously, not wanting to step over the edge of the cliff. Which, if an extra strong gust of wind had not blown the mist away, he would have done. The track had petered out into a patch of grass cropped smooth by the goats and the rabbits. They were on the brink of a sheer drop. There was no sign of the companions they thought they had been following.

'We're lost,' said Mattie despairingly. 'What shall we do?' Ben looked round and saw a tall standing stone with a fallen one, bench-like, beside it.

'Sit here and rest, Mattie. I'll see if I can find a track that looks worth following.' He left her and walked warily along the edge of the cliff. At last, he found a path of sorts and followed it away from the precipice. After thirty yards or so, it forked. He hesitated, then decided to take the path that sloped slightly upwards in the hope of seeing where they were, but he had only taken a few steps along when he heard voices approaching. He retreated to the ancient stones where he had left Mattie, but there was no sign of her. Desperately, he looked for cover. There was a cairn of stones at the point at which the path forked. He crept back to it and crouched, making himself as small as he could, his hand on the hilt of the short sword that hung from his belt. Two men came out of the mist, one in the livery of Reginald Mohun, the other in a long black gown. Ben recognised Marrack the reeve, who had been presented to Princess Alyce after they had arrived in the village.

'We've missed them,' said the liveried man in a voice Ben knew all too well. Guy Despenser. The smooth-talking snake who had seduced Mattie and betrayed them all. Who could, come to think of it, have started the fire at Crewkerne Manor that had almost seen his mistress and the other womenfolk burnt alive. And who Tamsin had seen watching Joseph Pek fall under the runaway cart on Stepcote Hill.

'We'd better separate,' he heard Despenser say. 'I'll go this way and you go that.'

'I'd rather we stayed together,' the man with him answered nervously. 'I've got no weapons.'

'Spineless coward,' growled Despenser. 'You've got a dagger. If you find them, grab the wench, hold it to her throat and shout for me.'

He must have given the still protesting man a shove as Ben heard him stumble and gasp. Then he saw his head pass by along the path he'd planned to take. Which meant that Guy would take the one Ben had come by, the one to where he had left Mattie. What to do? Follow Marrack and reduce the fighting odds against them, or follow Guy in case he found the frightened girl? Easy. Warily he raised his head. No sign of either man. Treading carefully, he stole after Guy.

But when he reached the great upright stone and its fallen

fellow, there was no sign of either of them, only the crash of waves on the cliffs below, and the ceaseless howl of the rising gale which was blowing away the thick mist. Bemused, he walked round the tall stone – only for a jagged stone hurled by Guy to hit his forehead at close range. He tumbled to his knees, blinded by blood running into his eyes. Raising his hands to wipe it away, he saw Guy striding forward, drawn sword in his hand. He groped for his own, but knew he was too late. Guy raised his arm to strike – only to be blinded as a cloak flew down and over him, then flattened by the small, determined body that followed it. Ben got to his feet, pulled Mattie out of the way and ran the point of his sword into the man struggling to untangle himself. It was not very chivalrous, he knew, but then he was no knight. Nor had Guy shown any sign of giving him time to recover before running him through.

'Look out!' Mattie's shout made him spin round – to see Guy's companion creeping towards them, dagger in hand. When he realised he'd been seen, the man turned and ran blindly away along the track Ben knew led only to a sudden drop. They heard a desperate scream, wavering into a series of shrieks. Then there was only silence. Ben dragged Mattie's cloak away from Guy's body, wrapped it around Mattie and held her tightly to his chest until her sobs subsided. Then he took her hand and led her away from the still body of her betrayer.

The wind had blown the mist away and the whole of the summit of the island was visible now – as was a procession of people in the distance. Ben ducked down flat, pulling Mattie down beside him.

'Why are we staying hidden?' she whispered. 'Isn't that our company?'

'Yes, but look – they aren't alone. There are guards in front and behind. They must be Sir Reginald's men. Let's keep down until they're out of sight. Then we'll go the way they came from. It'll lead to the schoolhouse Owen was taking us to. Hopefully we can shelter there.'

They watched as the long procession disappeared into the island castle, then emerged on the ridge to the mainland.

'We should be safe now,' said Ben. 'Mattie, that was bravely done, throwing your cloak over Despenser, then leaping down on top of him. How on earth did you get to the top of the stone?'

She gave him a cheeky grin. 'I'm an acrobat, remember. I can climb like a squirrel.' Then her face grew grim. 'And I relished revenging myself on Guy.'

He took her in his arms and hugged her. 'You can forget him now. If you'll let me, I'll bide by your side for good.'

Her face lit up with joy, then darkened as suddenly. She pulled away from him, shaking her head miserably. 'You wouldn't offer me that if you knew that in my belly I have a brat who could as well be Guy's as yours.'

He stared at her, blinking as he took in her meaning. Then, impulsive as ever, he took her in his arms again. 'It's you I want, Mattie. I'll take on this baby as joyfully as I will our future ones.'

As if in approval, the last of the mist blew away and sunshine poured out above the low bank of cloud that hedged the mainland's horizon. Clasping her strong little hand firmly in his, Ben led her to the westward side of the island, where they came to a low stone building.

'This must be the school,' said Ben, opening its door. Inside they saw chaos: stools fallen on their sides and writing tablets lying broken on the floor.

'It looks as if there's been a struggle,' said Ben. 'Or else wanton destruction.'

'What's through that door?' asked Mattie.

Ben went to the door and lifted its latch – only to be bowled over as a muscular young body cannoned into him, fell on top of him and began to strangle him.

'Ben!' Mattie screamed and began beating her fists on the attacker's back. To her surprise, he promptly let go his hold and stood up.

'Ben? Is that really you?' It was Wat's voice. Ben staggered to his feet, gasping for breath. Then another figure stepped out of the second room, and he recognised Simon. Behind him was a girl.

'Wat and I went to look for you when we realised you weren't with us,' said Simon. 'But then we saw Sir Reginald and his men being led to the school by Marrack the reeve, so we lay low. They took the whole company away. We decided the best thing was to go back to the school. Then we heard you coming, so we went into the inner room. We thought some of Mohun's men had returned.'

Ben rubbed his neck ruefully. 'Well, I'm glad I wasn't one of them.'

Simon took the girl's hand. 'Ben, this is Morwenna.' He paused, then added with a glow of pride, 'She's my wife. She was being led away with the others, but she made a break for it, and fortunately they didn't bother to chase after her.'

'Good for her,' said Ben. 'She's as bold as Mattie here – who I plan to make *my* wife. What do you think we should do now?'

'Sir Reginald will probably take Lady Alyce and her company first to Bodmin then to Lostwithiel along the Saints' Way,' said Simon. 'But it'll take him some time to organise such a journey. I think we should go in front of them and take any opportunity that offers to rescue at least some of them.'

'Suppose we joined up with the players?' suggested Mattie. 'Cabal will be with them by now. Denzil told me that he was going to join them in Camelford and go with them to Bodmin.'

Simon reflected for a moment, then nodded. 'That's a good idea. We can wait until dusk, then take the path to the haven and make our way east through the Trewarmett woods to Camelford.'

'As long as I find Tamsin again,' said Wat.

Bodmin

It wasn't until Monday morning that they set off from Tintagel. Alyce had piously declared to Mohun that she could not travel on a Sunday, earning her company a welcome day of rest – and giving Owen a chance to retrieve Tricksy and Hades from the Malthouse Inn. It was late afternoon before they reached Bodmin because Alyce had also demanded horse-drawn litters for herself and Joan Moulton. Uncertain of the fate of Ben, Mattie, Wat, Simon and Morwenna, she decided that the more time the young people had to get away safely the better. Although the snow had given way to fine, crisp weather, there were still high drifts on each side of the road across the moor, and she was grateful for the protection provided by the curtains of the litter and the furs she could heap around and over herself. Nones was being rung for afternoon prayers as Mohun ushered the company, prisoners in everything but name, into the great hall of St Petroc's Priory. The monks had already dined, but Prior Vyvyan ordered the cellarer to rouse the kitchen to provide for the unexpected guests.

As they sat down to eat, Harcourt advanced towards them, followed by a serving boy carrying a platter of salted codlings fried in butter and sprinkled with dried tansy petals. 'Sustenance well suited to delicate appetites,' he boomed, and pushed himself into the almost non-existent space between Joan and Tamsin. 'Tansy is excellent for the digestion, I believe.'

The stench of his ale-soaked breath made Tamsin gag and after a few minutes she excused herself, muttering about seeing to the disposal of their baggage. Wishing she could do the same but knowing it would be tactless, Joan forced herself to give Harcourt a warm smile, which had the unfortunate effect of making him move closer to her. What I do for a friend, she thought to herself as she pierced a juicy codling cheek with the tip of her knife and flirtatiously raised it to Harcourt's wet lips. He swallowed it, then belched. To her relief, Alyce chose this moment to call across the table to Mohun. 'If you've no objection, Sir Reginald, Sir Thomas has offered to read his latest tale of Arthur to myself, Mistress Moulton and my senior servants. Is there a warm room we could retire to? And would you both like to join us?'

As she had predicted, Mohun gave a snort of amusement at the idea of listening to Malory read. He shook his head. 'I've no interest in fanciful legends. Nor has Sir Robert. Why don't you ask the prior if you can use his private parlour? He said he'd show me and Harcourt the new church they're building before it gets dark.'

Alyce looked across at Prior Vyvyan, who nodded. 'Of course, your grace. I'd be honoured. There's a good fire there.' Harcourt hesitated, uninterested in architecture and suspicious of any private conference between Alyce and Malory.

Mohun took him by the arm. 'Come on, Sir Robert. After we've admired the church, the local tavern will provide more cheer than this joyless monastery.'

⚜

Once they had settled themselves in the parlour and the prior had retreated, Alyce took Madoc's parcel out of the pocket in her sleeve and spread its contents out on the table. Malory picked them up one by one. First, he looked at the family tree.

'The circles and squares are easily explained. Circles for kings, squares for the descent of a claim to the throne; red for Lancaster, black for York. The thicker ones show the nearest heir to the throne at the time this pedigree was drawn.'

'That's just what we thought,' said Alyce. 'Speculations that assumed that King Henry would have no children and that the Beaufort claim, for all their being barred from the succession, was superior to that of York. Which York would of course dispute.'

Malory took up the bill of sale. 'Robert Wennington and John Jay of Bristol and Thomas Neville of Guernsey. Sealed with the Neville saltire with a baton sinister. That's the device of Thomas, Bastard of Fauconberg. He has a fleet of warships which sails the coast as far east as King's Lynn and as far west as Dublin. He could well have acquired an interest in a ship like the *Nicholas*. I wonder who the former owners were.' He turned the bill over. 'Ah. Here they are. Thomas Courtenay, Earl of Devon, Henry Heydon of Rochester and…' He stopped, his eyes wide with shock. Swallowing hard, he read out the last name. 'Sir John Wenlock of Someries.'

Joan felt as if a chill fist had gripped her heart. 'John Wenlock? Are you sure? Where is that written? There was nothing there when we looked at it in Bossiney.'

'We didn't turn it over,' said Alyce. 'We just read the front, looked at the seal, then opened the velvet bag. This changes everything.'

'Perhaps. Perhaps not,' said Malory. 'We need to hear Wenlock's side of things. What else was in the parcel?'

Alyce handed him the scroll of verses. 'This was sealed with

313

Beaufort's seal, but the verses are surely by Richard Roos. I understand the coded allusions, but I don't understand what some of the comments refer to.'

After fingering the portcullis seal thoughtfully, Malory unrolled the scroll and read aloud. When he reached 'The Cart now is spokeless', Alyce interrupted.

'Buckingham's device is the Cart of course. But what does "spokeless" signify? And what was "the counsel that he gave"?'

'Well... from the reference to "the envy of the Ape Clog", it's clear that this was penned before your husband's fall. As to Buckingham being judged spokeless, he was in Wales so perhaps it means that any advice he had to offer King Henry was ineffectual – he wasn't in London when Suffolk was arraigned. So, much as I hated him, I can't see how he could have been an active mover in your husband's downfall.'

He studied the verses again. 'The White Lion. The Duke of Norfolk, my liege lord. He married his son and heir to Talbot's daughter.'

Alyce grimaced. 'Elizabeth Talbot. A vexatious piece of work who keeps her husband on a very tight rein. She's certainly no friend of mine. But she was only eight in 1450.'

'God's wounds!' Joan exclaimed. 'We've been forgetting the women. We of all people! Remember the old proverb: "The man is the head of the family, but the woman is the neck; she turns the head." Suppose the wives took action rather than their menfolk? Talbot and Edmund Beaufort were on pilgrimage at the time of Duke William's murder, but their wives were at court. Sisters, daughters of the legendary Sir Richard Beauchamp. They were as fond of books as their father was. They often visited the Sign of the Mole.'

Alyce nodded slowly. 'And as prone as their husbands to

demand respect of high rank. They looked down their haughty noses at William and me, grandchildren of a merchant of Hull and a baseborn poet who made good through marriage.'

'Are they still alive?' asked Tamsin.

Joan shook her head. 'They both died two years ago of the plague.'

'Then their secrets died with them,' said Malory.

Joan was enjoying the idea of women's involvement. '"The Falcon flieth and has no rest." York was in Ireland of course, but where was his wife Cecily?'

There was an appalled silence. Then Alyce said, 'Surely she was with him in Dublin. Her son George was born there in October 1449. And York didn't return to England until September 1450, five months after William's murder.'

'Cecily might have returned to London earlier than he did, though,' said Joan. 'And what about her sister Anne, the Duke of Buckingham's wife? They had a house in Bread Street then. She's very fond of books; she's still a good customer. And her husband resented Suffolk's closeness to King Henry.'

Malory looked daggers at her. 'Duchess Anne would never stoop so low.'

Alyce remembered the intensity with which he had spoken of his love for Buckingham's wife when they were riding along the River Parrett towards Montacute Priory.

'She might not have been aware of Buckingham's purpose,' she said tentatively. 'A wife has to carry out a husband's commands. It could merely have been a matter of passing on sealed letters.'

'What about the Bastard of Fauconberg?' said Tamsin. 'Perhaps he too had a wife in London.'

Malory shook his head. 'He was married to a Guernsey girl.

A pretty one too. I visited the island seven years ago after his father Thomas Fauconberg bailed me out of Newgate. Nor would he have anything to do with such a cowardly plot. And buying an interest in the *Nicholas* after Duke William's murder doesn't mean he had anything to do with it.'

Alyce clutched at the straw of hope his words offered. 'Perhaps Wenlock didn't know that his ship was involved in the murder. Perhaps he was abroad, as he so often is. Did you question him about it, Joan, as I asked you too?'

'I asked him, but he was his usual secretive self,' said Joan miserably, a catch in her voice. 'He muttered something about royal business.'

Malory picked up the velvet bag and took out the golden badge. He gave a gasp of surprise. 'Talbot, by the Rood. I can't believe he was involved. He was a fierce, hot-tempered man, but ever the soul of honour.'

'Then why was his badge included in the evidences?' said Joan.

Malory shook his head in bemusement. 'I served under Talbot at Gisors in 1436. He was resolution incarnate. We took that supposedly impregnable castle in less than a week.'

'Could it signal his wife, Margaret Beauchamp?' said Alyce. 'As Joan said, it may well be that women were the moving spirits in the plot against William.'

'She was certainly at court then,' said Joan. 'A redoubtable lady. John used to tell me tales of her battles with the Berkeleys. They sacked her son's manor at Wootton-under-Edge, and she came to appeal to the king. Suffolk gave her short shrift, apparently.'

'So she might well have had a grievance against him?'

Malory took up the story. 'Soon after his death, she sent

her son Viscount Lisle to lay siege to Berkeley Castle. It was something of a scandal that no action was taken against him after he sacked it, but as the son of the great Talbot he was high in royal favour. And that of Henry's new chief adviser, Edmund Beaufort.'

'What became of Viscount Lisle?' asked Tamsin.

'He left to join his father in the defence of Aquitaine a year later. And died with him there.'

'A dead end, then,' said Denzil ghoulishly.

Malory frowned at him. 'They were the finest men of their age. Their defeat meant the loss of France.'

He felt in the bag again and took out the gold ring.

Alyce winced. 'That was my husband's ring. Stolen from his corpse no doubt.'

Malory stroked the tiny leopard's head, then put on his eyeglasses and examined the ring's inside face. 'Whose are these initials?' he asked. '*CR* prettily interlaced with *EB*.'

'Give it to me,' said Alyce peremptorily. She stared at the initials, mystified. 'I'd no idea they were there. William never took it off his finger. He called it his luck. It was given to him by his sister Katherine, Abbess of Barking.'

'May I?' asked Joan, and Alyce handed it to her. She turned it round and round. 'Given the other evidences, it seems likely that *EB* stands for Edmund Beaufort. Everything points to his involvement. But I can't think of anyone with the initials *CR*.' She put it down on the table.

Owen, who had been examining each of the evidences as Malory laid them down, picked the ring up. 'Perhaps *CR* stands for Catherine Regina. My grandmother always used to say that the dowager queen had a high-born lover. This could be the key to his identity.'

Joan's ribald allusion to Edmund Beaufort as Catherine of Valois's lover suddenly replayed itself in Alyce's mind.

'Suppose the queen's marriage to Owen Tudor was a face-saver?' she said slowly. 'And that Edmund Tudor *was* Edmund Beaufort's bastard and was given the ring by his mother before she died in 1437? Edmund and his younger brother Jasper were put into the care of Abbess Katherine, who had long been a faithful friend to the queen. He could have presented it to her when he left the abbey. Suppose she realised the significance of the initials inside and explained it to her brother, my husband, when she gave it to him?'

'Or perhaps the queen gave the ring to the abbess herself,' said Joan. 'Whichever way it happened, having the ring gave Duke William a hold over Beaufort which enabled him to win the wardship of Margaret Beaufort and marry her to his own heir, Jack. Signing his own death warrant in the process because Beaufort wanted a quite different future for his niece Margaret – marriage to his illegitimate son Edmund Tudor, giving their children a claim to inherit the throne.'

Malory nodded. 'Which their son Henry Tudor has, although nothing is likely to come of it now that King Henry has a sixteen-year-old son, a vigorous lad by all accounts, who is said to talk of nothing but chopping off the heads of his enemies. And though King Henry is a captive in the Tower of London, the boy is safe with his mother in Lorraine.'

'But second in line is close indeed in these uncertain days,' said Joan. 'Wenlock told me before he left Ewelme for London that with two potential heirs, King Henry has never been nearer being restored to his throne.'

'I'm in a muddle,' said Tamsin. 'I don't know enough history.'

Joan smiled sympathetically. 'You aren't the only one. Far

too few of us know enough about history. Nor is what we're saying history; it's just guesswork.'

'But if our guesswork is right, it was Edmund Beaufort, Duke of Somerset, who engineered William's nemesis,' said Alyce hesitantly.

'Where is he now?' asked Tamsin, who had been studying the family tree. 'This doesn't show him at all.'

'That's because it only shows direct heirs, and Edmund was a younger brother,' said Alyce. 'He replaced William as King Henry's chief adviser, but he was killed five years later in the wars between York and Lancaster. At St Albans, when the Yorkists captured King Henry.'

Malory was looking thoughtful. 'So if you ask the all-important question, *cui bono?*, who benefited most from William's death, it was Somerset.'

'I never dreamt of suspecting him,' said Alyce. 'When the commons were clamouring for me to be deprived of all I had, he supported my cause with King Henry, and made sure I kept both my lands and wardship of Jack.'

'You were fortunate indeed that Jack fell in love with Bess of York,' Joan said meditatively. 'Had he not, you would never have kept your estates after the cause of Lancaster was lost in 1460 and her brother came to the throne.'

'So perhaps there's more behind the Harcourts' attacks on you than avarice,' said Malory. 'They've always been allies of the Beauforts. They want to bring you down in case William told you the truth of Edmund Tudor's parentage.'

'And Harcourt is still obsessed with doing so,' said Joan. 'When I was flirting with him at Whalesborough he told me he'd every hope of getting you convicted of treason. He sent his ship the *Peacock* to Fowey without him so that he could join Mohun in hunting Sir Thomas down and proving you knew who he was.'

They were still gazing at the scattered evidences when there was a sharp rap at the door. Alyce quickly gathered them up and slid them under a cushion on the settle, then pushed the ring onto her own finger and tucked Talbot's badge into her pocket. Sir Reginald entered, glancing suspiciously around.

'Not retired yet? Malory's tales must be good if he's kept you listening·this long. Or...' He took in their flushed faces and Tamsin's hurried arranging of the cushions on the settle.

'Or are you concealing weapons under those cushions?' He walked over to the settle and tugged them away. He picked up the evidences in triumph.

'These I think are what I was instructed to find and destroy. Without them nothing can be proved.' He tossed them into the fire, picked up a poker, and spread glowing embers over them. The wax seals sizzled fiercely, and flames leapt up, eagerly consuming the tinder-dry documents. He watched them shrivel to ashes, then strode out of the room.

Mesmerised, Alyce watched the precious evidences burn. She remembered just such a blaze in the hearth of her solar at Ewelme three years ago – and Joan's words as she threw the proof of John's birth into the flames: '"What's found is history. What's lost is mystery." Jack isn't the first and he won't be the last convenient arrival for a dynasty. Far greater families than yours have found an unofficial way of continuing their line. Lancaster among them, in all probability.'

Turning William's ring round and round on her finger, she remembered Joan's ribald allusion not just to an affair between Edmund Beaufort and Catherine of Valois but to a later affair altogether, one between Edmund Beaufort and

Margaret of Anjou. One that gave Henry VI an heir he thought miraculously begotten by the Holy Ghost.

'Of course,' she thought to herself. 'This has all been about bastardy. Not just Jack's, but that of both the Lancastrian heirs to the throne. She remembered her father, by then Cardinal Beaufort's right-hand man, saying that the Beauforts would triumph in the end. 'They aren't fighting men,' he'd said. 'But they've got the brains to make their way, by hook or by crook.'

Trewarmett Woods

'I can't walk another step,' groaned Mattie, and sat down on a snow-covered rock.

'Pick-a-back?' Ben offered. She brightened and sprang up.

Morwenna nudged Simon. 'Me too?' she said hopefully. 'Let's see which of us can go the fastest.'

Not a good idea. Within minutes, Ben was sprawling on the slushy track and Simon cannoned onto him and Mattie. Giggling, they sorted themselves out and proceeded more cautiously.

'Let's sing a song,' said Mattie. 'How about "Judas and Wenceslas"?'

They were happily carolling when Wat, who had been acting as rearguard, caught them up and grabbed Ben's arm.

'Shhh,' he warned. 'I can hear riders behind us.' They stopped abruptly, and the girls slipped down to the ground.

'Into the wood,' said Simon. They made their way through the frosty undergrowth and crouched down. Soon they all heard horses' hoofs and the jingling of harness. And, disastrously, the baying of sleuth hounds.

'Pray God they don't have a scent for the dogs to trail,' whispered Simon. 'Quick, Ben, let's lift the girls up into that tree.' He pointed to an ancient oak with enough low branches to allow Mattie and Morwenna to climb high into its bole. Hearts in mouth, the three young men watched through the gloaming as half a dozen horsemen trooped past, followed by a dog-boy with three reddish-brown hounds with drooping lips and long ears, their noses snuffling the ground as they loped along. Suddenly one bayed with excitement and almost tugged its lead out of the hand of the dog boy. He braced his feet firmly on the ground, hauled the dog back, and shouted to the leader of the riders. 'He's picked up a scent, Sir Patrick.'

'Let him go, then.' Tregoys called back. To the fugitives' horror, the hound came slobbering through the undergrowth towards them. Ben raised his sword, but then lowered it. Killing a knight's hunting dog carried serious penalties, and they were in enough trouble already. The hound reached them, and came to a halt, sniffing and dribbling over their garments, then passed on to the foot of the oak tree in which the girls had taken refuge. Stopping, it raised itself on its back legs, and put its forelegs as high as it could reach, scrabbling with its claws and whining for a few seconds before confidently giving tongue.

Within minutes, they were surrounded. Tregoys stared at Simon with recognition.

'So here you are, Brailles. Mohun will reward me generously for tracking you down. Tell whoever's up in that tree to come down. If the dog's to be believed he's Guy Despenser's murderer.'

Ben's heart sank. Mattie was wearing the cloak she had thrown over Despenser to blind him – the cloak through which Ben had stabbed him. It was still stained with Guy's blood.

He stepped forward, head held high.

'The honour of killing Despenser fell to me. It was self-defence.' He touched his hand to the scabby gash on his forehead. 'He hurled a rock that knocked me out, and if Mattie – she's the girl up the tree – hadn't thrown her cloak over him, he'd have run me through. His blood is still on her cloak; that's what your hound has scented.'

'So how came it to be there?' snarled Tregoys. 'Did she stab him?'

Ben shook his head. 'I did,' he said defiantly. 'And he richly deserved to die.'

He was still ashamed that he had denied Guy fair combat. But his head had been swimming with pain and he'd known the other man would return any minute. And in his own mind he was sure that Guy had been behind both the fire at the Paults' Crewkerne manor and the runaway horse that had killed Joseph Pek. He opened his mouth to explain, then closed it again. There was absolutely no likelihood that Tregoys would believe him.

'And what about Oswald Marrack?' said Tregoys. 'His body was found at the foot of the cliffs. Which of you pushed him over the brink?'

'He ran away when he saw Guy was dead,' said Mattie, dropping down from the oak tree. 'On a goat track that led nowhere. We heard him scream, but we had nothing to do with his death.'

'Unlikely,' scoffed Tregoys. He turned to Ben. 'You chased him, didn't you? I'm going to arraign you both for murder.' He turned to his men.

'Take his sword and bind his wrists behind his back,' he ordered. 'We'll take them both to Lostwithiel for judgment.' His men stepped forward to do so, but Simon stepped forward.

'Wait, Sir Patrick. Ben Bilton is steward to her grace the Duchess of Suffolk and a man of honour. I'm sure he'll give his word not to escape. He'll have had good reason for anything he did, and he deserves a fair hearing in her presence.'

As he spoke, Morwenna dropped down from the tree, and put her arm round Mattie.

'Mattie is also one of Princess Alyce's servants,' she said. 'She too deserves a fair hearing.'

Tregoys considered his options. Princess Alyce was not only the mother-in-law of King Edward's sister but a lady of legendary wealth. She was likely to give him a generous reward for treating her servant well. Mohun's reward for capturing the murderer of his squire would be miserly in comparison. 'So be it,' he said, mentally doubling his likely reward from Alyce. 'I'm taking you all to Lostwithiel. We'll get some more horses from the Trewarmett Inn.'

Ireland

Twelve-year-old Lionel Trevelyan was kneeling in front of Sir John Tiptoft and slathering his knee-high leather boots with a paste made from tallow, wax and fish oil to ensure they were waterproof, when the door of the chamber crashed open. He looked round in surprise, then delight spread across his face.

'Father!' he exclaimed, jumping up eagerly. Then he remembered his duty and crouched down again to finish his task.

Tiptoft looked up from a letter that had arrived late the night before by a special courier.

'Trevelyan, by all the saints! What brings you to Wexford unannounced?'

Managing to quell the impulse to hug Lionel, Trevelyan gave Tiptoft a respectful bow.

'Urgent developments, my lord,' he said. 'I judged it best to bring you the news myself. Princess Alyce insisted on going to Tintagel to search for the parcel that Madoc gave to Simon Brailles before the harbour master…'

He hesitated, looking down at Lionel. Tiptoft finished the sentence for him. 'Before the Welshman fell into the sea after a Wadebridge brawl. So where's her grace now?'

'Sir Reginald and Sir Robert Harcourt are escorting her and her company to Lostwithiel. Harcourt is insisting that she be tried for treason, as according to Mohun's squire Guy Despenser she was travelling with a known outlaw, Sir Thomas Malory. Who they also have under arrest.'

'Do they have the evidences with them?'

'Probably. My informant Sir Patrick Tregoys thinks they do, but doesn't know for sure.'

Though outwardly unmoved, Tiptoft was seething with anger. If Alyce had studied Madoc's evidences, then she would have discovered the plot he had managed to keep veiled in mystery for almost twenty years. He cared little for its perpetrators, but the reputation of the Talbots would be dragged in the mire, a mighty house undeservedly dishonoured by a scoundrel and a bevy of conniving women. Two lines from Alyce's grandfather's *Tales of Canterbury* beat in his brain.

Though hidden for a year, or two, or three,
Murder will out: that is my conclusion.

He looked at Trevelyan. 'I fear your friendship with her grace will not survive the revelations in those evidences, Sir John.' He waved his letter. 'Lord Wenlock has told me of your part in Suffolk's downfall.'

Trevelyan paled, and nodded miserably. 'He, more than anyone, knows the truth of the matter.' Then he rallied. 'My lord, I have had a thought. Nothing matters more to Princess Alyce than her relationship with her son. She might be minded to remain silent if it was in his interests that she did so.'

Tiptoft considered, recalling the contents of Wenlock's letter. How extraordinarily shrewd Trevelyan was. Though knowing little of the facts of the case, he had put his finger on the heart of the matter: the need to trade one secret for another, Talbot for Newton Montagu.

'It could well be,' he said thoughtfully. 'In any case, you and I must make haste to join them in Lostwithiel. Tomorrow, your ship can take us to Wadebridge, where we can hire fast horses for the journey. We'll arrive on Friday, God willing.'

'Can… can Lionel come with us?' Trevelyan asked. Tiptoft was about to refuse when Lisbet touched his arm.

'Why not, John? The boy's been desperately homesick.'

Looking down at her, and mindful of his hope that the child she was bearing would at last provide him with an heir, he relented.

'Very well.'

The Saints' Way

Reinforced by another eight men-at-arms, Mohun's cavalcade trooped out of Bodmin. The snow had cleared, and the sky was a brilliant blue. Alyce decided to abandon her litter and ride alongside Joan's. She found her friend depressed and silent, a state so unusual for her that Alyce couldn't help smiling.

'What are you grinning about?' Joan snapped. 'Here we are under armed guard, heading for trial for harbouring an outlaw. It doesn't just concern you and me. The others have also been in his company.'

'It all depends whether my guilt can be proved,' put in Malory, who had spurred forward to reach them. 'I've suggested to Mohun and Harcourt that we break our fast at St Benet's Abbey, in Lanlivet. It's early to stop, but we'll eat better there than anywhere else on the road to Restormel. They have a pilgrim's hospice, so they can cope with our numbers, and Father Solomon at Temple told me that the abbey's cook is renowned for his delicacies.'

Joan brightened, as she always did at the prospect of good food. 'Good idea. It's high time we had a squadron meal.' She looked up at Alyce. 'You did tell me we'd suffer privations on our journey west, but I didn't realise we'd be living on pottage.'

Father Solomon had been right about the talents of the St Benet's cook, but Alyce had little appetite for his pork, chicken and ginger pie and honey-sweetened bone-marrow custard.

It was served with a cider that made their heads spin as they took to the road once again.

The next part of their journey was the loveliest. A straight track ran along the backbone of a ridge. Beaten smooth by countless herds of cattle and flocks of sheep, as well as the feet of pilgrims, it wound around a high tor, once an ancient encampment and still fortified by massive stones.

Tamsin looked up at it longingly. 'I expect you can see for miles from up there.'

'Let's go and find out,' said Denzil. 'May we, your grace?'

Alyce considered. The more slowly they journeyed, the more time it gave the missing members of their company to catch them up. On the other hand, she was bone-weary, and longed for the famed comforts of Restormel. The decision was made for her by the sound of a horn. Three long blasts. Mohun had told his page to call the *arrêt*.

'Time for easement,' he announced. 'We'll stop for an hour.'

The men in front of and behind them dismounted. Some merely turned their backs, others disappeared behind rocks and bushes.

Alyce called to Mohun. 'These two have a mind to climb the tor. I give my word they'll return when your page sounds the horn for us to ride on again.'

Mohun sniffed. 'Rather them than me. But they'll need an escort.' He motioned to two of his men to go with them.

Alyce nodded at Tamsin and Denzil. 'Up you go. And look out for anyone following us.'

Pulling her skirt up through her belt to give herself more freedom, Tamsin scrambled eagerly to the top of the tor, and found a huge flat rock to perch on. Denzil climbed up beside her. Their much less agile escorts clambered up more slowly, stopping twenty feet or so below them to sit down and swig ale.

The view was staggering. Immediately below were the pits and waste mounds of tin-streamers, who worked the land for its rich ores. To the east was a tall church tower, and beyond it a startlingly white circular keep, rising above a walled bailey crowded with buildings.

'That must be Restormel,' said Denzil. 'The Black Prince's famous White Castle.'

'Who's the Black Prince?' asked Tamsin.

'Who *was* he, rather,' Denzil answered. 'Edward III's oldest son, Earl of Cornwall, and the greatest paladin of his age. For tournaments he wore black armour and carried a black shield with three white ostrich feathers. White was his other favourite colour. Get Malory to tell you some of the tales about him.'

Beyond Restormel was a township that straddled a river, which widened as it wound down to the sea, where a curved bastion formed a well-protected harbour. In it was a forest of masts and sails.

'By the Mass, Warwick's fleet has arrived!' Denzil exclaimed. 'His authority as Admiral in time of war easily overrides that of Mohun as deputy sheriff. But it means I'll have to abandon you all. As soon as I let him know I'm here, he'll summon me back to my ship.'

'What about Lady Alyce and Malory?' said Tamsin. 'Could – would – Warwick use his authority on their behalf?'

'I don't know,' said Denzil. 'We'll find out in time. But I rather doubt it. No one knows for sure where Warwick's sympathies lie. He's as hidden a man as Sir John Wenlock. Once he was all for York, but rumour has it that he's lost faith in him. If he's beginning to favour Lancaster, then both Malory and Lady Alyce could have a chance.'

They turned round and looked to the west. In the distance they could see the sea beyond Wadebridge; closer by was the stumpy tower of Lanlivet Abbey. And below them, winding in and out of sight on the track they had come by, a dozen or so horsemen.

'Look! Riders not far behind us,' said Tamsin. 'And isn't that a girl riding pillion behind one of them? It could be Mattie.'

'And there's another girl, behind the next horseman,' said Denzil. 'Perhaps it's Morwenna.'

They heard the horn again, the rapid blasts of the *réchasse*.

'They're preparing to mount up,' said Denzil. 'We'd better get back.'

As soon as they were on the move again, Tamsin told Alyce and Joan about the riders behind them.

'There are two girls with them. So it could be Simon, Ben and Wat with Morwenna and Mattie. But they aren't alone. It looks as if they're under armed escort.'

Ahead they saw the lofty, pinnacled tower of a church, and soon they were riding into a village.

'This must be Lanlivery,' said Joan. 'The abbot of St Benet's said it has the highest church tower in Cornwall and an excellent tavern, the Crown Inn. And that behind it is a well holy to St Brevita, patron saint of women travellers. Two good reasons to call a halt again.' She called to Mohun.

'Sir Reginald, her grace and I could not ease ourselves decently at the last halt, and we require refreshment. Moreover, her grace has it in mind to send up a prayer at St Brevita's Well.'

Harcourt gave a snort of impatience. 'This is absurd, Mohun. We won't be at Restormel until nightfall at this rate.'

Mohun shrugged. 'We can't deny our distinguished charges any reasonable request. And, for my own part, I'm chilled to the bone. I wouldn't mind warming up in the Crown and drinking some decent ale instead of the sour stuff in my flask.' He signed to his page, who blew the notes for a halt once again.

The Crown Inn was every bit as good as the abbot had promised, but when Alyce asked the way to St Brevita's well, the alewife warned them that it was sadly neglected.

'There are so many shrines to saints in these parts that folk forget the nourishing of their souls in favour of nourishing their bodies in my inn,' she said as she ladled hot broth into bowls and mulled ale into wooden tankards. 'And who can blame them when it's as cold as this?' She waved at the icicles hanging from the roof of a nearby barn. 'I'll get my scullion to show you the way.'

She went back into the kitchen. When she re-emerged she was dragging a skinny urchin by his ear. 'Take these ladies to Bryvyth's well, Ulf. And don't let them step in the mire.'

The path to the well was trodden hard, not just by human feet but by the hoofs of horses and cattle. The well house was a high rounded hump, thick with ferns and hung around with votive offerings. Around its stonework plinth was a boggy morass. Ulf beckoned to them to follow him, then skirted the sea of mud until he came to a place where stepping stones led to the open mouth of the well house. An image of a hooded woman holding something in her arms had been carved into the stone on its right-hand side. Joan grimaced.

'This is close enough for me. I'm sure St Brevita will be able to hear my prayers from here.' She muttered for a while, then tossed a penny into the darkness. They heard a tiny splash.

'That's cheating,' said Alyce crisply. 'You need to be touching

St Brevita's feet for your prayers to work.' She put her foot on the first stepping stone, which wobbled perilously. Ulf grabbed her arm and pulled her back to safety, shaking his head. Alyce was about to protest when they heard the jangle of harness and the sound of horses' hoofs.

'That must be the band of riders I told you Denzil and I saw from the top of the tor,' said Tamsin. 'With two girls who could be Morwenna and Mattie.'

'Let's go back to the tavern,' said Joan.

'First I want to leave an offering to St Brevita,' insisted Alyce. 'We need all the help we can get from the saints.'

'Then let me take it for you,' said Tamsin. Alyce felt in her girdle pouch and handed her a few pence, and Tamsin set off across the stepping stones. She had just reached the lip of the well when a dark shape hurtled towards her, only to slip on the wobbly first stone and fall face-down into the mire. When it raised itself, wiping mud from its eyes, nose and mouth, Tamsin could only laugh as Wat looked adoringly up at her.

They returned to find Morwenna and Mattie sitting with Simon and Ben at a table outside the tavern. They jumped to their feet, as Alyce advanced with an eager smile, only for Joan to pull at her sleeve, pointing to the tavern. Mohun and Harcourt were coming out of the inn deep in conversation with a third man. They came towards her.

'Your grace, can I present Sir Patrick Tregoys?' said Mohun. 'He has apprehended four of your servants. Two of them admit that they caused the death of my squire Guy Despenser, and Tregoys believes they are also guilty of the murder of Tintagel's reeve, Oswald Marrack. He's bringing them to Lostwithiel to stand trial.' Tregoys. The name rang a distant bell in Alyce's memory. Where had she heard it before?

As he bowed, Harcourt stepped forward. 'I've been up the church tower,' he said. 'There's a splendid view of Fowey harbour. The Earl of Warwick's fleet has arrived, and so has my own ship, the *Peacock*. My banner far outdoes any other in size and colour.'

'It's less than three miles to Restormel,' said Mohun. 'We'll be there for vespers.'

Two hours later, as dusk was falling, the company rode over a drawbridge and through the gatehouse of a moated and walled bailey the size of a small village, then across another drawbridge and up through a second gatehouse into the magnificent white-painted keep of Restormel Castle. Mohun had sent harbingers to warn of their arrival, and the smell of roasting meats made their mouths water as they passed the kitchen on their way to the chapel to give thanks for their safe journey.

After vespers, the castle chamberlain showed Alyce, Joan and the three girls to a spacious guest chamber, one of a series of rooms in the circular attic storey that ran round the keep. As his knightly rank required, Malory and his squire were also given quarters in the attic storey, but the rest of their company were taken down into Restormel's notorious dungeon.

Tamsin went to a window and leant out. Looking right, she could see over the bailey, busy as a disturbed ant's nest as quarters were found for Mohun's and Tregoys's retainers and supplies sent up to the keep. Looking left, she saw the far away masthead lanterns of the ships massed in Golant and Fowey. Well, she reflected, she was certainly having an adventure. Though it might well turn out to be her last one if Princess Alyce was convicted of harbouring a traitor, as Harcourt intended. Would she too be deemed guilty? And what was the penalty?

Lostwithiel

The Duchy Palace was the crowning glory of Lostwithiel, Cornwall's capital. Built two hundred years ago by Edmund, Earl of Cornwall, and spreading over two acres of the town, it was the headquarters of his administration and exchequer, housing a great hall and ancillary lodgings, the shire court, an office for maritime affairs, the stannary hall, which administered Cornwall's tin industry, a smelting house, the coinage court and a prison.

Alyce shivered as Sir Reginald Mohun escorted her into the courtroom. It was both grand and gloomy, with a high hammer-beamed roof from which hung three cartwheel chandeliers and a succession of triple lancet windows around the walls. At the north end there was a high dais on which was placed a judge's chair of state. In front of the dais were long desks and benches occupied by court officials and copyists, and in front of them was the long rail known as the bar, to which defendants and plaintiffs would be summoned The edges of the room were already crowded with chattering townsfolk.

The court would begin sitting at noon, he was explaining as he showed her to a padded chair of state standing beside the benches allotted to the women in her company on the left side of the courtroom.

'I believe proceedings will start with the case against Sir Thomas Malory, who has not denied that he is a fugitive from justice. Once they have passed sentence on him, I fear that you will be arraigned for knowingly harbouring an outlaw. Together with Mistress Moulton and the rest of your company.'

'What about Simon Brailles and Morwenna?' she asked. 'Surely they've committed no crimes?'

'Er... that remains to be seen. Tregoys is claiming that they had something to do with the disappearance of two of his men in the hills above Tintagel.' Mohun sounded far less bombastically sure of himself than he had when they reached Restormel on Tuesday.

Though the castle was as luxurious as he had promised, Alyce had spent her days there on tenterhooks, anxiously rehearsing justifications for her actions and those of her friends and followers, wondering at the busy comings and goings of messengers, and puzzled on Thursday by the sight of Sir Reginald riding away with Denzil Caerleon under guard behind him and returning yesterday without him. At dinner time, he had been morose, not speaking except to bid her goodnight and say, distinctly apologetically, that he hoped she would agree that he had treated her with every courtesy.

Now he was looking positively shifty as he strode away to join Harcourt and Tregoys, who were sitting in seats on the right side of the court. The judge's chair of state on the dais was empty but, as Alyce settled into her seat, two more chairs of state were carried in and placed one on each side of it. Who, she wondered, were they to be tried by?

There was a shuffle of feet and the clink of chains and Ben, Simon, Jem and Wat were escorted in and led to a large dock on the right-hand side of the room. Next, Malory was led in, Owen behind him, and shown into a smaller dock. When he saw Alyce, he bowed, giving her an encouraging smile as he straightened up.

A trumpet blew a fanfare, and the door at the side of the dais opened to admit the commanding figure of Sir Richard Neville, Earl of Warwick, Admiral of the Royal Fleet. Bronzed and bearded and attended by two seamen, he exuded power and decisiveness as he seated himself on the left-hand chair. Then came a second fanfare, and Alyce watched with amazement as Lord Tiptoft entered, wearing the purple robe of a justiciar. Sir John Trevelyan and a boy of about twelve in Tiptoft's livery followed behind him. Lionel, Alyce guessed. The boy Tiptoft had taken hostage to ensure Trevelyan's obedience. What, she wondered, as Tiptoft took the central chair, did their presence here mean?

Then came a third, prolonged fanfare announcing someone of higher rank than either of them. To Alyce's utter astonishment, Jack entered, splendidly apparelled from his gold-buckled riding boots to his ducal coronet and attended by her grandson John. Alyce was stupefied. She had never seen him so confident and at his ease. For the first time she realised how he appeared to others. Rising thirty, no longer plump and dandified but an acclaimed jouster who had been singled out for favour last year by the Duke of Burgundy. One of the four remaining royal dukes. Certainly the man with more authority than any other in the county of Cornwall.

Jack gave her a respectful bow before settling himself in the chair on Tiptoft's right. Little John doffed his feathered cap with an elaborate flourish, then gave his grandmother a cheery wave as he took up his position beside his father's chair. A ripple of laughter ran through the onlookers.

Joan nudged Alyce. 'Didn't I tell you that there was more to Jack than you gave him credit for? Look at him now. Every inch a foremost peer of the realm. I'll bet he's going to save our bacon.' She sat back complacently, only to sit forward again with a gasp of shock as Lord Wenlock strode up the central aisle, and bowed at the lords on the dais. As he took a seat next to Mohun, Tregoys and Harcourt, he caught her eye and gave her a bland nod which told her absolutely nothing.

The steward of the court thumped his staff on the tiled floor for silence as Tiptoft rose. He bowed to Warwick, Jack and Alyce, then addressed the court.

'As Lord Deputy and Justiciar of Ireland, I claim authority to pass judgment on the cases brought before the Duchy Court in Lostwithiel. The first case to be considered is that of Sir Thomas Malory, exempted from the general pardon offered by his majesty King Edward last July and accused of damnable, malicious and most hateful deceptions. Although no case has yet been proven against him, he has broken the law in attempting to flee the country. He was apprehended in Tintagel by Sir Reginald Mohun.' He looked across to where Malory stood.

'Do you have anything to say in your defence, Sir Thomas?'

Malory shook his head, but Lord Wenlock sprang to his feet.

'My lords, may I speak for Sir Thomas? I was his lord for several years.'

Tiptoft gave a nod.

'The accusations made against Sir Thomas are being appealed in London. Although he did wrong in attempting to flee the country, he is not yet proven to be a traitor. I will undertake to escort him back to London and see him lodged in whichever prison your lordships deem appropriate.'

'Are we agreed that this is a reasonable request?' said Tiptoft, looking first at Jack and then at Warwick. They both gave approving nods.

'In that case, I authorise Lord Wenlock of Someries to take Sir Thomas into custody and escort him back to London to remain in Newgate until his guilt has been ascertained or disproved.'

As guards led Malory out of the courtroom, Sir Robert Harcourt sprang to his feet. 'And what of the Dowager Duchess of Suffolk and her companions, who knowingly harboured an enemy of York?'

Tiptoft frowned. 'There is no evidence that either Princess Alyce or her companions knew of Sir Thomas's exclusion from pardon.'

'Balderdash!' exclaimed Harcourt. 'They were heard discussing it by Sir Reginald Mohun's squire Guy Despenser, who rode with them from Stourton Castle to Exeter. He told both me and Sir Reginald Mohun of it. Didn't he, Mohun? And Trevelyan, you heard him too.'

Mohun looked vague and muttered something inaudible. Trevelyan frowned, and looked puzzled. 'I'm sorry, Sir Robert, but I wasn't listening to your conversation. I was telling my son to go and get himself and his brothers and sisters ready for dinner.'

Tiptoft raised his eyebrows. 'Then this is mere hearsay, Sir Robert. We need to hear it from the lips of an accredited witness. Where is Guy Despenser?'

Tregoys rose. 'His fate concerns the next case to be heard, my lord. He was murdered by two members of the duchess's own company. By their own admission. We apprehended them in Trewarmett Woods and have brought them and their companions here for trial.'

'Bring them to the bar,' said Tiptoft. A court clerk led Ben forward. Exhausted and begrimed after two days of running with his wrists tied behind one of Tregoys's men, he still managed to shuffle forward with dignity and to hold his head high. At the sound of his chains, Tiptoft frowned.

'Who ordered the prisoner to be chained?' There was silence. Tregoys turned to Mohun, who remained silent, staring at the floor.

'Remove the chains,' ordered Tiptoft. As a guard did so, another led Mattie from her seat beside Tamsin to join Ben at the bar. A head shorter than he was, she looked meek as a mouse in her dun-coloured gown, her curly hair tucked under a wimple.

'Your names?' demanded the clerk. They gave them in turn.

'Ben Bilton of Ewelme Palace, Oxfordshire, steward to Princess Alyce, Dowager Duchess of Suffolk.'

'Matilda Lovejoy, also of Ewelme, laundrymaid to the Palace.'

Tiptoft regarded them sternly. 'And what is your answer to this accusation?'

'It was self-defence,' said Ben resolutely. 'We were trying to find our way back to Princess Alyce's company when Despenser attacked without warning. He threw a rock at my head and knocked me out. This scar on my head is the proof of it. Then he raised his sword to run me through, but Mattie threw her cloak down from where she was hiding. It fell over him and then she jumped on top of him.'

Titters of laughter and admiring murmurs came from the crowd and the steward banged his staff for silence.

'And then?' said Tiptoft.

'I could hear his companion returning and knew that we had no chance against two of them,' Ben continued. 'So I picked up his sword and ran him through.'

'*His* sword?' queried Tiptoft. 'You had no weapon of your own?' Ben shook his head.

'And what of this companion?'

It was Mattie's turn to speak. 'He saw that Guy was dead and that Ben had a sword and he fled. But in the mist he fell over the cliff. We just heard his screams.'

At this point, Princess Alyce rose to her feet. 'I would speak, my lord.' Tiptoft inclined his head.

'If Guy Despenser were not dead, he would be standing in this court himself, accused of causing the death of my servant Joseph Pek,' she announced in clear, ringing tones. 'We have several witnesses who saw him send a horse and cart careering down Stepcote Hill in Exeter towards us. If it wasn't for Joseph Pek, I myself could have died.'

A hubbub rose from the onlookers, and the steward had to bang down his staff repeatedly before it subsided.

'Thank you, your grace,' said Tiptoft. 'In view of your testimony, the fact that the defendants were not carrying arms and the absence of witnesses to the death of Despenser's companion, I declare Ben Bilton and Matilda Lovejoy have no case to answer. They are free to go, and so are those apprehended with them.'

There were cheers from the onlookers. The steward raised his staff angrily. 'The court will proceed *in camera* if there are any more interruptions,' he announced, bringing it down on the floor with a thud. 'Call the next plaintiff.'

To general surprise, it was one of the former prisoners who stepped up to the bar.

'Your name?' asked the steward.

'Simon Brailles, formerly secretary of her grace of Ewelme, presently ordinand of Father Gregory, vicar of Tintagel.'

340

'And what is your plea?' said Tiptoft, face inscrutable.

'I was kidnapped by the deputy sheriff Sir Reginald Mohun on Candlemas Eve and stranded on an Irish island.'

'Do you have any witnesses to this?'

Simon hesitated. 'Not exactly. Sir Reginald had men with him, but I don't know their names. Or those of the Irishmen who stranded me. But Denzil Caerleon, who rescued me from Little Saltee, will corroborate my story.' He gestured to Denzil, who now standing beside Wenlock. Morwenna gripped Tamsin's hand as he strode forward and stood beside Simon.

'Your name?' demanded the steward.

'Denzil Caerleon, Captain in the Royal Fleet under its Admiral the Earl of Warwick.' He looked towards Warwick, who gave him a nod of approval.

When Tiptoft asked him how he had come to rescue Simon. Denzil spoke with confidence.

'I had taken passage to Wexford to visit a Knight Hospitaller friend in the preceptory of Crook, and I saw Brailles waving from Little Saltee. He told me that he'd been abducted from Tintagel by Sir Reginald Mohun and stranded on Great Saltee. He was in great fear of his life.'

'Is there proof that Mohun was involved?' demanded Tiptoft. When Denzil admitted that there wasn't, Tiptoft dismissed him with a wave of his hand, and beckoned to Mohun. He rose sullenly and took up a place at the bar.

'Is there any truth in this man's claim that you were involved in his kidnap?' asked Tiptoft.

'Absolutely none,' mumbled Mohun. 'I suspect that it was a practical joke of some kind. The tinners of Tintagel are notoriously pagan. Perhaps they resented the ordinand's attempts to convert them and found some heathen who superficially resembled me.' There were jeers of disbelief from the crowd, but Tiptoft quelled the uproar with a stern glance, then turned back to Mohun.

'Since Brailles is now safe and sound, I'm going to dismiss his appeal against you. However, the court awards him compensation of £20 in view of the privations he suffered. And it awards Denzil Caerleon £10 for restoring him. Both to be paid from the shire fund.' Mohun opened his mouth to protest but, at a quelling glance from Tiptoft, subsided sulkily.

The steward stepped forward again. 'Are there any more cases to be heard?'

Harcourt stalked to the stand. 'I wish to raise an issue which may have to be taken beyond this court and into that of the highest in the land, that of the Lords Spiritual and Temporal in Westminster. It concerns the legitimacy of...'

'Stop!' commanded Jack, before Harcourt could finish his sentence. He rose to his feet. 'If it is a matter for the Lords, then it is not one to be discussed here. You will have to take your plea and the proofs necessary to justify it to London.' Harcourt began to object, only for Warwick to rise.

'Not for some time, however,' said Warwick. 'Both Sir Robert and Denzil Caerleon are captains in the Royal Fleet. And as Admiral I have given orders that we are to sail for France on tomorrow's tide.'

Alyce suddenly realised that the entire proceedings had been just as carefully orchestrated as those at Whalesborough when Mohun and Harcourt had made their moves against her. But this time true friends were operating unstoppably in her favour.

The steward gave a final tattoo on the floor with his staff. 'The court will rise.'

After bowing to Princess Alyce, the lords on the dais processed out of the room, led by Jack, his head held high. His poise and dignity reminded Alyce vividly of that of her husband Thomas Montagu, who had given judgment forty years ago in this very courtroom on – of course, that's why the name Tregoys was familiar – one Richard Tregoys for maiming a neighbour and creating general mayhem. He must have been Sir Patrick's father.

Mohun, Tregoys and Harcourt marched down the aisle and out of the court without glancing at Alyce, let alone giving her the bow that courtesy demanded. But Wenlock came over to her and bowed over the hand Alyce held out for him to kiss. Then he turned to Joan with the crooked smile that she had grown to love and opened his arms wide. Forgetting the suspicions still seething in her mind, she stepped into his embrace.

Alyce was not mollified. She met Wenlock's eyes over Joan's cradled head with a challenging stare. 'Explanations are in order, Sir John. Firstly, how came you and Jack to be here at all, and secondly why did you never tell me that you were a part-owner of the *Nicholas* at the time of William's death?'

'Ah,' said Wenlock. 'You've retrieved the evidences. Presumably they included the *Nicholas*'s bill of sale?' Alyce's angry reply was interrupted by the return of Jack, now attended by Trevelyan. Behind them came Lionel and Little John, clearly already firm friends.

Jack strode over to Alyce and for the first time ever took her into his arms and hugged her. Face pressed to his chest, she closed her eyes, overcome with a confusion of feelings: puzzlement at his presence, anger at Wenlock, suspicion of Trevelyan – but also, stronger than any of these, a sense of

343

relief and a singing awareness of being loved by this splendid young man whom she had misunderstood for so long.

'Time, undoubtedly, for explanations,' said Wenlock, and chuckled as Alyce's grandson nudged his father out of the way and flung his own arms around his grandmother's waist. 'We need somewhere more comfortable and private than this to embark on them. I suggest the Trevelyans' manor of St Veep, just across the river. Malory and Owen have already been taken there. Under guard, of course,' he added blandly.

'My wife is even now preparing to receive you,' said Trevelyan, once more his exuberant self. 'Our barge is at the bridge.'

He offered Alyce his arm and led her out of the courtroom. As soon as they appeared, an elderly cleric made his way out of the crowd of onlookers and came bustling up to them, followed by Simon and Morwenna. Alyce greeted him with an affectionate smile.

'Father Gregory! It's good to see you fully recovered. Though I fear the promising ordinand I sent you has other plans. How he intends to achieve them, I don't know.' She looked sternly at Simon, whose face fell.

'I have a solution, your grace, if you'll permit it,' said Gregory. 'Tintagel would welcome Simon's appointment as reeve in place of Oswald Marrack, who as you've heard had an unfortunate accident on the cliffs of the castle island. A small house adjoining the vicarage comes with the position, and there's a modest stipend, doubled if the reeve happens to be married.'

Alyce could almost feel Simon and Morwenna holding their breath. She hesitated for a moment, then gave a gracious nod. 'So be it. Together with the monies Lord Tiptoft awarded

Simon in compensation for his privations on the Saltees, and the reward he has earned from me for his discovery of the evidences, they will have plenty to live on.' She held out a bulging purse and a book.

Simon gasped. Glowing with happiness, he gave Alyce a deep bow as he took the purse. Then he opened the book and read its title: *Bartholomew for Little Minds*. Leafing through it, he smiled in delight at the lively illustrations opposite each entry. He looked up at Alyce gratefully. 'Thank you, your grace. I remember you telling me long ago that you had this made for the teaching of children in your school. It'll be the foundation stone of our own school's library. And perhaps the book from which one day our own child will learn to read.' Alyce saw a blush rise to Morwenna's cheek. Impulsively, she stepped forward, pulled a ring off her own finger, and presented it to her. Then she held her hand out for the girl to kiss in farewell.

As she did so, Trevelyan fumbled in his doublet pocket and pulled out his own purse. He held it out to Morwenna, smiling. 'A woman needs something of her own if she is to be wed. This is for you – with my blessing. You and Simon will always be welcome at Whalesborough. And I'd relish standing godfather to your first child.'

As Morwenna smiled back at him, Alyce blinked, struck by the startling similarity of their smiles. She was twenty or so… Had Trevelyan romped with her mother before he married Elizabeth as Joan had surmised? Very possibly, she reflected wryly.

She watched as they followed Gregory, bound for Tintagel and a new life. How little she had understood Simon's needs, she reflected. Leaving Ewelme and coming to Cornwall had been the making of him; nor could he have found a better wife than Morwenna, whether or not she was a by-blow of John Trevelyan. And with a baby already due, the sooner they settled down into the reeve's house next to the vicarage the better.

Whistling cheerfully, Trevelyan led Alyce's company down the hill from the Duchy Palace to Lostwithiel's many-arched stone bridge. Just downstream of it a barge was moored. Denzil was standing beside it.

'I have to bid you all farewell,' he said. 'The Earl of Warwick's barge is waiting for me on the other side of the river; he's ordered both Harcourt and me to go with him to Golant, where his flagship is moored.'

Joan went up to him and gave him a warm hug. 'God be with you. You've the luck of the devil too, so between the two of them you should survive.'

When it was Alyce's turn to wish Denzil well, she took his hand firmly in her own.

'There will always be a welcome for you at Ewelme, Denzil. Make sure you come back to us one day.' The pang of regret she felt at his departing was mixed with relief. To have even considered a match with this rash young adventurer had been madness. Then she remembered the person she had begun to realise was much better suited to him, and she looked round for Tamsin. She could only see Mattie, sitting happily beside Ben.

'Where's Tamsin?' she asked.

'She's with Wat,' said Mattie, pointing to the bridge. Tamsin and Wat were leaning over it, watching the fish sheltering under its arches.

'Go and bid Tamsin farewell,' she said to Denzil. 'And tell her and Wat to come on board the barge.'

Hugely relieved at being taken back into Alyce's favour, Denzil bowed, then walked onto the bridge. Tamsin looked up with a smile as he reached them.

'Look, Denzil! We think that big one is the king of the river. Nowhere near as big as that sturgeon you brought to Ewelme, but what a feast he'd make! Are you coming with us to St Veep?'

He shook his head. 'No, I wish I could, but I'm commanded to the Earl of Warwick's barge. As he said, we sail on to-morrow's tide.' He looked at her, eyes dancing. 'I'm going to miss our adventures.'

On an impulse, Tamsin felt in her pocket for the little wooden mouse that he had bought for her to give Wat long ago in Oxford, and which Wat had given her to cheer her up on the journey from Exeter. She took it out and handed it to him. 'Here,' she said. 'It's your turn to have this. It's brought both Wat and me luck. I hope it'll keep you safe. Bring it back to me some day.'

He considered her thoughtfully as he took it. 'I will, as soon as we defeat the enemy. That's a promise.'

Then he felt in his own pocket and took out the little holly-wood cross that he had bought from the Irish sailor Angus when they were waiting for the tide to go out in Kilmore. 'Here's a talisman in return. To keep you safe until I can.' He put it into her hand and bent to kiss her forehead. Then he turned and walked away.

She blinked in surprise. What could he mean? He was twice her age and a man of good family, educated and ex-perienced and a captain in the Earl of Warwick's fleet. They had been thrown together by chance, and she had assumed he would not give her another thought. 'I'm going to miss our adventures,' he had said. Though still heartsore and confused after Will Stonor's rough wooing, Tamsin put her finger to where Denzil's lips had touched and realised that so would she.

St Veep

Elizabeth Whalesborough had made sure that a splendid welcome met them in St Veep. Comfortable quarters had been allotted to everyone in its new apartments, but dinner was to be served in the ancient hall they had retained at the heart of the house. 'So much cosier for winter feasts than the draughty great chamber in the new part,' Elizabeth explained as she and Trevelyan led them inside. Its walls were over a yard thick, and its windows tiny. There was no ceremonial dais, just a huge hearth heaped with blazing logs. Chairs of state for Jack and Alyce had been placed at each end of a long wooden table. Everyone else sat on benches along its length.

Alyce looked down the table with a sigh of satisfaction. Apart from the tragic loss of Joseph Pek and the departure of Cabal and Godith, her company was as complete as it was when they left Andover. Malory sat on her right, with Owen at his side, and Wenlock on her left, with Joan beside him. At the other end of the table sat Jack. On his right was Elizabeth Whalesborough, on his right John Trevelyan, Artie as always on his shoulder. In between, Tamsin and Wat sat facing Ben and Mattie. Little John and Lionel were acting as pages. Having offered bowls of warm water and towels, they helped Jem and the St Veep servants bring round the food. Fish dishes predominated: little soft-shelled crabs to be crunched up whole, mussels in a broth thickened with bread crusts and seasoned with saffron and garlic, and loach and tench chopped up and fried and served with a sweet and sour sauce made from vinegar, cloves, currants and raisins. There was also a spicy rabbit stew and a great pie full of quails flavoured with honey and pine nuts.

Once the meal was over, the two proud little pages followed Jem, Wat and the Trevelyans' servants to the kitchen. Alyce looked at Jack and Wenlock.

'Well?'

They looked at each other. 'You first,' said Jack to Wenlock. 'You've a deal more to explain than I have.'

Wenlock gave a wry smile. 'Indeed. But first I'd like to know just what was in the parcel that Madoc gave to Simon Brailles.'

'As would I,' said Jack.

'We can tell you, but not show you,' said Alyce. 'Mohun burst in on us when we were examining them and tossed them into the fire. I only managed to save two things.' She felt in her pocket for the Talbot badge, pulled the gold ring off her finger, and laid them both on the table.

Trevelyan leant forward and picked up the badge. 'Ah. Just as Lord Tiptoft feared.'

'Does it mean that Talbot was involved in Duke William's murder?' asked Joan.

'Not Talbot himself,' said Wenlock. 'He would never have stooped so low. I believe the badge was given as a pledge of faith by his wife Margaret Beauchamp. Her sister was married to Edmund Beaufort, and they were the foremost of the plotters.'

'I knew it!' said Joan triumphantly. 'We needed to look to the ladies. But why was Tiptoft concerned to protect her?'

'His father's first wife was Philippa Talbot,' said Wenlock.

349

'You know how passionate Tiptoft is on matters of honour. He was concerned that no smear of shame should be attached to the Talbot family. With your permission, I'll hand this badge over to him before he returns to Ireland and reassure him that the Talbots' name is unsullied. In return, I'm sure he'll cease inquiring into any mysteries concerning Newton Montagu.'

'What else was in the parcel?' asked Trevelyan.

'Verses written before William's death by Sir Richard Roos,' said Alyce. 'They declared who was loyal to King Henry and who was not. Among the latter was "the Cornish chough" who "had made our eagle blind".' She glared at Trevelyan. He hung his head.

'They also absolved both Talbot as being in captivity and the Duke of York, who was in Ireland at the time.'

Wenlock brightened. 'That will please Tiptoft. Besides being an ardent defender of the Talbots' honour, he's heart and soul for York.'

'What about the bill of sale of the *Nicholas*?' said Joan coldly. 'Showing that you were one of its owners.'

Wenlock shrugged. 'And so I was. The truth is that I had no idea that my ship had been commandeered and sent to intercept Suffolk. But I can't prove that. Or the involvement of the person who was most to blame and had most to gain. Wasn't there anything else in the parcel?'

'There was a family tree which showed that Margaret Beaufort had the closest Lancastrian claim to the throne if the Beauforts' ban from the succession was ignored,' said Alyce. 'And there was this ring.' She picked it up and handed it to him with an air of triumph.

Wenlock examined it with a puzzled frown. 'What's so special about it?'

'William always wore it,' said Alyce. 'John Wyte, the captain of the *Nicolas*, must have taken it off his corpse and added it to the other assurances he'd insisted on being given.'

'Inside it there are two sets of initials,' said Joan. '*EB* for Edmund Beaufort. And *CR* for Catherine Regina. We're guessing now, but we think it is evidence of an affair between Henry V's queen and Edmund Beaufort.'

'God's teeth!' Wenlock exclaimed. 'How did it come to be in Suffolk's possession?'

'His sister Katherine, Abbess of Barking, gave it to him,' said Alyce. 'She and the queen were very close, and she became the guardian of Catherine's sons. We think Edmund gave her the ring, or perhaps the queen herself did. She would have guessed its significance. My guess is that she told her brother, my husband, what that was.'

'And we think that he used it to force Beaufort to agree to Jack's marriage to his niece Margaret,' said Joan. 'Not realising that the ring was evidence that Beaufort would and did kill for. He wanted Margaret to marry his son by Catherine, Edmund Tudor.'

'That would certainly make sense,' said Wenlock. 'But how did Captain Wyte know the ring was important?'

'Could it be that he didn't?' said Joan. 'Suppose whoever gave Wyte his orders did, though, and told him to take the ring off Suffolk's finger and return it to them? And that Wyte put it for safety with his other evidences in the parcel which Madoc stole?'

'We decided in the end that everything pointed to the involvement of Edmund Beaufort,' said Alyce. 'The verses accused him and his brother John of losing France. The family tree emphasised Beaufort claims. The ring revealed his close-ness to Queen Catherine.'

Wenlock nodded slowly. 'Edmund Beaufort certainly had the most to gain from Suffolk's downfall. And he achieved it through the machinations of his women folk.'

'But what about you owning the *Nicholas*?' said Joan, glaring at Wenlock.

'What about its other owners?' interposed Malory. 'The Earl of Devon's wife was Edmund Beaufort's youngest sister.'

Wenlock sighed. 'Yes. Understood rightly, the bill of sale again pointed to Beaufort – but overtly it pointed to me. As Margaret Beauchamp pointed out when I came close to discovering the degree of her involvement in Suffolk's murder. "Directly or indirectly, the evidences incriminate everyone involved in the plot," she told me. "They are devised so that only we ourselves understand their significance and nobody can betray anyone else without implicating themselves." She said they were put together when Captain Wyte demanded a surety that he'd be exonerated. Giving them to Wyte to hold ensured both his safety and that of the plotters. They distrusted each other, with good reason. They split into differ-ent camps during the civil wars of the 1450s. After Wyte was killed at sea and the *Nicholas* reduced to a hulk, they hoped, as I did, that the evidences would never be seen again. But long ago I told Tiptoft that Margaret Beauchamp had been involved. Which made him anxious for the Talbots' good name, and determined to destroy the evidences when he heard Madoc had sold them to Brailles.'

Jack had been listening, fascinated. 'So in all likelihood, my father was betrayed by the Beauforts and Talbot's wife Margaret Beauchamp, but we cannot prove it. Edmund Beaufort is dead, as are Margaret Beauchamp and the Countess of Devon.' He rose and walked the length of the table to where Alyce sat, then knelt at her feet.

'The one person not involved was you, mother,' he declared. 'For seventeen years I believed you were, and because of that I treated you abominably. Thank the Lord that Bess has helped me understand all that you've done for me. And that Wenlock and I arrived in Fowey in time to save you from unjust persecution.'

Confused and close to tears, Alyce raised him to his feet – and found herself folded in his arms again. Once released, she gave him a tremulous smile and deliberately chose the words that would best please him.

'I thank you, my son.' He gave her a long, tender look, bowed deeply, then walked back to his chair.

Joan tugged at Wenlock's sleeve impatiently. 'Enough of surmise, satisfying as it has proved to be. I'd dearly love to know how you and Jack *did* happen to arrive in Fowey in the nick of time. And why Sir Reginald Mohun looked like a punctured football bladder in the Duchy Court and refused to support Harcourt.'

Wenlock and Jack looked at each other. This was too public a place to enter in on the happenings at Bampton and Newton Montagu.

'A happy chance,' Wenlock said blandly. 'I'd been alerted by letters from you and Malory as to your misfortunes on your journey, and I decided to join the Earl of Warwick's fleet, which was about to sail from Southampton to Fowey. I overnighted at Amesbury Priory where Prioress Joanna told me that Jack had passed by on his way to Newton Montagu. Since I knew that the Earl of Warwick was preparing to leave Southampton for Fowey with the royal fleet, I rode hard for Newton Montagu, told Jack the news, and suggested that he sailed with me to Cornwall. He sent his squire Dick Quartermain back to Ewelme to explain to Duchess Bess, and I sent a courier to Warwick. Two days later, the Earl's fleet anchored off Bridport to take us aboard. Once we arrived in Fowey, I sent a letter to Lord Tiptoft to tell him what was afoot.'

Trevelyan took up the story, Artie nibbling at his ear. 'Tiptoft was still reading Lord Wenlock's letter when I arrived in Wexford to give him the news that Tregoys had sent me of Mohun's and Harcourt's arrest of Princess Alyce and her company. He was furious with Mohun for far exceeding his brief. I also told him that Tregoys thought that Princess Alyce had been given the parcel Brailles bought from Madoc. We set out for Wadebridge the next morning and reached Fowey on Wednesday. The young duke, Lord Wenlock and Warwick had already arrived. Tiptoft and they hatched plans to save Princess Alyce, scotch Harcourt and preserve some – er, some significant reputations. On Thursday they summoned Mohun from Restormel, reproved him sternly and gave him certain instructions. And today – well, you all know what happened today.' Once more his cocksure self, he gave them all conspiratorial smile. On his shoulder, Artie gave a triumphant caw.

Wenlock gave him a sardonic look. 'Trevelyan, I would recommend that you tell Princess Alyce and her son exactly how your robbing of King Henry rebounded on Suffolk.' Trevelyan's cocksure pose disappeared, as did his smile. He swallowed nervously.

'I... I arranged an ambush to rob the Bishop of Chichester, Adam Moleyns, as he rode to Portsmouth in January 1450 with the long overdue wages of the soldiers who were to join Talbot's forces in Normandy. When he told them he'd been robbed, they tore him to pieces. The Pope excommunicated the people of Portsmouth, which appalled the king, and Edmund Beaufort accused Suffolk of not sending the money. Suffolk was sent to the Tower, and his downfall followed.'

Alyce stared at him, dumbfounded.

'Cousin Alyce, John had no idea that Suffolk, who had always stood his friend, would be blamed.' Elizabeth Whalesborough had sprung to her husband's defence. 'Or of the plot to have him murdered. And he used all his influence with King Henry and Queen Margaret to ensure that you kept your estates.'

'As did Beaufort, of course,' put in Wenlock. 'He'd achieved his purpose in contriving Suffolk's death, but he didn't want you looking into it.'

Alyce's memories of that terrible time shifted shape. She had always known that she had only been able to keep hold of all her estates and the wardship of Jack because Trevelyan and Beaufort had backed her cause. And when they had told her not to risk provoking the enemies who had brought about his murder by investigating his ghastly death, she had agreed that it was best to lie low, bending like the willow to avoid snapping like the elm, just as her mother had long ago advised. But Jack, mere boy that he was, had misinterpreted her inaction as proof of her involvement. Thank the Lord that he now knew otherwise.

Joan was still intent on worrying out more of the day's surprising events. 'So how did Tiptoft bring Mohun to heel?' she asked Wenlock as they sat down.

'He sacked him as deputy sheriff and warned him that if he stepped out of line during the hearing he'd find himself arraigned for dereliction of duty by Sir Avery Cornbury, who has been summoned to return to take up his shrieval duties. And he forbad him to warn Harcourt.'

Joan gave a guffaw. 'Wasn't Sir Robert's face a picture when Mohun mumbled of pagan tinners?'

Alyce fingered the ring that lay on the table beside her. Now that Wenlock had taken the gold Talbot badge, it was the only remaining clue to the death of her husband. What should become of it?'

As if in answer there was a sudden whirr of wings and Artie hurtled down the table towards her. Picking up the ring in his beak, he flew out of hall and into the buttery. Everyone sprang to their feet and followed. Trevelyan was first out of the room, whistling Artie's recall frantically, but the bird was already in the kitchen. Startled by the uproar he was causing, he fluttered round the lofty ceiling a couple of times and then vanished through the central smoke hole.

'Outside!' shouted Trevelyan, pushing the kitchen door wide and hurrying into the courtyard. Looking up, he saw the chough wheeling higher and higher, heading for the river.

The others caught up with him and followed his gaze. The sun was low in the sky but Artie was silhouetted against the silvered water of the river like a black comma as he followed its meanderings towards the sea. They watched until the bird vanished from sight, then trooped back into the manorial hall in shocked silence.

Once they were all seated, Alyce rose to her feet and looked round at them. 'Now nothing remains but our surmises of how the murder of my husband, Jack's father, came about. Perhaps it is just as well. What matters is that Jack and I are at last in accord. He can take pride in his father's merits without his death's dark shadow obscuring them.'

She raised her cup. 'My grandfather once wrote that "murder will out, though hidden for a year, or two, or three." It's been nearly twenty, in fact. But I believe we see clearly now. To Truth!'

They all stood up, raised their own cups and echoed her toast: 'To Truth.'

As the toast rang around the table, her weary grey eyes met Jack's alert blue ones. They both smiled.

Epilogue

'You didn't tell me it was going to stink, Farhang,' Alyce complained as she stepped back from admiring the spectacular red flower that had opened exuberantly from the long stalk of one of the bulbs she had last seen showing only tips of green.

'It is perhaps more attractive at a distance,' admitted Farhang. 'Like so many people.'

'As I've learnt only too well,' said Alyce. 'I should never have put so much trust in Trevelyan – though, as matters turned out, he helped to save the day.'

'*Ashk-e-Siavash* has another name in Europe,' said Farhang. 'According to the Italian gardener employed to beautify the grounds of Magdalen, Bishop Wayneflete's new college, it is known as the "crown imperial". It is certainly a right royal flower.'

Alyce gazed at it. 'I wonder. Maybe it heralds the return of England's rightful king.'

There was a sudden commotion from the far side of the garden. Yapping shrilly, a four-legged ball of silky soft black fur raced towards her, hotly pursued by her grandsons. Alyce looked round and flinched as the puppy leapt at her eagerly, raking her embroidered kirtle with its claws.

'Get off, Pan,' shrieked Ned.

'Down, sir!' commanded John, hauling the excited little dog away by its collar. He looked up at his grandmother abashed.

'Sorry Grandmother, he escaped. We haven't had time to

train him properly. But Job Smith says he'll be well fitted for both house and hunt once you take him over. He's for you. To make up for losing Leo. We called him Pan because we think that when he grows to full size he'll be like the panther Grandmother Cecily showed us in Uncle Edward's Lion Tower in London.'

Alyce was torn between anger at the idea of any dog being able to fill the hole in her heart made by Leo's death, her desire not to disappoint her well-meaning grandsons and instinctive admiration for the bold little hound. She managed a smile.

'Darlings, how thoughtful of you.' She swallowed hard, then continued. 'He's exactly the companion I need.'

She looked at Farhang, who gave her a slow smile. 'Things do not always turn out as we expect – but not always for the worse.'

'Is that Rumi?' she asked.

'No – but it's a favourite of mine.'

Tamsin stood a little apart from the scene. She had returned to Ewelme with mixed feelings, happy to be home but also hoping that a new adventure would not be long in coming. Far from daunting her with its dangers, the journey to Cornwall had made her long to go further, to cross the sea to France, even. Who knew what her future would hold? She thought of Will Stonor, still far away in Exeter, and of the letter, blotched with tears, that she'd found waiting for her at Ewelme, apologising for his behaviour. Then she put her hand in her pocket and stroked the intricate carving on the holly-wood cross that Denzil had given her. Her jaw tightened. 'Hold to your truth, and you'll go far.'

THE END

Afterword

The third of Lucy Morton's inspired covers for the Alyce books refers to the fight for the throne. Crown imperials signify the rightful king Henry VI, imprisoned at the time of this story but restored in October 1470. Christian tradition tells that, of all the flowers, only the proud crown imperial refused to bow its head at the crucifixion – it has bowed and wept ever since. The flowers emit a distinctly foxy smell, reputed to repel mice and moles. The yellow branches of broom, *planta genista*, are for the Plantagenet pretender Edward IV of York. The Cornish chough, owing allegiance to neither, is a pointer to the significance in the story of John Trevelyan.

Details of Tintagel and the endpaper maps come from the third folio volume of a magnificent work of nineteenth-century scholarship, Sir John MacLean's *Parochial and Family History of the Deanery of Trigg Minor in the County of Cornwall* (Nichols & Son, London, 1879). MacLean also gives interesting details of the former Hospitaller presbytery at Temple. The verses in the evidences are from Thomas Wright's *Political Poems Relating to English History*, Longman, London, 1861.

Trehane, near Trevalga, is a real farm, providing rooms and camping huts and the best home-cooked breakfast in Cornwall. All that is left of Newton Montagu is Round Chimney's Farm, near Glanville's Wootton, Dorset. You can stay there for a holiday, or just visit its cafe and shop.

As in *The Serpent of Division* and *The Book of the Duchess*, facts inform my fiction. New research into the owners and fate of the *Nicholas of the Tower* was published by Jan Mulrenan in *The Ricardian Bulletin*, December 2022, the magazine of the Richard III Society. I invented the battered hull of the original ship disappearing into Ireland as Sir John Tiptoft's presence there, because being deputy governor made his re-entering the story so opportune.

Alyce did indeed hold the advowson to Tintagel church, and John Gregory was its vicar. She also owned tin mines in the county. Hennes Kleineke mentions Alyce having to appeal for the return of her Cornish tin mines in 'Mine's a Mine', an essay for the History of Parliament online. In another essay, 'Why the West was Wild' (*Fifteenth Century III*, edited by Linda Clark, 2003), Kleineke also discovered that Alyce's second husband Sir Thomas Montagu, Earl of Salisbury, was in Lostwithiel in August 1428 during the arrest of Richard Tregoys. He must have been with Alyce, as she was in France with him when he died in October 1428 while besieging Joan of Arc in Orléans. In my biography of Sir Thomas Malory I speculate that he might have visited Cornwall as a young man, as his uncle Sir John Chetwynd was once Constable of Tintagel.

As to my Big Reveal, the notion that Edmund Beaufort, Duke of Somerset was behind the murder of William, Duke of Suffolk, because of his interest in promoting his niece Margaret Beaufort and his putative grandson Henry Tudor, it might seem far-fetched but there have been murmurings of it for centuries. It is, however, true that a parliamentary statute regulating the remarriage of queens of England was passed in

1428, and it is just possible that Henry V's widow Catherine of Valois (1401–1437) married Owen Tudor to avoid visiting its penalties on Edmund Beaufort. The eminent historian Gerard Harriss raises the notion in his biography of Edmund's uncle Cardinal Beaufort:

> By its very nature the evidence for the parentage of Edmund 'Tudor' is less than conclusive, but such facts as can be assembled permit the agreeable possibility that Edmund 'Tudor' and Margaret Beaufort were first cousins and that the royal house of 'Tudor' sprang in fact from Beauforts on both sides.
>
> It might seem unlikely that Edmund Beaufort would have taken so great a political risk as getting the queen dowager with child, but he was a dashing young man (recently released from prison) as well as a Beaufort, and Catherine, who had fulfilled the only role open to her by immediately producing a son for the Lancastrian dynasty, was a lonely Frenchwoman in England, and at thirty or thereabouts was, the rumour ran, oversexed. Many stranger things have happened, and the idea of renaming sixteenth-century England is an appealing one.
>
> G.L. Harriss, *Cardinal Beaufort: A Study of Lancastrian Ascendancy and Decline*, Clarendon Press, Oxford, 1988, p. 178 n34.)

Joan Moulton's suggestion that Edmund Beaufort had also been the lover of Margaret of Anjou has also been seriously considered, since much uncertainty surrounded the parentage of the child born to her in 1453. Told of her only pregnancy since their marriage eight years earlier, her husband King Henry VI exclaimed that he must have been conceived of the Holy Ghost, losing his wits for eighteen months; once Edward IV took the throne, the Yorkists claimed that Edward was a bastard. Described by the modern historian T.B. Pugh as 'unscrupulous and resourceful', Beaufort was certainly thrown into the Tower soon after the child's birth. Edward of Lancaster grew up with his mother in Kœur, Lorraine, and was said to 'talk of nothing but chopping off heads'. He was killed at the age of eighteen at the Battle of Tewkesbury.

The story arc of the trilogy, solving the murder of Alyce's third husband William, Duke of Suffolk, is now complete. But my characters, real and imagined, live on in my head. First, the history. Rebellions against Edward IV engineered by Richard, Earl of Warwick, began two months after *Murder Will Out* ends, and in September 1470 Edward IV fled to Bruges. Warwick released King Henry VI from the Tower of London and put him back on the throne. Queen Margaret of Anjou and her son Edward of Lancaster prepared to sail for England and landed at Weymouth on 24 March 1471. But by then Edward IV had landed in Lincolnshire, gathered an army and defeated and killed her most powerful ally, the Earl of Warwick. Margaret led her own army at the Battle of Tewkesbury, but she was defeated. Edward of Lancaster was killed and Margaret captured. Henry VI was imprisoned in the Tower, then quietly murdered. Edward IV remained on the throne for another twelve years. But his sons did not inherit it. It was seized by his brother, who was crowned Richard III in 1483, and the two young princes disappeared into the Tower.

What of my imagined characters, real and invented? Several of the real ones died at the Battle of Tewkesbury in 1471. Margaret of Anjou was imprisoned in Wallingford Castle in the custody of – Princess Alyce. Remembering that Alyce had gone to France to bring back the fifteen-year-old Margaret of Anjou to marry King Henry VI in 1445, it's an irresistible temptation to imagine how they both felt. What will happen to Joan Moulton after she loses her beloved Wenlock? And how about Tamsin? Does Will Stonor come up to scratch? What about Denzil Caerleon? What happened to Sir John Tiptoft? To Sir Thomas Malory? To Sir Robert Harcourt? To Sir John Trevelyan?

If a Real Publisher felt that word-of-mouth enthusiasm and excellent sales for the privately published Alyce trilogy merited bringing her adventures out to a wider public, I would set to work gleefully on a fourth book about Alyce. I will probably do so anyway.

Christina Hardyment
Oxford, October 2024

ACKNOWLEDGEMENTS

My thanks again go to family, friends and experts who have helped so much with encouragement and proofreading. Without Claire Bodanis I would have faltered at the first hurdle. Nicolas Soames not only read all three books before publication but engineered the production of an audiobook of *The Serpent of Division*, read by Claire Wille and available in public libraries and on Audible. Phil 'Hawkeye' Tabor improved this as he did both of the earlier books. Henry Oakeley, Garden Fellow of the Royal College of Physicians, kept me straight on the naturalisation of snowdrops, crown imperials and medieval herbal lore. Local historian Jon Baker advised on Glanville Wootton and Newton Montagu's history, as did the erudite investigator Timothy J. Connor. Professor Peter Field steered me away from egregious errors concerning Sir Thomas Malory and again winked at my embroiderings of his doings. Paul Heiney advised on voyaging to the Saltees and Wexford. Professor Nicolas Orme advised on my account of Exeter Cathedral; Dr Linda Clark, editor of the fifteenth-century biographies in the History of Parliament project, made very helpful comments; and Dr Rowena Archer, well known for her scholarly articles about my heroine, spotted a dramatic point at which to end my story. Maybe the lost bit will end up in *Alyce 4*... Finally my designer Lucy Morton and copy-editor Robin Gable of illuminati books once again worked wonders of accuracy and elegance. Any remaining faults and inaccuracies are all my own work.

Other stalwarts have been Richard Mayon-White, to whom this book is dedicated, Fiona Maddocks, Martin Meredith and Gillian Crampton Smith. Lucy and Andrew Penny's house on the slopes of the Brecon Beacons was again a marvellous retreat, as was Phil and Ros Danby's Arnside bungalow, and the Gladstone Library at Hawarden. Oxford's Bodleian Library and The London Library, St James's Square, were as always invaluable. My four daughters Tilly, Daisy, Ellie and Susie, and their ten wonderful children, make life worth living.